AWA UPSHOT
PRESENTS

AMERICAN RONIN

PETER MILLIGAN
Writer

ACO
Artist & Cover Artist

DAVID LORENZO
Inker

DEAN WHITE
Colorist

SAL CIPRIANO
Letterer

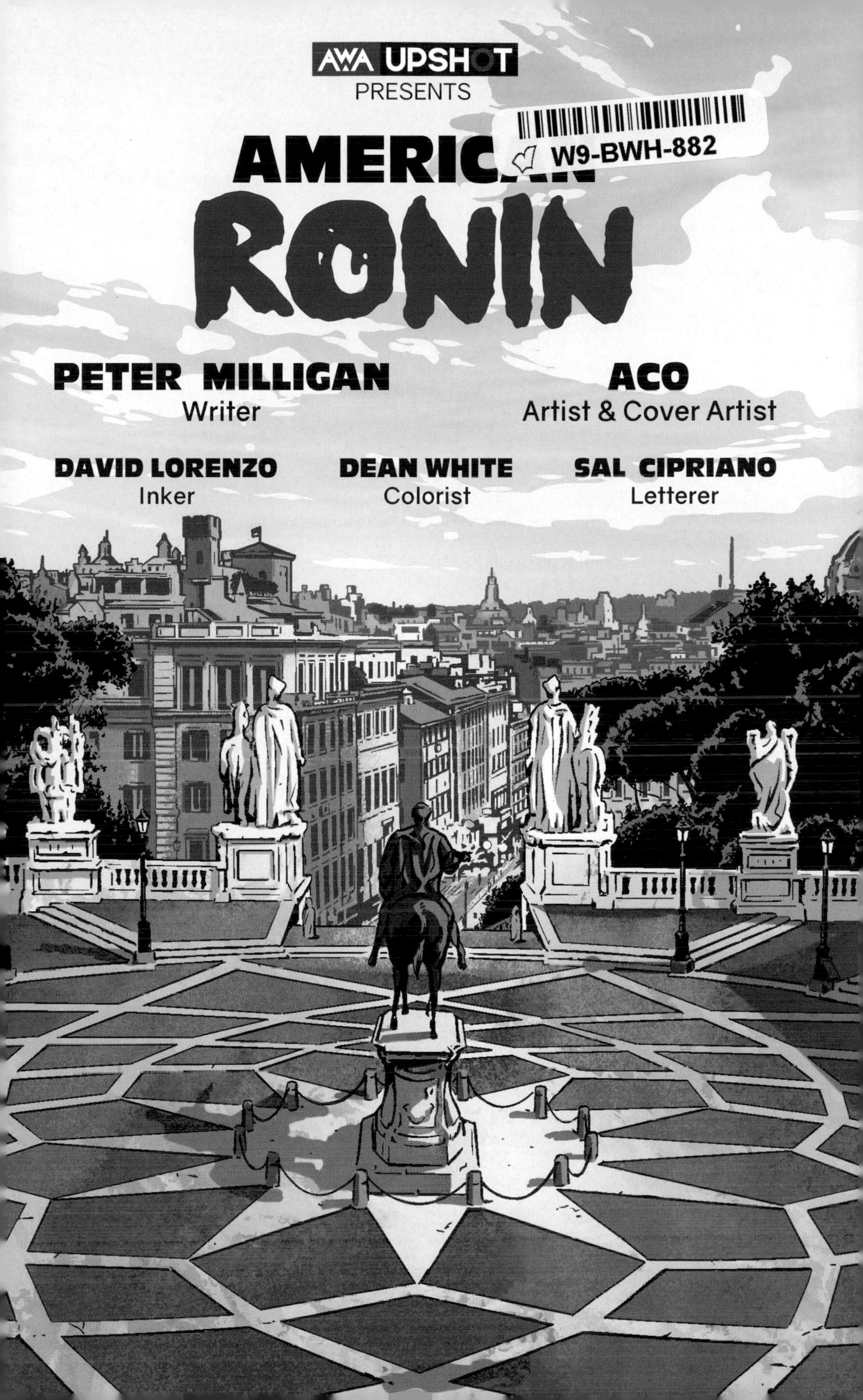

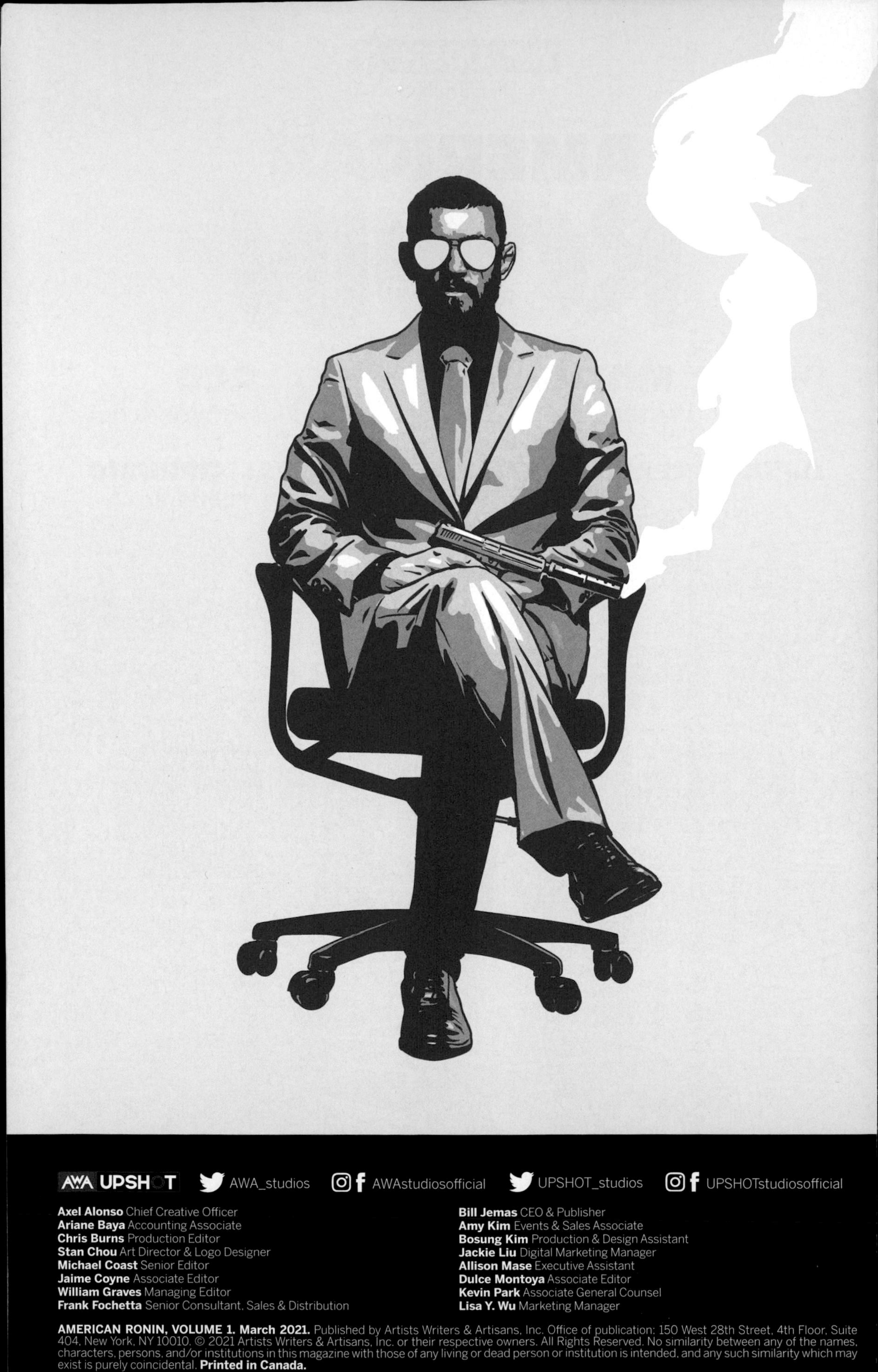

AWA UPSHOT AWA_studios AWAstudiosofficial UPSHOT_studios UPSHOTstudiosofficial

Axel Alonso Chief Creative Officer
Ariane Baya Accounting Associate
Chris Burns Production Editor
Stan Chou Art Director & Logo Designer
Michael Coast Senior Editor
Jaime Coyne Associate Editor
William Graves Managing Editor
Frank Fochetta Senior Consultant, Sales & Distribution
Bill Jemas CEO & Publisher
Amy Kim Events & Sales Associate
Bosung Kim Production & Design Assistant
Jackie Liu Digital Marketing Manager
Allison Mase Executive Assistant
Dulce Montoya Associate Editor
Kevin Park Associate General Counsel
Lisa Y. Wu Marketing Manager

AMERICAN RONIN, VOLUME 1. March 2021. Published by Artists Writers & Artisans, Inc. Office of publication: 150 West 28th Street, 4th Floor, Suite 404, New York, NY 10010. **Printed in Canada.**

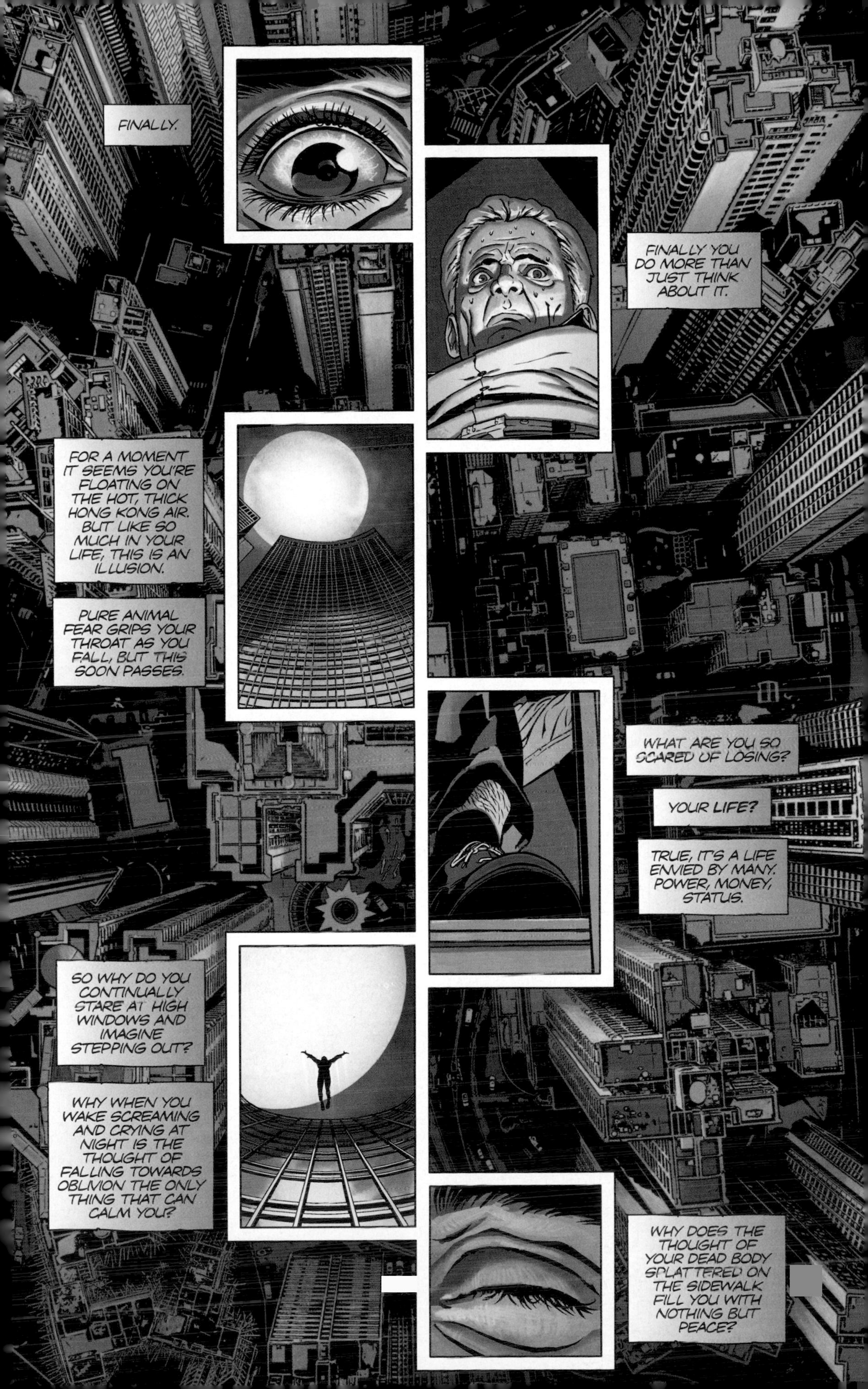
FINALLY.
FINALLY YOU DO MORE THAN JUST THINK ABOUT IT.
FOR A MOMENT IT SEEMS YOU'RE FLOATING ON THE HOT, THICK HONG KONG AIR. BUT LIKE SO MUCH IN YOUR LIFE, THIS IS AN ILLUSION.
PURE ANIMAL FEAR GRIPS YOUR THROAT AS YOU FALL, BUT THIS SOON PASSES.
WHAT ARE YOU SO SCARED OF LOSING?
YOUR LIFE?
TRUE, IT'S A LIFE ENVIED BY MANY. POWER, MONEY, STATUS.
SO WHY DO YOU CONTINUALLY STARE AT HIGH WINDOWS AND IMAGINE STEPPING OUT?
WHY WHEN YOU WAKE SCREAMING AND CRYING AT NIGHT IS THE THOUGHT OF FALLING TOWARDS OBLIVION THE ONLY THING THAT CAN CALM YOU?
WHY DOES THE THOUGHT OF YOUR DEAD BODY SPLATTERED ON THE SIDEWALK FILL YOU WITH NOTHING BUT PEACE?

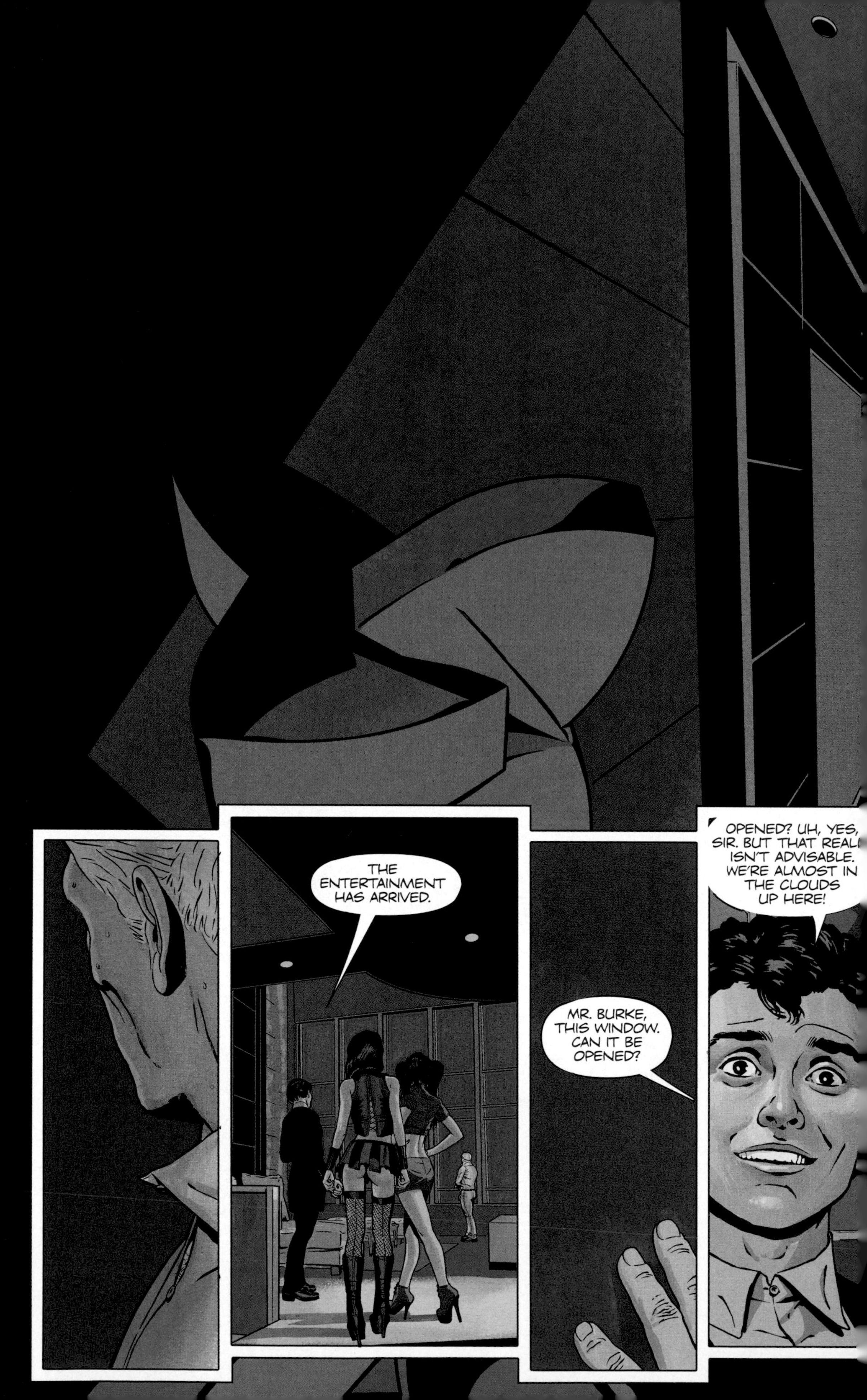
THE ENTERTAINMENT HAS ARRIVED.
MR. BURKE, THIS WINDOW. CAN IT BE OPENED?
OPENED? UH, YES, SIR. BUT THAT REALL ISN'T ADVISABLE. WE'RE ALMOST IN THE CLOUDS UP HERE!

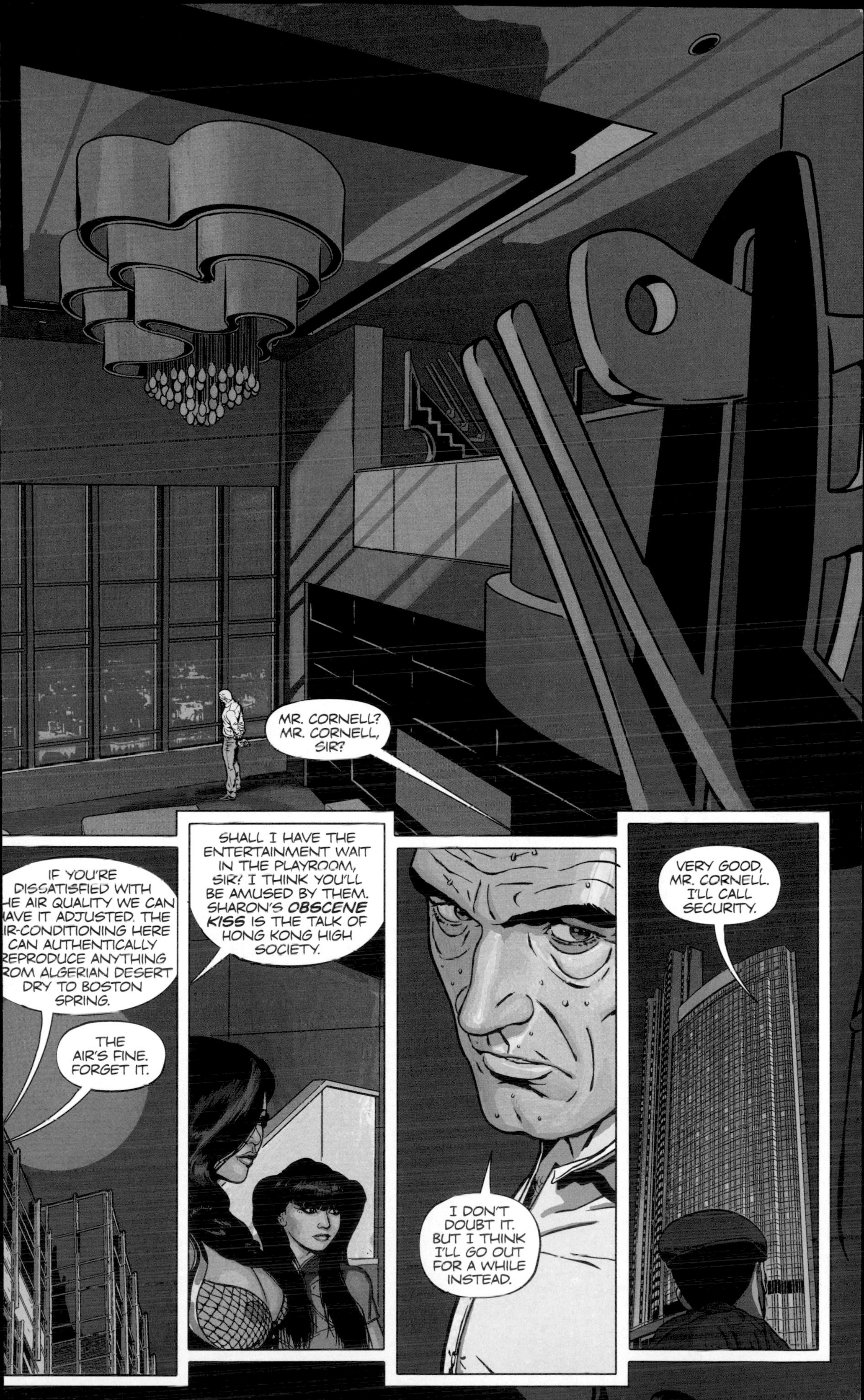
MR. CORNELL? MR. CORNELL, SIR?
IF YOU'RE DISSATISFIED WITH HE AIR QUALITY WE CAN HAVE IT ADJUSTED. THE IR-CONDITIONING HERE CAN AUTHENTICALLY REPRODUCE ANYTHING ROM ALGERIAN DESERT DRY TO BOSTON SPRING.
THE AIR'S FINE. FORGET IT.
SHALL I HAVE THE ENTERTAINMENT WAIT IN THE PLAYROOM, SIR? I THINK YOU'LL BE AMUSED BY THEM. SHARON'S *OBSCENE KISS* IS THE TALK OF HONG KONG HIGH SOCIETY.
I DON'T DOUBT IT. BUT I THINK I'LL GO OUT FOR A WHILE INSTEAD.
VERY GOOD, MR. CORNELL. I'LL CALL SECURITY.

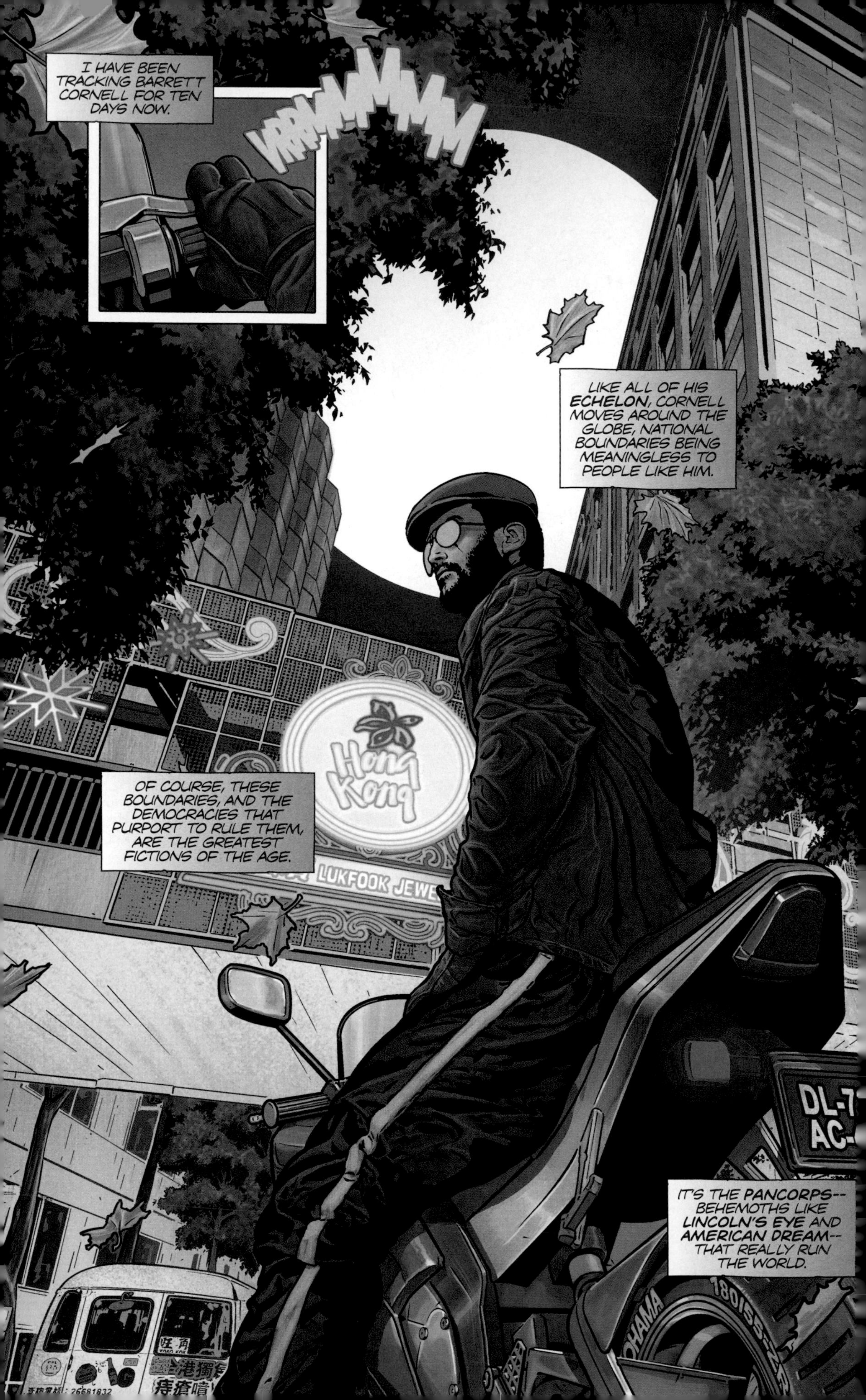
I HAVE BEEN TRACKING BARRETT CORNELL FOR TEN DAYS NOW.
VRRMMMMMMM
LIKE ALL OF HIS ECHELON, CORNELL MOVES AROUND THE GLOBE, NATIONAL BOUNDARIES BEING MEANINGLESS TO PEOPLE LIKE HIM.
Hong Kong
OF COURSE, THESE BOUNDARIES, AND THE DEMOCRACIES THAT PURPORT TO RULE THEM, ARE THE GREATEST FICTIONS OF THE AGE.
LUKFOOK JEWE
IT'S THE PANCORPS-- BEHEMOTHS LIKE LINCOLN'S EYE AND AMERICAN DREAM-- THAT REALLY RUN THE WORLD.

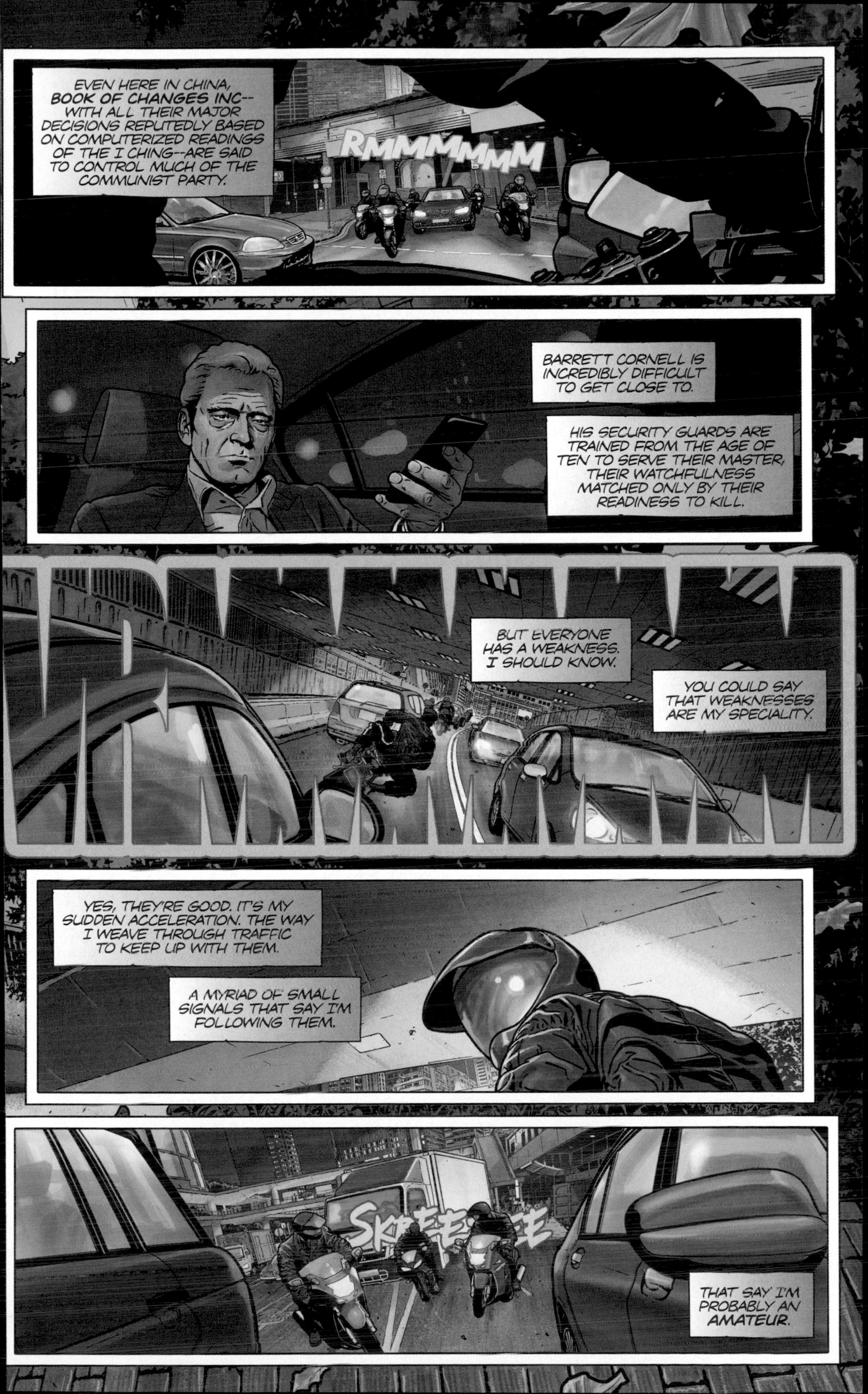
EVEN HERE IN CHINA, BOOK OF CHANGES INC-- WITH ALL THEIR MAJOR DECISIONS REPUTEDLY BASED ON COMPUTERIZED READINGS OF THE I CHING--ARE SAID TO CONTROL MUCH OF THE COMMUNIST PARTY.
RMMMMMMM
BARRETT CORNELL IS INCREDIBLY DIFFICULT TO GET CLOSE TO.
HIS SECURITY GUARDS ARE TRAINED FROM THE AGE OF TEN TO SERVE THEIR MASTER, THEIR WATCHFULNESS MATCHED ONLY BY THEIR READINESS TO KILL.
BUT EVERYONE HAS A WEAKNESS. I SHOULD KNOW.
YOU COULD SAY THAT WEAKNESSES ARE MY SPECIALITY.
YES, THEY'RE GOOD. IT'S MY SUDDEN ACCELERATION. THE WAY I WEAVE THROUGH TRAFFIC TO KEEP UP WITH THEM.
A MYRIAD OF SMALL SIGNALS THAT SAY I'M FOLLOWING THEM.
THAT SAY I'M PROBABLY AN AMATEUR.

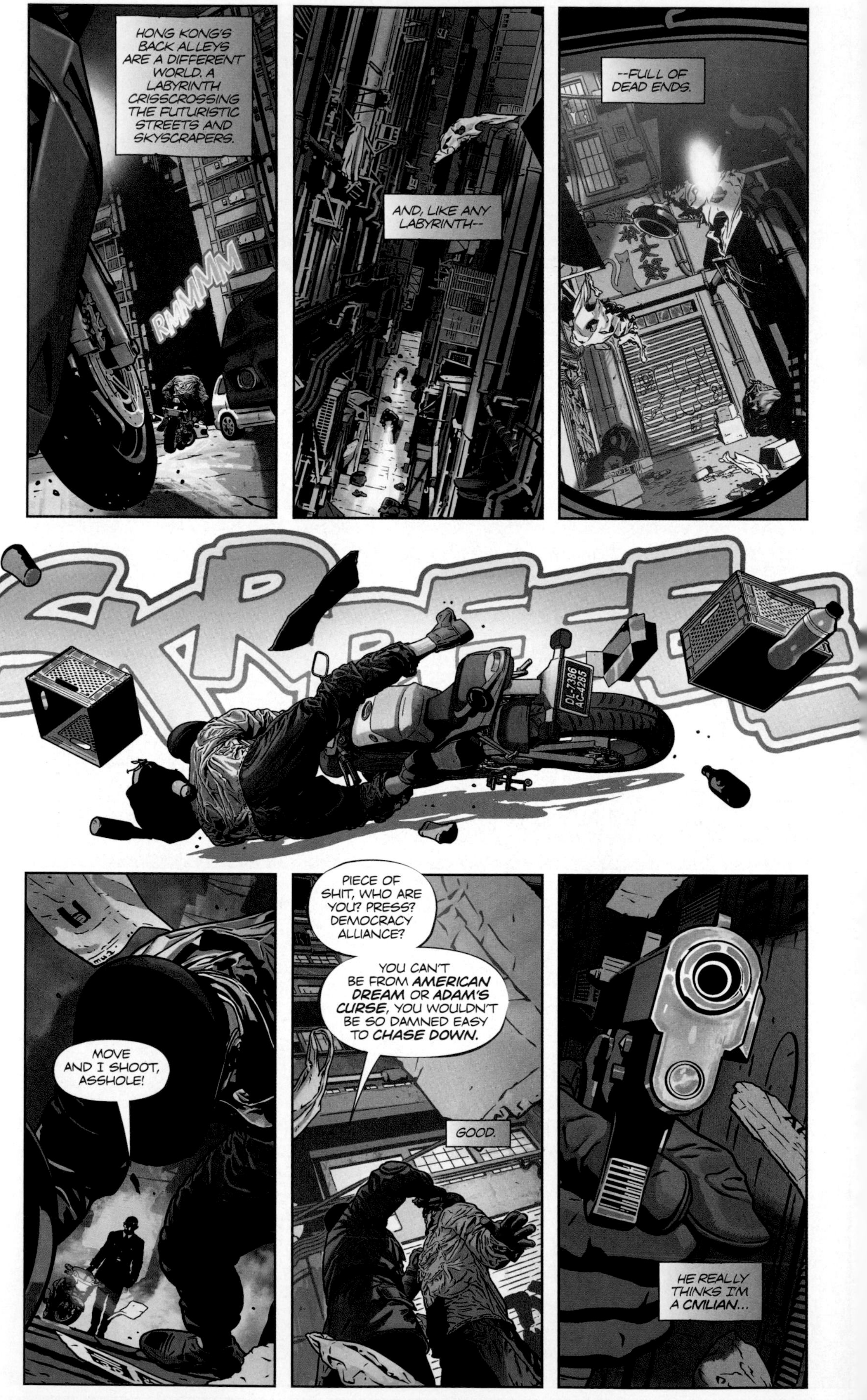
HONG KONG'S BACK ALLEYS ARE A DIFFERENT WORLD. A LABYRINTH CRISSCROSSING THE FUTURISTIC STREETS AND SKYSCRAPERS.
RMMMM
AND, LIKE ANY LABYRINTH--
--FULL OF DEAD ENDS.
SKREEE
DL-7386
AC-4285
MOVE AND I SHOOT, ASSHOLE!
PIECE OF SHIT, WHO ARE YOU? PRESS? DEMOCRACY ALLIANCE?
YOU CAN'T BE FROM AMERICAN DREAM OR ADAM'S CURSE, YOU WOULDN'T BE SO DAMNED EASY TO CHASE DOWN.
GOOD.
HE REALLY THINKS I'M A CIVILIAN...

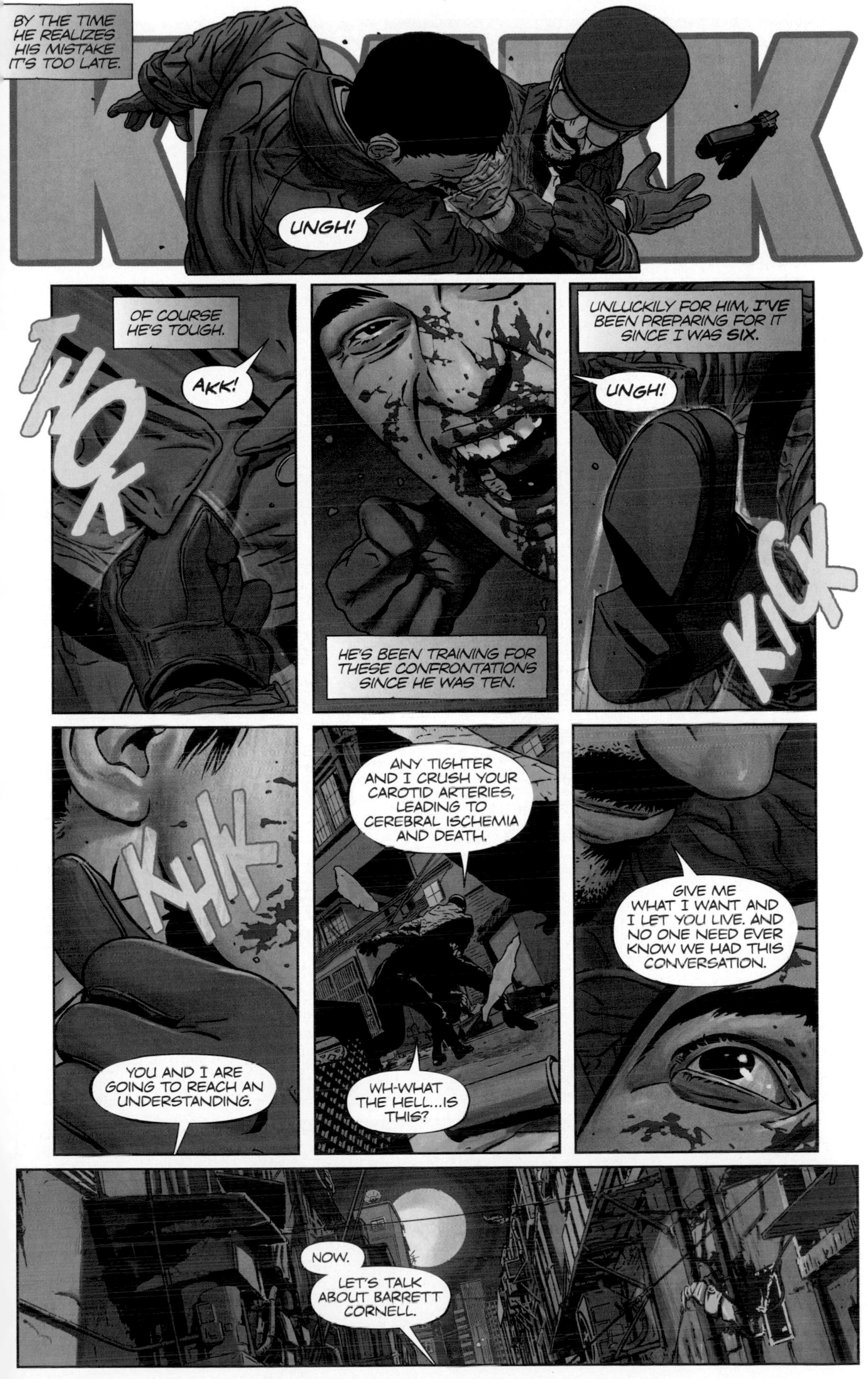
BY THE TIME HE REALIZES HIS MISTAKE IT'S TOO LATE.
KRAKK
UNGH!
OF COURSE HE'S TOUGH.
AKK!
THOK
HE'S BEEN TRAINING FOR THESE CONFRONTATIONS SINCE HE WAS TEN.
UNLUCKILY FOR HIM, I'VE BEEN PREPARING FOR IT SINCE I WAS SIX.
UNGH!
KICK
KHK
YOU AND I ARE GOING TO REACH AN UNDERSTANDING.
ANY TIGHTER AND I CRUSH YOUR CAROTID ARTERIES, LEADING TO CEREBRAL ISCHEMIA AND DEATH.
WH-WHAT THE HELL...IS THIS?
GIVE ME WHAT I WANT AND I LET YOU LIVE. AND NO ONE NEED EVER KNOW WE HAD THIS CONVERSATION.
NOW.
LET'S TALK ABOUT BARRETT CORNELL.

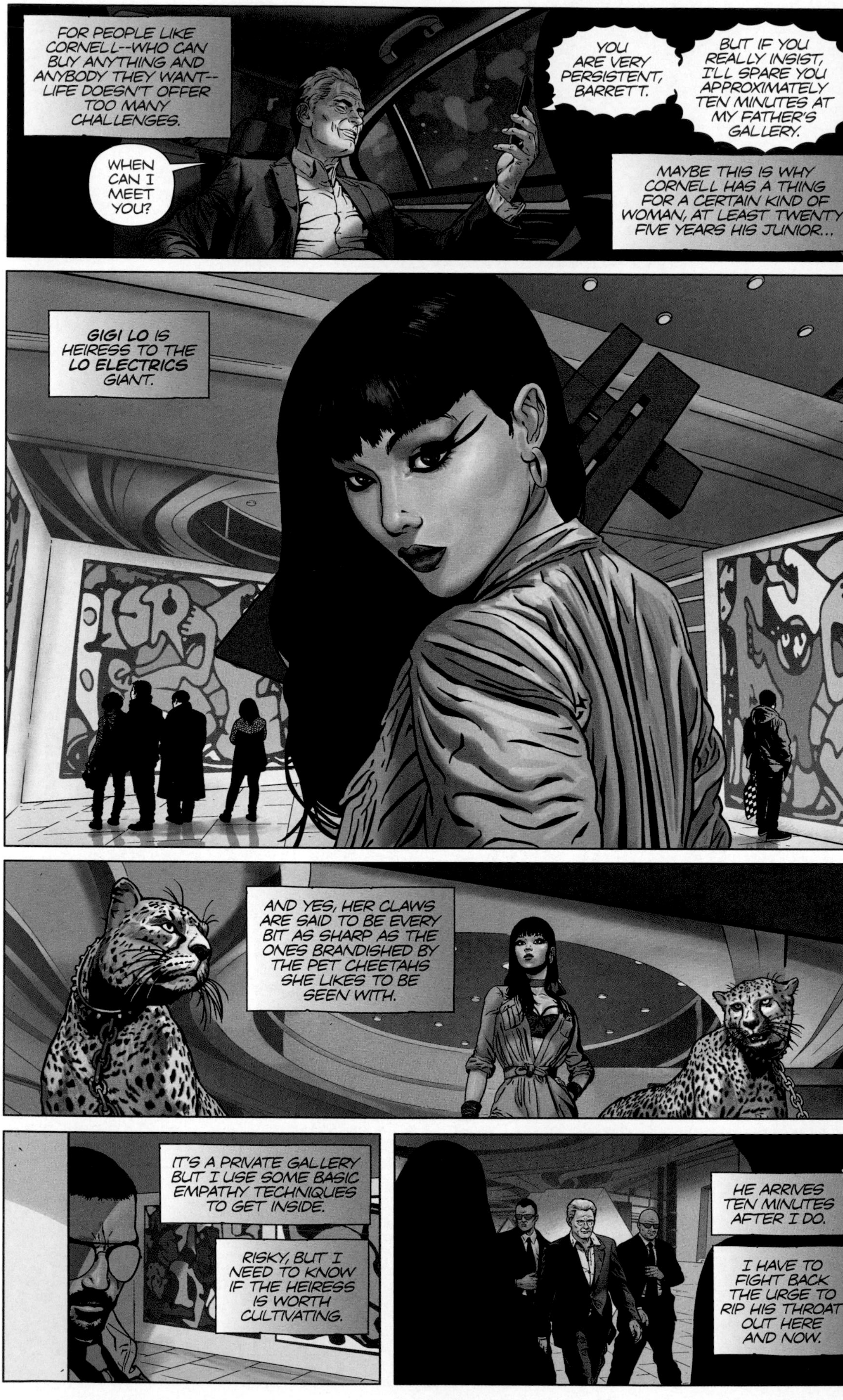

FOR PEOPLE LIKE CORNELL--WHO CAN BUY ANYTHING AND ANYBODY THEY WANT--LIFE DOESN'T OFFER TOO MANY CHALLENGES.
WHEN CAN I MEET YOU?
YOU ARE VERY PERSISTENT, BARRETT.
BUT IF YOU REALLY INSIST, I'LL SPARE YOU APPROXIMATELY TEN MINUTES AT MY FATHER'S GALLERY.
MAYBE THIS IS WHY CORNELL HAS A THING FOR A CERTAIN KIND OF WOMAN, AT LEAST TWENTY-FIVE YEARS HIS JUNIOR...
GIGI LO IS HEIRESS TO THE LO ELECTRICS GIANT.
AND YES, HER CLAWS ARE SAID TO BE EVERY BIT AS SHARP AS THE ONES BRANDISHED BY THE PET CHEETAHS SHE LIKES TO BE SEEN WITH.
IT'S A PRIVATE GALLERY BUT I USE SOME BASIC EMPATHY TECHNIQUES TO GET INSIDE.
RISKY, BUT I NEED TO KNOW IF THE HEIRESS IS WORTH CULTIVATING.
HE ARRIVES TEN MINUTES AFTER I DO.
I HAVE TO FIGHT BACK THE URGE TO RIP HIS THROAT OUT HERE AND NOW.

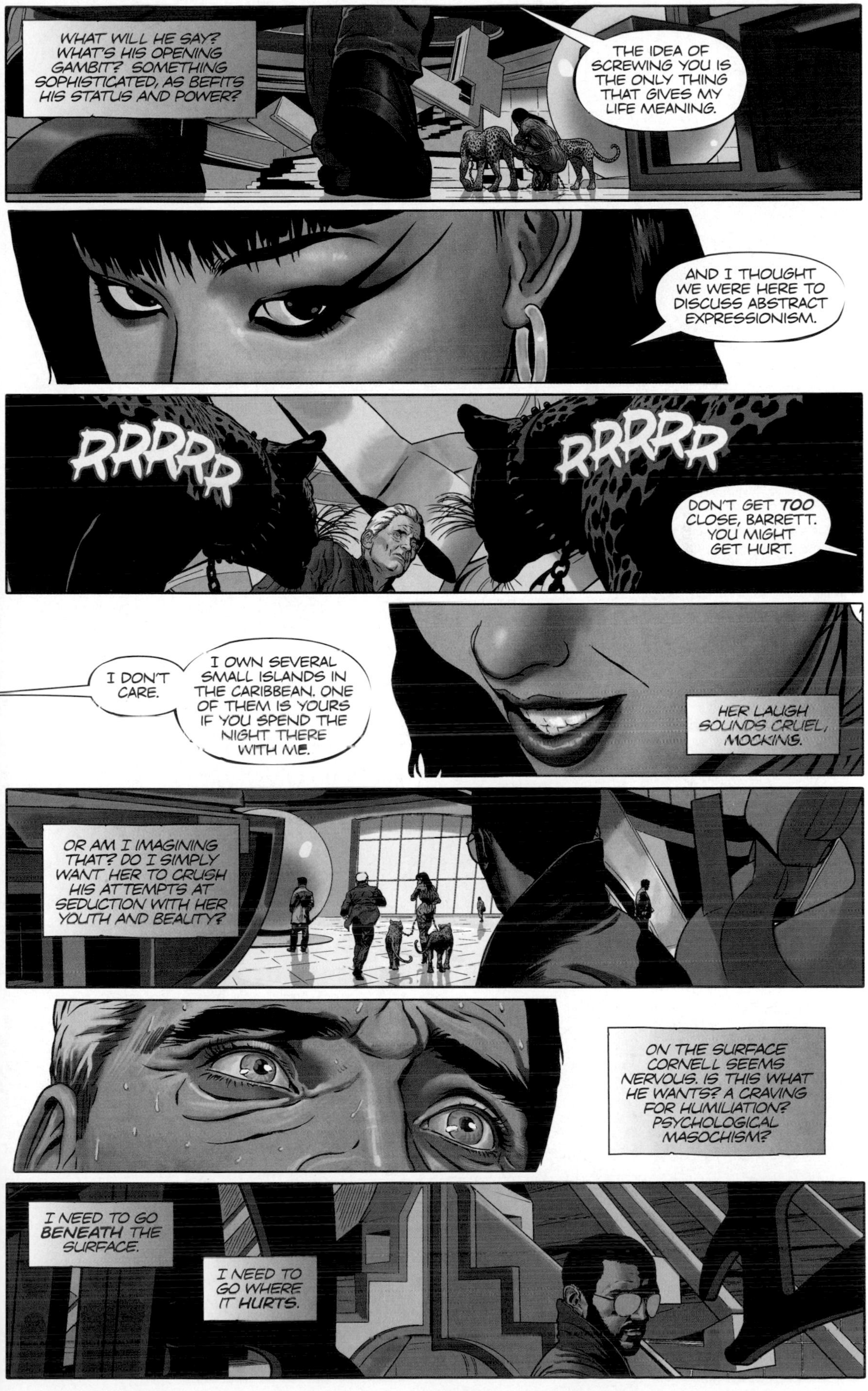
WHAT WILL HE SAY? WHAT'S HIS OPENING GAMBIT? SOMETHING SOPHISTICATED, AS BEFITS HIS STATUS AND POWER?
THE IDEA OF SCREWING YOU IS THE ONLY THING THAT GIVES MY LIFE MEANING.
AND I THOUGHT WE WERE HERE TO DISCUSS ABSTRACT EXPRESSIONISM.
RRRRR
RRRRR
DON'T GET TOO CLOSE, BARRETT. YOU MIGHT GET HURT.
I DON'T CARE.
I OWN SEVERAL SMALL ISLANDS IN THE CARIBBEAN. ONE OF THEM IS YOURS IF YOU SPEND THE NIGHT THERE WITH ME.
HER LAUGH SOUNDS CRUEL, MOCKING.
OR AM I IMAGINING THAT? DO I SIMPLY WANT HER TO CRUSH HIS ATTEMPTS AT SEDUCTION WITH HER YOUTH AND BEAUTY?
ON THE SURFACE CORNELL SEEMS NERVOUS. IS THIS WHAT HE WANTS? A CRAVING FOR HUMILIATION? PSYCHOLOGICAL MASOCHISM?
I NEED TO GO BENEATH THE SURFACE.
I NEED TO GO WHERE IT HURTS.

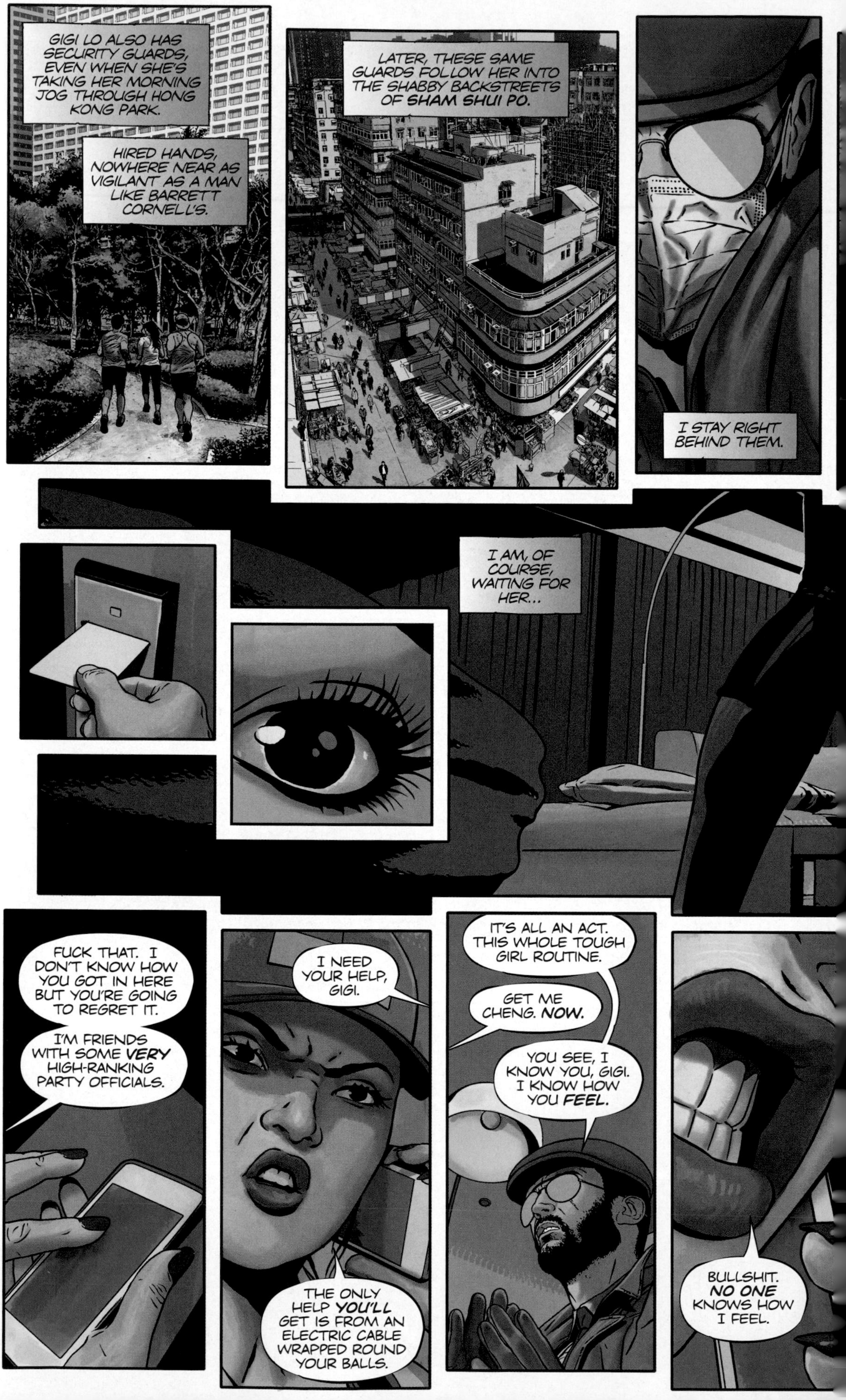
GIGI LO ALSO HAS SECURITY GUARDS, EVEN WHEN SHE'S TAKING HER MORNING JOG THROUGH HONG KONG PARK.
HIRED HANDS, NOWHERE NEAR AS VIGILANT AS A MAN LIKE BARRETT CORNELL'S.
LATER, THESE SAME GUARDS FOLLOW HER INTO THE SHABBY BACKSTREETS OF SHAM SHUI PO.
I STAY RIGHT BEHIND THEM.
I AM, OF COURSE, WAITING FOR HER...
FUCK THAT. I DON'T KNOW HOW YOU GOT IN HERE BUT YOU'RE GOING TO REGRET IT.
I'M FRIENDS WITH SOME VERY HIGH-RANKING PARTY OFFICIALS.
I NEED YOUR HELP, GIGI.
THE ONLY HELP YOU'LL GET IS FROM AN ELECTRIC CABLE WRAPPED ROUND YOUR BALLS.
IT'S ALL AN ACT. THIS WHOLE TOUGH GIRL ROUTINE.
GET ME CHENG. NOW.
YOU SEE, I KNOW YOU, GIGI. I KNOW HOW YOU FEEL.
BULLSHIT. NO ONE KNOWS HOW I FEEL.

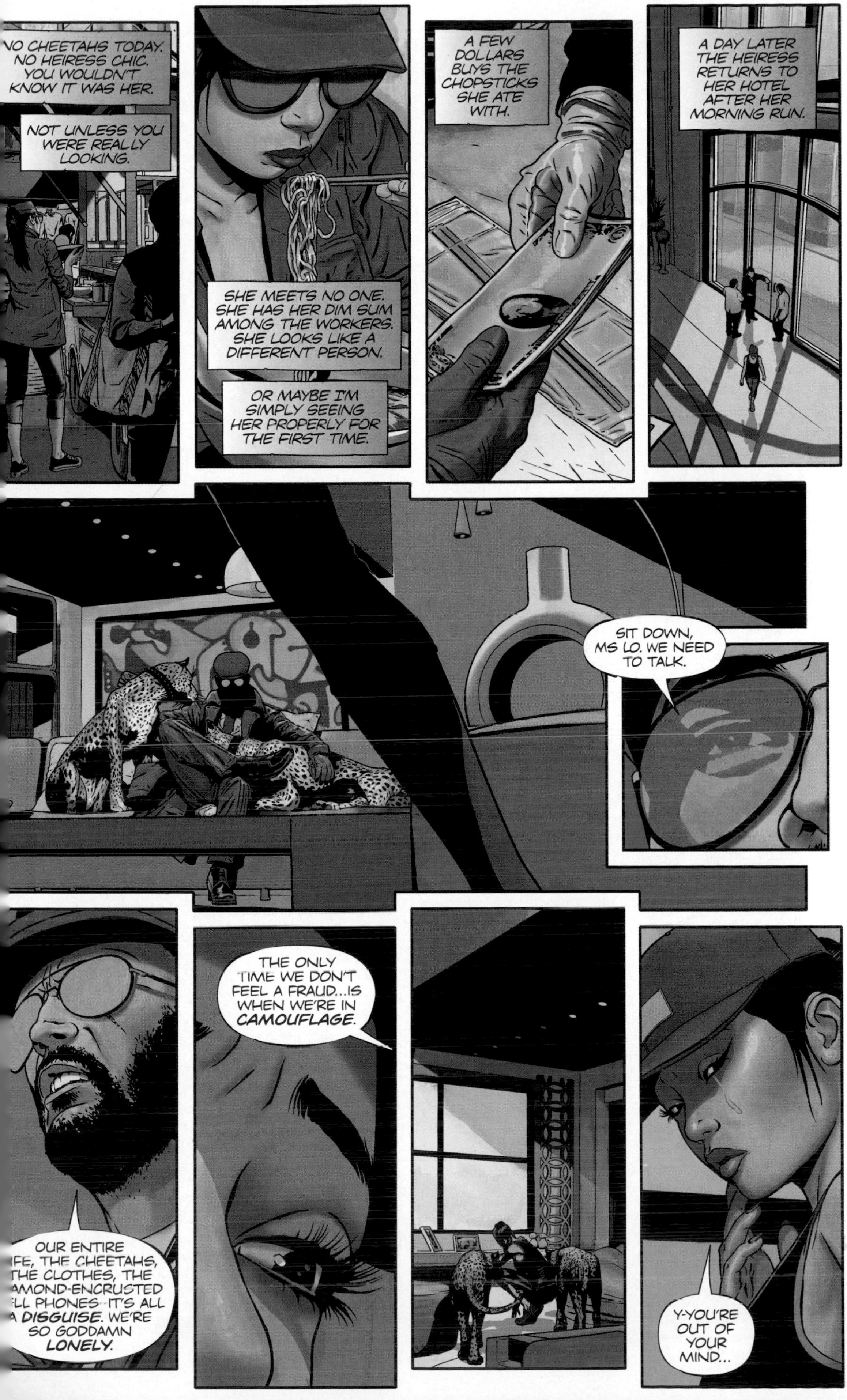
NO CHEETAHS TODAY. NO HEIRESS CHIC. YOU WOULDN'T KNOW IT WAS HER.
NOT UNLESS YOU WERE REALLY LOOKING.
SHE MEETS NO ONE. SHE HAS HER DIM SUM AMONG THE WORKERS. SHE LOOKS LIKE A DIFFERENT PERSON.
OR MAYBE I'M SIMPLY SEEING HER PROPERLY FOR THE FIRST TIME.
A FEW DOLLARS BUYS THE CHOPSTICKS SHE ATE WITH.
A DAY LATER THE HEIRESS RETURNS TO HER HOTEL AFTER HER MORNING RUN.
SIT DOWN, MS LO. WE NEED TO TALK.
OUR ENTIRE IFE, THE CHEETAHS, THE CLOTHES, THE AMOND-ENCRUSTED ELL PHONES--IT'S ALL A **DISGUISE**. WE'RE SO GODDAMN **LONELY**.
THE ONLY TIME WE DON'T FEEL A FRAUD...IS WHEN WE'RE IN **CAMOUFLAGE**.
Y-YOU'RE OUT OF YOUR MIND...

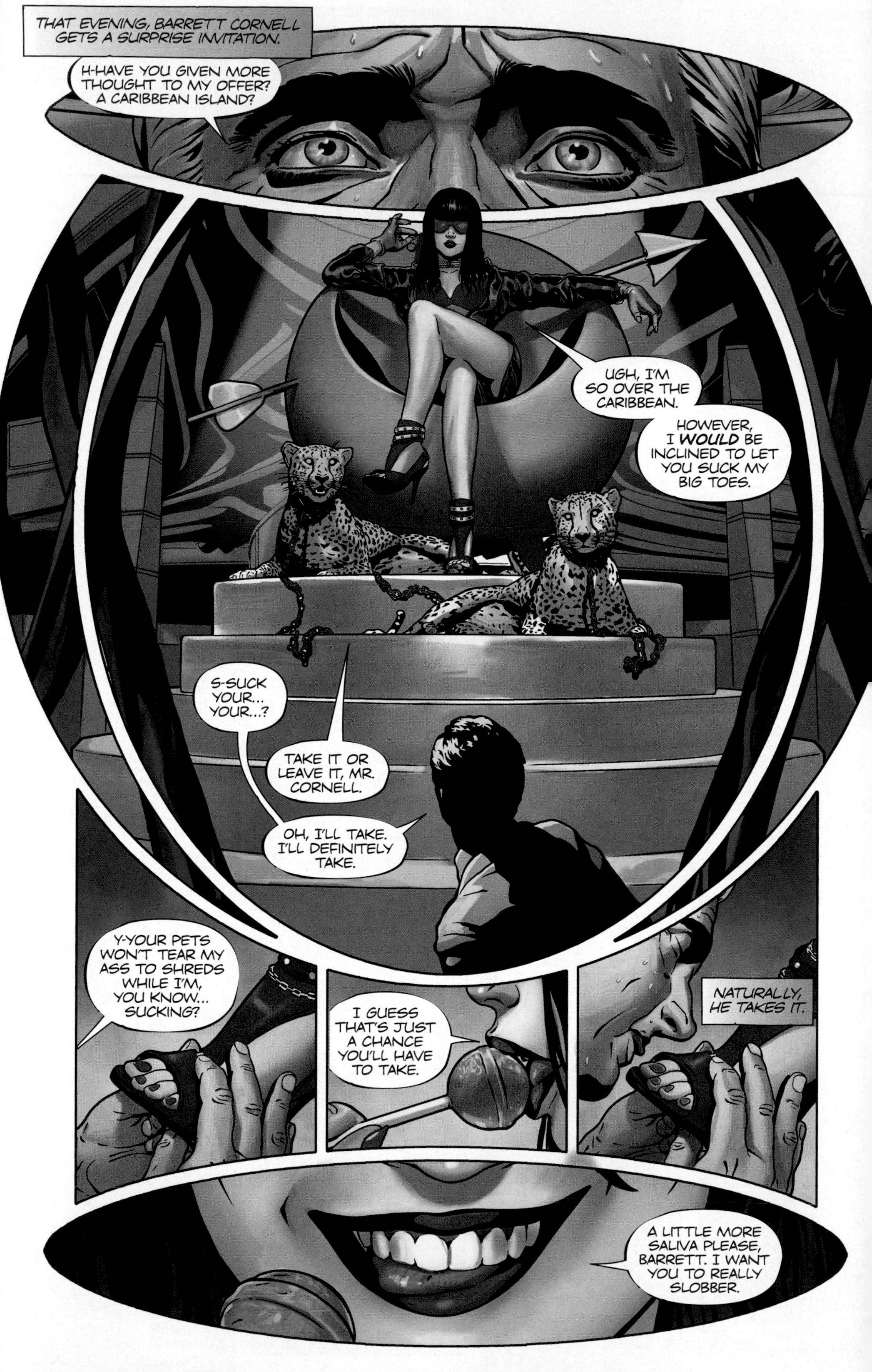
THAT EVENING, BARRETT CORNELL GETS A SURPRISE INVITATION.
H-HAVE YOU GIVEN MORE THOUGHT TO MY OFFER? A CARIBBEAN ISLAND?
UGH, I'M SO OVER THE CARIBBEAN.
HOWEVER, I WOULD BE INCLINED TO LET YOU SUCK MY BIG TOES.
S-SUCK YOUR... YOUR...?
TAKE IT OR LEAVE IT, MR. CORNELL.
OH, I'LL TAKE. I'LL DEFINITELY TAKE.
Y-YOUR PETS WON'T TEAR MY ASS TO SHREDS WHILE I'M, YOU KNOW... SUCKING?
I GUESS THAT'S JUST A CHANCE YOU'LL HAVE TO TAKE.
NATURALLY, HE TAKES IT.
A LITTLE MORE SALIVA PLEASE, BARRETT. I WANT YOU TO REALLY SLOBBER.

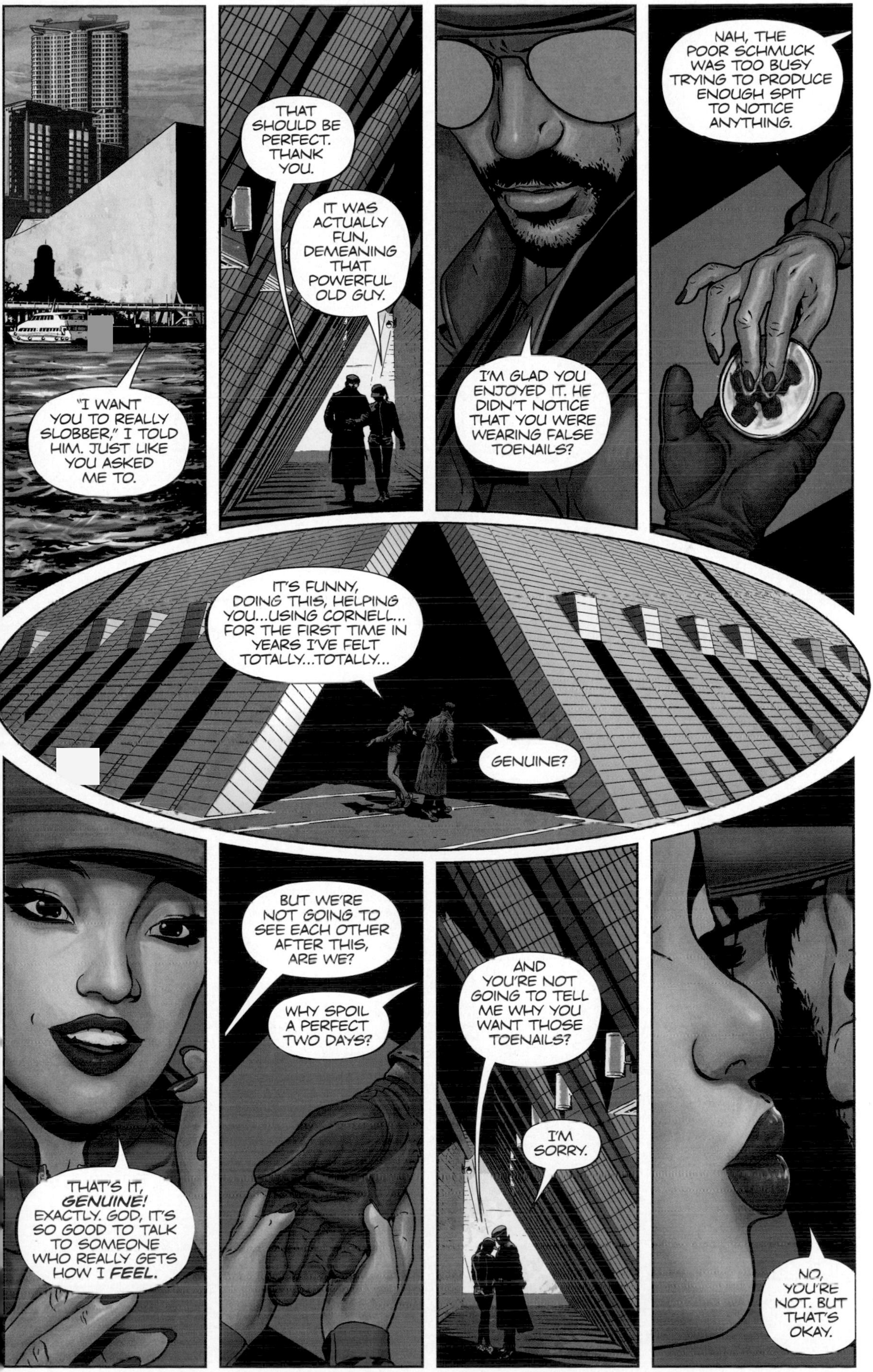
"I WANT YOU TO REALLY SLOBBER," I TOLD HIM. JUST LIKE YOU ASKED ME TO.
THAT SHOULD BE PERFECT. THANK YOU.
IT WAS ACTUALLY FUN, DEMEANING THAT POWERFUL OLD GUY.
I'M GLAD YOU ENJOYED IT. HE DIDN'T NOTICE THAT YOU WERE WEARING FALSE TOENAILS?
NAH, THE POOR SCHMUCK WAS TOO BUSY TRYING TO PRODUCE ENOUGH SPIT TO NOTICE ANYTHING.
IT'S FUNNY, DOING THIS, HELPING YOU...USING CORNELL... FOR THE FIRST TIME IN YEARS I'VE FELT TOTALLY...TOTALLY...
GENUINE?
THAT'S IT, *GENUINE!* EXACTLY. GOD, IT'S SO GOOD TO TALK TO SOMEONE WHO REALLY GETS HOW I *FEEL*.
BUT WE'RE NOT GOING TO SEE EACH OTHER AFTER THIS, ARE WE?
WHY SPOIL A PERFECT TWO DAYS?
AND YOU'RE NOT GOING TO TELL ME WHY YOU WANT THOSE TOENAILS?
I'M SORRY.
NO, YOU'RE NOT. BUT THAT'S OKAY.

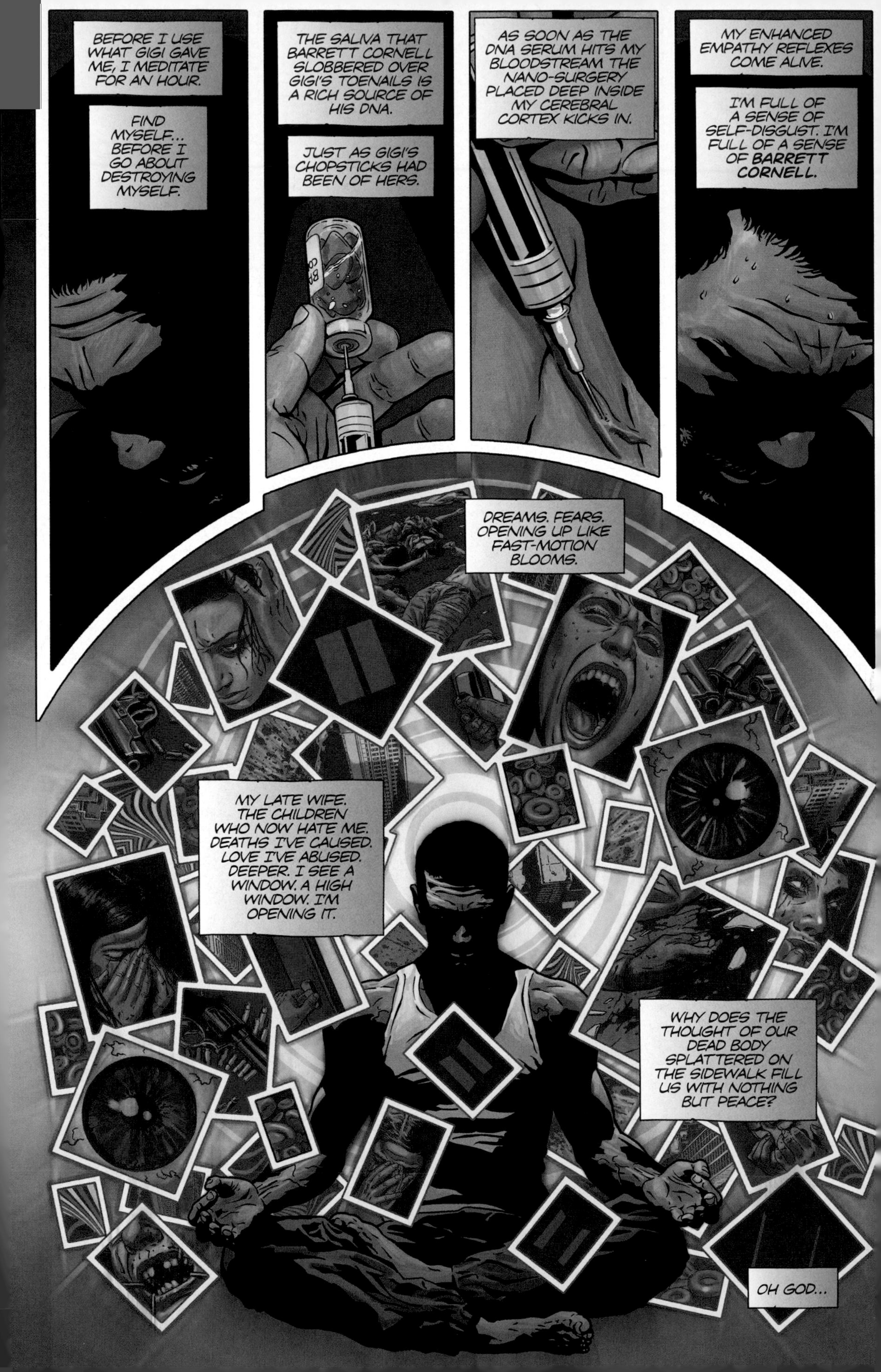
BEFORE I USE WHAT GIGI GAVE ME, I MEDITATE FOR AN HOUR.
FIND MYSELF... BEFORE I GO ABOUT DESTROYING MYSELF.
THE SALIVA THAT BARRETT CORNELL SLOBBERED OVER GIGI'S TOENAILS IS A RICH SOURCE OF HIS DNA.
JUST AS GIGI'S CHOPSTICKS HAD BEEN OF HERS.
AS SOON AS THE DNA SERUM HITS MY BLOODSTREAM THE NANO-SURGERY PLACED DEEP INSIDE MY CEREBRAL CORTEX KICKS IN.
MY ENHANCED EMPATHY REFLEXES COME ALIVE.
I'M FULL OF A SENSE OF SELF-DISGUST. I'M FULL OF A SENSE OF **BARRETT CORNELL**.
DREAMS. FEARS. OPENING UP LIKE FAST-MOTION BLOOMS.
MY LATE WIFE. THE CHILDREN WHO NOW HATE ME. DEATHS I'VE CAUSED. LOVE I'VE ABUSED. DEEPER. I SEE A WINDOW. A HIGH WINDOW. I'M OPENING IT.
WHY DOES THE THOUGHT OF OUR DEAD BODY SPLATTERED ON THE SIDEWALK FILL US WITH NOTHING BUT PEACE?
OH GOD...

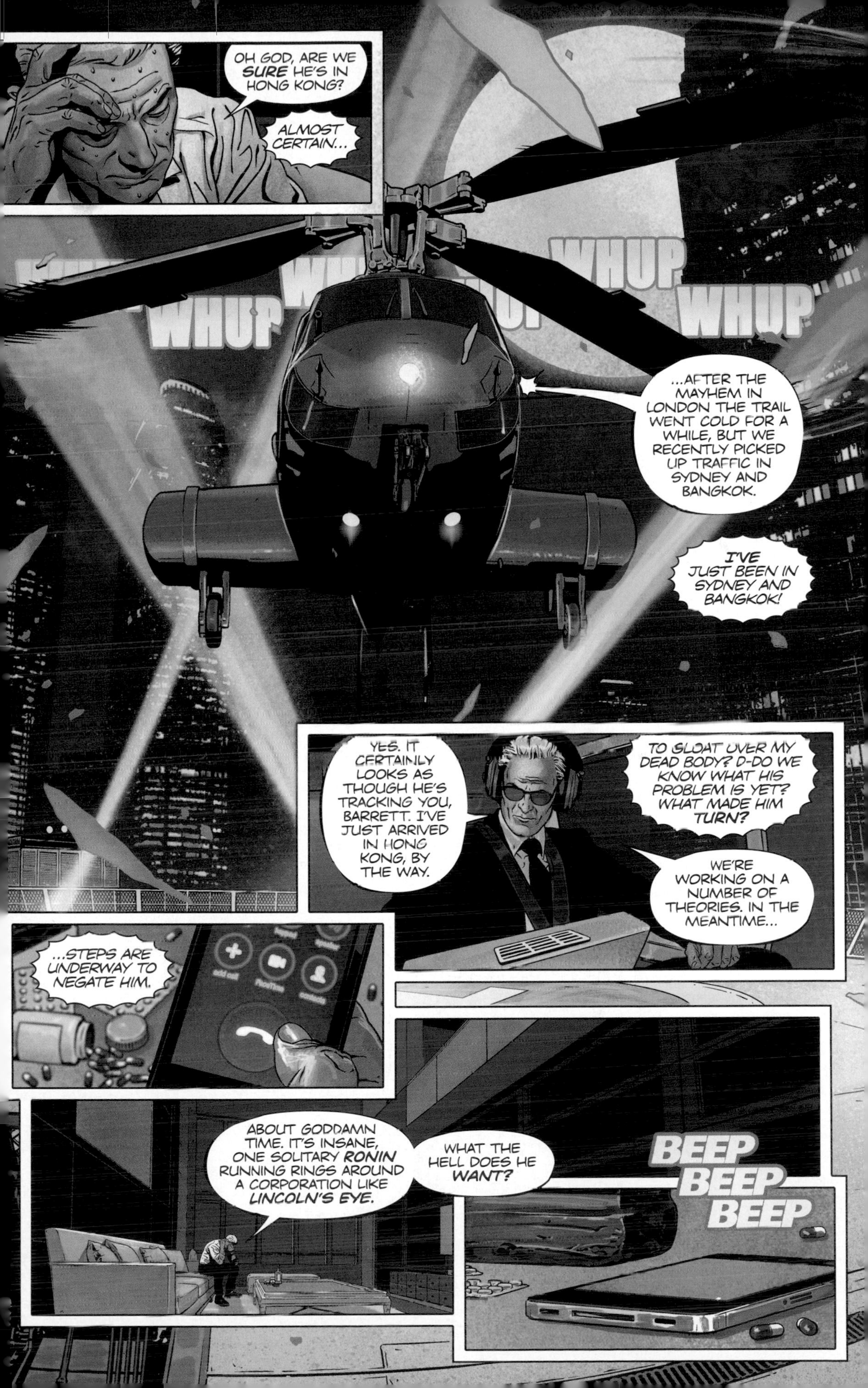

OH GOD, ARE WE *SURE* HE'S IN HONG KONG?
ALMOST CERTAIN...
WHUP WHUP WHUP WHUP WHUP
...AFTER THE MAYHEM IN LONDON THE TRAIL WENT COLD FOR A WHILE, BUT WE RECENTLY PICKED UP TRAFFIC IN SYDNEY AND BANGKOK.
I'VE JUST BEEN IN SYDNEY AND BANGKOK!
YES. IT CERTAINLY LOOKS AS THOUGH HE'S TRACKING YOU, BARRETT. I'VE JUST ARRIVED IN HONG KONG, BY THE WAY.
TO GLOAT OVER MY DEAD BODY? D-DO WE KNOW WHAT HIS PROBLEM IS YET? WHAT MADE HIM *TURN?*
WE'RE WORKING ON A NUMBER OF THEORIES. IN THE MEANTIME...
...STEPS ARE UNDERWAY TO NEGATE HIM.
ABOUT GODDAMN TIME. IT'S INSANE, ONE SOLITARY *RONIN* RUNNING RINGS AROUND A CORPORATION LIKE *LINCOLN'S EYE.*
WHAT THE HELL DOES HE *WANT?*
BEEP BEEP BEEP

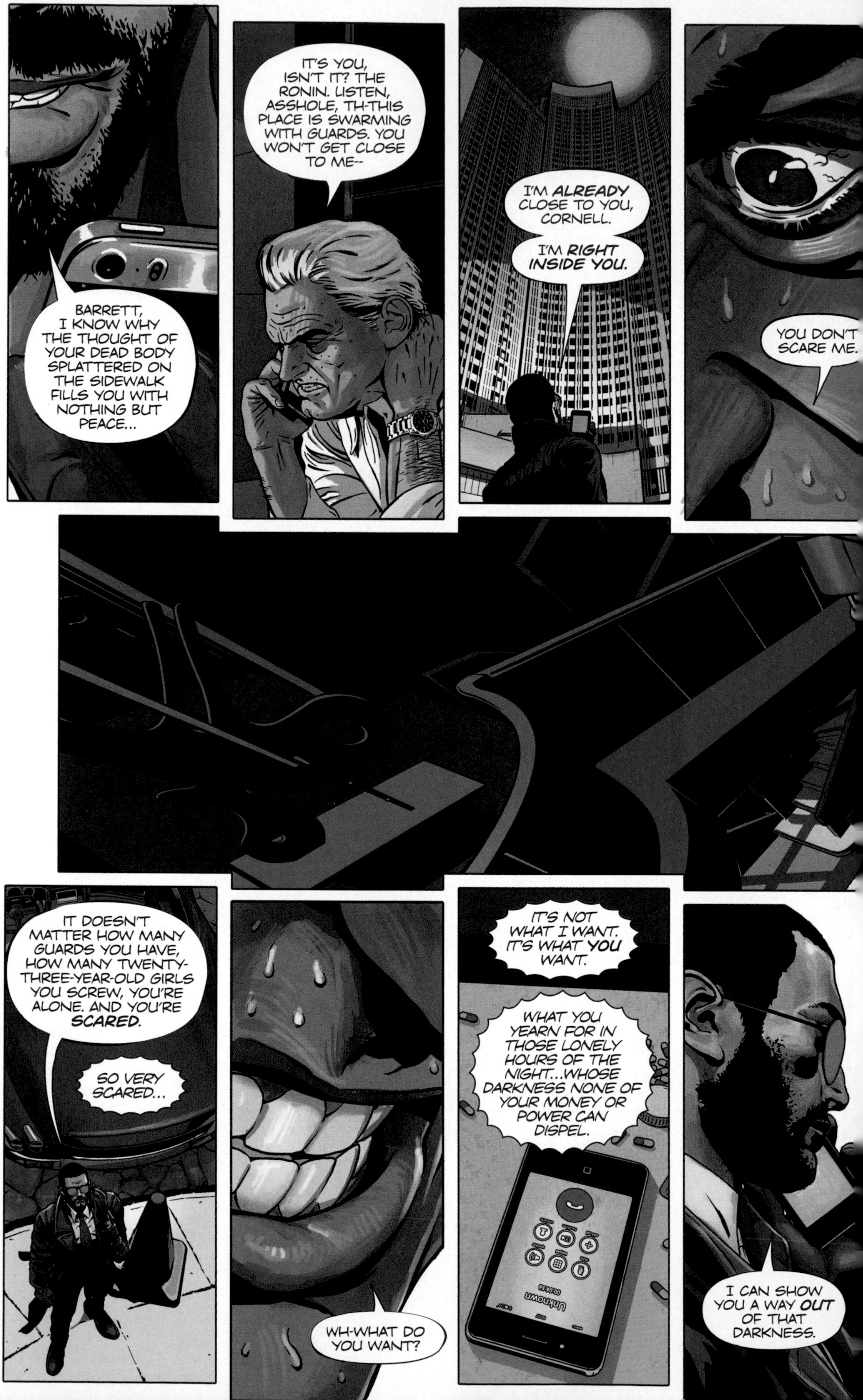
BARRETT, I KNOW WHY THE THOUGHT OF YOUR DEAD BODY SPLATTERED ON THE SIDEWALK FILLS YOU WITH NOTHING BUT PEACE...
IT'S YOU, ISN'T IT? THE RONIN. LISTEN, ASSHOLE, TH-THIS PLACE IS SWARMING WITH GUARDS. YOU WON'T GET CLOSE TO ME--
I'M ALREADY CLOSE TO YOU, CORNELL.
I'M RIGHT INSIDE YOU.
YOU DON'T SCARE ME.
IT DOESN'T MATTER HOW MANY GUARDS YOU HAVE, HOW MANY TWENTY-THREE-YEAR-OLD GIRLS YOU SCREW, YOU'RE ALONE. AND YOU'RE SCARED.
SO VERY SCARED...
WH-WHAT DO YOU WANT?
IT'S NOT WHAT I WANT. IT'S WHAT YOU WANT.
WHAT YOU YEARN FOR IN THOSE LONELY HOURS OF THE NIGHT...WHOSE DARKNESS NONE OF YOUR MONEY OR POWER CAN DISPEL.
I CAN SHOW YOU A WAY OUT OF THAT DARKNESS.

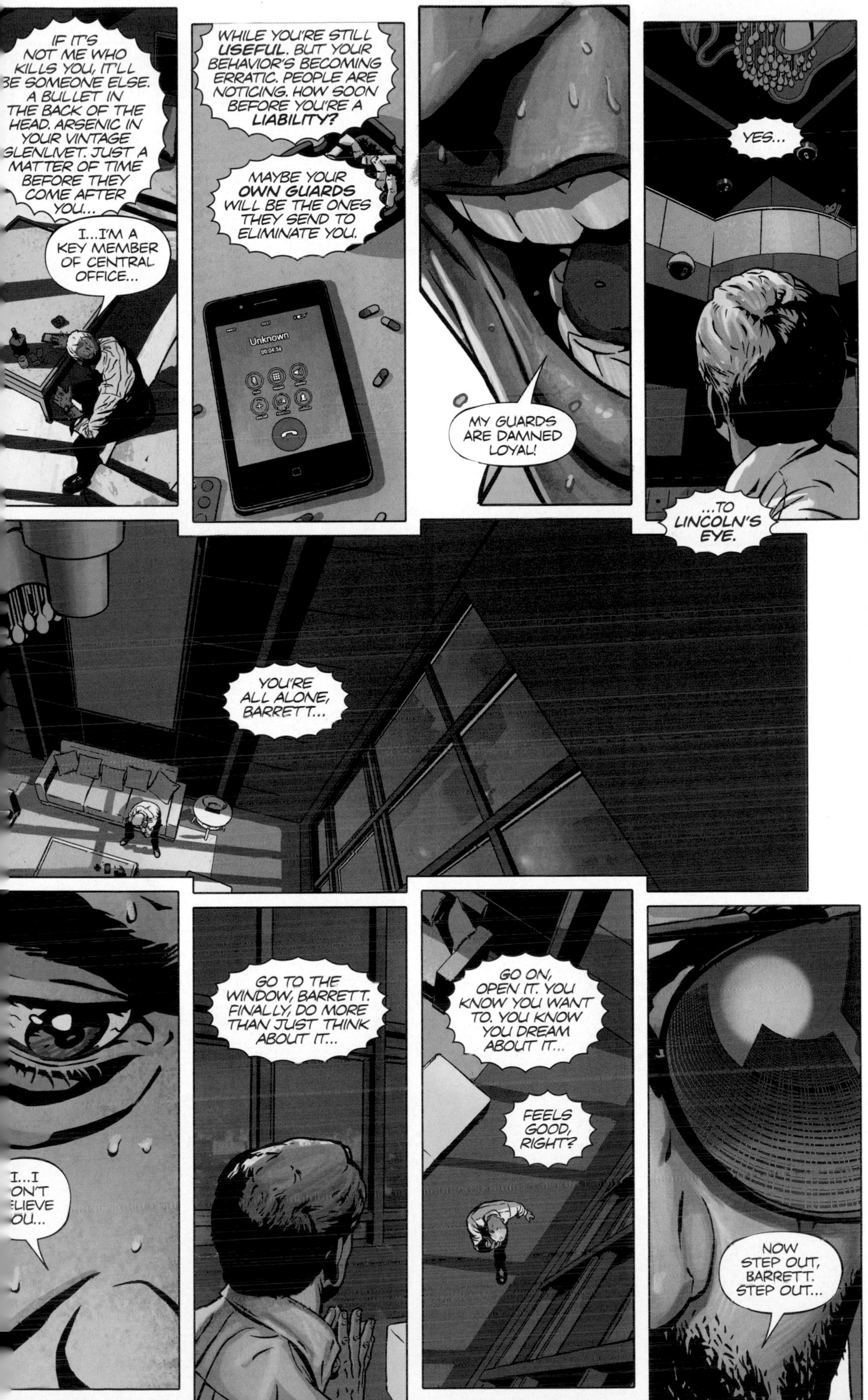
IF IT'S NOT ME WHO KILLS YOU, IT'LL BE SOMEONE ELSE. A BULLET IN THE BACK OF THE HEAD. ARSENIC IN YOUR VINTAGE GLENLIVET. JUST A MATTER OF TIME BEFORE THEY COME AFTER YOU...
I...I'M A KEY MEMBER OF CENTRAL OFFICE...
WHILE YOU'RE STILL **USEFUL**. BUT YOUR BEHAVIOR'S BECOMING ERRATIC. PEOPLE ARE NOTICING. HOW SOON BEFORE YOU'RE A **LIABILITY?**
MAYBE YOUR **OWN GUARDS** WILL BE THE ONES THEY SEND TO ELIMINATE YOU.
Unknown
00:04:56
MY GUARDS ARE DAMNED LOYAL!
YES...
...TO LINCOLN'S EYE.
YOU'RE ALL ALONE, BARRETT...
I...I ON'T ELIEVE OU...
GO TO THE WINDOW, BARRETT. FINALLY, DO MORE THAN JUST THINK ABOUT IT...
GO ON, OPEN IT. YOU KNOW YOU WANT TO. YOU KNOW YOU DREAM ABOUT IT...
FEELS GOOD, RIGHT?
NOW STEP OUT, BARRETT. STEP OUT...

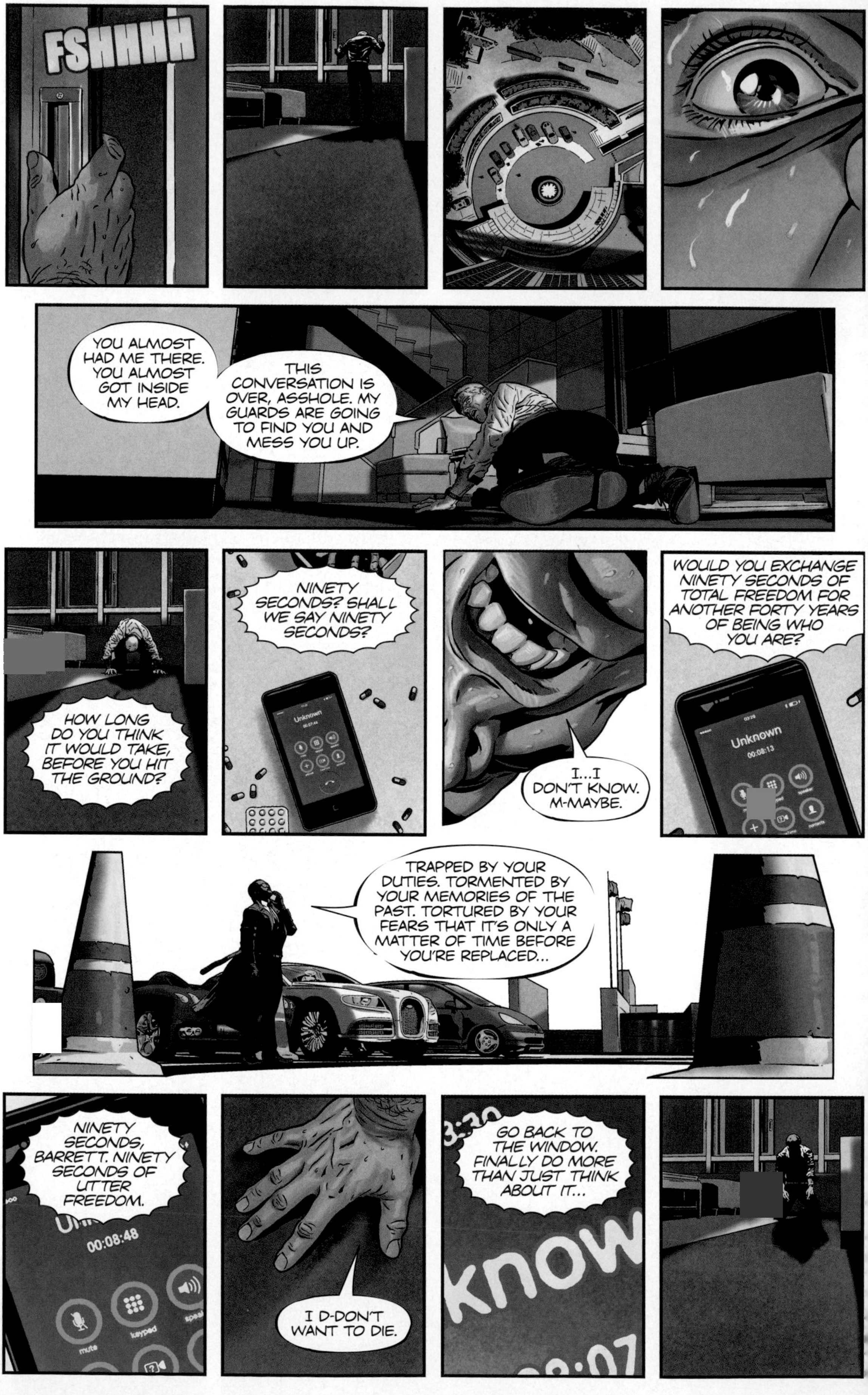
FSHHHH
YOU ALMOST HAD ME THERE. YOU ALMOST GOT INSIDE MY HEAD.
THIS CONVERSATION IS OVER, ASSHOLE. MY GUARDS ARE GOING TO FIND YOU AND MESS YOU UP.
HOW LONG DO YOU THINK IT WOULD TAKE, BEFORE YOU HIT THE GROUND?
NINETY SECONDS? SHALL WE SAY NINETY SECONDS?
Unknown
I...I DON'T KNOW. M-MAYBE.
WOULD YOU EXCHANGE NINETY SECONDS OF TOTAL FREEDOM FOR ANOTHER FORTY YEARS OF BEING WHO YOU ARE?
Unknown
00:08:13
TRAPPED BY YOUR DUTIES. TORMENTED BY YOUR MEMORIES OF THE PAST. TORTURED BY YOUR FEARS THAT IT'S ONLY A MATTER OF TIME BEFORE YOU'RE REPLACED...
NINETY SECONDS, BARRETT. NINETY SECONDS OF UTTER FREEDOM.
00:08:48
mute
keypad
I D-DON'T WANT TO DIE.
GO BACK TO THE WINDOW. FINALLY DO MORE THAN JUST THINK ABOUT IT...
known

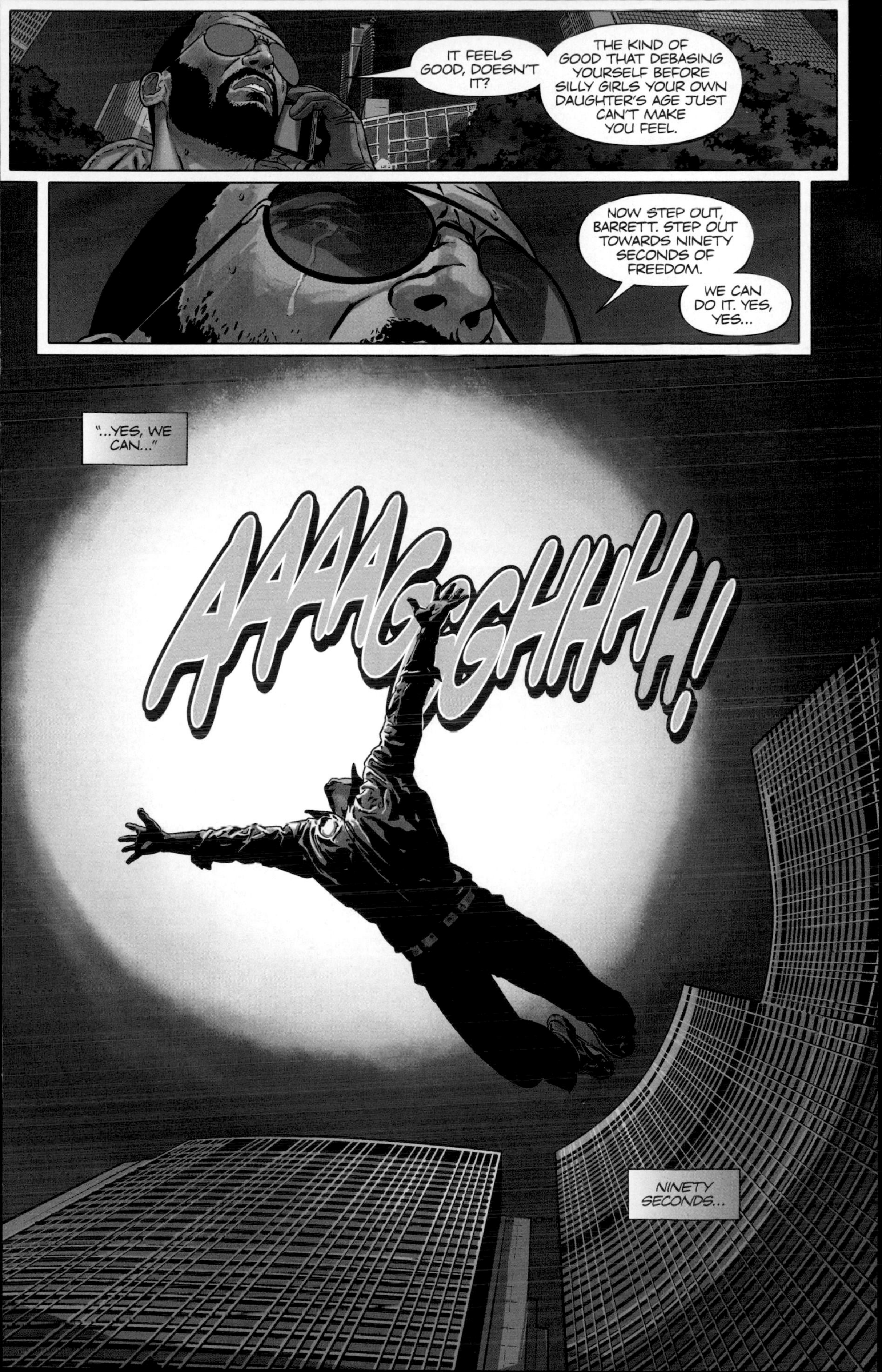
IT FEELS GOOD, DOESN'T IT?
THE KIND OF GOOD THAT DEBASING YOURSELF BEFORE SILLY GIRLS YOUR OWN DAUGHTER'S AGE JUST CAN'T MAKE YOU FEEL.
NOW STEP OUT, BARRETT. STEP OUT TOWARDS NINETY SECONDS OF FREEDOM.
WE CAN DO IT. YES, YES...
"...YES, WE CAN..."
AAAAGGGHHHH!
NINETY SECONDS...

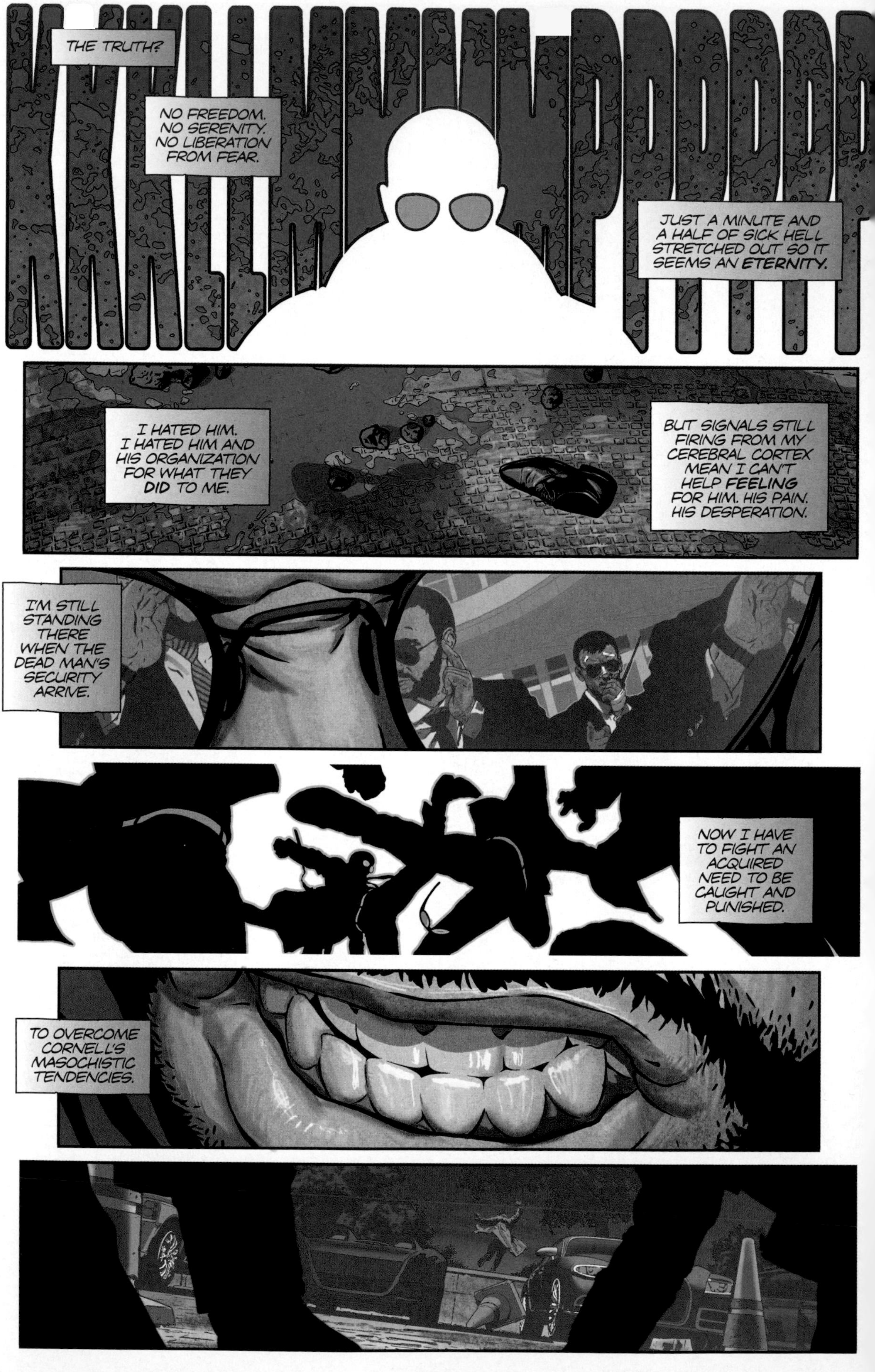
KKKLLMMMMMPPPPPP
THE TRUTH?
NO FREEDOM. NO SERENITY. NO LIBERATION FROM FEAR.
JUST A MINUTE AND A HALF OF SICK HELL STRETCHED OUT SO IT SEEMS AN ETERNITY.
I HATED HIM. I HATED HIM AND HIS ORGANIZATION FOR WHAT THEY DID TO ME.
BUT SIGNALS STILL FIRING FROM MY CEREBRAL CORTEX MEAN I CAN'T HELP FEELING FOR HIM. HIS PAIN. HIS DESPERATION.
I'M STILL STANDING THERE WHEN THE DEAD MAN'S SECURITY ARRIVE.
NOW I HAVE TO FIGHT AN ACQUIRED NEED TO BE CAUGHT AND PUNISHED.
TO OVERCOME CORNELL'S MASOCHISTIC TENDENCIES.

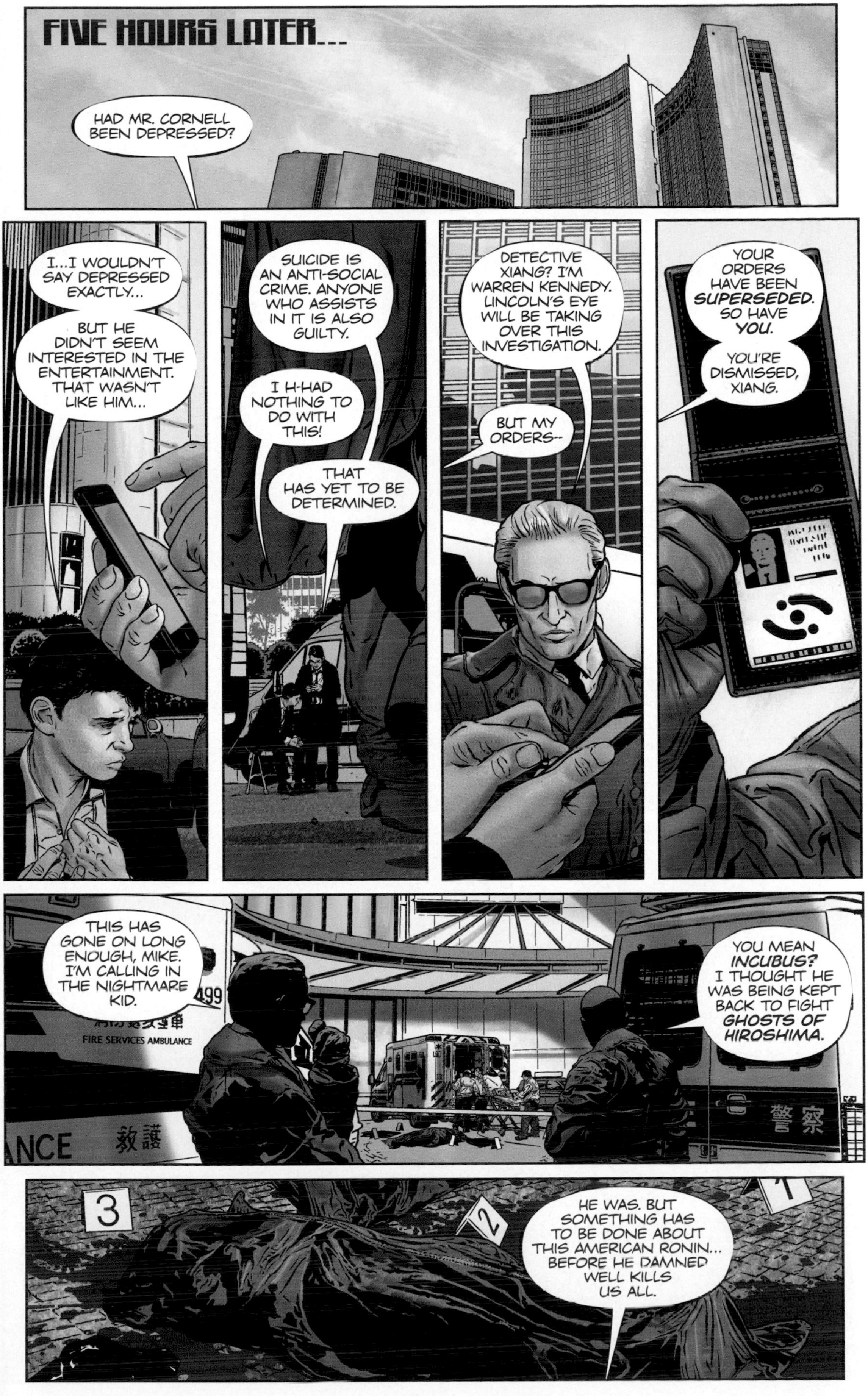
FIVE HOURS LATER...
HAD MR. CORNELL BEEN DEPRESSED?
I...I WOULDN'T SAY DEPRESSED EXACTLY...
BUT HE DIDN'T SEEM INTERESTED IN THE ENTERTAINMENT. THAT WASN'T LIKE HIM...
SUICIDE IS AN ANTI-SOCIAL CRIME. ANYONE WHO ASSISTS IN IT IS ALSO GUILTY.
I H-HAD NOTHING TO DO WITH THIS!
THAT HAS YET TO BE DETERMINED.
DETECTIVE XIANG? I'M WARREN KENNEDY. LINCOLN'S EYE WILL BE TAKING OVER THIS INVESTIGATION.
BUT MY ORDERS--
YOUR ORDERS HAVE BEEN SUPERSEDED. SO HAVE YOU.
YOU'RE DISMISSED, XIANG.
THIS HAS GONE ON LONG ENOUGH, MIKE. I'M CALLING IN THE NIGHTMARE KID.
YOU MEAN INCUBUS? I THOUGHT HE WAS BEING KEPT BACK TO FIGHT GHOSTS OF HIROSHIMA.
FIRE SERVICES AMBULANCE
ANCE 救護
警察
3
2
1
HE WAS. BUT SOMETHING HAS TO BE DONE ABOUT THIS AMERICAN RONIN... BEFORE HE DAMNED WELL KILLS US ALL.

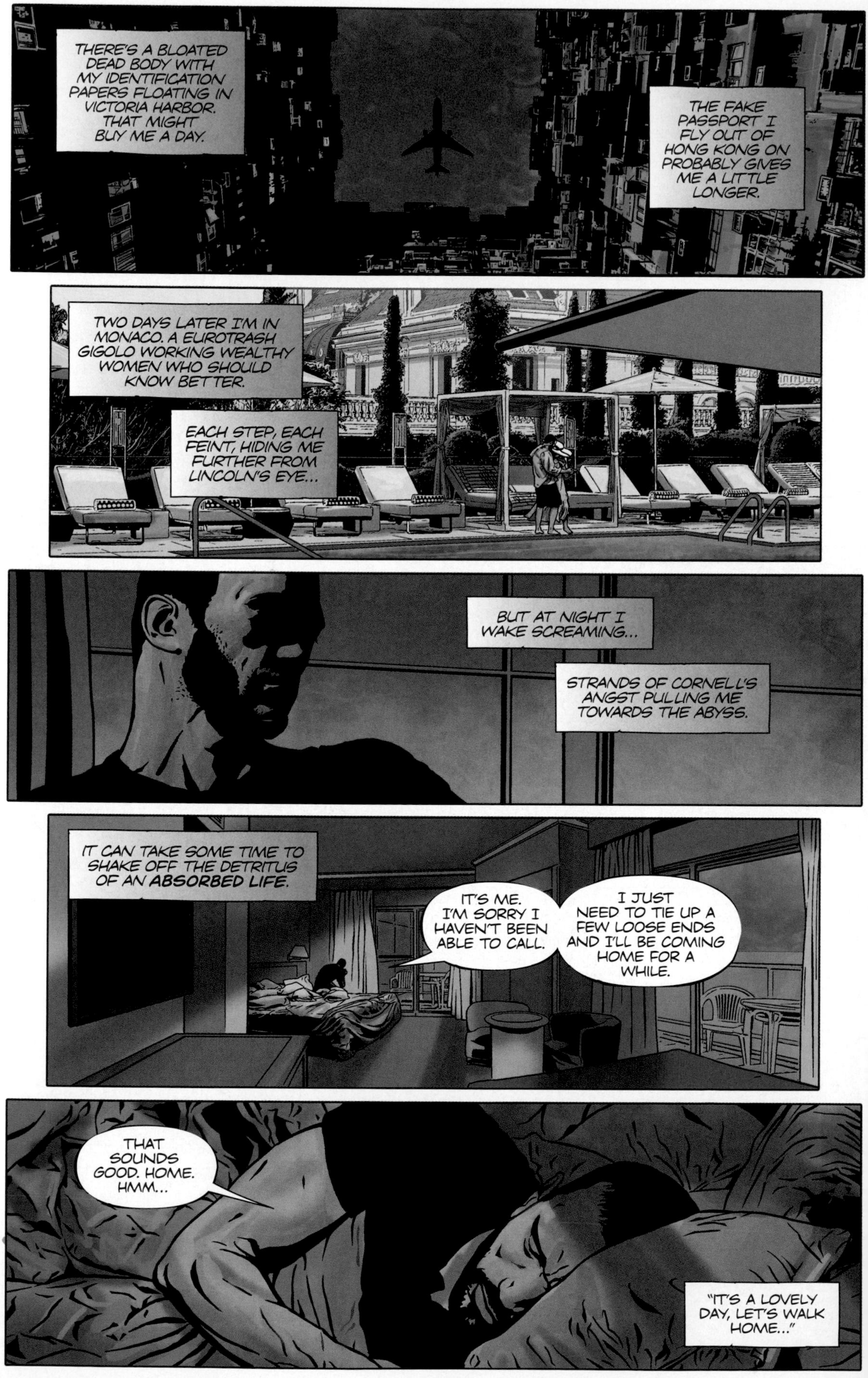
THERE'S A BLOATED DEAD BODY WITH MY IDENTIFICATION PAPERS FLOATING IN VICTORIA HARBOR. THAT MIGHT BUY ME A DAY.
THE FAKE PASSPORT I FLY OUT OF HONG KONG ON PROBABLY GIVES ME A LITTLE LONGER.
TWO DAYS LATER I'M IN MONACO. A EUROTRASH GIGOLO WORKING WEALTHY WOMEN WHO SHOULD KNOW BETTER.
EACH STEP, EACH FEINT, HIDING ME FURTHER FROM LINCOLN'S EYE...
BUT AT NIGHT I WAKE SCREAMING...
STRANDS OF CORNELL'S ANGST PULLING ME TOWARDS THE ABYSS.
IT CAN TAKE SOME TIME TO SHAKE OFF THE DETRITUS OF AN ABSORBED LIFE.
IT'S ME. I'M SORRY I HAVEN'T BEEN ABLE TO CALL.
I JUST NEED TO TIE UP A FEW LOOSE ENDS AND I'LL BE COMING HOME FOR A WHILE.
THAT SOUNDS GOOD. HOME. HMM...
"IT'S A LOVELY DAY, LET'S WALK HOME..."

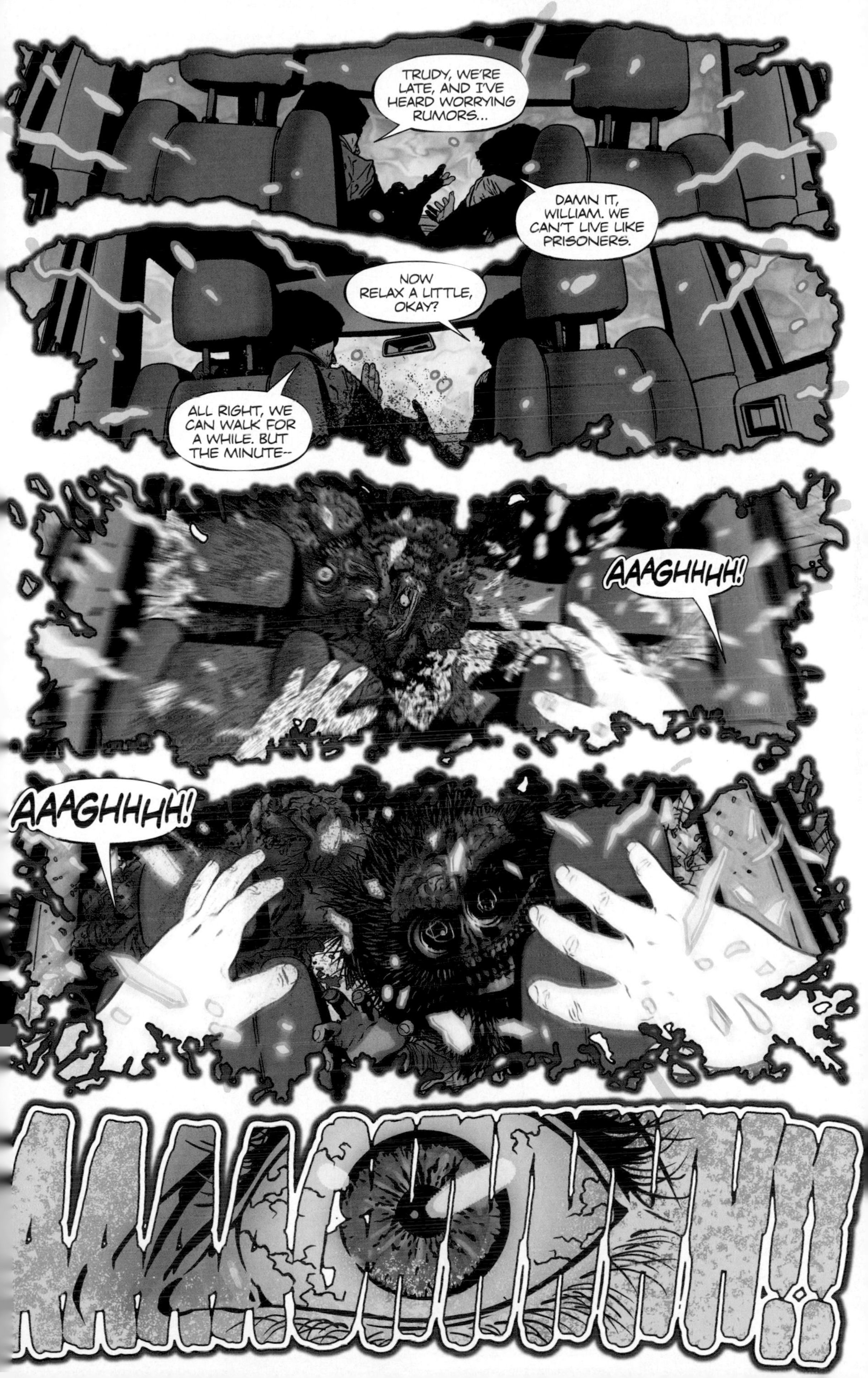
TRUDY, WE'RE LATE, AND I'VE HEARD WORRYING RUMORS...
DAMN IT, WILLIAM. WE CAN'T LIVE LIKE PRISONERS.
NOW RELAX A LITTLE, OKAY?
ALL RIGHT, WE CAN WALK FOR A WHILE. BUT THE MINUTE--
AAAGHHHH!
AAAGHHHH!

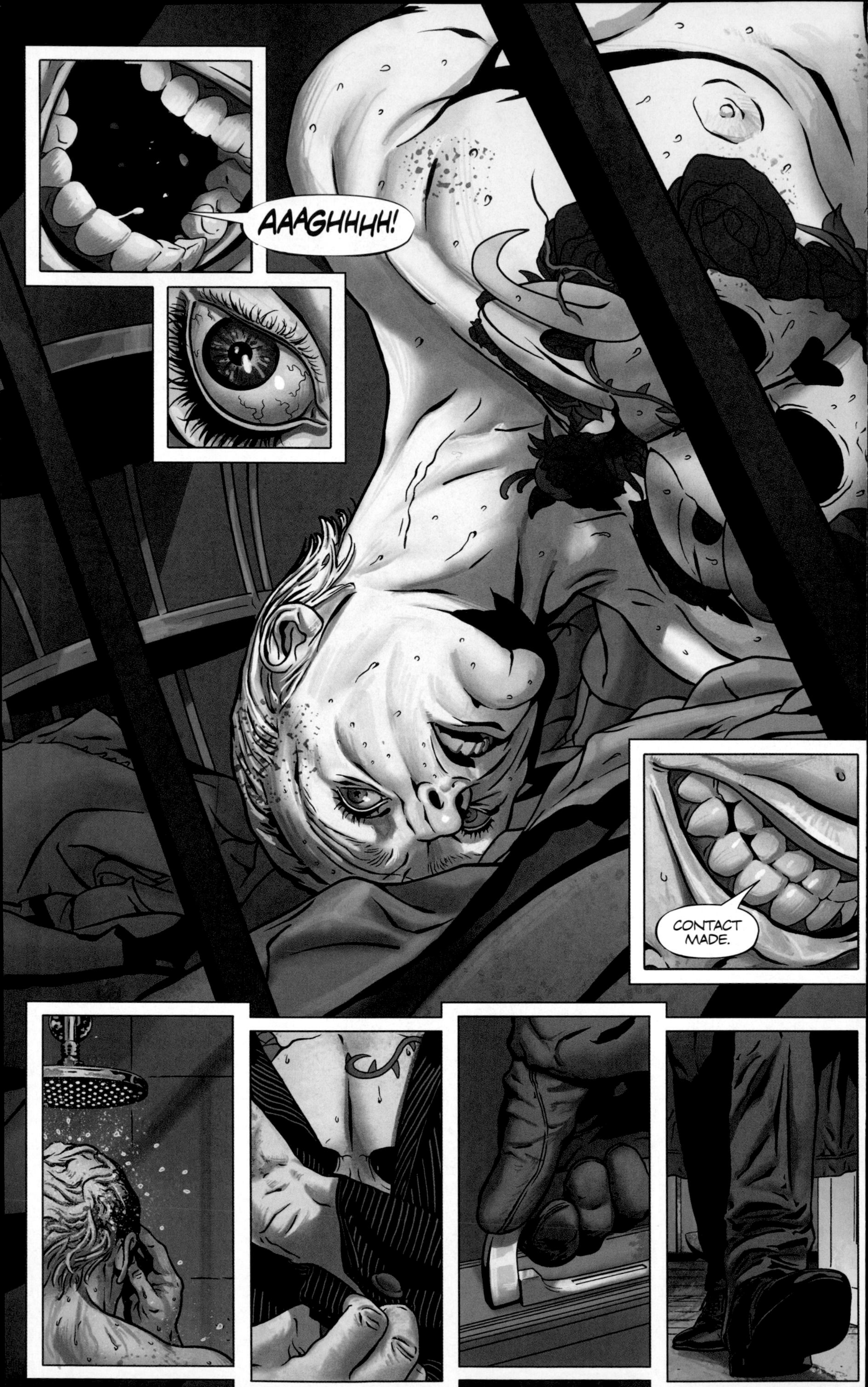
AAAGHHHH!
CONTACT MADE.

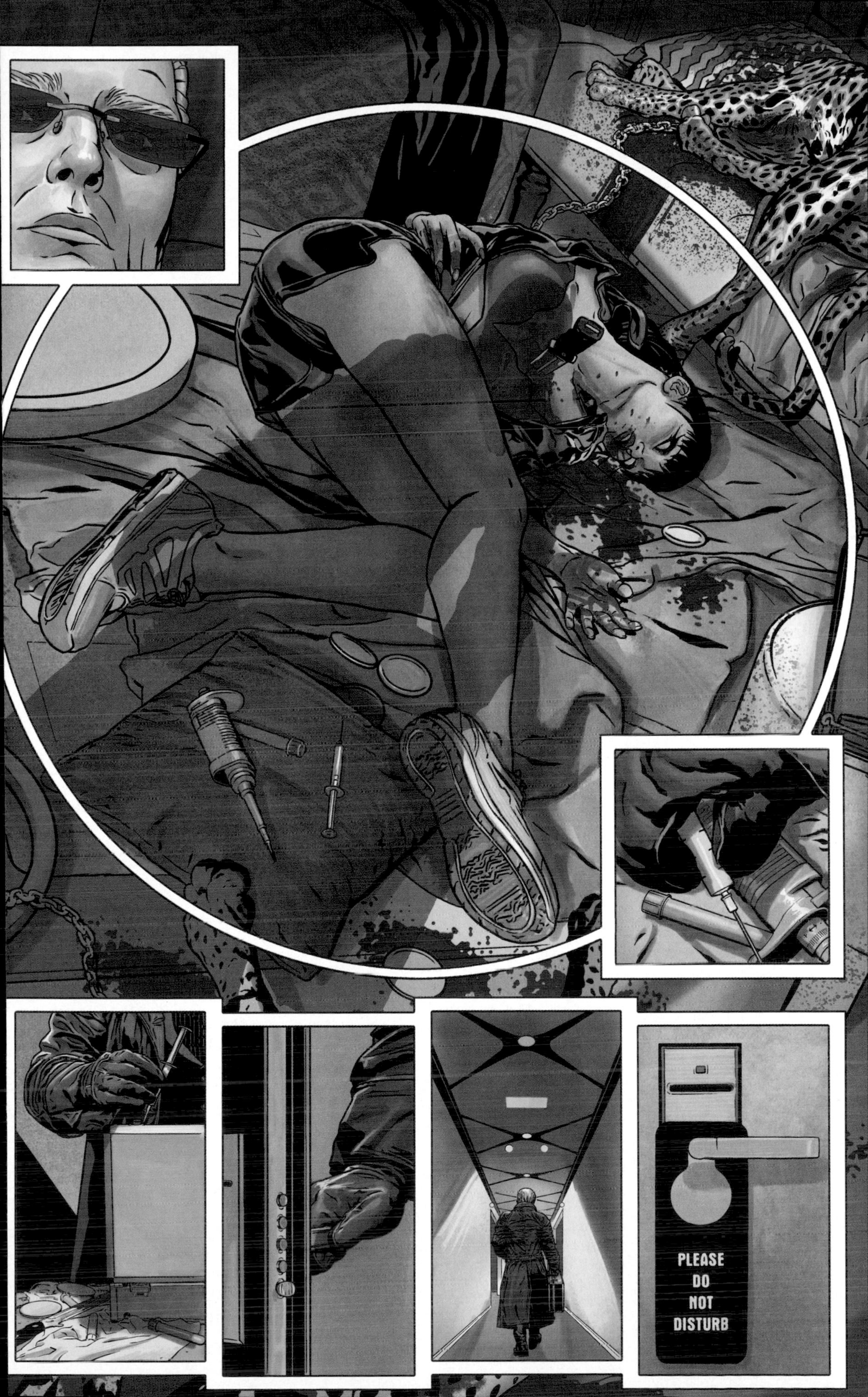
PLEASE DO NOT DISTURB

TARGET #2

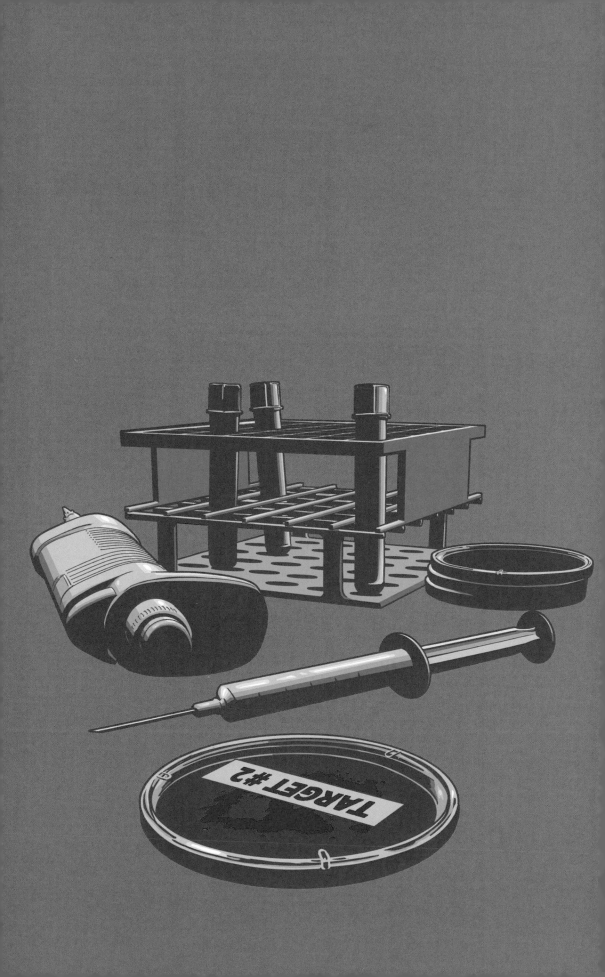

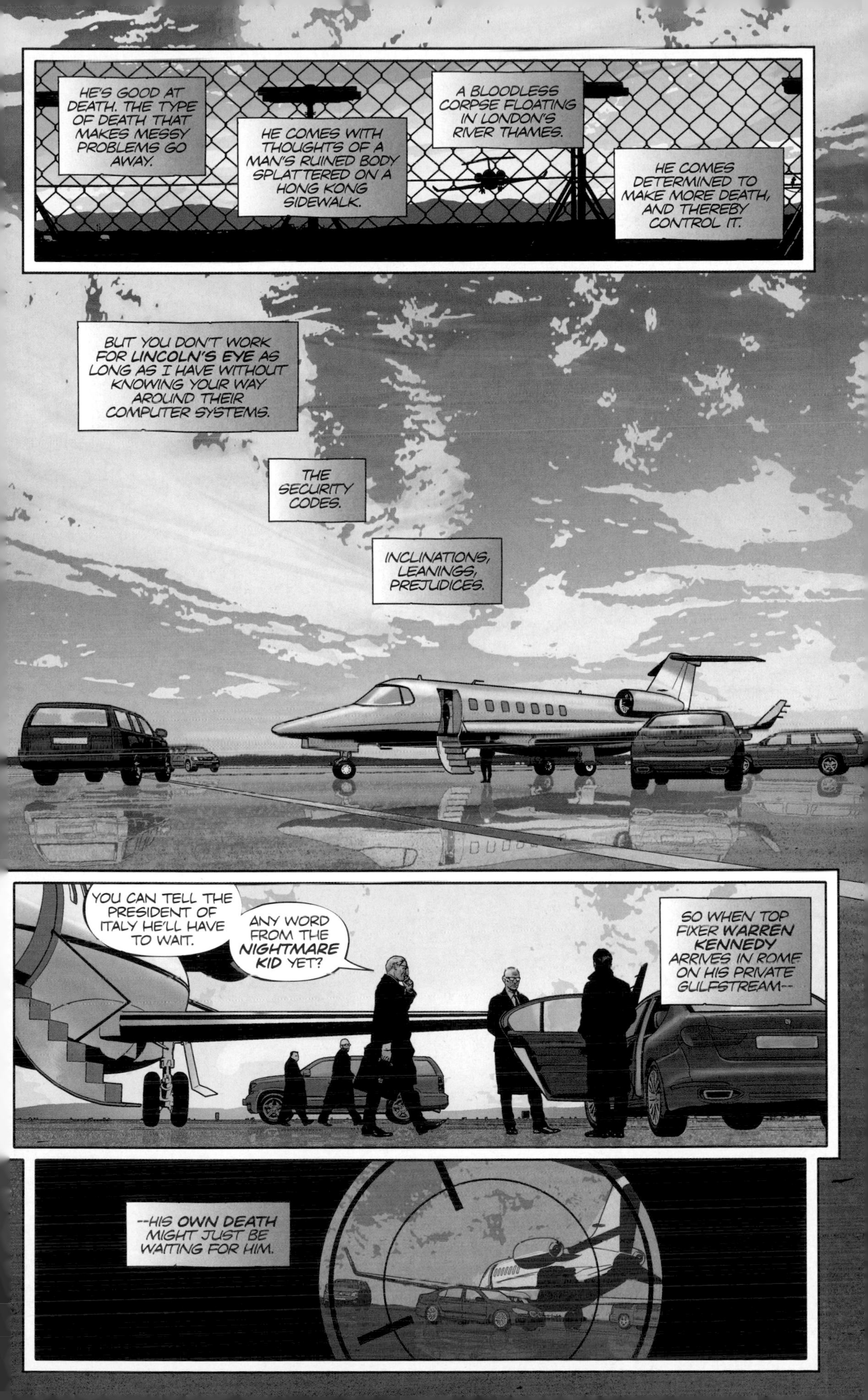
HE'S GOOD AT DEATH. THE TYPE OF DEATH THAT MAKES MESSY PROBLEMS GO AWAY.
HE COMES WITH THOUGHTS OF A MAN'S RUINED BODY SPLATTERED ON A HONG KONG SIDEWALK.
A BLOODLESS CORPSE FLOATING IN LONDON'S RIVER THAMES.
HE COMES DETERMINED TO MAKE MORE DEATH, AND THEREBY CONTROL IT.
BUT YOU DON'T WORK FOR LINCOLN'S EYE AS LONG AS I HAVE WITHOUT KNOWING YOUR WAY AROUND THEIR COMPUTER SYSTEMS.
THE SECURITY CODES.
INCLINATIONS, LEANINGS, PREJUDICES.
YOU CAN TELL THE PRESIDENT OF ITALY HE'LL HAVE TO WAIT.
ANY WORD FROM THE NIGHTMARE KID YET?
SO WHEN TOP FIXER WARREN KENNEDY ARRIVES IN ROME ON HIS PRIVATE GULFSTREAM--
--HIS OWN DEATH MIGHT JUST BE WAITING FOR HIM.

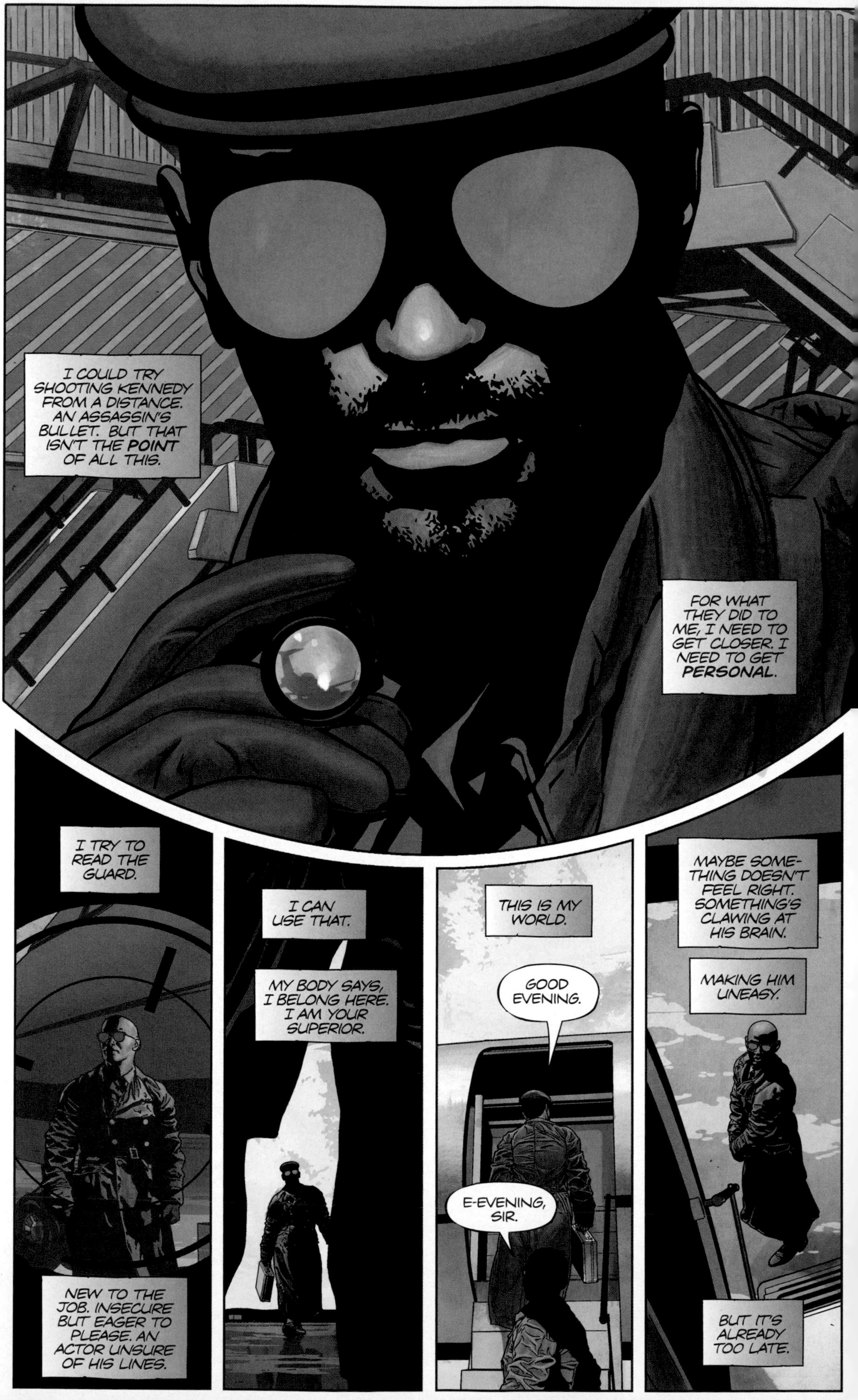
I COULD TRY SHOOTING KENNEDY FROM A DISTANCE. AN ASSASSIN'S BULLET. BUT THAT ISN'T THE POINT OF ALL THIS.
FOR WHAT THEY DID TO ME, I NEED TO GET CLOSER. I NEED TO GET PERSONAL.
I TRY TO READ THE GUARD.
NEW TO THE JOB. INSECURE BUT EAGER TO PLEASE. AN ACTOR UNSURE OF HIS LINES.
I CAN USE THAT.
MY BODY SAYS, I BELONG HERE. I AM YOUR SUPERIOR.
THIS IS MY WORLD.
GOOD EVENING.
E-EVENING, SIR.
MAYBE SOMETHING DOESN'T FEEL RIGHT. SOMETHING'S CLAWING AT HIS BRAIN.
MAKING HIM UNEASY.
BUT IT'S ALREADY TOO LATE.

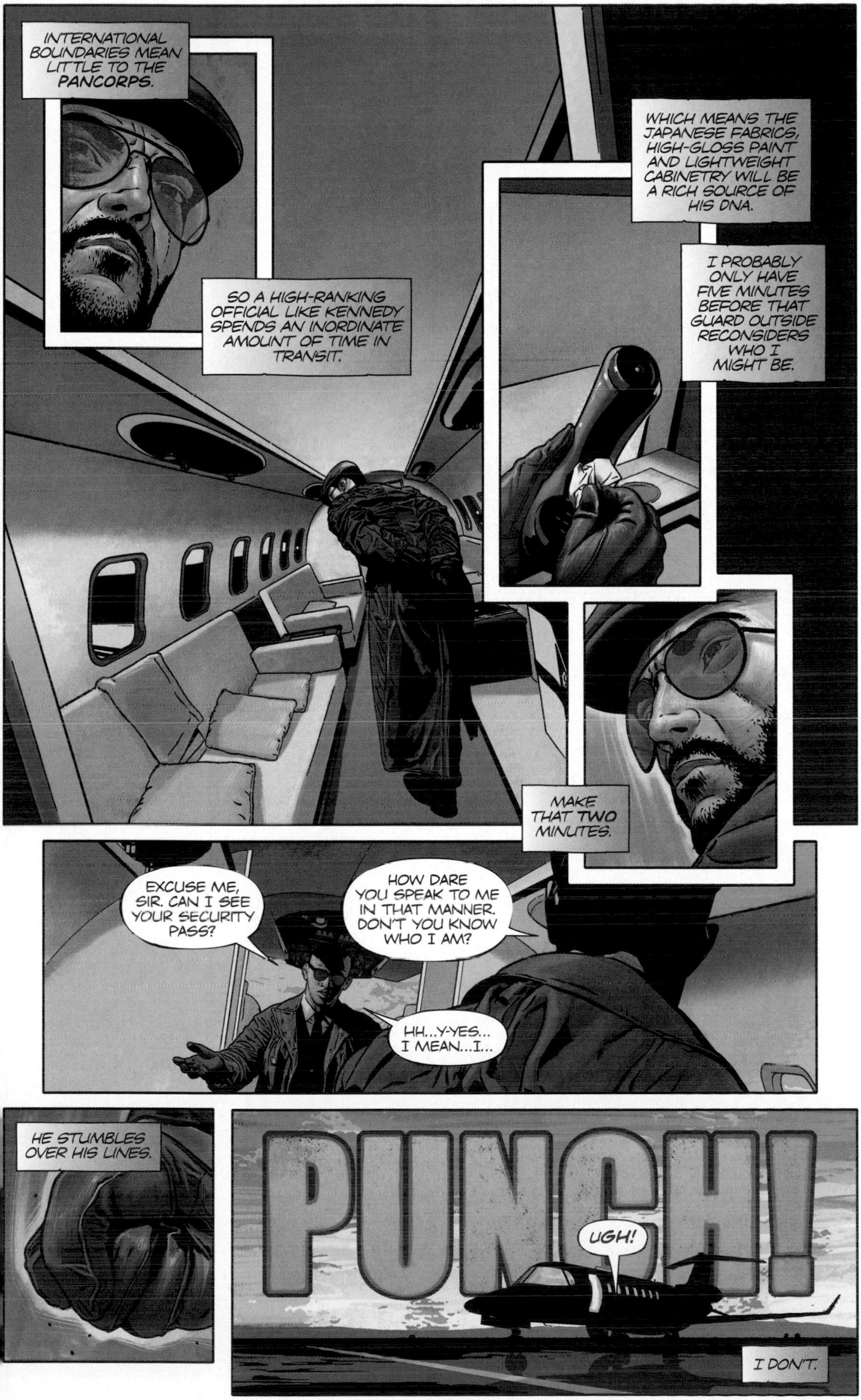
INTERNATIONAL BOUNDARIES MEAN LITTLE TO THE PANCORPS.
SO A HIGH-RANKING OFFICIAL LIKE KENNEDY SPENDS AN INORDINATE AMOUNT OF TIME IN TRANSIT.
WHICH MEANS THE JAPANESE FABRICS, HIGH-GLOSS PAINT AND LIGHTWEIGHT CABINETRY WILL BE A RICH SOURCE OF HIS DNA.
I PROBABLY ONLY HAVE FIVE MINUTES BEFORE THAT GUARD OUTSIDE RECONSIDERS WHO I MIGHT BE.
MAKE THAT TWO MINUTES.
EXCUSE ME, SIR. CAN I SEE YOUR SECURITY PASS?
HOW DARE YOU SPEAK TO ME IN THAT MANNER. DON'T YOU KNOW WHO I AM?
HH...Y-YES... I MEAN...I...
HE STUMBLES OVER HIS LINES.
PUNCH!
UGH!
I DON'T.

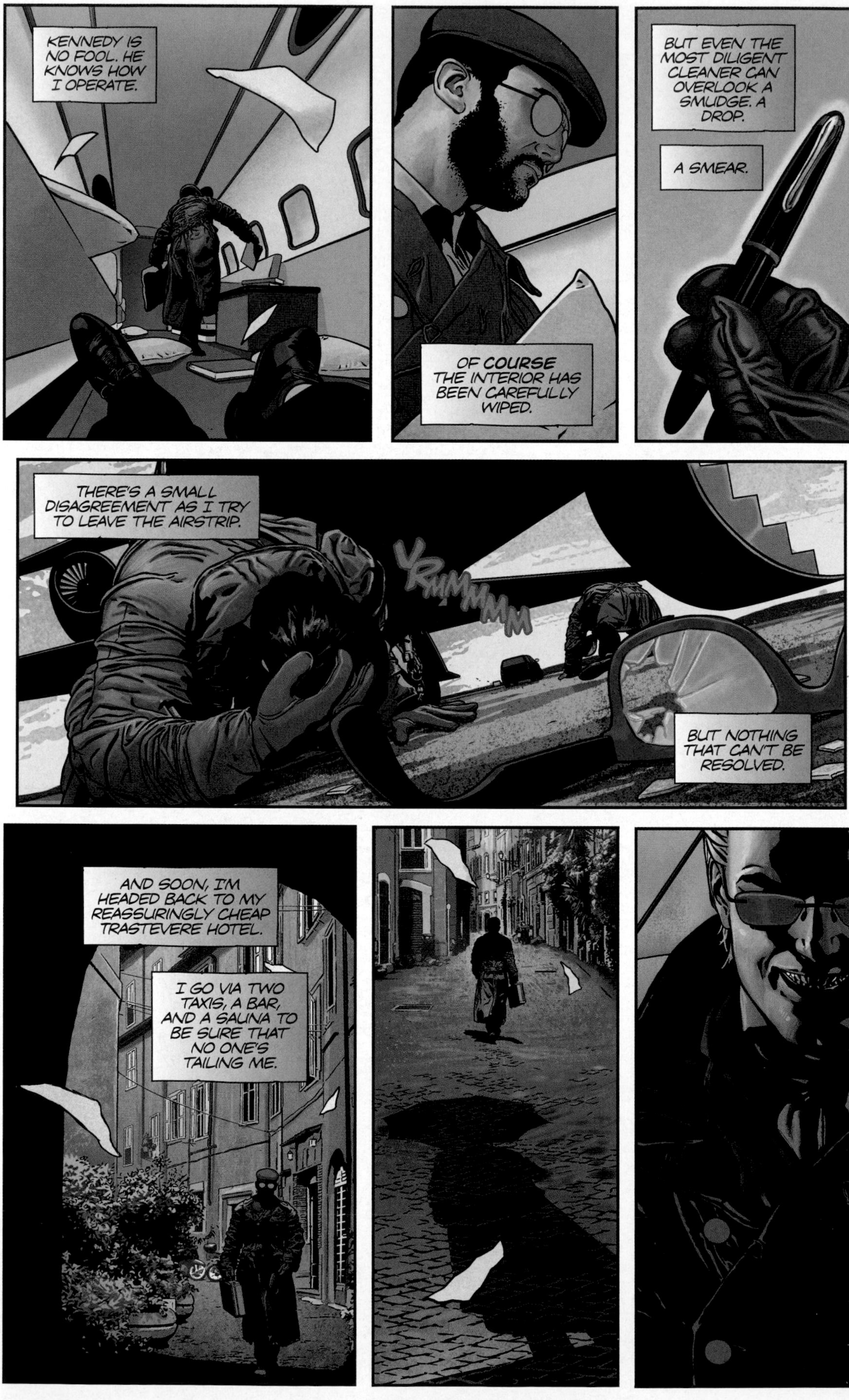

KENNEDY IS NO FOOL. HE KNOWS HOW I OPERATE.
OF COURSE THE INTERIOR HAS BEEN CAREFULLY WIPED.
BUT EVEN THE MOST DILIGENT CLEANER CAN OVERLOOK A SMUDGE. A DROP.
A SMEAR.
THERE'S A SMALL DISAGREEMENT AS I TRY TO LEAVE THE AIRSTRIP.
VRUMMMMM
BUT NOTHING THAT CAN'T BE RESOLVED.
AND SOON, I'M HEADED BACK TO MY REASSURINGLY CHEAP TRASTEVERE HOTEL.
I GO VIA TWO TAXIS, A BAR, AND A SAUNA TO BE SURE THAT NO ONE'S TAILING ME.

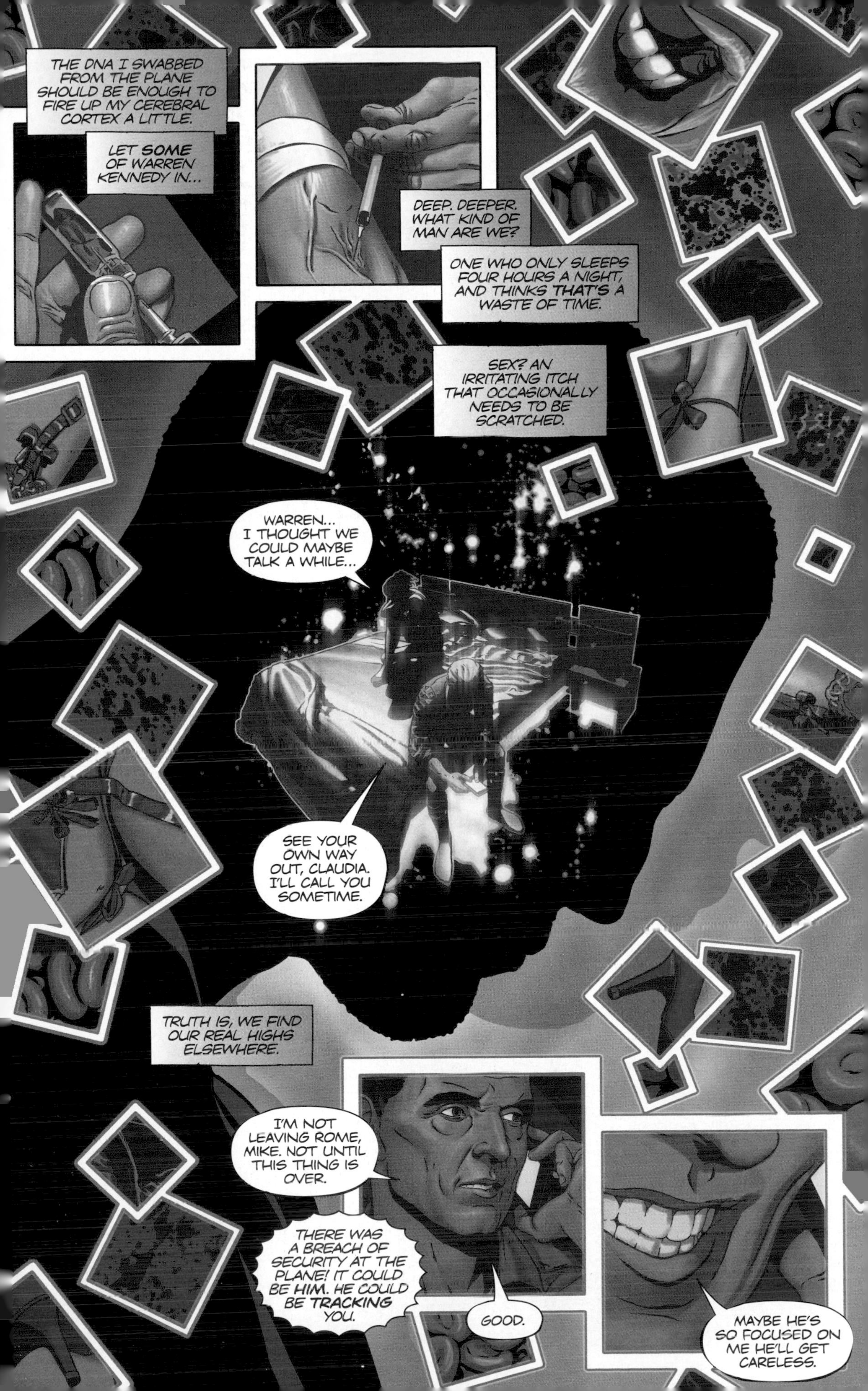
THE DNA I SWABBED FROM THE PLANE SHOULD BE ENOUGH TO FIRE UP MY CEREBRAL CORTEX A LITTLE.
LET SOME OF WARREN KENNEDY IN...
DEEP. DEEPER. WHAT KIND OF MAN ARE WE?
ONE WHO ONLY SLEEPS FOUR HOURS A NIGHT, AND THINKS THAT'S A WASTE OF TIME.
SEX? AN IRRITATING ITCH THAT OCCASIONALLY NEEDS TO BE SCRATCHED.
WARREN... I THOUGHT WE COULD MAYBE TALK A WHILE...
SEE YOUR OWN WAY OUT, CLAUDIA. I'LL CALL YOU SOMETIME.
TRUTH IS, WE FIND OUR REAL HIGHS ELSEWHERE.
I'M NOT LEAVING ROME, MIKE. NOT UNTIL THIS THING IS OVER.
THERE WAS A BREACH OF SECURITY AT THE PLANE! IT COULD BE HIM. HE COULD BE TRACKING YOU.
GOOD.
MAYBE HE'S SO FOCUSED ON ME HE'LL GET CARELESS.

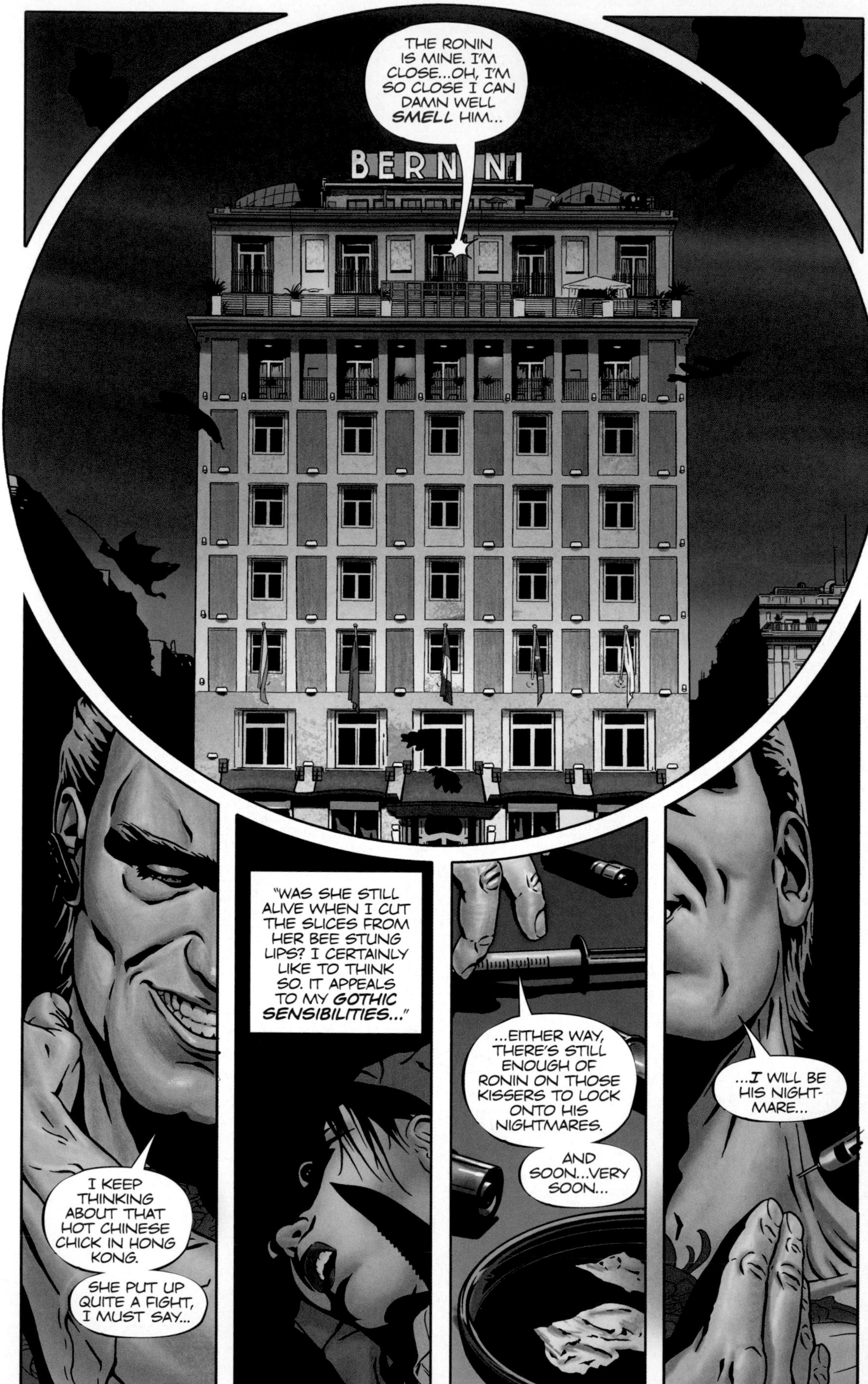
THE RONIN IS MINE. I'M CLOSE...OH, I'M SO CLOSE I CAN DAMN WELL **SMELL** HIM...
BERNINI
I KEEP THINKING ABOUT THAT HOT CHINESE CHICK IN HONG KONG.
SHE PUT UP QUITE A FIGHT, I MUST SAY...
"WAS SHE STILL ALIVE WHEN I CUT THE SLICES FROM HER BEE STUNG LIPS? I CERTAINLY LIKE TO THINK SO. IT APPEALS TO MY **GOTHIC SENSIBILITIES...**"
...EITHER WAY, THERE'S STILL ENOUGH OF RONIN ON THOSE KISSERS TO LOCK ONTO HIS NIGHTMARES.
AND SOON...VERY SOON...
...*I* WILL BE HIS NIGHT-MARE...

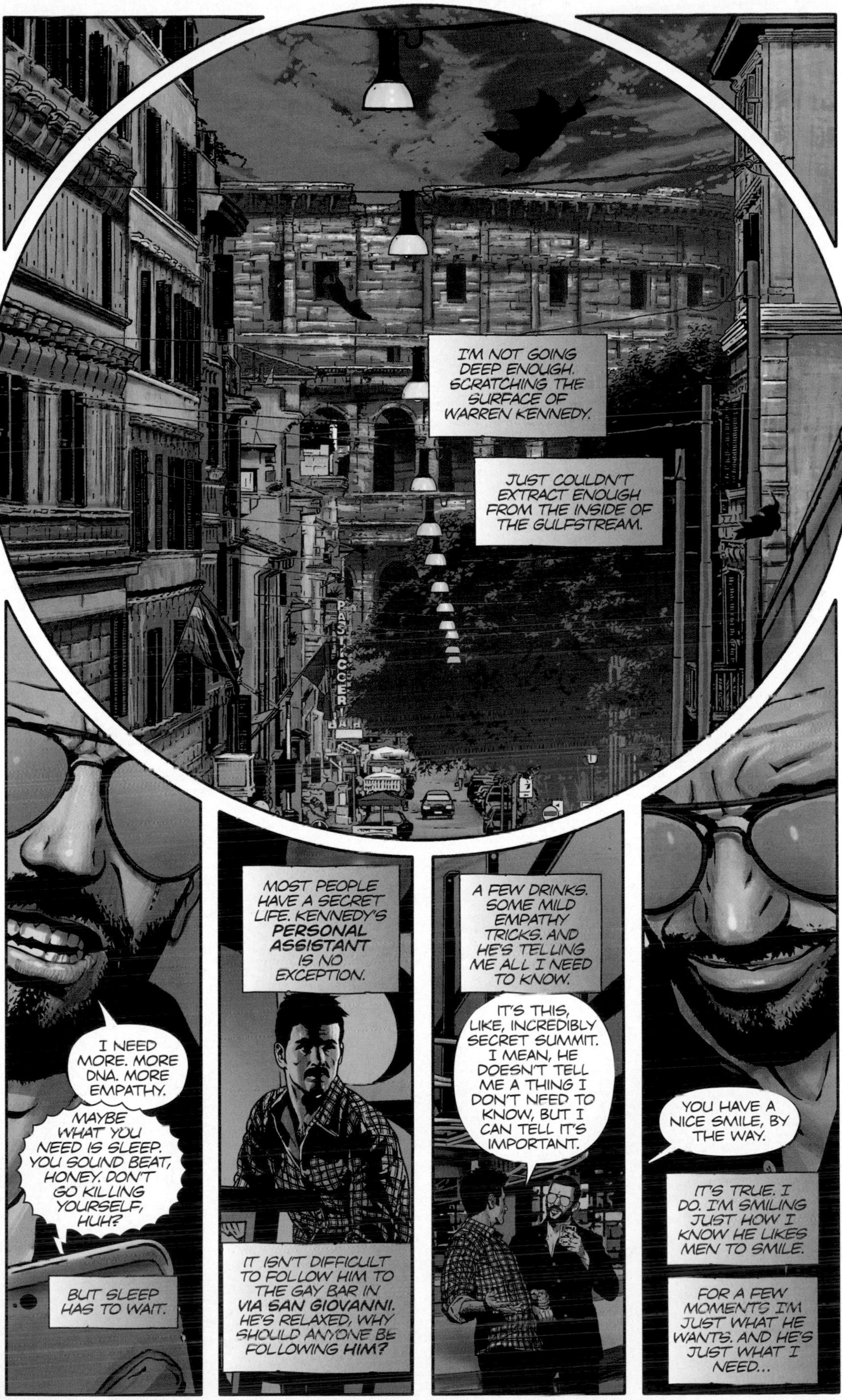
I'M NOT GOING DEEP ENOUGH. SCRATCHING THE SURFACE OF WARREN KENNEDY.
JUST COULDN'T EXTRACT ENOUGH FROM THE INSIDE OF THE GULFSTREAM.
PASTICCERIA
I NEED MORE. MORE DNA. MORE EMPATHY.
MAYBE WHAT YOU NEED IS SLEEP. YOU SOUND BEAT, HONEY. DON'T GO KILLING YOURSELF, HUH?
BUT SLEEP HAS TO WAIT.
MOST PEOPLE HAVE A SECRET LIFE. KENNEDY'S PERSONAL ASSISTANT IS NO EXCEPTION.
IT ISN'T DIFFICULT TO FOLLOW HIM TO THE GAY BAR IN VIA SAN GIOVANNI. HE'S RELAXED, WHY SHOULD ANYONE BE FOLLOWING HIM?
A FEW DRINKS. SOME MILD EMPATHY TRICKS. AND HE'S TELLING ME ALL I NEED TO KNOW.
IT'S THIS, LIKE, INCREDIBLY SECRET SUMMIT. I MEAN, HE DOESN'T TELL ME A THING I DON'T NEED TO KNOW, BUT I CAN TELL IT'S IMPORTANT.
YOU HAVE A NICE SMILE, BY THE WAY.
IT'S TRUE. I DO. I'M SMILING JUST HOW I KNOW HE LIKES MEN TO SMILE.
FOR A FEW MOMENTS I'M JUST WHAT HE WANTS. AND HE'S JUST WHAT I NEED...

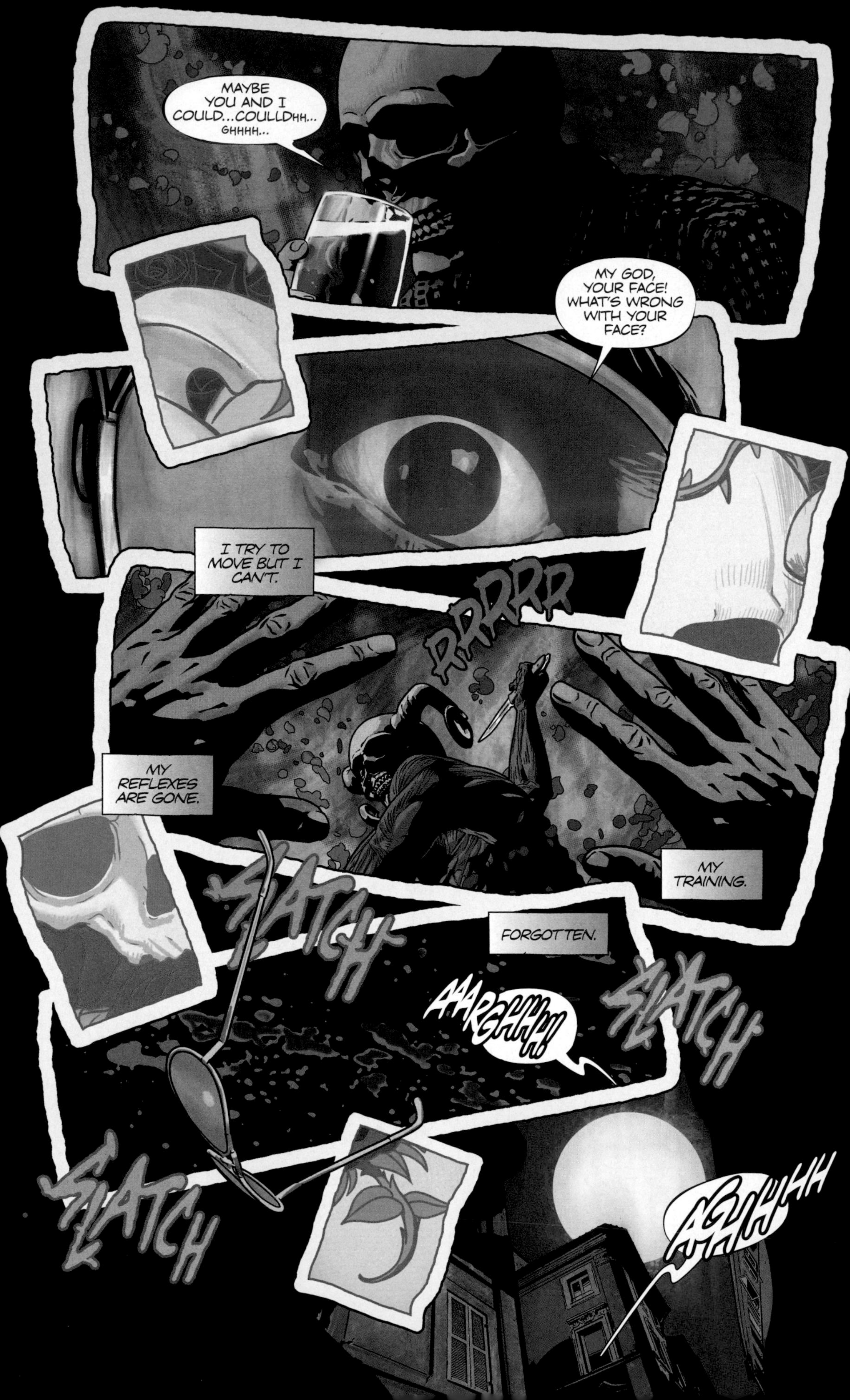
MAYBE YOU AND I COULD...COULLDHH... GHHHH...
MY GOD, YOUR FACE! WHAT'S WRONG WITH YOUR FACE?
I TRY TO MOVE BUT I CAN'T.
RRRRR
MY REFLEXES ARE GONE.
MY TRAINING.
FORGOTTEN.
SLATCH
AAARGHHH!
SLATCH
SLATCH
AGHHHHH

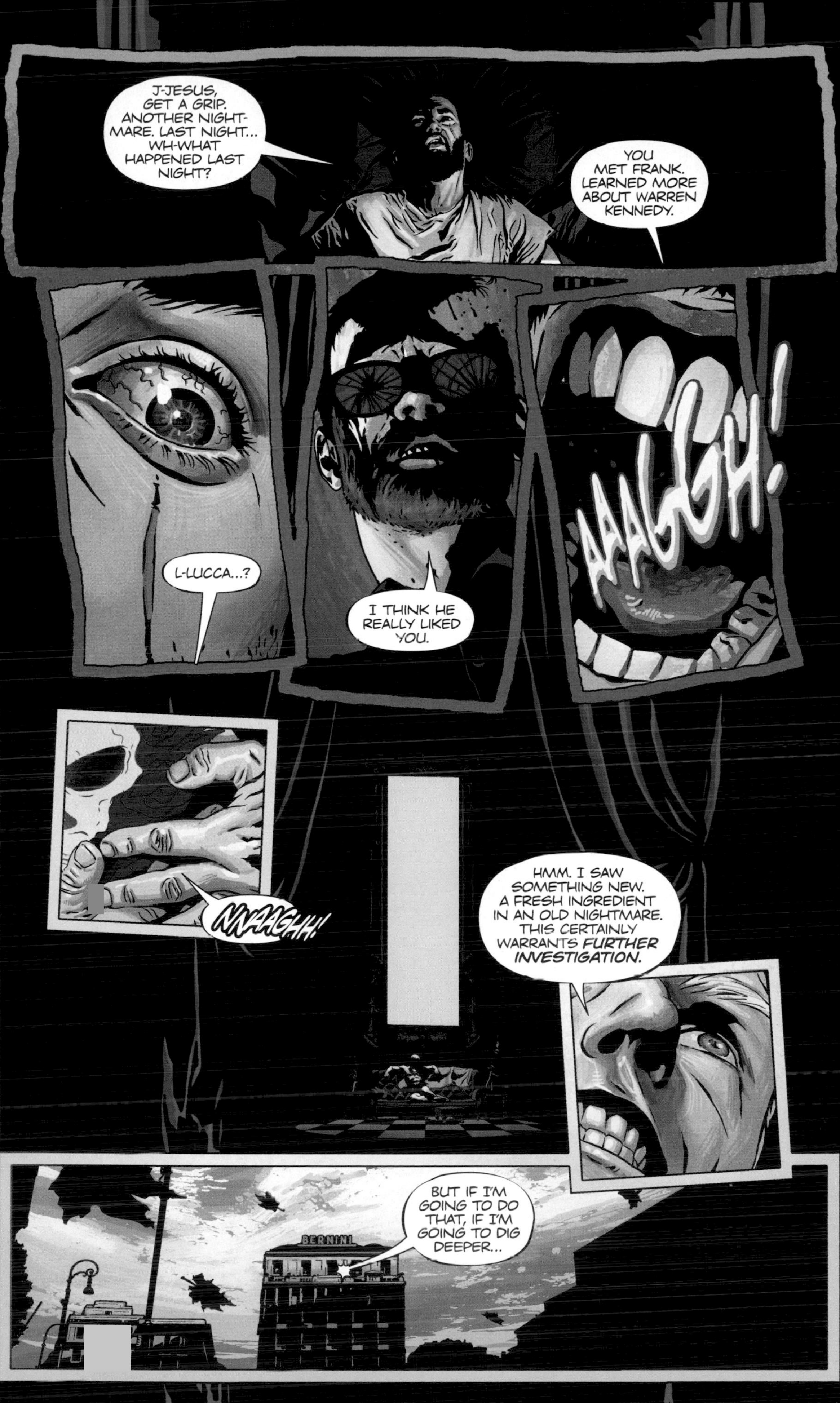

J-JESUS, GET A GRIP. ANOTHER NIGHT-MARE. LAST NIGHT... WH-WHAT HAPPENED LAST NIGHT?
YOU MET FRANK. LEARNED MORE ABOUT WARREN KENNEDY.
L-LUCCA...?
I THINK HE REALLY LIKED YOU.
AAAGGH!
NNAAGHH!
HMM. I SAW SOMETHING NEW. A FRESH INGREDIENT IN AN OLD NIGHTMARE. THIS CERTAINLY WARRANTS FURTHER INVESTIGATION.
BERNINI
BUT IF I'M GOING TO DO THAT, IF I'M GOING TO DIG DEEPER...

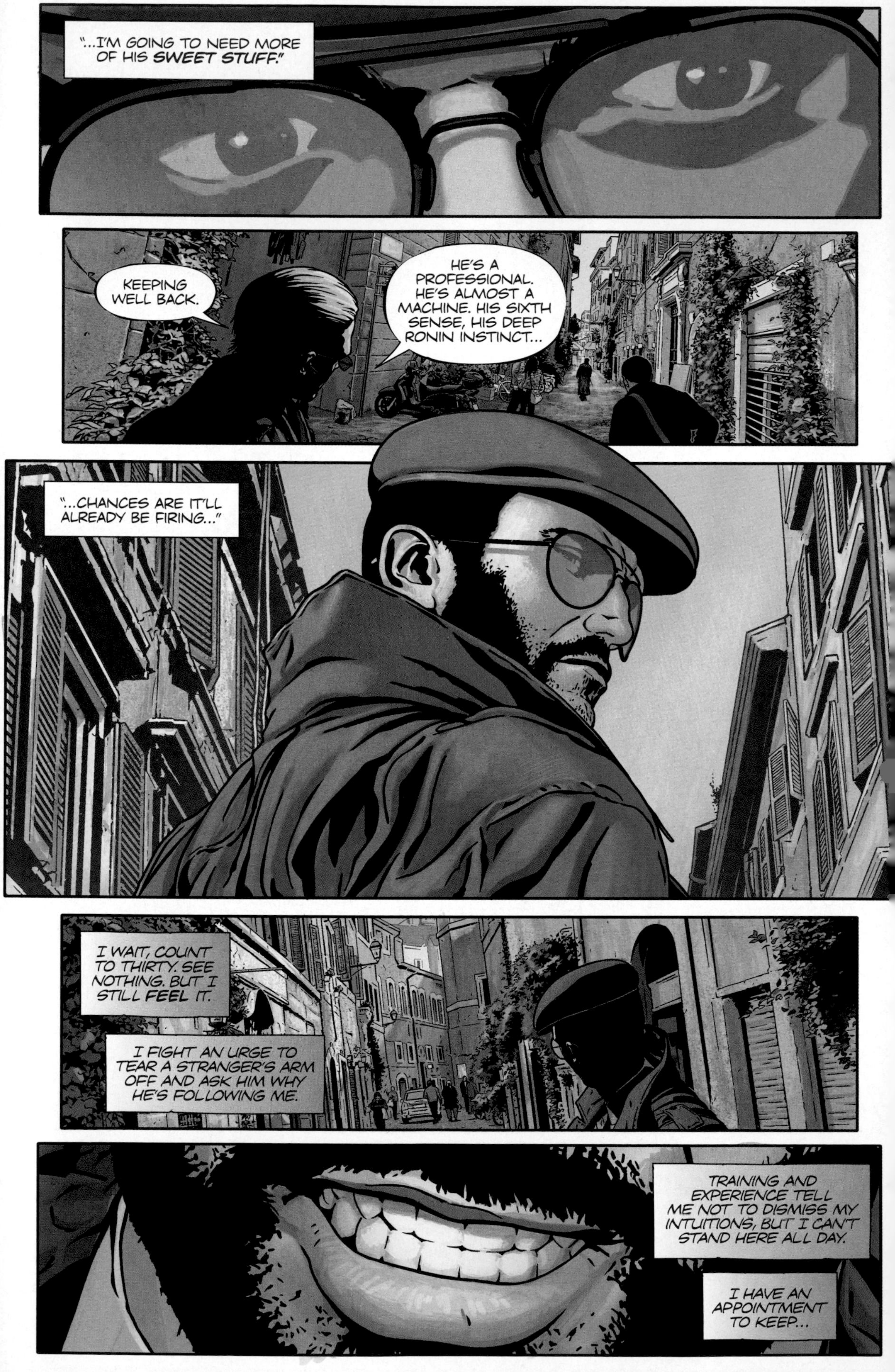
"...I'M GOING TO NEED MORE OF HIS SWEET STUFF."
KEEPING WELL BACK.
HE'S A PROFESSIONAL. HE'S ALMOST A MACHINE. HIS SIXTH SENSE, HIS DEEP RONIN INSTINCT...
"...CHANCES ARE IT'LL ALREADY BE FIRING..."
I WAIT, COUNT TO THIRTY. SEE NOTHING. BUT I STILL FEEL IT.
I FIGHT AN URGE TO TEAR A STRANGER'S ARM OFF AND ASK HIM WHY HE'S FOLLOWING ME.
TRAINING AND EXPERIENCE TELL ME NOT TO DISMISS MY INTUITIONS, BUT I CAN'T STAND HERE ALL DAY.
I HAVE AN APPOINTMENT TO KEEP...

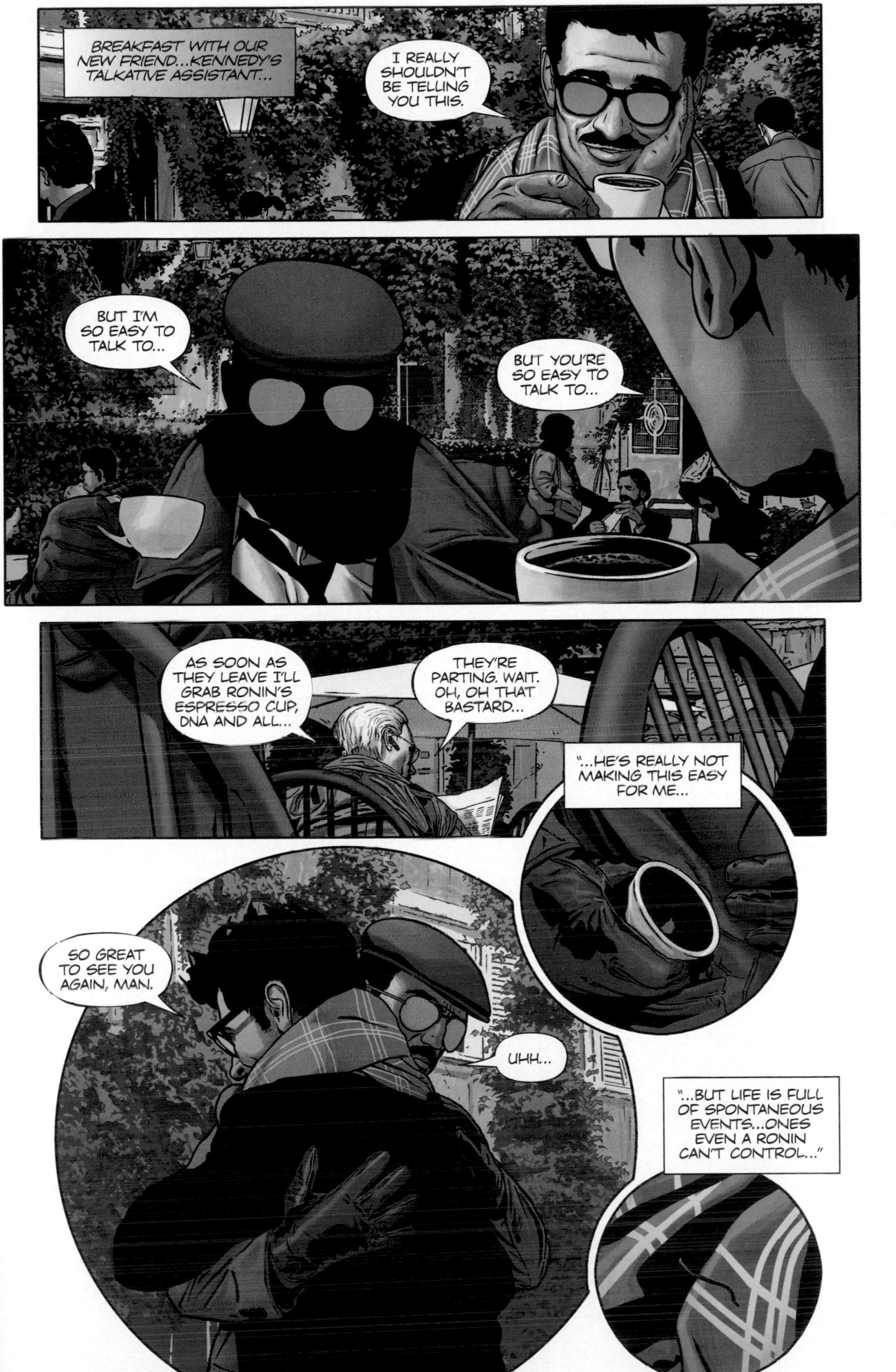
BREAKFAST WITH OUR NEW FRIEND...KENNEDY'S TALKATIVE ASSISTANT...
I REALLY SHOULDN'T BE TELLING YOU THIS.
BUT I'M SO EASY TO TALK TO...
BUT YOU'RE SO EASY TO TALK TO...
AS SOON AS THEY LEAVE I'LL GRAB RONIN'S ESPRESSO CUP, DNA AND ALL...
THEY'RE PARTING. WAIT. OH, OH THAT BASTARD...
"...HE'S REALLY NOT MAKING THIS EASY FOR ME...
SO GREAT TO SEE YOU AGAIN, MAN.
UHH...
"...BUT LIFE IS FULL OF SPONTANEOUS EVENTS...ONES EVEN A RONIN CAN'T CONTROL..."

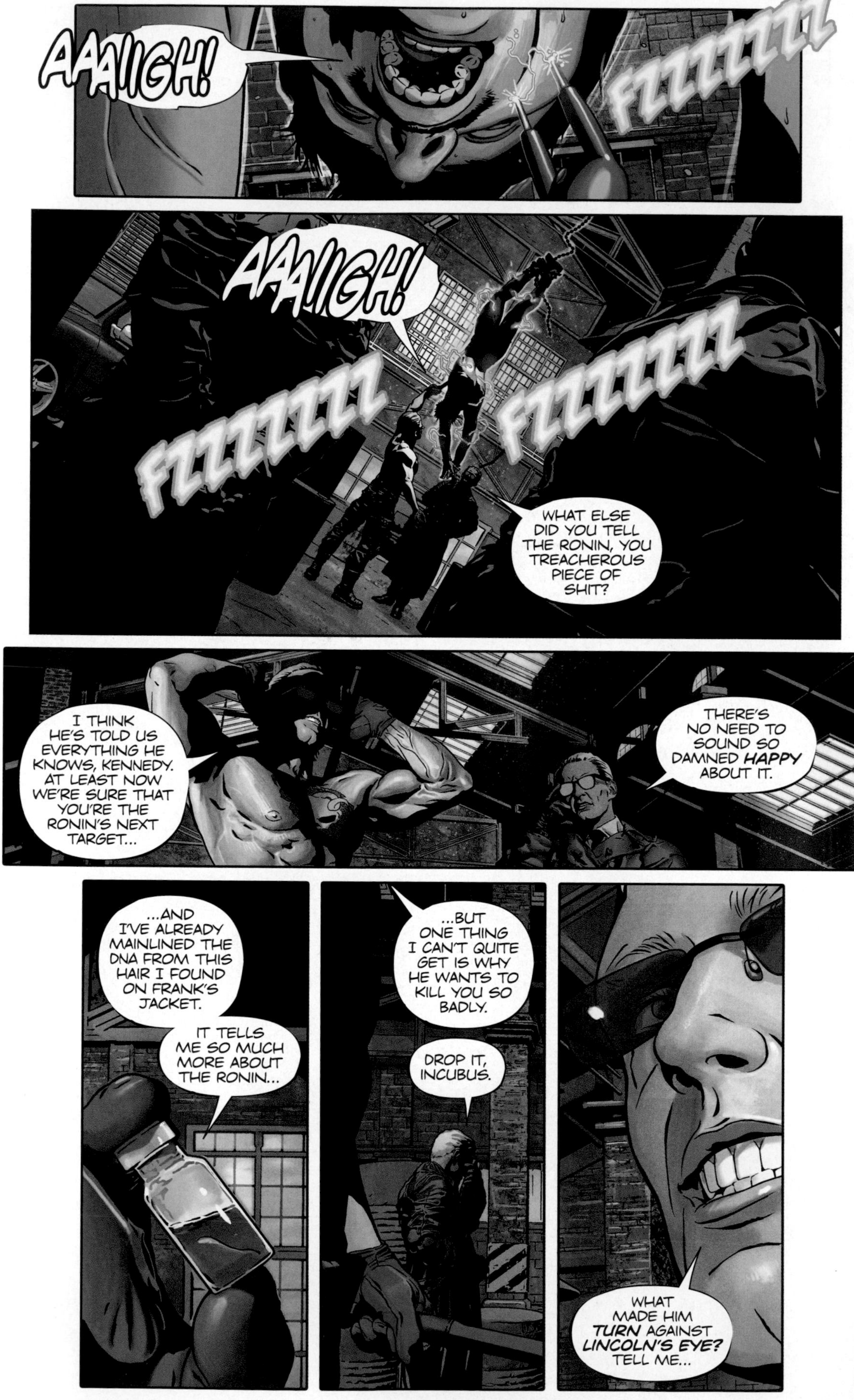
AAAIIGH!
FZZZZZZZZ
AAAIIGH!
FZZZZZZZZ
FZZZZZZZZ
WHAT ELSE DID YOU TELL THE RONIN, YOU TREACHEROUS PIECE OF SHIT?
I THINK HE'S TOLD US EVERYTHING HE KNOWS, KENNEDY. AT LEAST NOW WE'RE SURE THAT YOU'RE THE RONIN'S NEXT TARGET...
THERE'S NO NEED TO SOUND SO DAMNED *HAPPY* ABOUT IT.
...AND I'VE ALREADY MAINLINED THE DNA FROM THIS HAIR I FOUND ON FRANK'S JACKET.
IT TELLS ME SO MUCH MORE ABOUT THE RONIN...
...BUT ONE THING I CAN'T QUITE GET IS WHY HE WANTS TO KILL YOU SO BADLY.
DROP IT, INCUBUS.
WHAT MADE HIM *TURN* AGAINST *LINCOLN'S EYE?* TELL ME...

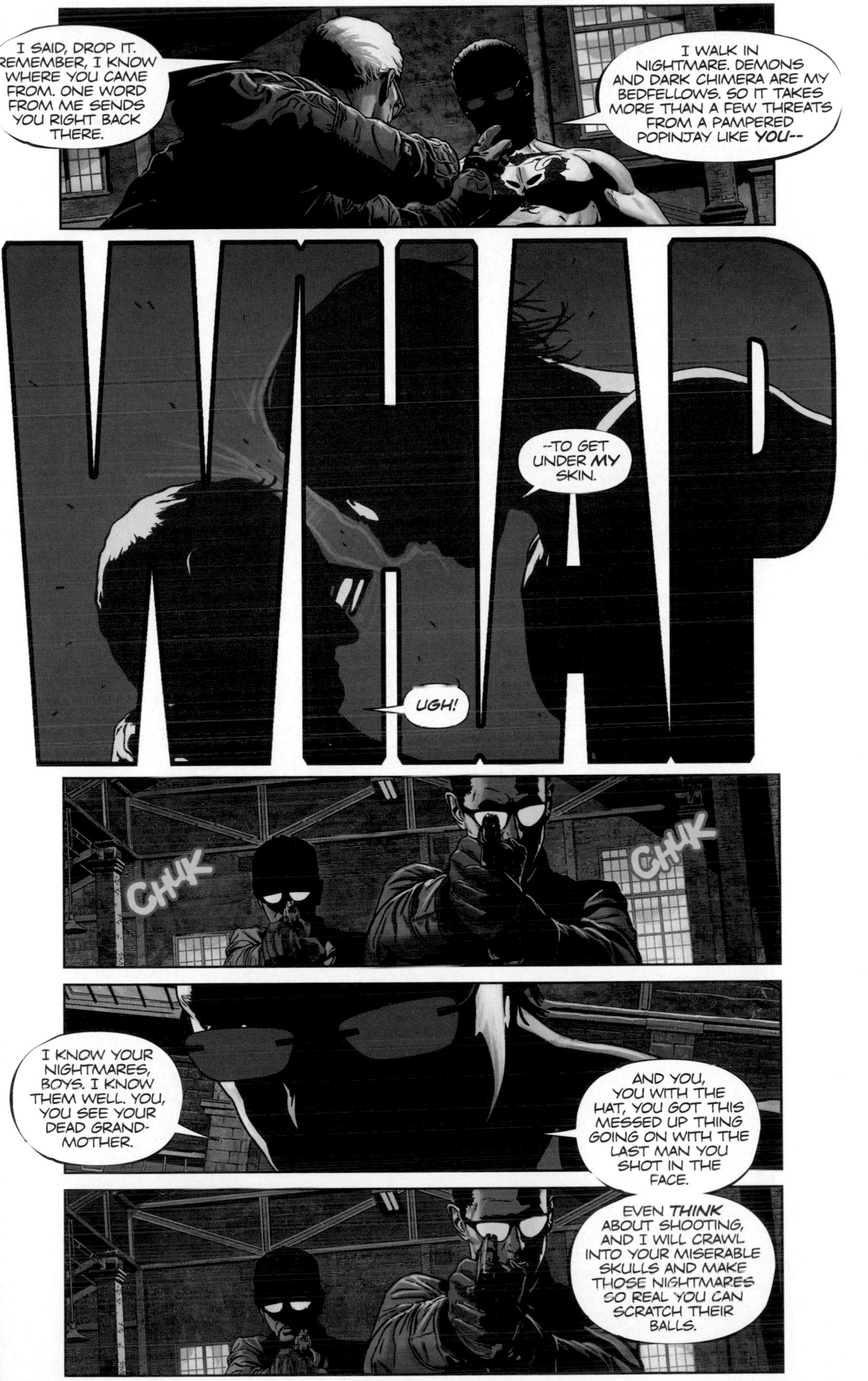
I SAID, DROP IT. REMEMBER, I KNOW WHERE YOU CAME FROM. ONE WORD FROM ME SENDS YOU RIGHT BACK THERE.
I WALK IN NIGHTMARE. DEMONS AND DARK CHIMERA ARE MY BEDFELLOWS. SO IT TAKES MORE THAN A FEW THREATS FROM A PAMPERED POPINJAY LIKE YOU--
WHAP
--TO GET UNDER MY SKIN.
UGH!
CHUK
CHUK
I KNOW YOUR NIGHTMARES, BOYS. I KNOW THEM WELL. YOU, YOU SEE YOUR DEAD GRAND-MOTHER.
AND YOU, YOU WITH THE HAT, YOU GOT THIS MESSED UP THING GOING ON WITH THE LAST MAN YOU SHOT IN THE FACE.
EVEN THINK ABOUT SHOOTING, AND I WILL CRAWL INTO YOUR MISERABLE SKULLS AND MAKE THOSE NIGHTMARES SO REAL YOU CAN SCRATCH THEIR BALLS.

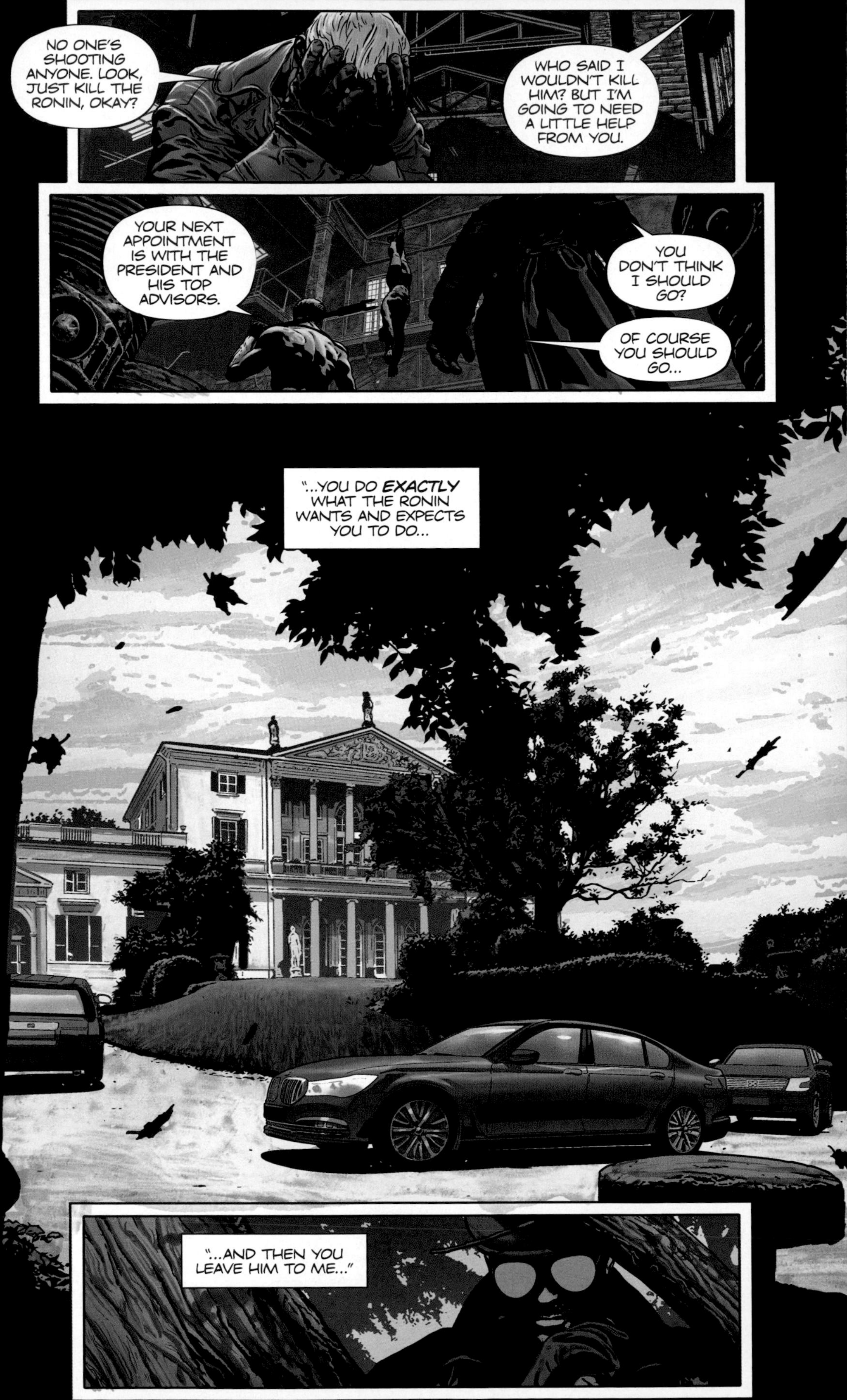
NO ONE'S SHOOTING ANYONE. LOOK, JUST KILL THE RONIN, OKAY?
WHO SAID I WOULDN'T KILL HIM? BUT I'M GOING TO NEED A LITTLE HELP FROM YOU.
YOUR NEXT APPOINTMENT IS WITH THE PRESIDENT AND HIS TOP ADVISORS.
YOU DON'T THINK I SHOULD GO?
OF COURSE YOU SHOULD GO...
"...YOU DO EXACTLY WHAT THE RONIN WANTS AND EXPECTS YOU TO DO...
"...AND THEN YOU LEAVE HIM TO ME..."

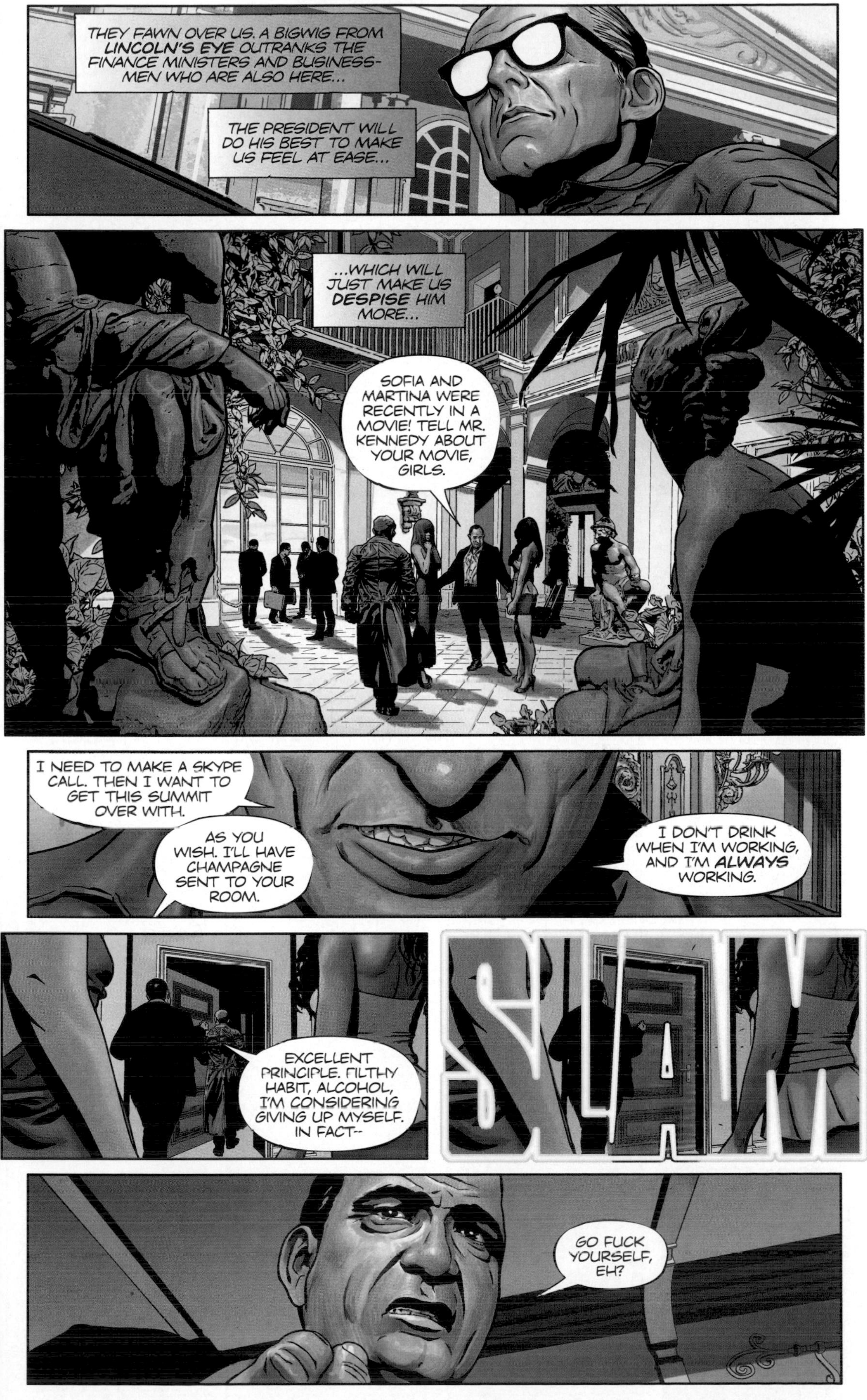

THEY FAWN OVER US. A BIGWIG FROM LINCOLN'S EYE OUTRANKS THE FINANCE MINISTERS AND BUSINESS-MEN WHO ARE ALSO HERE...
THE PRESIDENT WILL DO HIS BEST TO MAKE US FEEL AT EASE...
...WHICH WILL JUST MAKE US DESPISE HIM MORE...
SOFIA AND MARTINA WERE RECENTLY IN A MOVIE! TELL MR. KENNEDY ABOUT YOUR MOVIE, GIRLS.
I NEED TO MAKE A SKYPE CALL. THEN I WANT TO GET THIS SUMMIT OVER WITH.
AS YOU WISH. I'LL HAVE CHAMPAGNE SENT TO YOUR ROOM.
I DON'T DRINK WHEN I'M WORKING, AND I'M ALWAYS WORKING.
EXCELLENT PRINCIPLE. FILTHY HABIT, ALCOHOL, I'M CONSIDERING GIVING UP MYSELF. IN FACT--
SLAM
GO FUCK YOURSELF, EH?

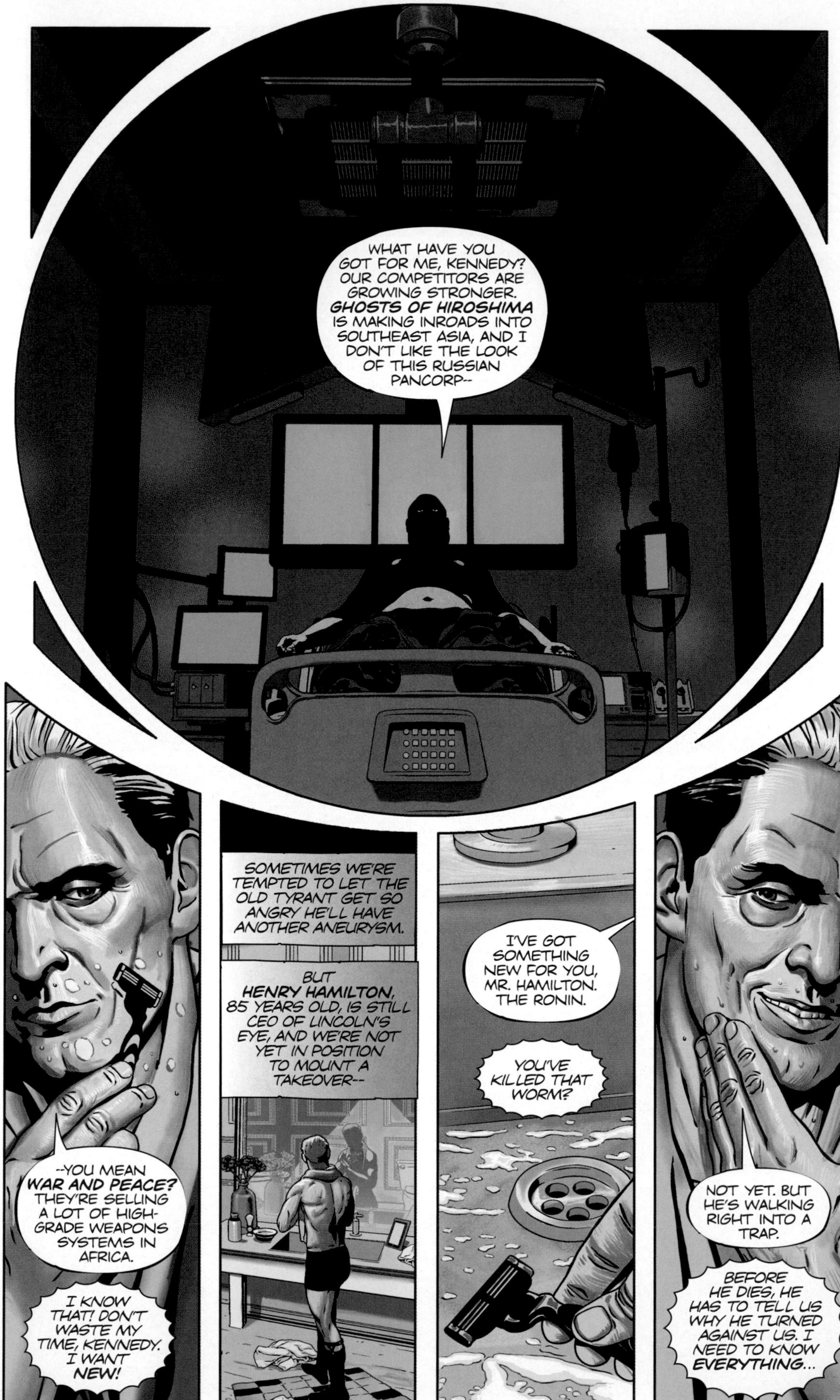
WHAT HAVE YOU GOT FOR ME, KENNEDY? OUR COMPETITORS ARE GROWING STRONGER. GHOSTS OF HIROSHIMA IS MAKING INROADS INTO SOUTHEAST ASIA, AND I DON'T LIKE THE LOOK OF THIS RUSSIAN PANCORP--
--YOU MEAN WAR AND PEACE? THEY'RE SELLING A LOT OF HIGH-GRADE WEAPONS SYSTEMS IN AFRICA.
I KNOW THAT! DON'T WASTE MY TIME, KENNEDY. I WANT NEW!
SOMETIMES WE'RE TEMPTED TO LET THE OLD TYRANT GET SO ANGRY HE'LL HAVE ANOTHER ANEURYSM.
BUT HENRY HAMILTON, 85 YEARS OLD, IS STILL CEO OF LINCOLN'S EYE, AND WE'RE NOT YET IN POSITION TO MOUNT A TAKEOVER--
I'VE GOT SOMETHING NEW FOR YOU, MR. HAMILTON. THE RONIN.
YOU'VE KILLED THAT WORM?
NOT YET. BUT HE'S WALKING RIGHT INTO A TRAP.
BEFORE HE DIES, HE HAS TO TELL US WHY HE TURNED AGAINST US. I NEED TO KNOW EVERYTHING...

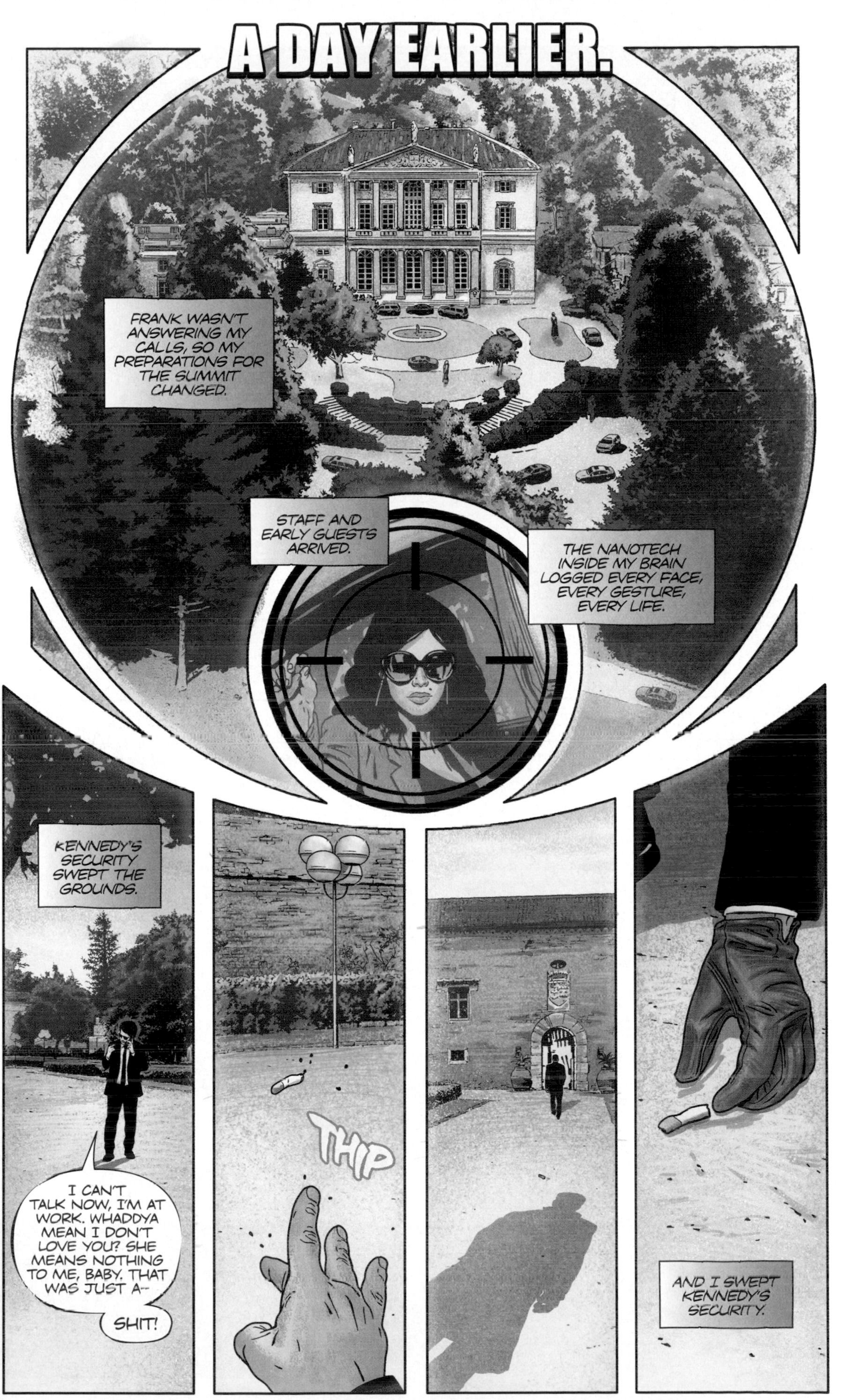
A DAY EARLIER.
FRANK WASN'T ANSWERING MY CALLS, SO MY PREPARATIONS FOR THE SUMMIT CHANGED.
STAFF AND EARLY GUESTS ARRIVED.
THE NANOTECH INSIDE MY BRAIN LOGGED EVERY FACE, EVERY GESTURE, EVERY LIFE.
KENNEDY'S SECURITY SWEPT THE GROUNDS.
I CAN'T TALK NOW, I'M AT WORK. WHADDYA MEAN I DON'T LOVE YOU? SHE MEANS NOTHING TO ME, BABY. THAT WAS JUST A--
SHIT!
THIP
AND I SWEPT KENNEDY'S SECURITY.

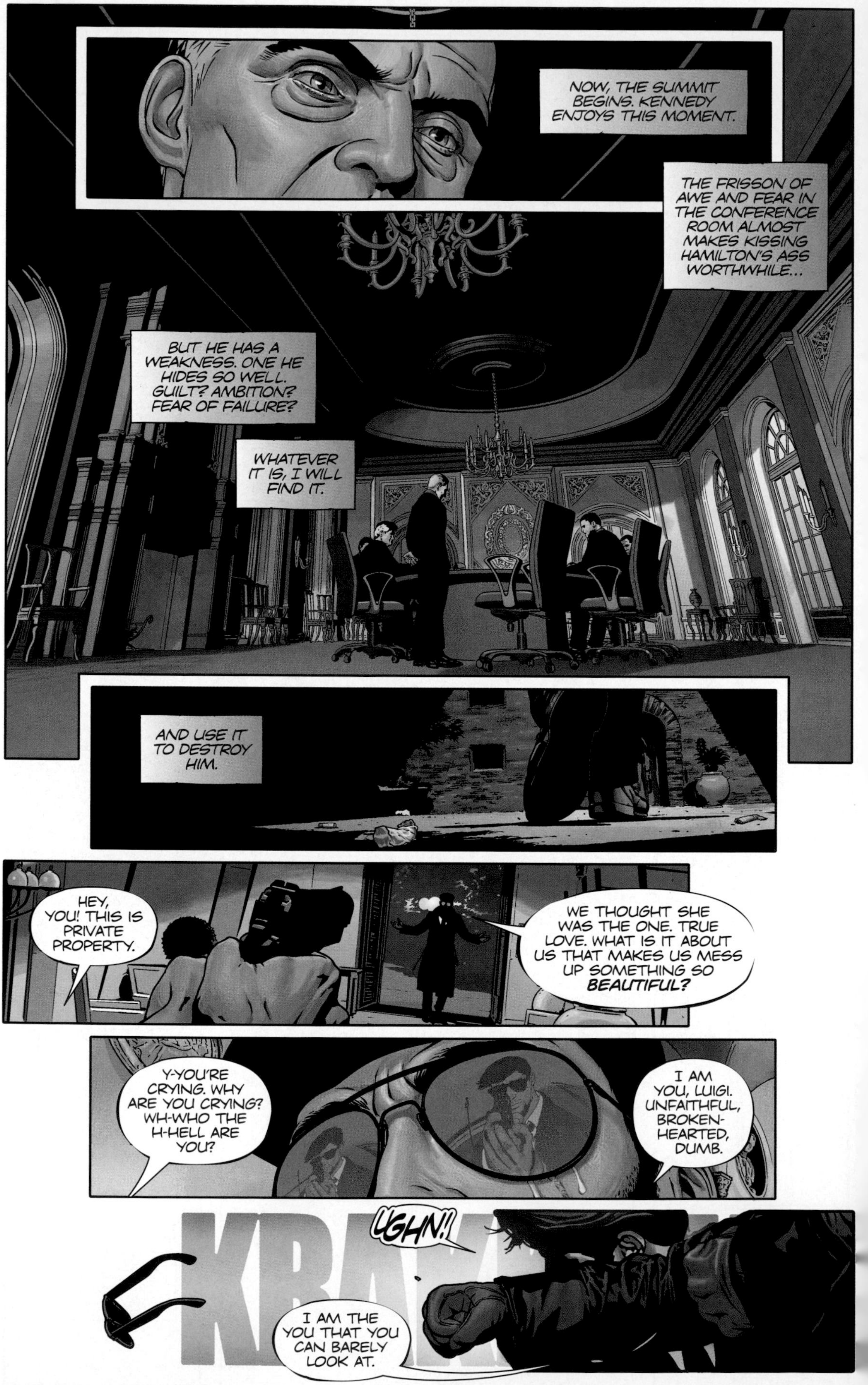
NOW, THE SUMMIT BEGINS. KENNEDY ENJOYS THIS MOMENT.
THE FRISSON OF AWE AND FEAR IN THE CONFERENCE ROOM ALMOST MAKES KISSING HAMILTON'S ASS WORTHWHILE...
BUT HE HAS A WEAKNESS. ONE HE HIDES SO WELL. GUILT? AMBITION? FEAR OF FAILURE?
WHATEVER IT IS, I WILL FIND IT.
AND USE IT TO DESTROY HIM.
HEY, YOU! THIS IS PRIVATE PROPERTY.
WE THOUGHT SHE WAS THE ONE. TRUE LOVE. WHAT IS IT ABOUT US THAT MAKES US MESS UP SOMETHING SO BEAUTIFUL?
Y-YOU'RE CRYING. WHY ARE YOU CRYING? WH-WHO THE H-HELL ARE YOU?
I AM YOU, LUIGI. UNFAITHFUL, BROKEN-HEARTED, DUMB.
UGHN!!
I AM THE YOU THAT YOU CAN BARELY LOOK AT.

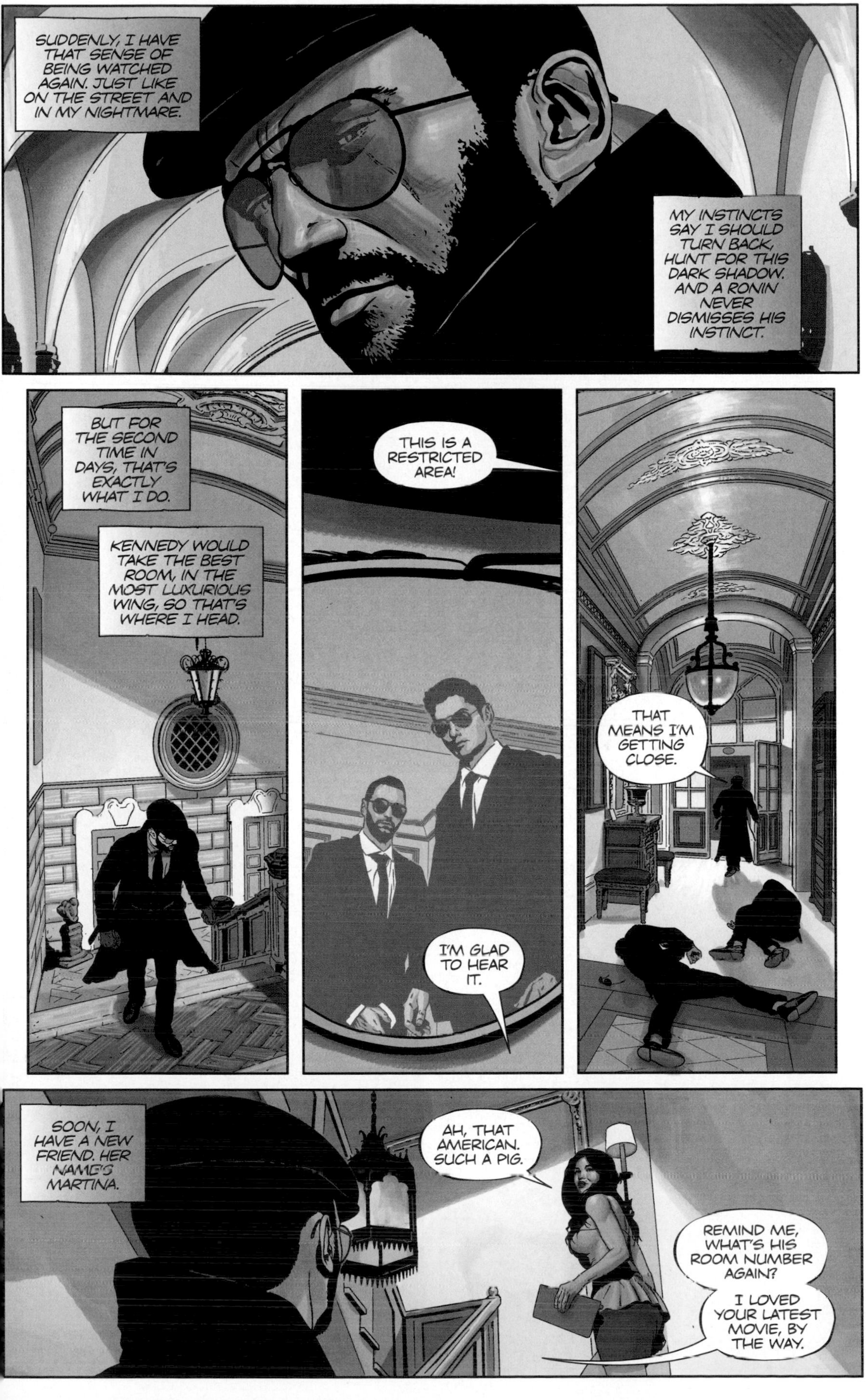
SUDDENLY, I HAVE THAT SENSE OF BEING WATCHED AGAIN. JUST LIKE ON THE STREET AND IN MY NIGHTMARE.
MY INSTINCTS SAY I SHOULD TURN BACK, HUNT FOR THIS DARK SHADOW. AND A RONIN NEVER DISMISSES HIS INSTINCT.
BUT FOR THE SECOND TIME IN DAYS, THAT'S EXACTLY WHAT I DO.
KENNEDY WOULD TAKE THE BEST ROOM, IN THE MOST LUXURIOUS WING, SO THAT'S WHERE I HEAD.
THIS IS A RESTRICTED AREA!
I'M GLAD TO HEAR IT.
THAT MEANS I'M GETTING CLOSE.
SOON, I HAVE A NEW FRIEND. HER NAME'S MARTINA.
AH, THAT AMERICAN. SUCH A PIG.
REMIND ME, WHAT'S HIS ROOM NUMBER AGAIN?
I LOVED YOUR LATEST MOVIE, BY THE WAY.

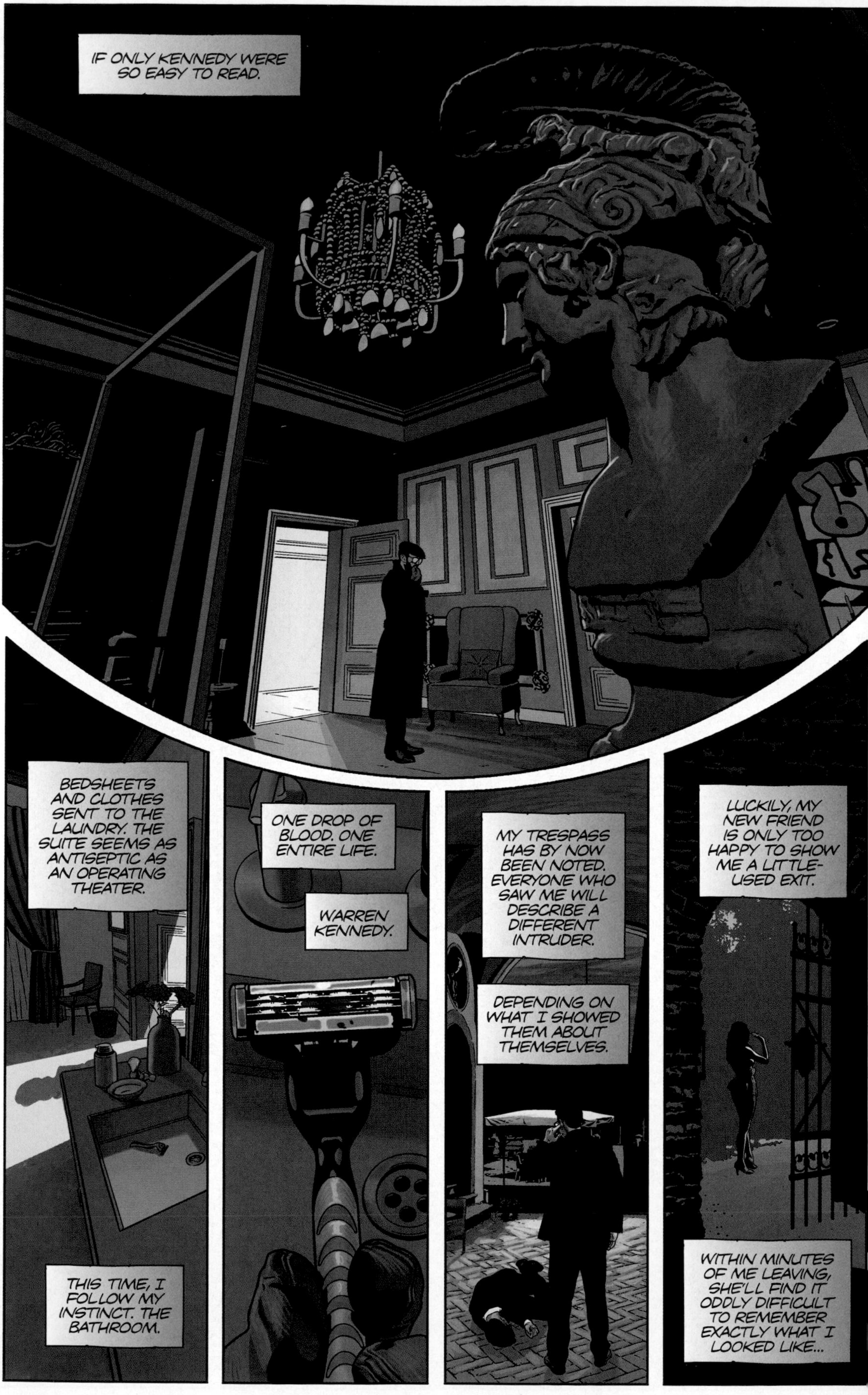
IF ONLY KENNEDY WERE SO EASY TO READ.
BEDSHEETS AND CLOTHES SENT TO THE LAUNDRY. THE SUITE SEEMS AS ANTISEPTIC AS AN OPERATING THEATER.
THIS TIME, I FOLLOW MY INSTINCT. THE BATHROOM.
ONE DROP OF BLOOD. ONE ENTIRE LIFE.
WARREN KENNEDY.
MY TRESPASS HAS BY NOW BEEN NOTED. EVERYONE WHO SAW ME WILL DESCRIBE A DIFFERENT INTRUDER.
DEPENDING ON WHAT I SHOWED THEM ABOUT THEMSELVES.
LUCKILY, MY NEW FRIEND IS ONLY TOO HAPPY TO SHOW ME A LITTLE-USED EXIT.
WITHIN MINUTES OF ME LEAVING, SHE'LL FIND IT ODDLY DIFFICULT TO REMEMBER EXACTLY WHAT I LOOKED LIKE...

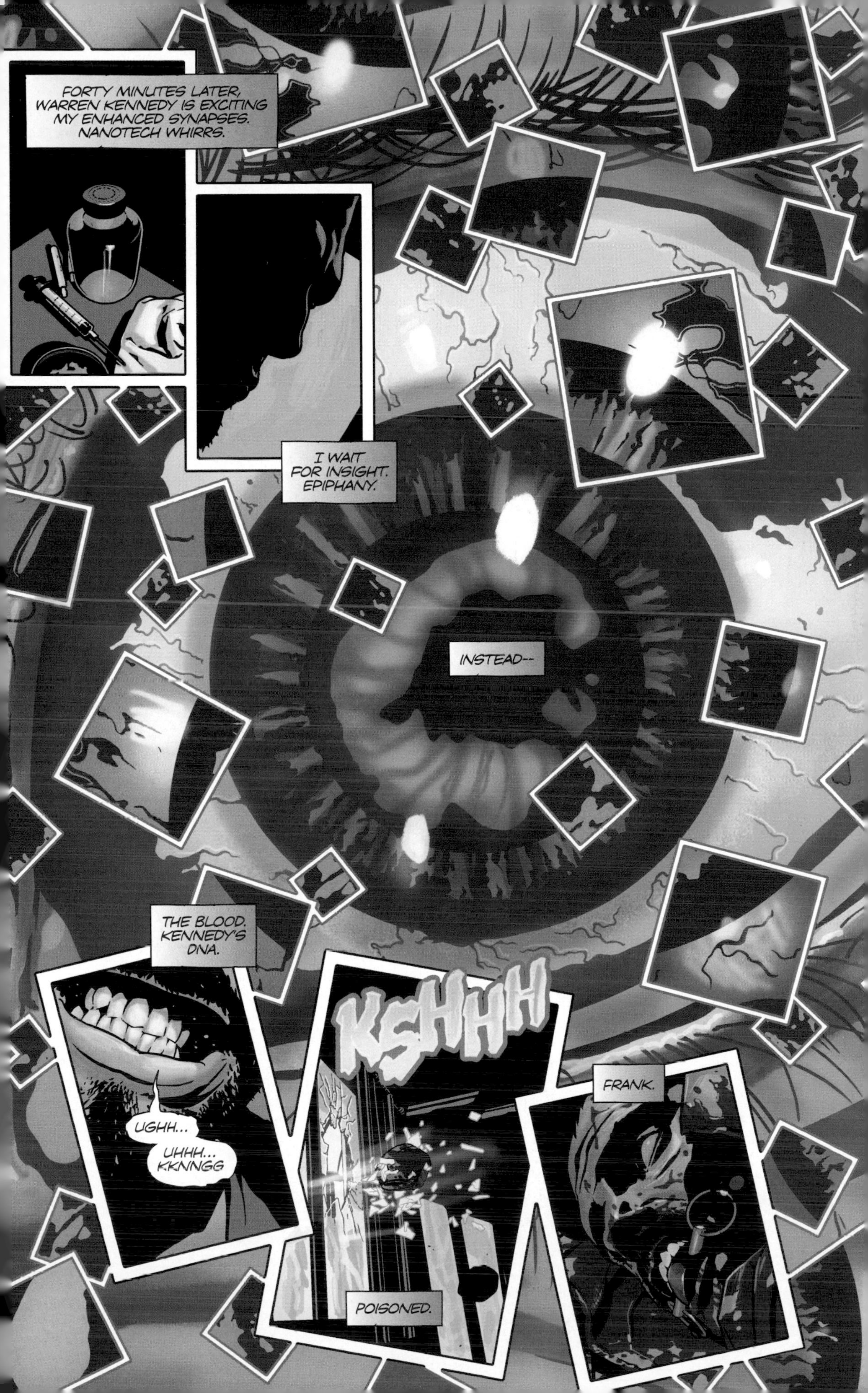
FORTY MINUTES LATER, WARREN KENNEDY IS EXCITING MY ENHANCED SYNAPSES. NANOTECH WHIRRS.
I WAIT FOR INSIGHT. EPIPHANY.
INSTEAD--
THE BLOOD. KENNEDY'S DNA.
UGHH... UHHH... KKNNGG
KSHHHH
POISONED.
FRANK.

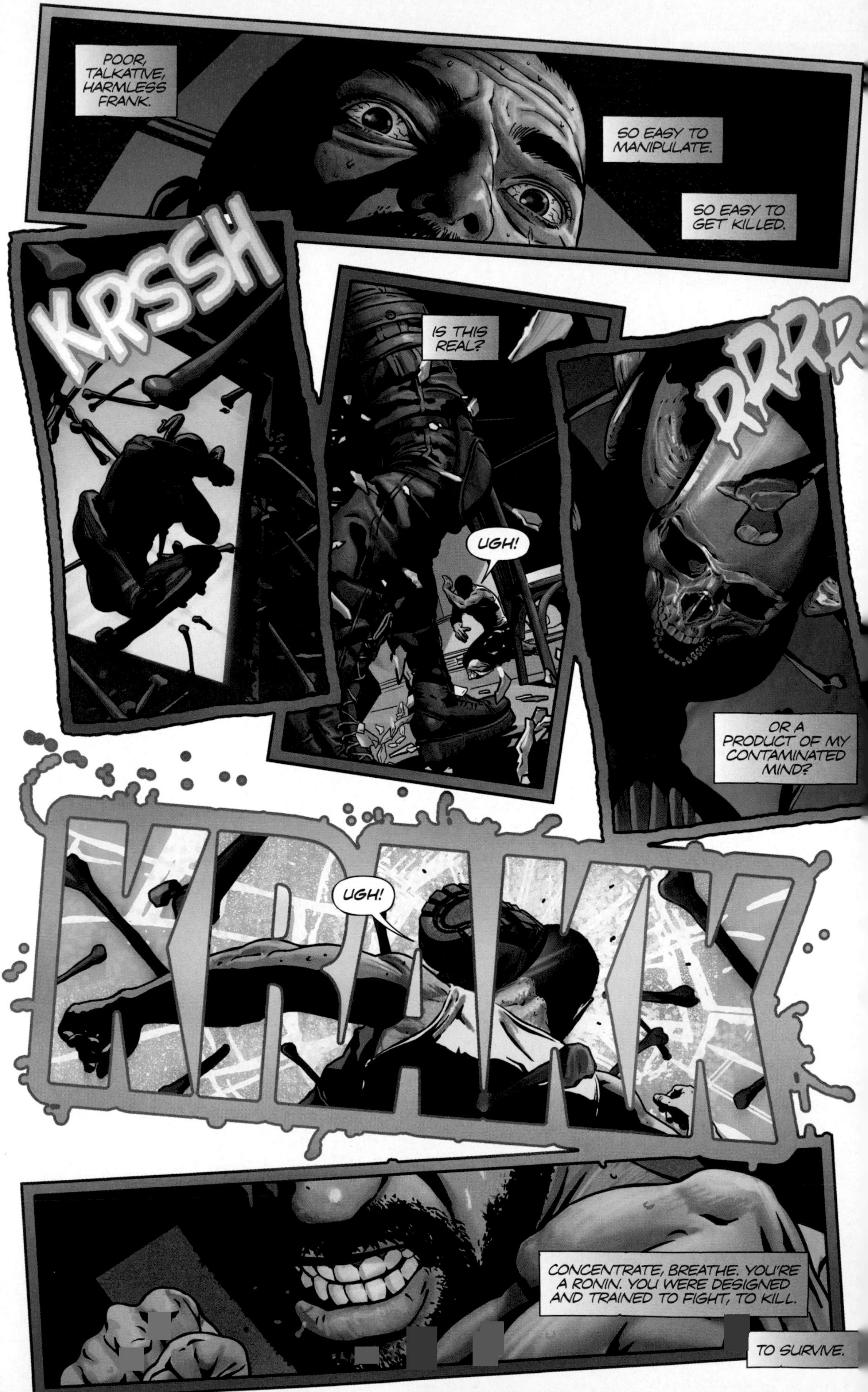
POOR, TALKATIVE, HARMLESS FRANK.
SO EASY TO MANIPULATE.
SO EASY TO GET KILLED.
KRSSH
IS THIS REAL?
UGH!
OR A PRODUCT OF MY CONTAMINATED MIND?
UGH!
CONCENTRATE, BREATHE. YOU'RE A RONIN. YOU WERE DESIGNED AND TRAINED TO FIGHT, TO KILL.
TO SURVIVE.

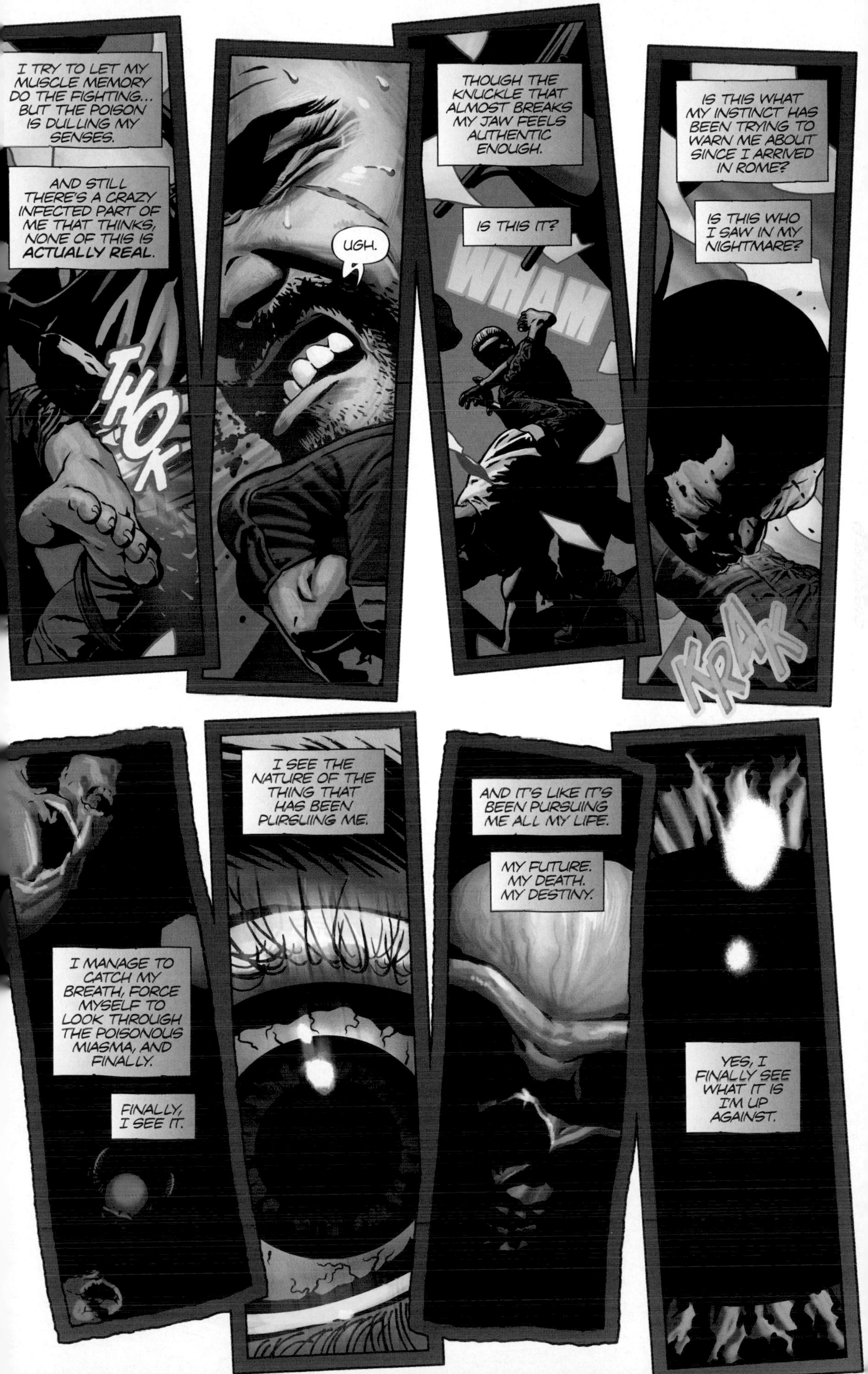
I TRY TO LET MY MUSCLE MEMORY DO THE FIGHTING... BUT THE POISON IS DULLING MY SENSES.
AND STILL THERE'S A CRAZY INFECTED PART OF ME THAT THINKS, NONE OF THIS IS ACTUALLY REAL.
THOK
UGH.
THOUGH THE KNUCKLE THAT ALMOST BREAKS MY JAW FEELS AUTHENTIC ENOUGH.
IS THIS IT?
WHAM
IS THIS WHAT MY INSTINCT HAS BEEN TRYING TO WARN ME ABOUT SINCE I ARRIVED IN ROME?
IS THIS WHO I SAW IN MY NIGHTMARE?
KRAK
I MANAGE TO CATCH MY BREATH, FORCE MYSELF TO LOOK THROUGH THE POISONOUS MIASMA, AND FINALLY.
FINALLY, I SEE IT.
I SEE THE NATURE OF THE THING THAT HAS BEEN PURSUING ME.
AND IT'S LIKE IT'S BEEN PURSUING ME ALL MY LIFE.
MY FUTURE. MY DEATH. MY DESTINY.
YES, I FINALLY SEE WHAT IT IS I'M UP AGAINST.

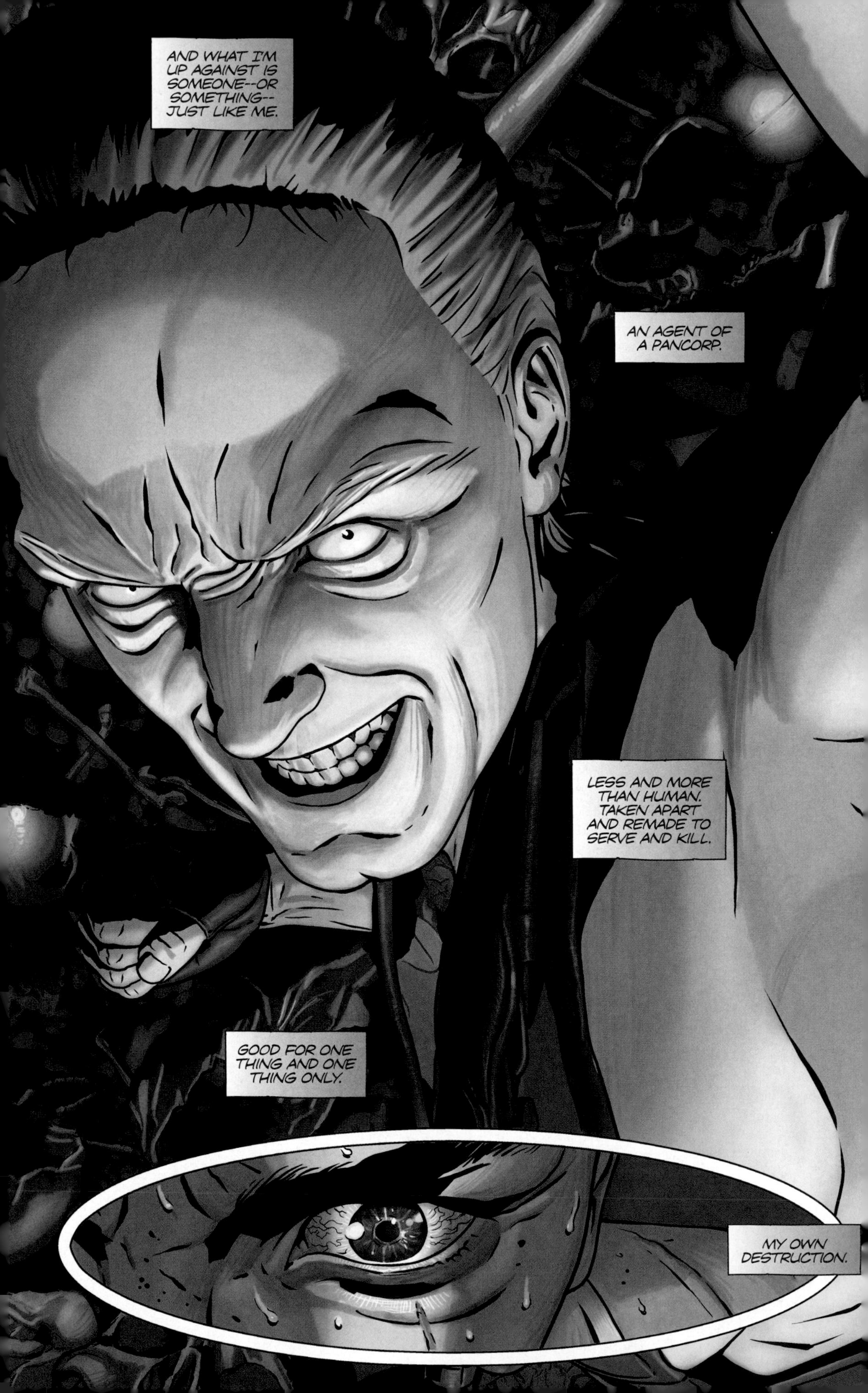
AND WHAT I'M UP AGAINST IS SOMEONE--OR SOMETHING--JUST LIKE ME.
AN AGENT OF A PANCORP.
LESS AND MORE THAN HUMAN. TAKEN APART AND REMADE TO SERVE AND KILL.
GOOD FOR ONE THING AND ONE THING ONLY.
MY OWN DESTRUCTION.

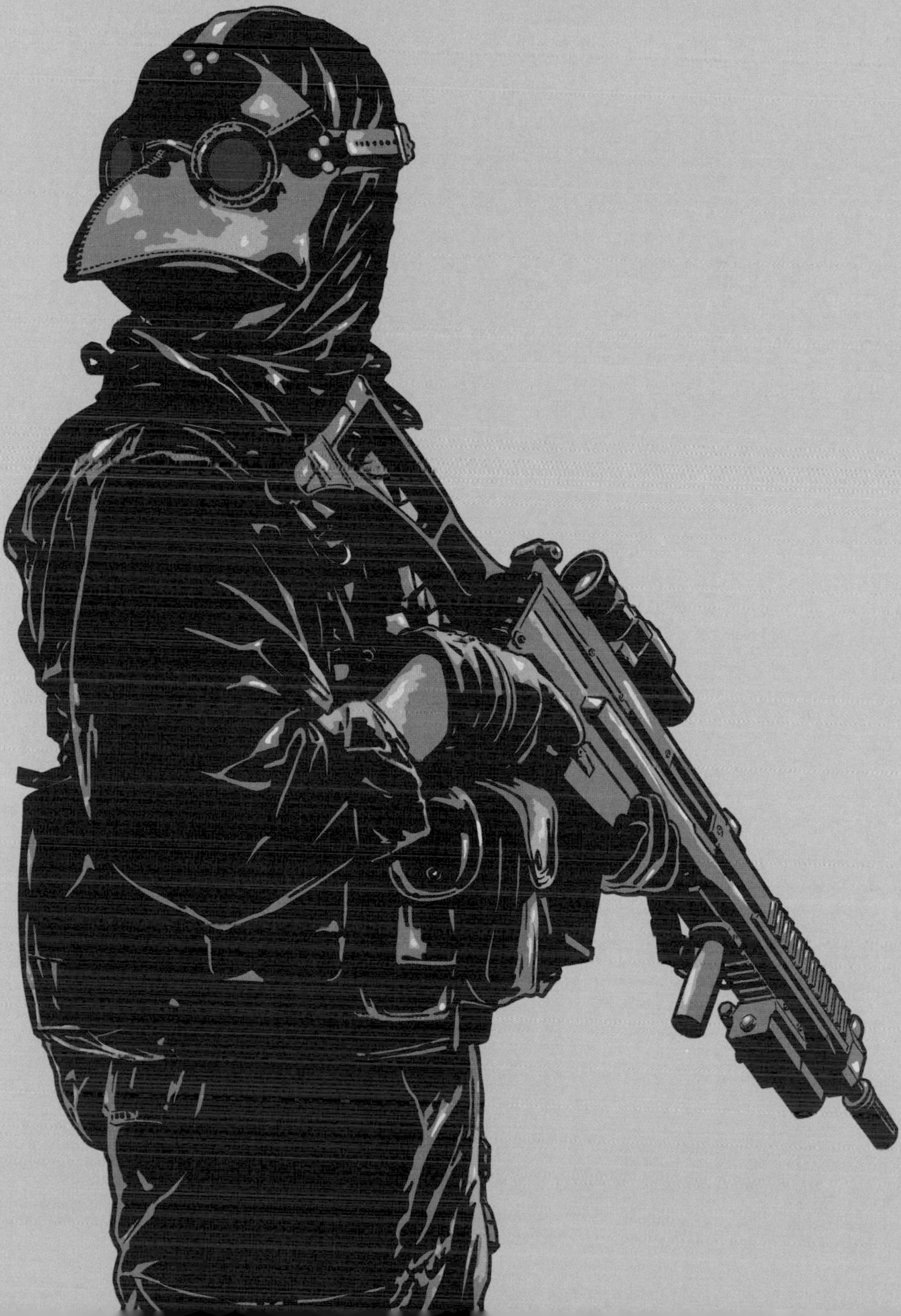

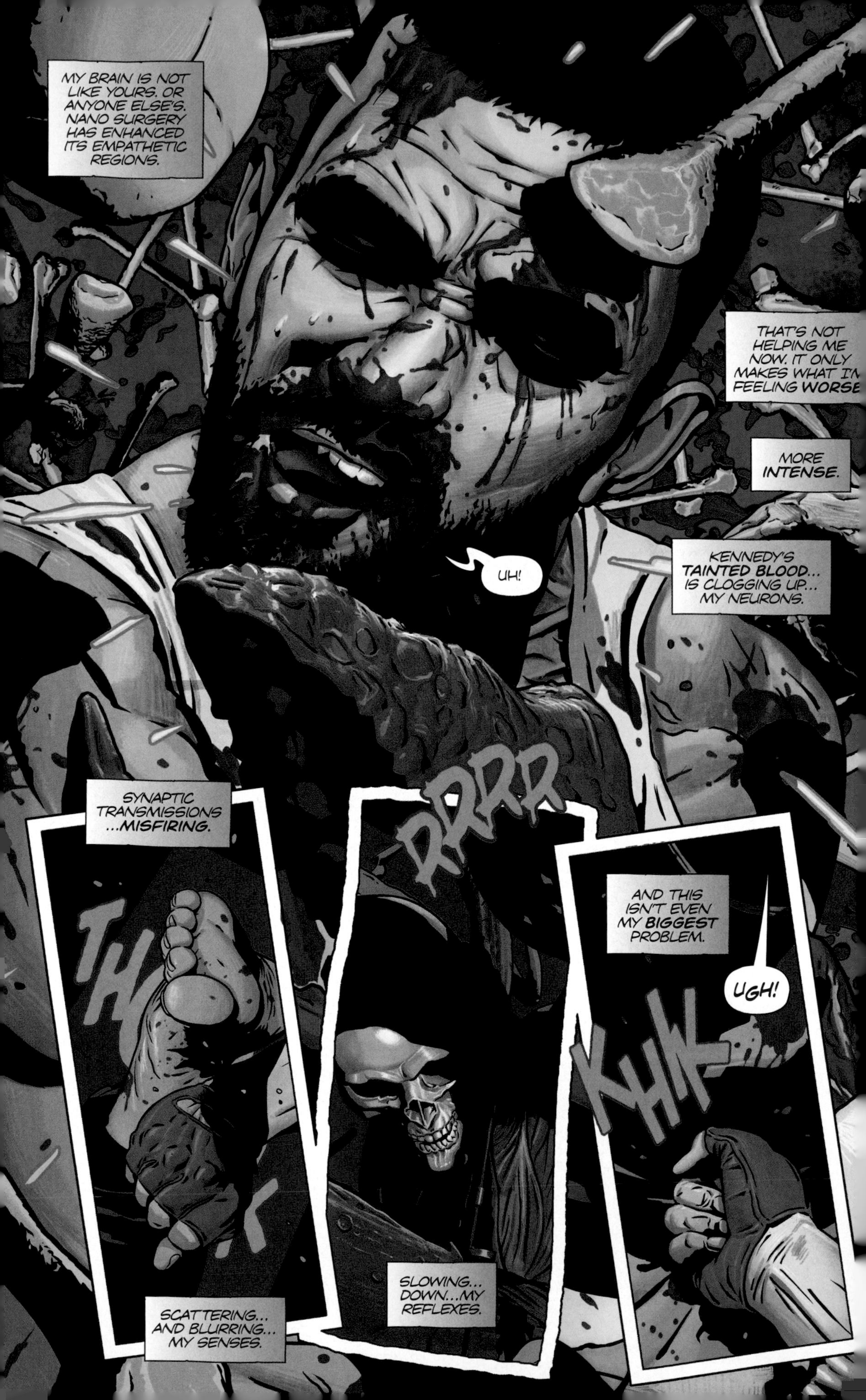
MY BRAIN IS NOT LIKE YOURS. OR ANYONE ELSE'S. NANO SURGERY HAS ENHANCED ITS EMPATHETIC REGIONS.
THAT'S NOT HELPING ME NOW. IT ONLY MAKES WHAT I'M FEELING WORSE.
MORE INTENSE.
UH!
KENNEDY'S TAINTED BLOOD... IS CLOGGING UP... MY NEURONS.
SYNAPTIC TRANSMISSIONS ...MISFIRING.
THK
SCATTERING... AND BLURRING... MY SENSES.
RRRR
SLOWING... DOWN...MY REFLEXES.
AND THIS ISN'T EVEN MY BIGGEST PROBLEM.
UGH!
KHK

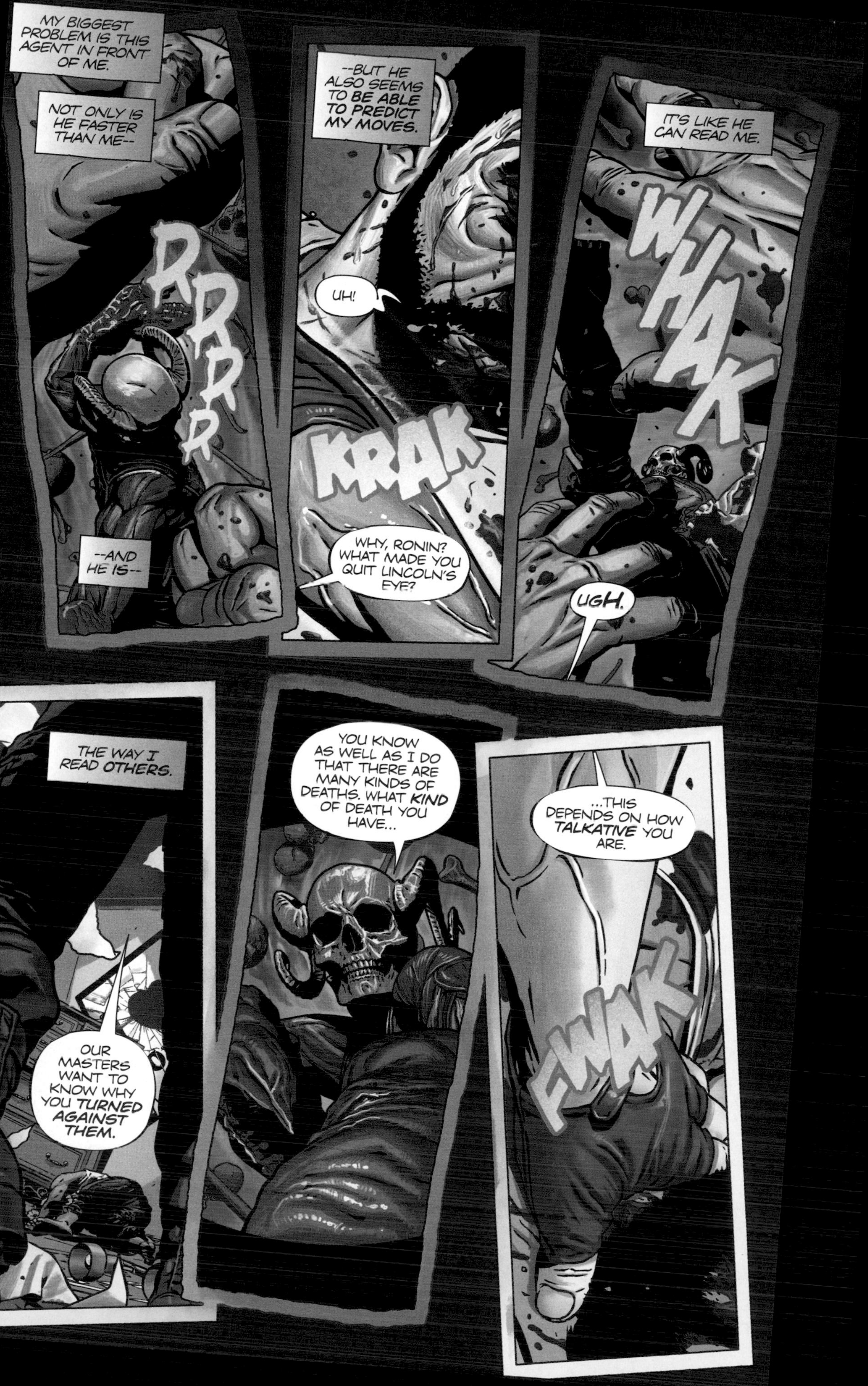

MY BIGGEST PROBLEM IS THIS AGENT IN FRONT OF ME.
NOT ONLY IS HE FASTER THAN ME--
RRRRR
--AND HE IS--
--BUT HE ALSO SEEMS TO BE ABLE TO PREDICT MY MOVES.
UH!
KRAK
WHY, RONIN? WHAT MADE YOU QUIT LINCOLN'S EYE?
IT'S LIKE HE CAN READ ME.
WHAK
UGH.
THE WAY I READ OTHERS.
OUR MASTERS WANT TO KNOW WHY YOU TURNED AGAINST THEM.
YOU KNOW AS WELL AS I DO THAT THERE ARE MANY KINDS OF DEATHS. WHAT KIND OF DEATH YOU HAVE...
...THIS DEPENDS ON HOW TALKATIVE YOU ARE.
FWAK

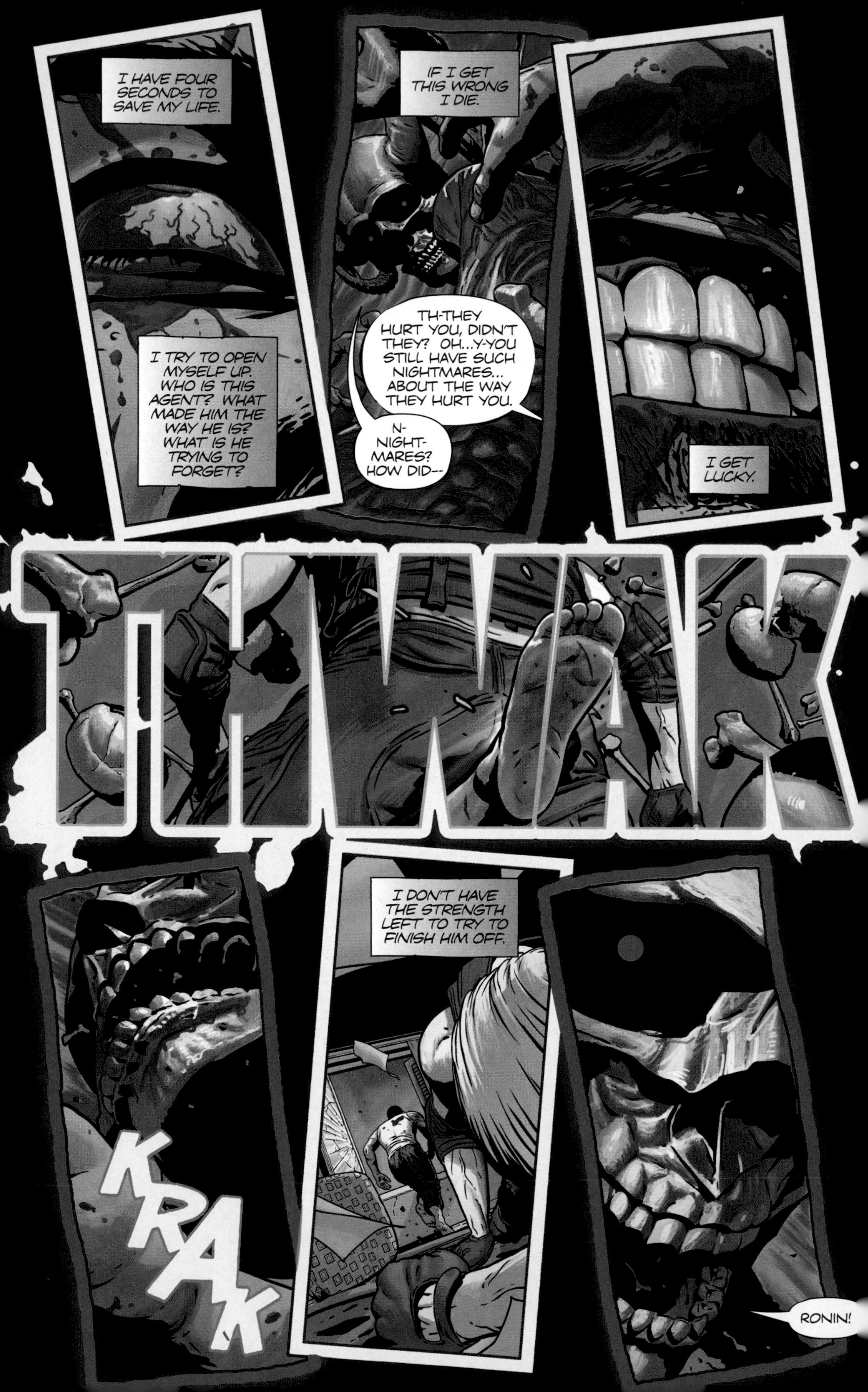
I HAVE FOUR SECONDS TO SAVE MY LIFE.
I TRY TO OPEN MYSELF UP. WHO IS THIS AGENT? WHAT MADE HIM THE WAY HE IS? WHAT IS HE TRYING TO FORGET?
IF I GET THIS WRONG I DIE.
TH-THEY HURT YOU, DIDN'T THEY? OH...Y-YOU STILL HAVE SUCH NIGHTMARES... ABOUT THE WAY THEY HURT YOU.
N-NIGHT-MARES? HOW DID--
I GET LUCKY.
THWAK
KRAK
I DON'T HAVE THE STRENGTH LEFT TO TRY TO FINISH HIM OFF.
RONIN!

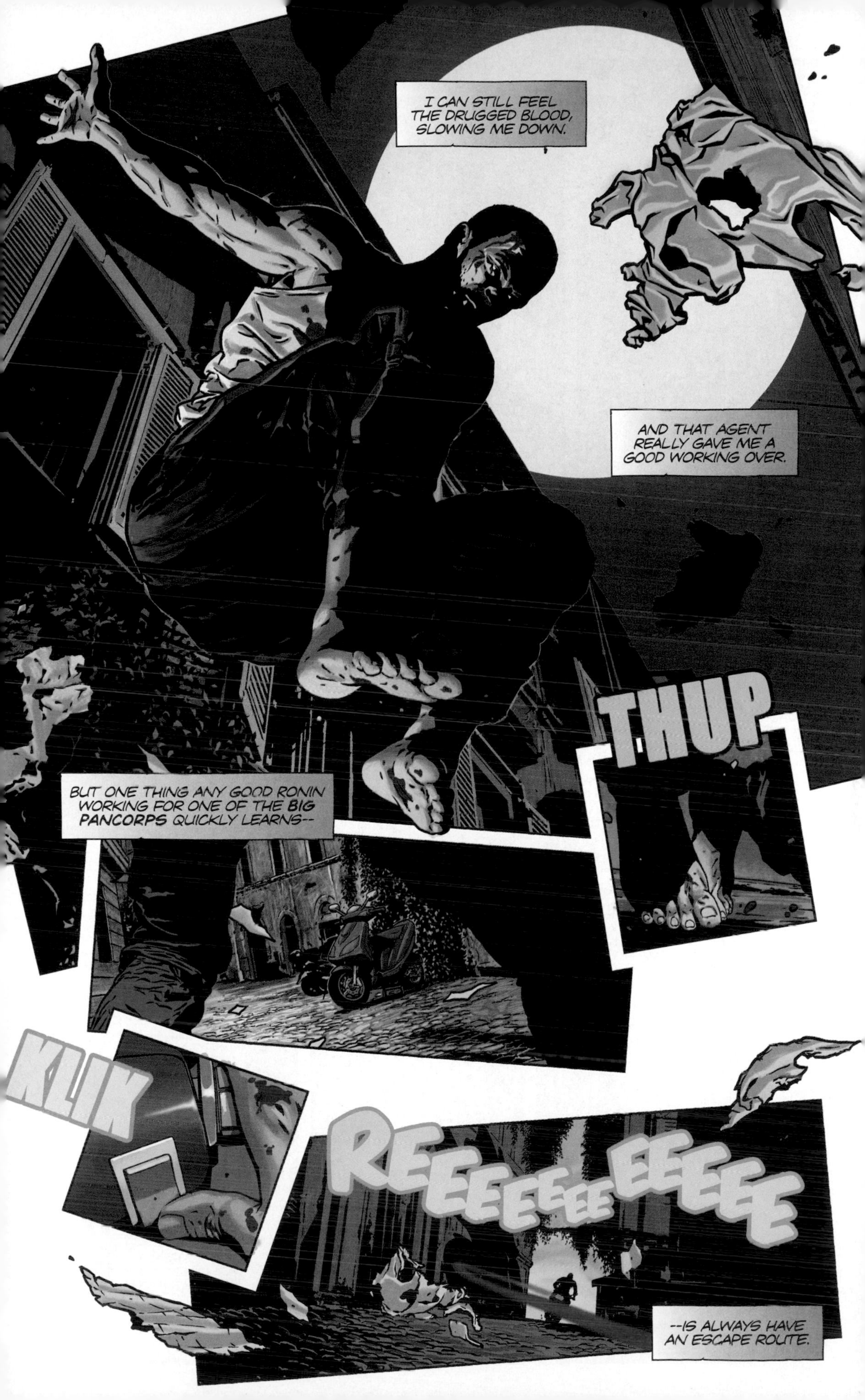
I CAN STILL FEEL THE DRUGGED BLOOD, SLOWING ME DOWN.
AND THAT AGENT REALLY GAVE ME A GOOD WORKING OVER.
THUP
BUT ONE THING ANY GOOD RONIN WORKING FOR ONE OF THE BIG PANCORPS QUICKLY LEARNS--
KLIK
REEEEEEEEEEEEEE
--IS ALWAYS HAVE AN ESCAPE ROUTE.

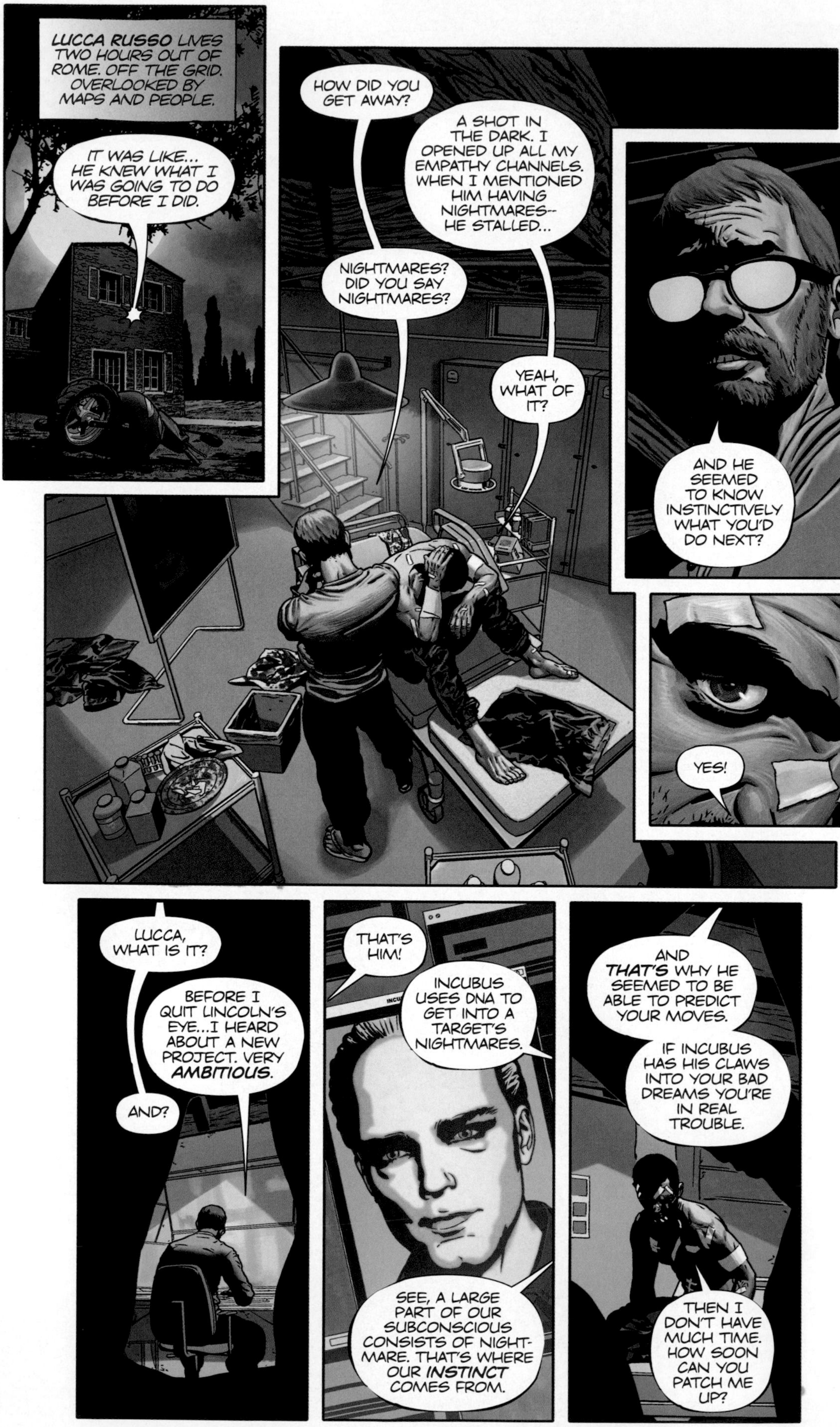
LUCCA RUSSO LIVES TWO HOURS OUT OF ROME. OFF THE GRID. OVERLOOKED BY MAPS AND PEOPLE.
IT WAS LIKE... HE KNEW WHAT I WAS GOING TO DO BEFORE I DID.
HOW DID YOU GET AWAY?
A SHOT IN THE DARK. I OPENED UP ALL MY EMPATHY CHANNELS. WHEN I MENTIONED HIM HAVING NIGHTMARES-- HE STALLED...
NIGHTMARES? DID YOU SAY NIGHTMARES?
YEAH, WHAT OF IT?
AND HE SEEMED TO KNOW INSTINCTIVELY WHAT YOU'D DO NEXT?
YES!
LUCCA, WHAT IS IT?
BEFORE I QUIT LINCOLN'S EYE...I HEARD ABOUT A NEW PROJECT. VERY AMBITIOUS.
AND?
THAT'S HIM!
INCUBUS USES DNA TO GET INTO A TARGET'S NIGHTMARES.
SEE, A LARGE PART OF OUR SUBCONSCIOUS CONSISTS OF NIGHT-MARE. THAT'S WHERE OUR INSTINCT COMES FROM.
AND THAT'S WHY HE SEEMED TO BE ABLE TO PREDICT YOUR MOVES.
IF INCUBUS HAS HIS CLAWS INTO YOUR BAD DREAMS YOU'RE IN REAL TROUBLE.
THEN I DON'T HAVE MUCH TIME. HOW SOON CAN YOU PATCH ME UP?

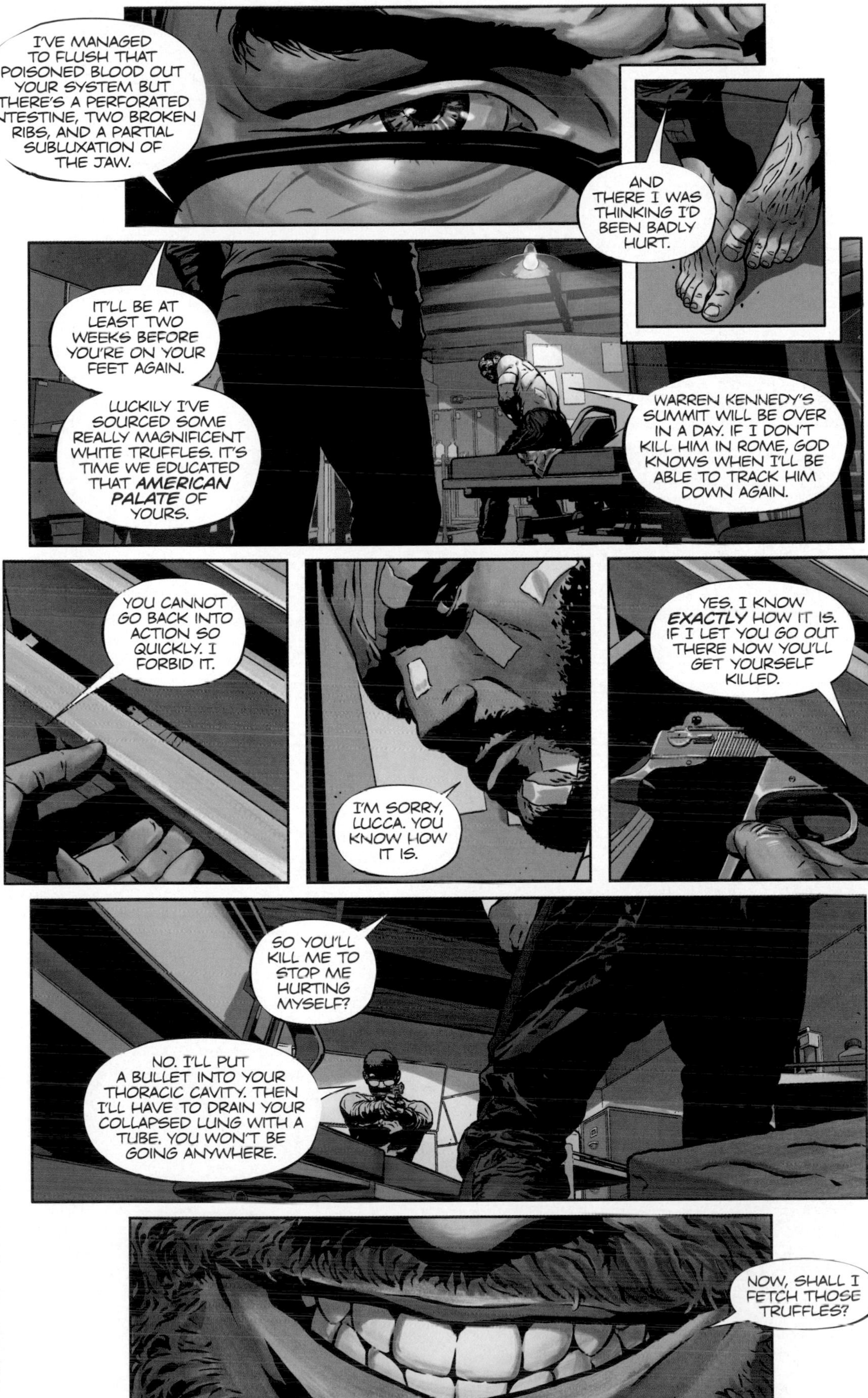
I'VE MANAGED TO FLUSH THAT POISONED BLOOD OUT YOUR SYSTEM BUT THERE'S A PERFORATED INTESTINE, TWO BROKEN RIBS, AND A PARTIAL SUBLUXATION OF THE JAW.
AND THERE I WAS THINKING I'D BEEN BADLY HURT.
IT'LL BE AT LEAST TWO WEEKS BEFORE YOU'RE ON YOUR FEET AGAIN.
LUCKILY I'VE SOURCED SOME REALLY MAGNIFICENT WHITE TRUFFLES. IT'S TIME WE EDUCATED THAT ***AMERICAN PALATE*** OF YOURS.
WARREN KENNEDY'S SUMMIT WILL BE OVER IN A DAY. IF I DON'T KILL HIM IN ROME, GOD KNOWS WHEN I'LL BE ABLE TO TRACK HIM DOWN AGAIN.
YOU CANNOT GO BACK INTO ACTION SO QUICKLY. I FORBID IT.
I'M SORRY, LUCCA. YOU KNOW HOW IT IS.
YES. I KNOW ***EXACTLY*** HOW IT IS. IF I LET YOU GO OUT THERE NOW YOU'LL GET YOURSELF KILLED.
SO YOU'LL KILL ME TO STOP ME HURTING MYSELF?
NO. I'LL PUT A BULLET INTO YOUR THORACIC CAVITY. THEN I'LL HAVE TO DRAIN YOUR COLLAPSED LUNG WITH A TUBE. YOU WON'T BE GOING ANYWHERE.
NOW, SHALL I FETCH THOSE TRUFFLES?

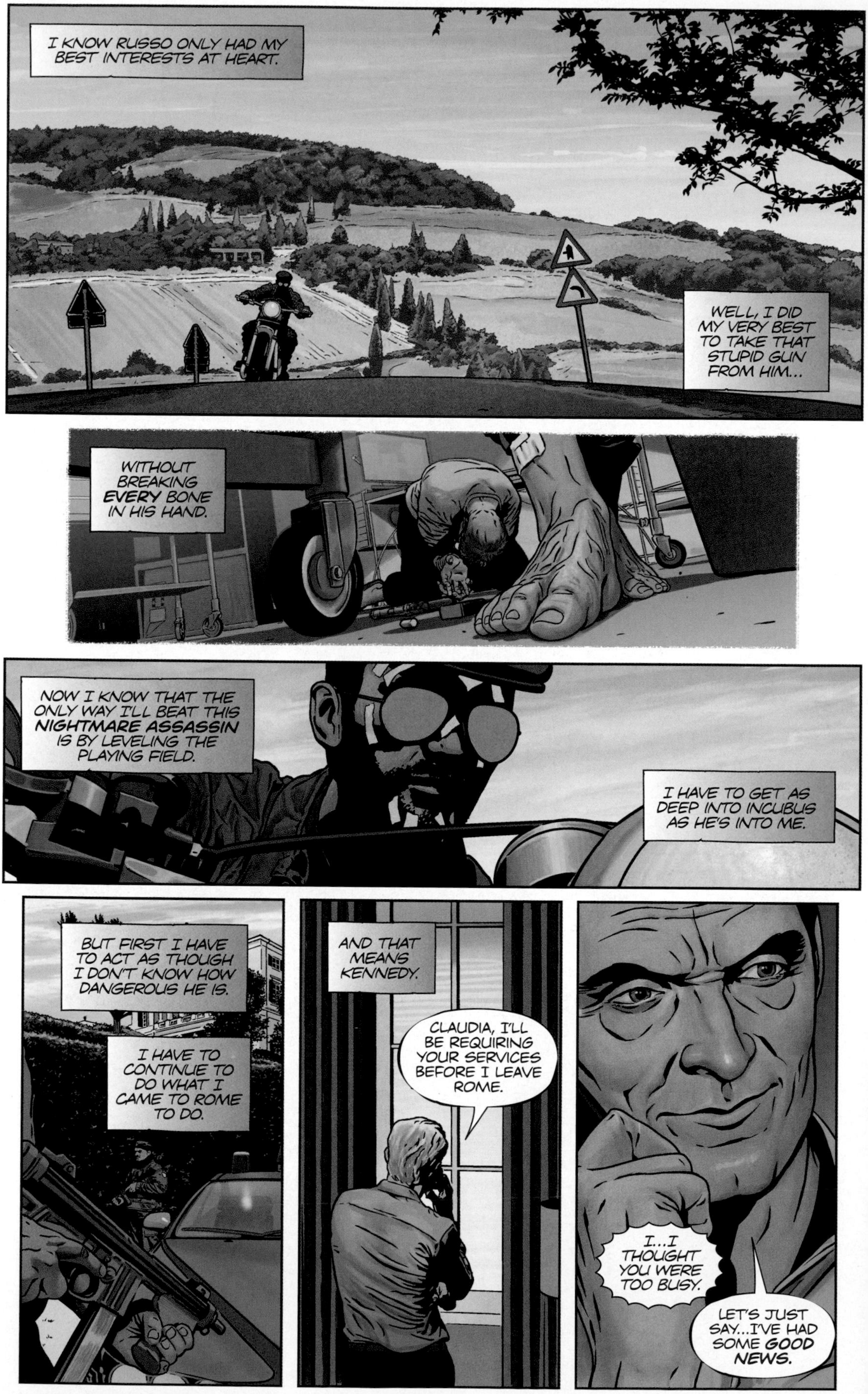
I KNOW RUSSO ONLY HAD MY BEST INTERESTS AT HEART.
WELL, I DID MY VERY BEST TO TAKE THAT STUPID GUN FROM HIM...
WITHOUT BREAKING EVERY BONE IN HIS HAND.
NOW I KNOW THAT THE ONLY WAY I'LL BEAT THIS NIGHTMARE ASSASSIN IS BY LEVELING THE PLAYING FIELD.
I HAVE TO GET AS DEEP INTO INCUBUS AS HE'S INTO ME.
BUT FIRST I HAVE TO ACT AS THOUGH I DON'T KNOW HOW DANGEROUS HE IS.
I HAVE TO CONTINUE TO DO WHAT I CAME TO ROME TO DO.
AND THAT MEANS KENNEDY.
CLAUDIA, I'LL BE REQUIRING YOUR SERVICES BEFORE I LEAVE ROME.
I...I THOUGHT YOU WERE TOO BUSY.
LET'S JUST SAY...I'VE HAD SOME GOOD NEWS.

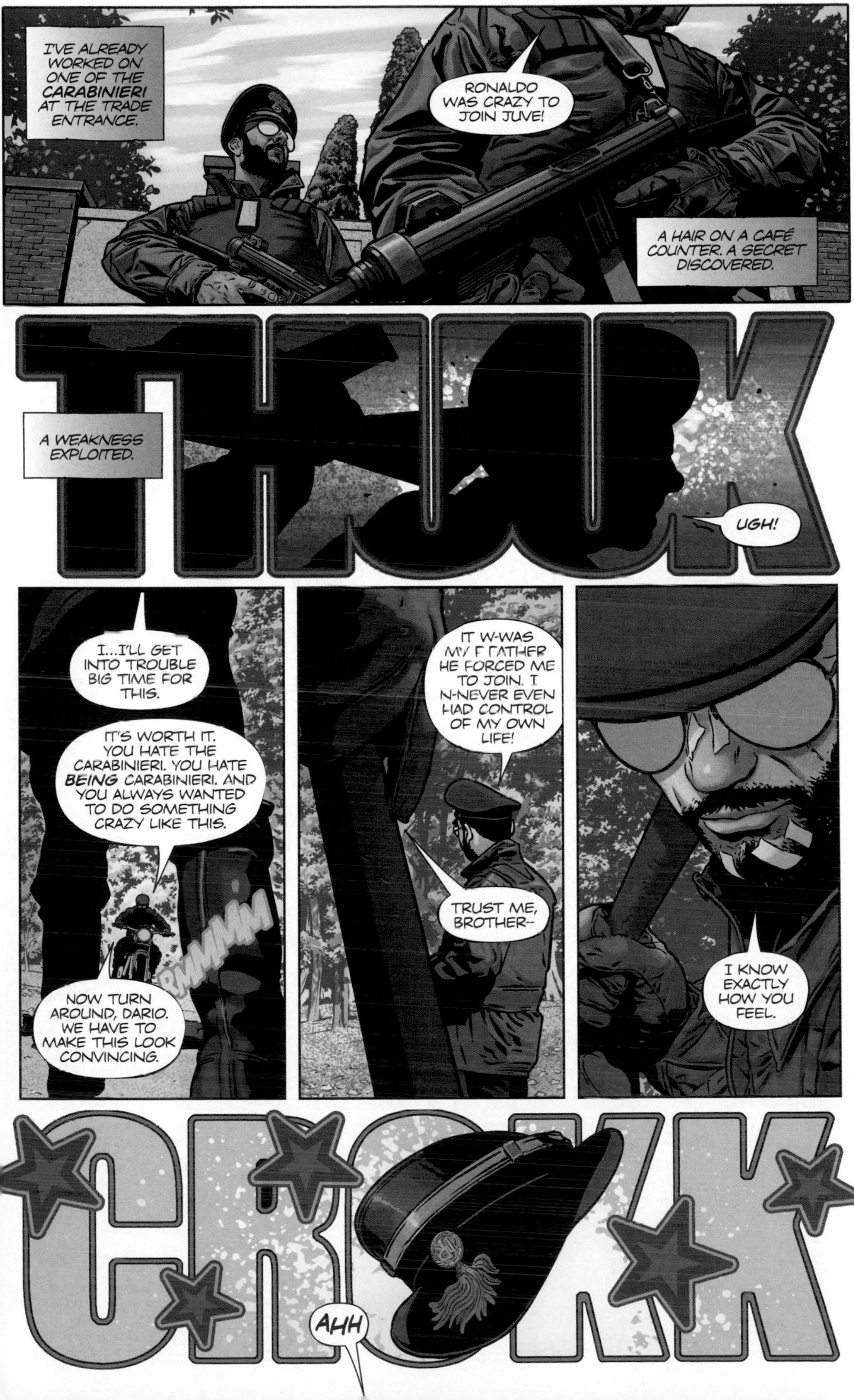

I'VE ALREADY WORKED ON ONE OF THE CARABINIERI AT THE TRADE ENTRANCE.
RONALDO WAS CRAZY TO JOIN JUVE!
A HAIR ON A CAFÉ COUNTER. A SECRET DISCOVERED.
THUK
A WEAKNESS EXPLOITED.
UGH!
I...I'LL GET INTO TROUBLE BIG TIME FOR THIS.
IT'S WORTH IT. YOU HATE THE CARABINIERI. YOU HATE BEING CARABINIERI. AND YOU ALWAYS WANTED TO DO SOMETHING CRAZY LIKE THIS.
BRMMMMM
NOW TURN AROUND, DARIO. WE HAVE TO MAKE THIS LOOK CONVINCING.
IT W-WAS MY F-FATHER. HE FORCED ME TO JOIN. I N-NEVER EVEN HAD CONTROL OF MY OWN LIFE!
TRUST ME, BROTHER--
I KNOW EXACTLY HOW YOU FEEL.
CRACK
AHH

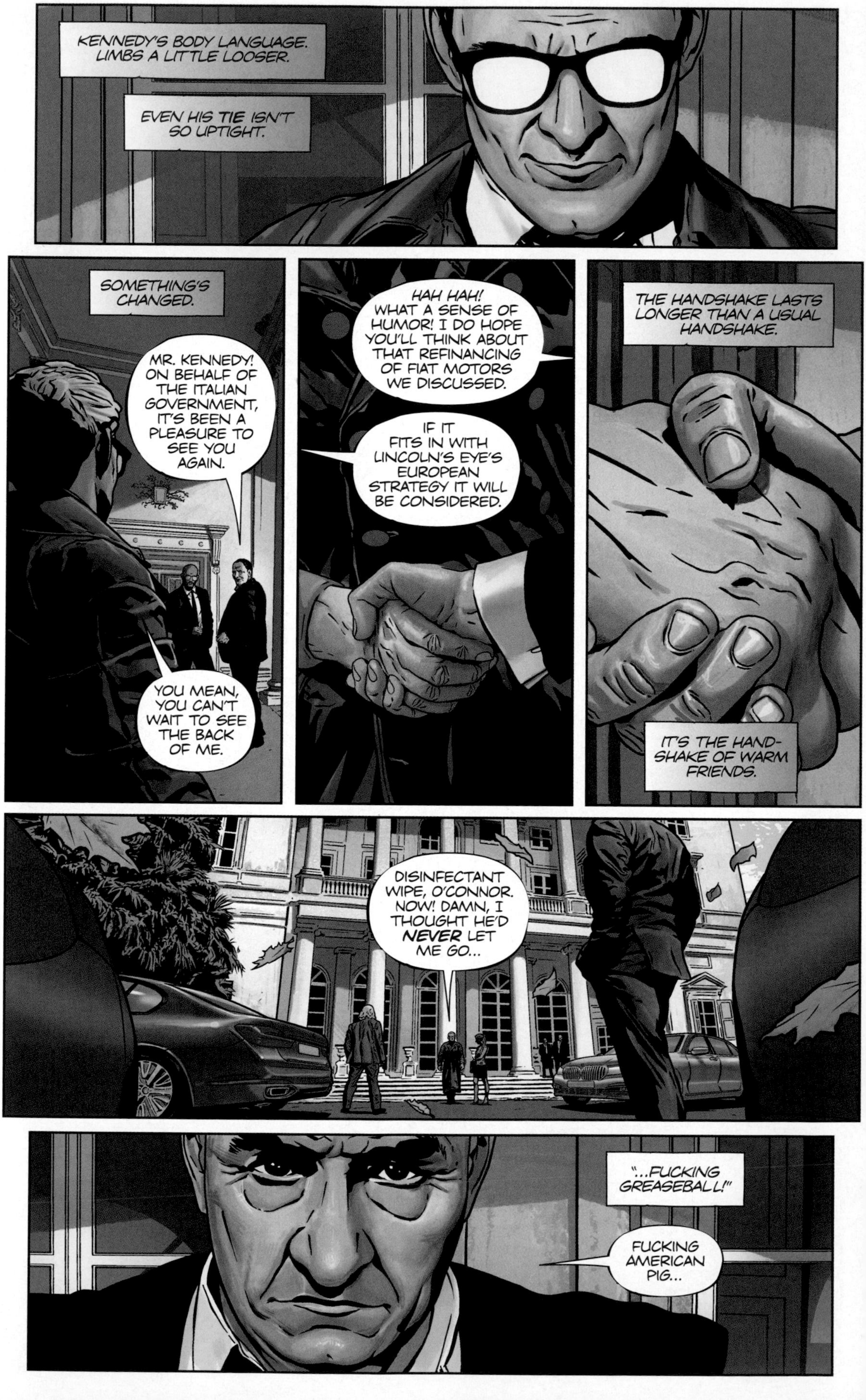
KENNEDY'S BODY LANGUAGE. LIMBS A LITTLE LOOSER.
EVEN HIS TIE ISN'T SO UPTIGHT.
SOMETHING'S CHANGED.
MR. KENNEDY! ON BEHALF OF THE ITALIAN GOVERNMENT, IT'S BEEN A PLEASURE TO SEE YOU AGAIN.
YOU MEAN, YOU CAN'T WAIT TO SEE THE BACK OF ME.
HAH HAH! WHAT A SENSE OF HUMOR! I DO HOPE YOU'LL THINK ABOUT THAT REFINANCING OF FIAT MOTORS WE DISCUSSED.
IF IT FITS IN WITH LINCOLN'S EYE'S EUROPEAN STRATEGY IT WILL BE CONSIDERED.
THE HANDSHAKE LASTS LONGER THAN A USUAL HANDSHAKE.
IT'S THE HAND-SHAKE OF WARM FRIENDS.
DISINFECTANT WIPE, O'CONNOR. NOW! DAMN, I THOUGHT HE'D NEVER LET ME GO...
"...FUCKING GREASEBALL!"
FUCKING AMERICAN PIG...

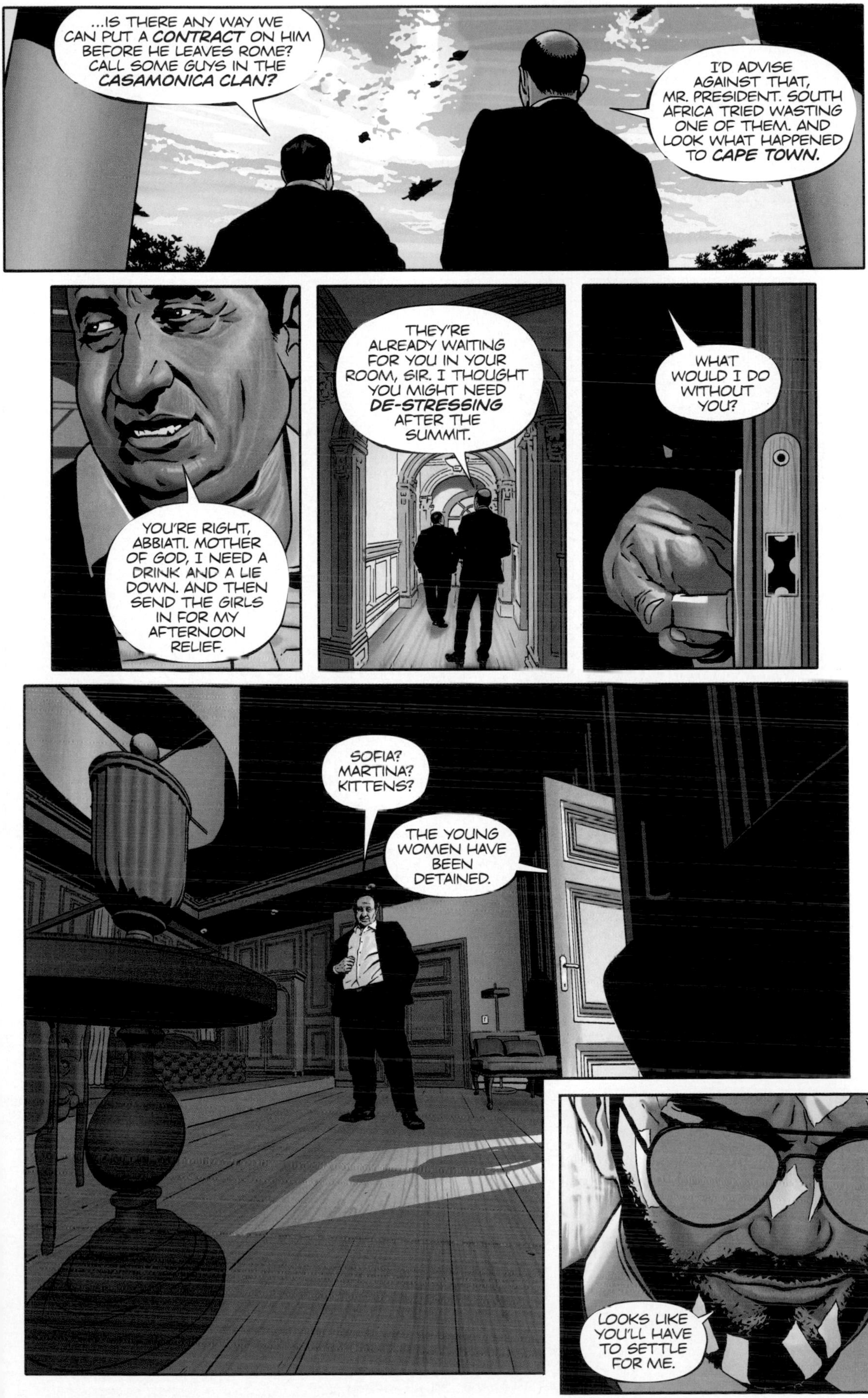
...IS THERE ANY WAY WE CAN PUT A CONTRACT ON HIM BEFORE HE LEAVES ROME? CALL SOME GUYS IN THE CASAMONICA CLAN?
I'D ADVISE AGAINST THAT, MR. PRESIDENT. SOUTH AFRICA TRIED WASTING ONE OF THEM. AND LOOK WHAT HAPPENED TO CAPE TOWN.
YOU'RE RIGHT, ABBIATI. MOTHER OF GOD, I NEED A DRINK AND A LIE DOWN. AND THEN SEND THE GIRLS IN FOR MY AFTERNOON RELIEF.
THEY'RE ALREADY WAITING FOR YOU IN YOUR ROOM, SIR. I THOUGHT YOU MIGHT NEED DE-STRESSING AFTER THE SUMMIT.
WHAT WOULD I DO WITHOUT YOU?
SOFIA? MARTINA? KITTENS?
THE YOUNG WOMEN HAVE BEEN DETAINED.
LOOKS LIKE YOU'LL HAVE TO SETTLE FOR ME.

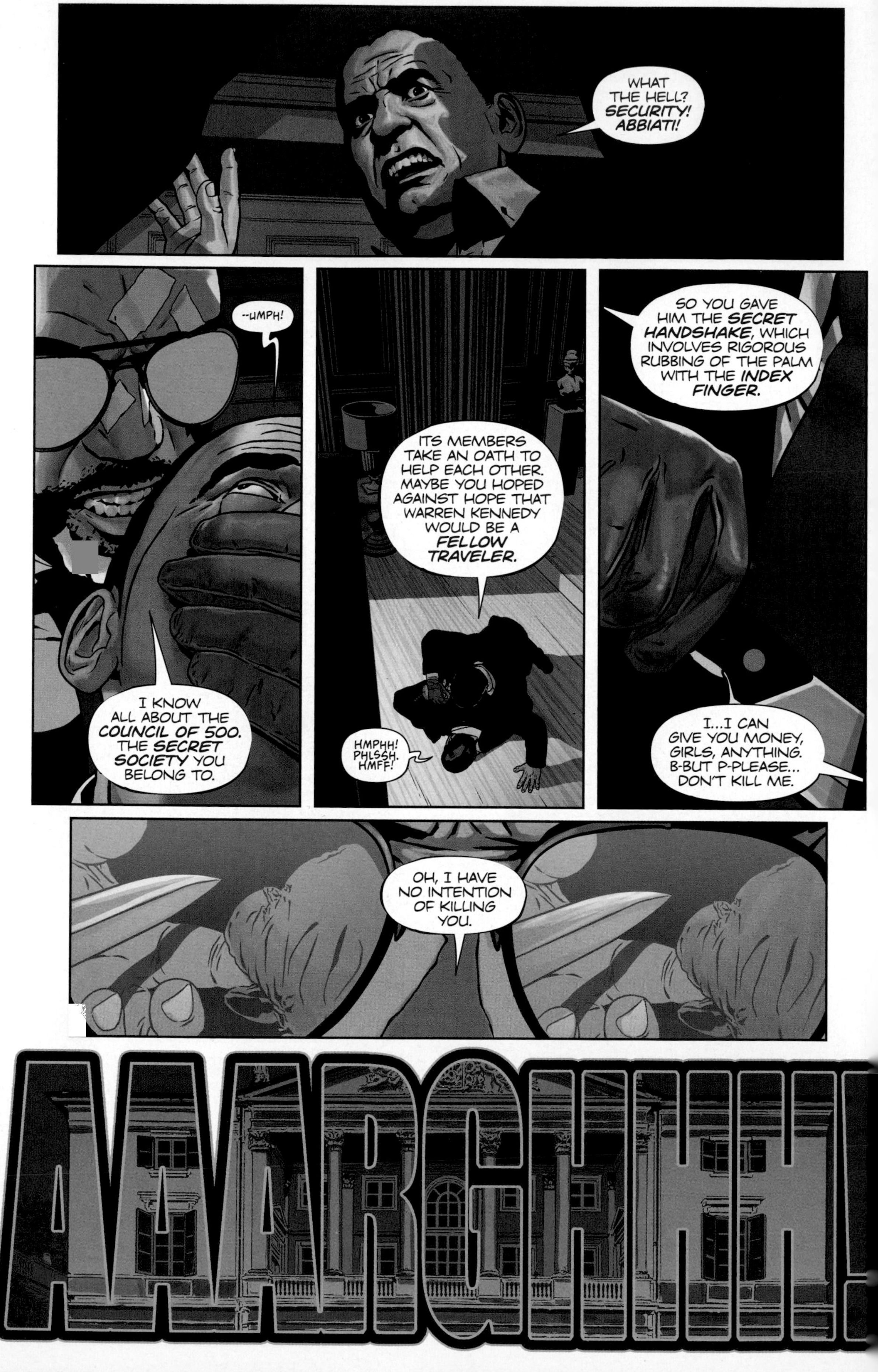
WHAT THE HELL? SECURITY! ABBIATI!
--UMPH!
I KNOW ALL ABOUT THE COUNCIL OF 500. THE SECRET SOCIETY YOU BELONG TO.
ITS MEMBERS TAKE AN OATH TO HELP EACH OTHER. MAYBE YOU HOPED AGAINST HOPE THAT WARREN KENNEDY WOULD BE A FELLOW TRAVELER.
HMPHH! PHLSSH. HMFF!
SO YOU GAVE HIM THE SECRET HANDSHAKE, WHICH INVOLVES RIGOROUS RUBBING OF THE PALM WITH THE INDEX FINGER.
I...I CAN GIVE YOU MONEY, GIRLS, ANYTHING. B-BUT P-PLEASE... DON'T KILL ME.
OH, I HAVE NO INTENTION OF KILLING YOU.
AAARGHHH!

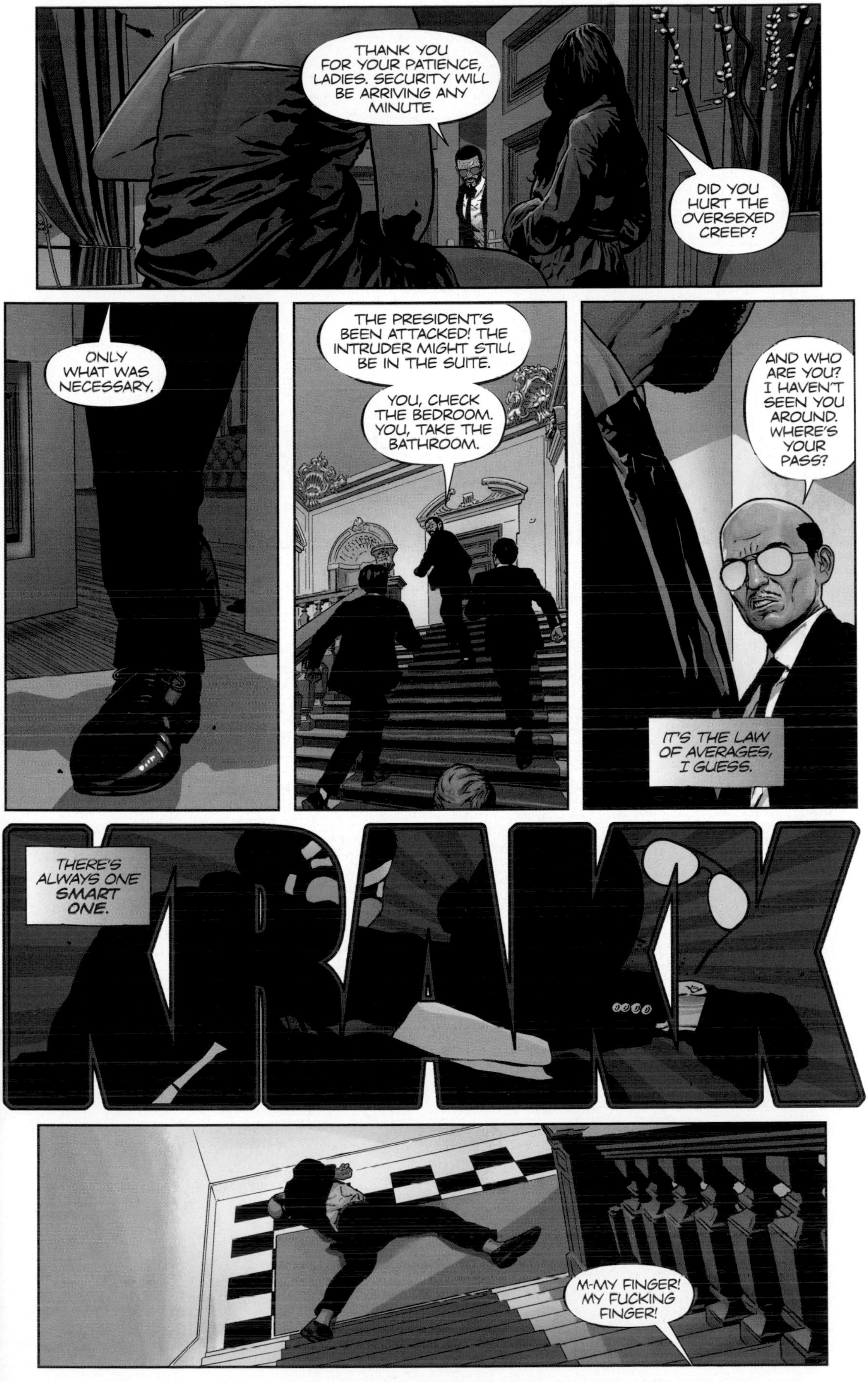
THANK YOU FOR YOUR PATIENCE, LADIES. SECURITY WILL BE ARRIVING ANY MINUTE.
DID YOU HURT THE OVERSEXED CREEP?
ONLY WHAT WAS NECESSARY.
THE PRESIDENT'S BEEN ATTACKED! THE INTRUDER MIGHT STILL BE IN THE SUITE.
YOU, CHECK THE BEDROOM. YOU, TAKE THE BATHROOM.
AND WHO ARE YOU? I HAVEN'T SEEN YOU AROUND. WHERE'S YOUR PASS?
IT'S THE LAW OF AVERAGES, I GUESS.
THERE'S ALWAYS ONE SMART ONE.
KRAKK
M-MY FINGER! MY FUCKING FINGER!

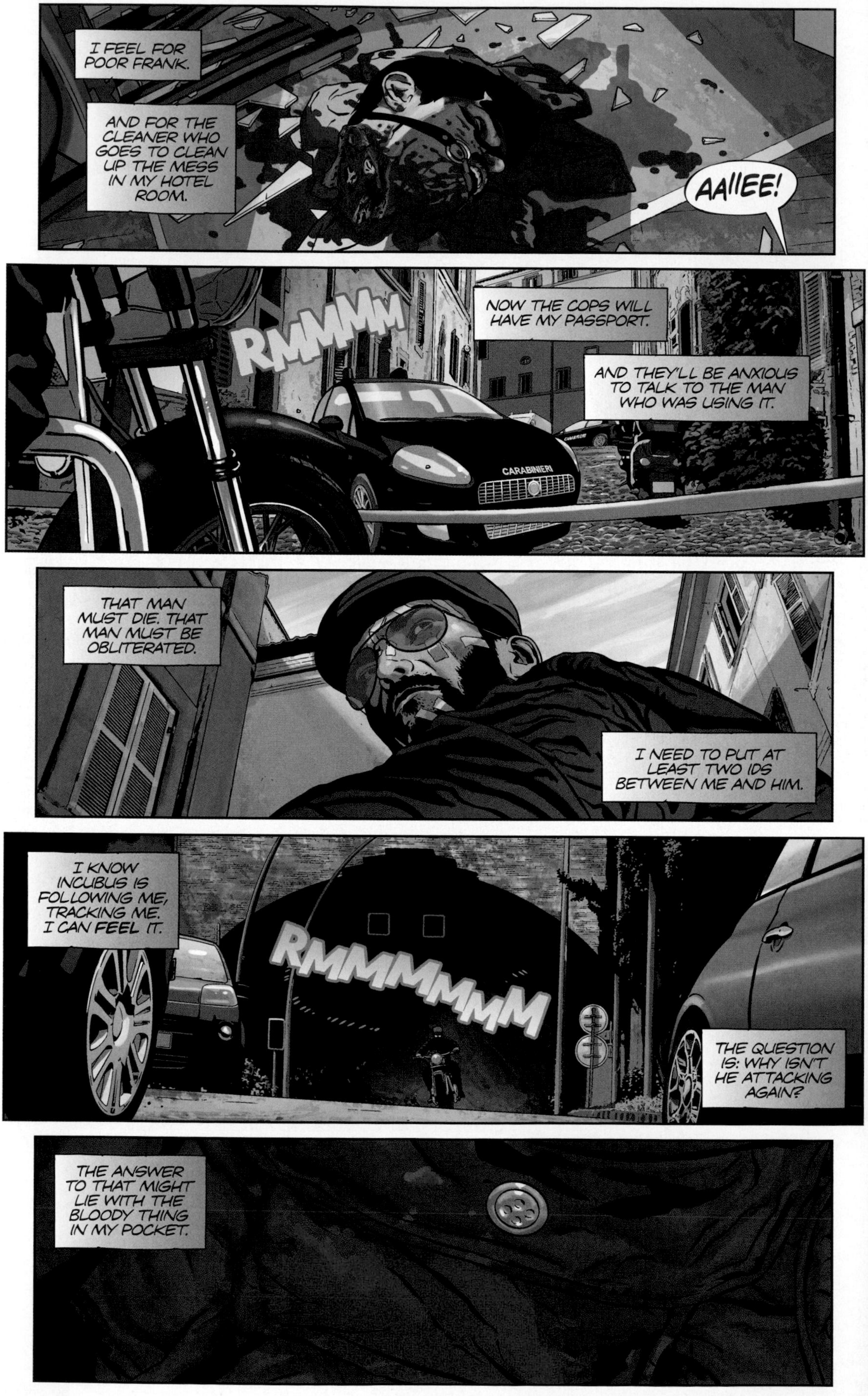
I FEEL FOR POOR FRANK.
AND FOR THE CLEANER WHO GOES TO CLEAN UP THE MESS IN MY HOTEL ROOM.
AAIIEE!
RMMMM
NOW THE COPS WILL HAVE MY PASSPORT.
AND THEY'LL BE ANXIOUS TO TALK TO THE MAN WHO WAS USING IT.
CARABINIERI
THAT MAN MUST DIE. THAT MAN MUST BE OBLITERATED.
I NEED TO PUT AT LEAST TWO IDS BETWEEN ME AND HIM.
I KNOW INCUBUS IS FOLLOWING ME, TRACKING ME. I CAN FEEL IT.
RMMMMMMM
THE QUESTION IS: WHY ISN'T HE ATTACKING AGAIN?
THE ANSWER TO THAT MIGHT LIE WITH THE BLOODY THING IN MY POCKET.

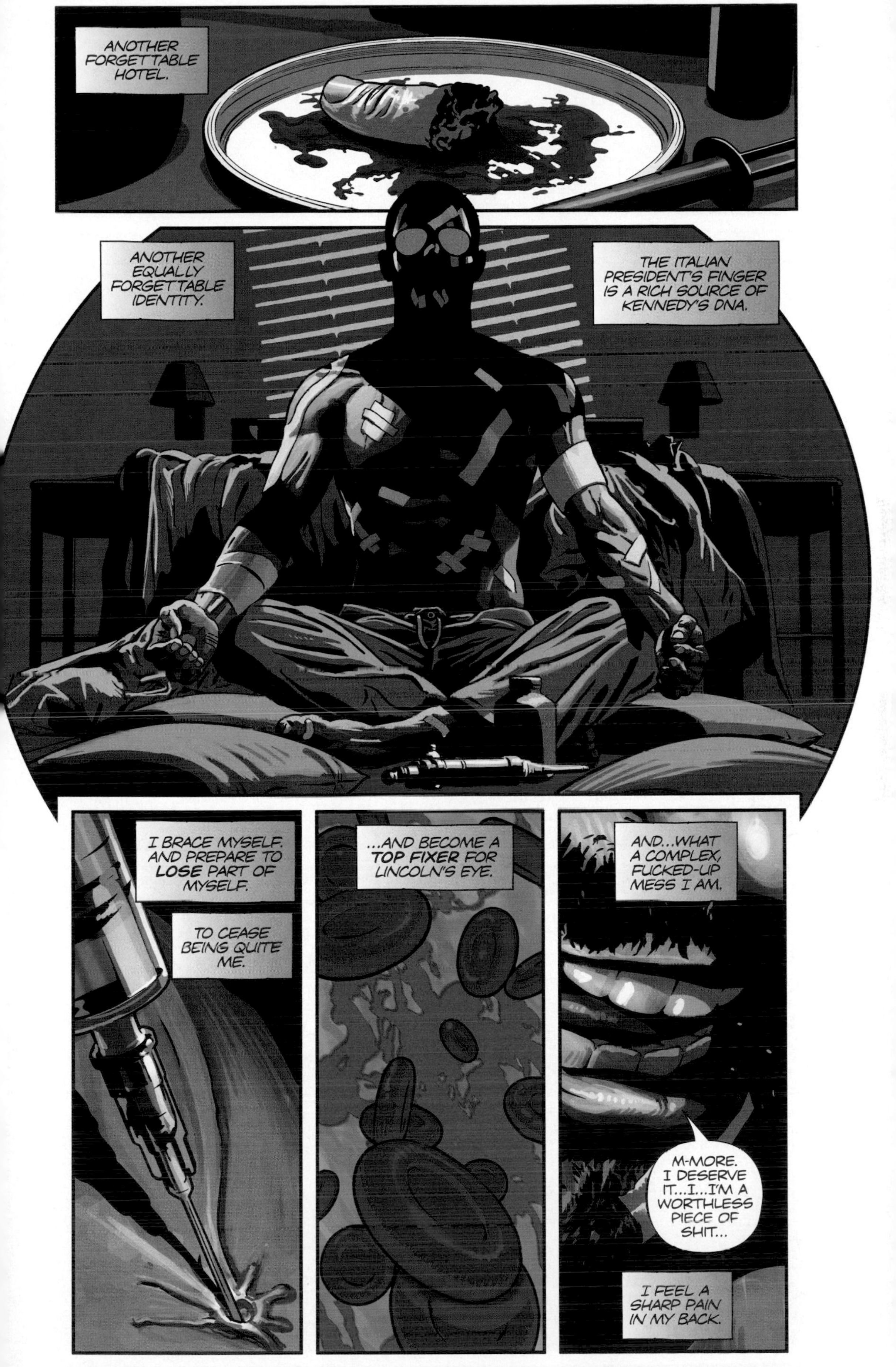
ANOTHER FORGETTABLE HOTEL.
ANOTHER EQUALLY FORGETTABLE IDENTITY.
THE ITALIAN PRESIDENT'S FINGER IS A RICH SOURCE OF KENNEDY'S DNA.
I BRACE MYSELF. AND PREPARE TO LOSE PART OF MYSELF.
TO CEASE BEING QUITE ME.
...AND BECOME A TOP FIXER FOR LINCOLN'S EYE.
AND...WHAT A COMPLEX, FUCKED-UP MESS I AM.
M-MORE. I DESERVE IT...I...I'M A WORTHLESS PIECE OF SHIT...
I FEEL A SHARP PAIN IN MY BACK.

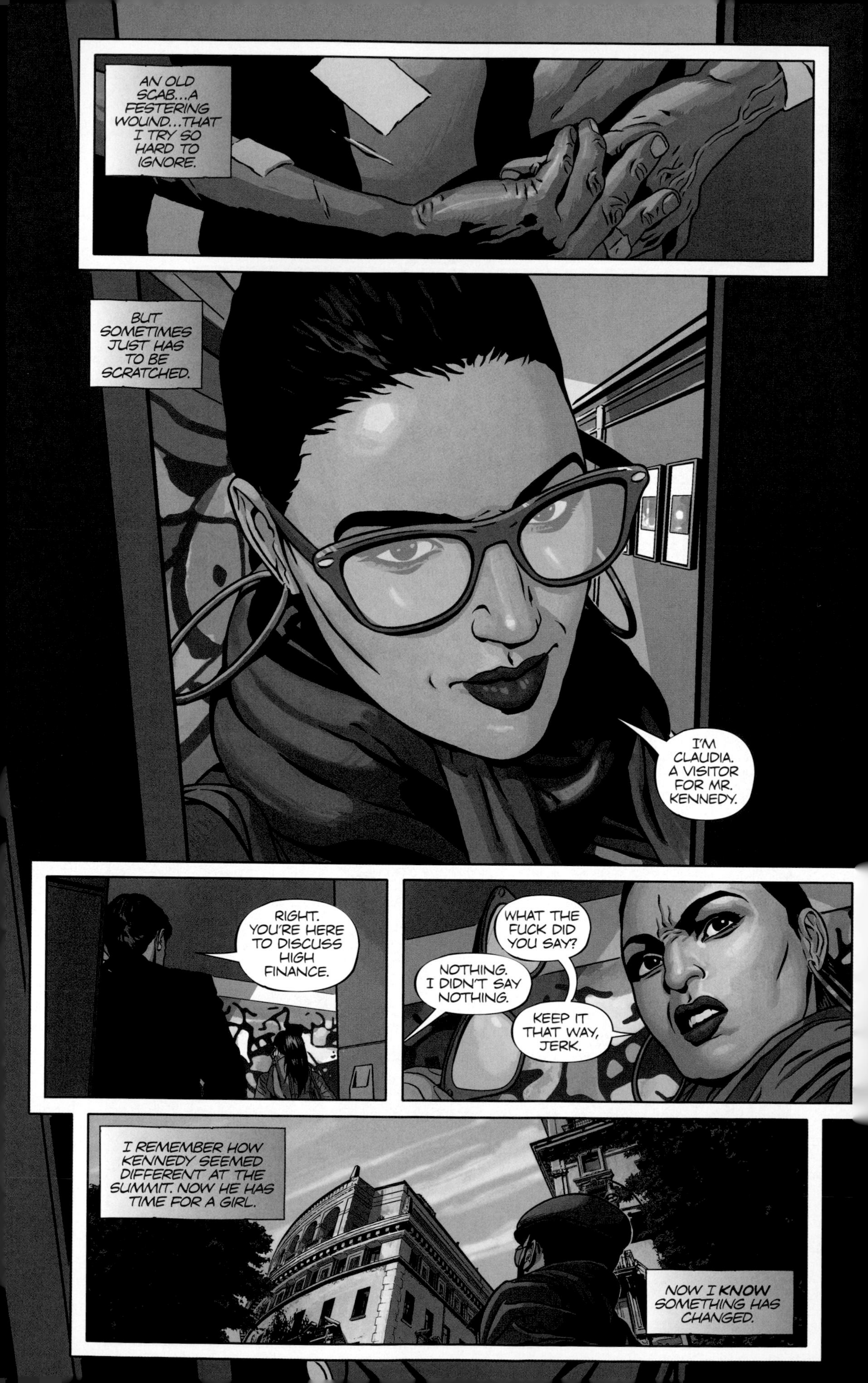
AN OLD SCAB...A FESTERING WOUND...THAT I TRY SO HARD TO IGNORE.
BUT SOMETIMES JUST HAS TO BE SCRATCHED.
I'M CLAUDIA. A VISITOR FOR MR. KENNEDY.
RIGHT. YOU'RE HERE TO DISCUSS HIGH FINANCE.
WHAT THE FUCK DID YOU SAY?
NOTHING. I DIDN'T SAY NOTHING.
KEEP IT THAT WAY, JERK.
I REMEMBER HOW KENNEDY SEEMED DIFFERENT AT THE SUMMIT. NOW HE HAS TIME FOR A GIRL.
NOW I KNOW SOMETHING HAS CHANGED.

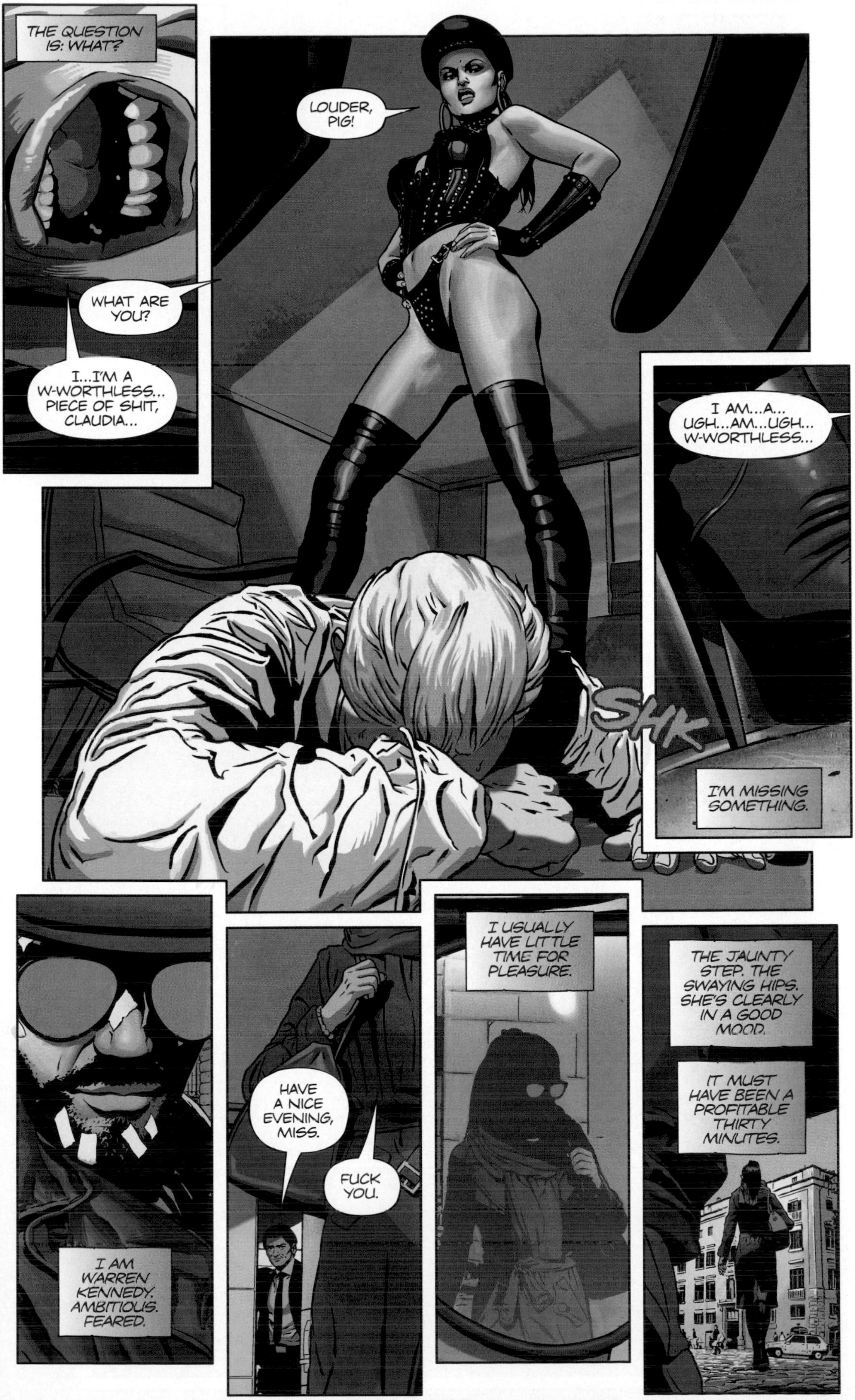
THE QUESTION IS: WHAT?
LOUDER, PIG!
WHAT ARE YOU?
I...I'M A W-WORTHLESS... PIECE OF SHIT, CLAUDIA...
I AM...A... UGH...AM...UGH... W-WORTHLESS...
SHK
I'M MISSING SOMETHING.
I AM WARREN KENNEDY. AMBITIOUS. FEARED.
HAVE A NICE EVENING, MISS.
FUCK YOU.
I USUALLY HAVE LITTLE TIME FOR PLEASURE.
THE JAUNTY STEP. THE SWAYING HIPS. SHE'S CLEARLY IN A GOOD MOOD.
IT MUST HAVE BEEN A PROFITABLE THIRTY MINUTES.

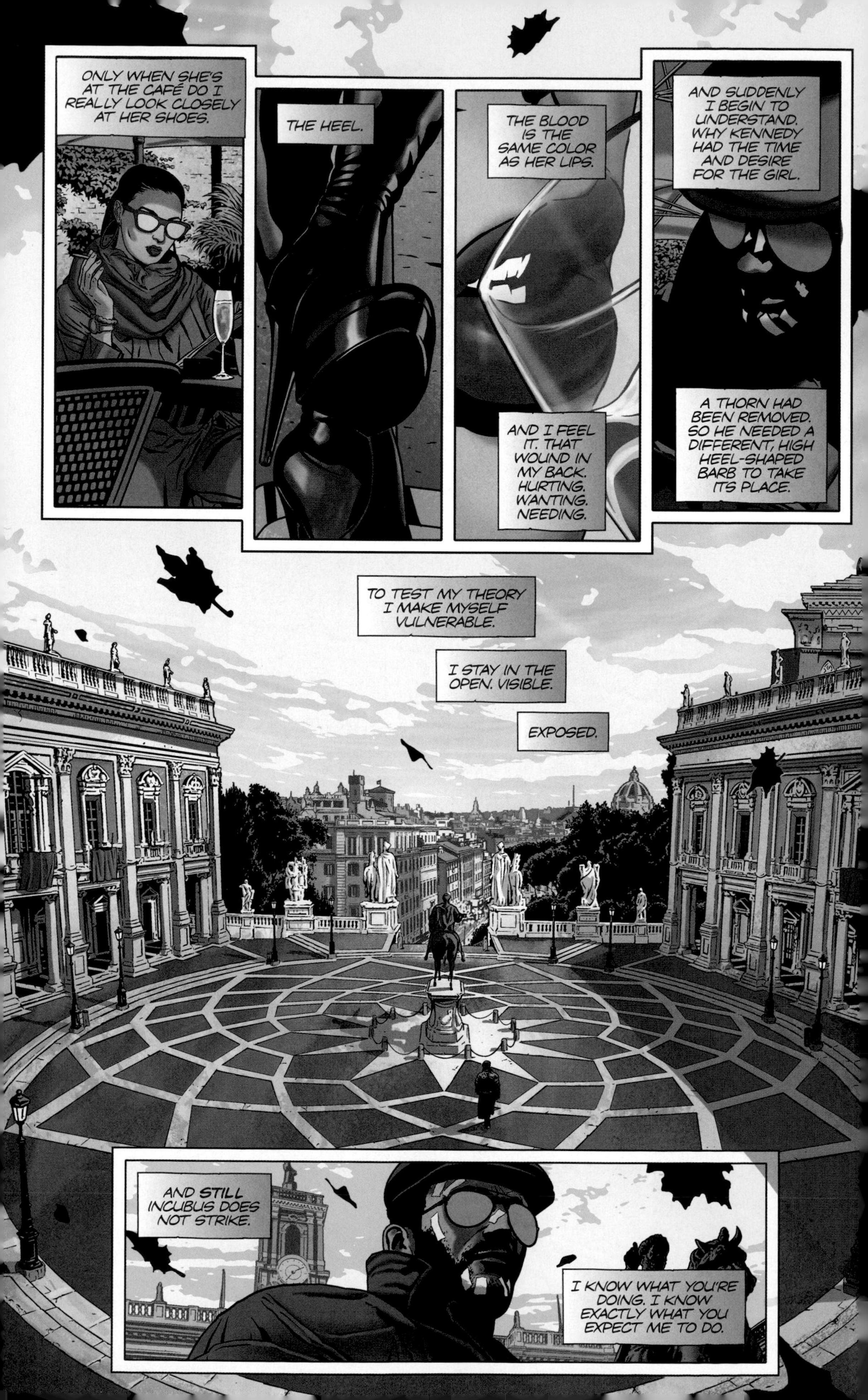
ONLY WHEN SHE'S AT THE CAFÉ DO I REALLY LOOK CLOSELY AT HER SHOES.
THE HEEL.
THE BLOOD IS THE SAME COLOR AS HER LIPS.
AND I FEEL IT. THAT WOUND IN MY BACK. HURTING. WANTING. NEEDING.
AND SUDDENLY I BEGIN TO UNDERSTAND. WHY KENNEDY HAD THE TIME AND DESIRE FOR THE GIRL.
A THORN HAD BEEN REMOVED. SO HE NEEDED A DIFFERENT, HIGH HEEL-SHAPED BARB TO TAKE ITS PLACE.
TO TEST MY THEORY I MAKE MYSELF VULNERABLE.
I STAY IN THE OPEN. VISIBLE.
EXPOSED.
AND STILL INCUBUS DOES NOT STRIKE.
I KNOW WHAT YOU'RE DOING. I KNOW EXACTLY WHAT YOU EXPECT ME TO DO.

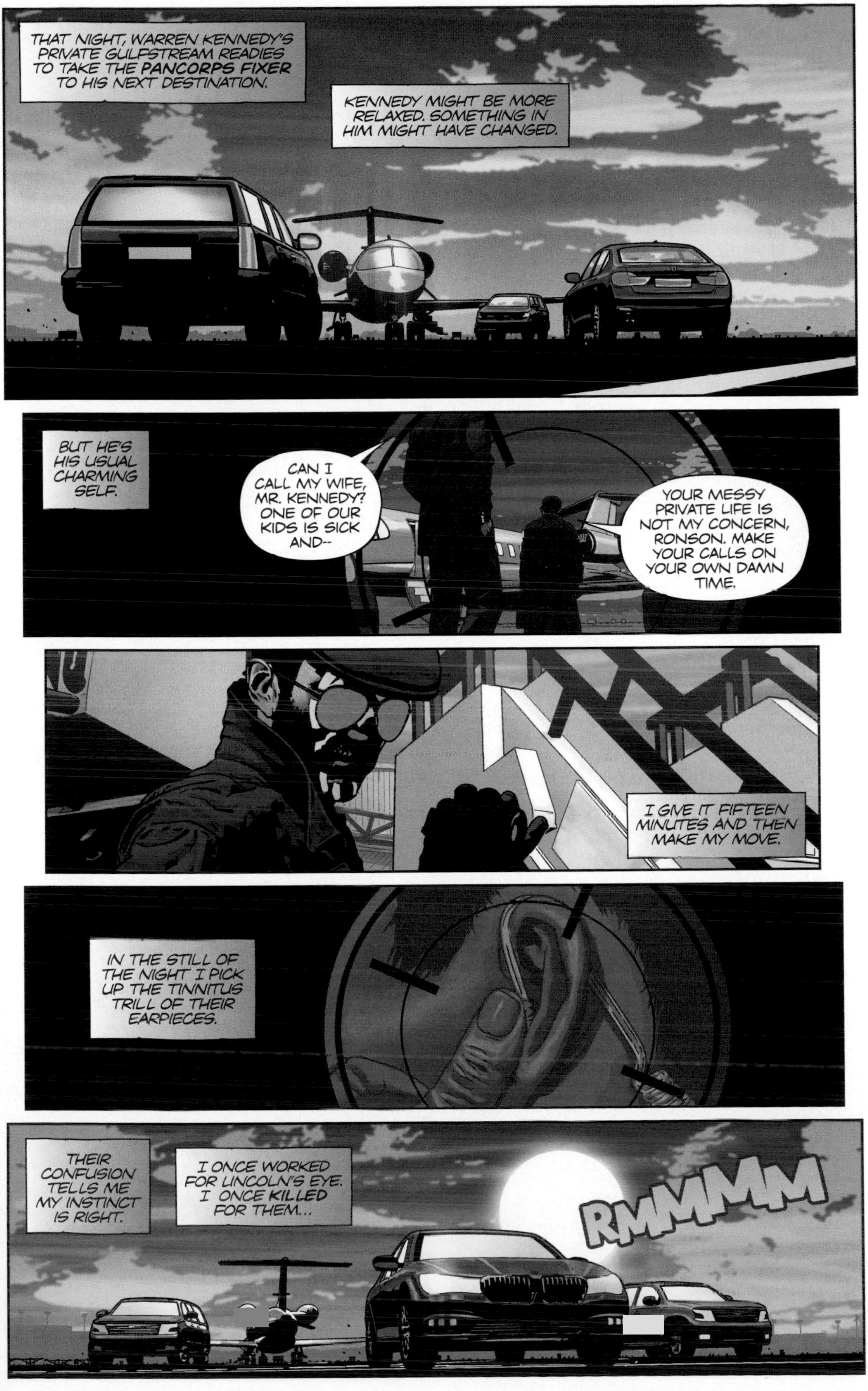
THAT NIGHT, WARREN KENNEDY'S PRIVATE GULFSTREAM READIES TO TAKE THE **PANCORPS FIXER** TO HIS NEXT DESTINATION.
KENNEDY MIGHT BE MORE RELAXED. SOMETHING IN HIM MIGHT HAVE CHANGED.
BUT HE'S HIS USUAL CHARMING SELF.
CAN I CALL MY WIFE, MR. KENNEDY? ONE OF OUR KIDS IS SICK AND--
YOUR MESSY PRIVATE LIFE IS NOT MY CONCERN, RONSON. MAKE YOUR CALLS ON YOUR OWN DAMN TIME.
I GIVE IT FIFTEEN MINUTES AND THEN MAKE MY MOVE.
IN THE STILL OF THE NIGHT I PICK UP THE TINNITUS TRILL OF THEIR EARPIECES.
THEIR CONFUSION TELLS ME MY INSTINCT IS RIGHT.
I ONCE WORKED FOR LINCOLN'S EYE. I ONCE **KILLED** FOR THEM...
RMMMMM

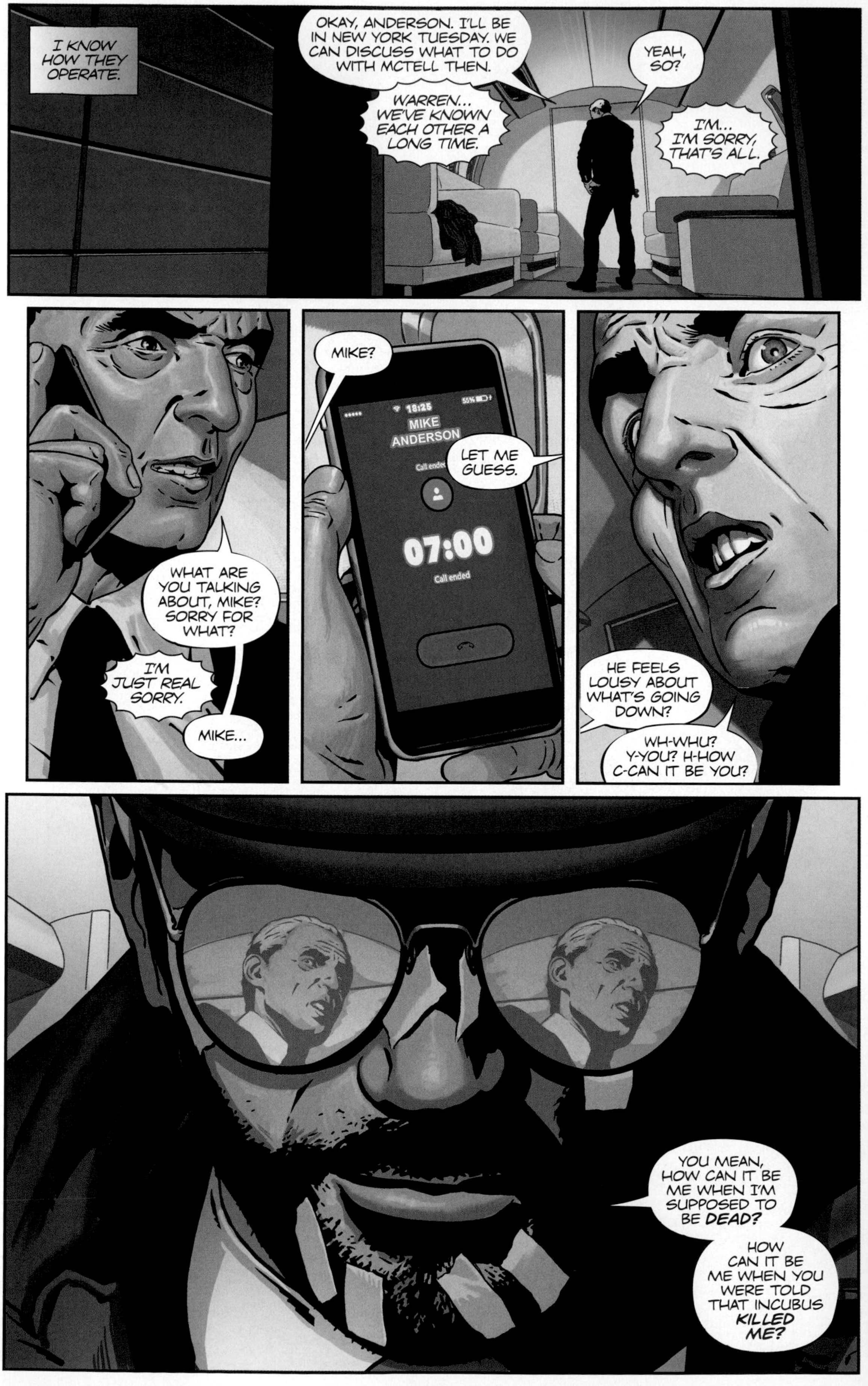
I KNOW HOW THEY OPERATE.
OKAY, ANDERSON. I'LL BE IN NEW YORK TUESDAY. WE CAN DISCUSS WHAT TO DO WITH MCTELL THEN.
WARREN... WE'VE KNOWN EACH OTHER A LONG TIME.
YEAH, SO?
I'M... I'M SORRY, THAT'S ALL.
WHAT ARE YOU TALKING ABOUT, MIKE? SORRY FOR WHAT?
I'M JUST REAL SORRY.
MIKE...
MIKE?
18:25
MIKE ANDERSON
Call ended
07:00
Call ended
LET ME GUESS.
HE FEELS LOUSY ABOUT WHAT'S GOING DOWN?
WH-WHU? Y-YOU? H-HOW C-CAN IT BE YOU?
YOU MEAN, HOW CAN IT BE ME WHEN I'M SUPPOSED TO BE **DEAD?**
HOW CAN IT BE ME WHEN YOU WERE TOLD THAT INCUBUS **KILLED ME?**

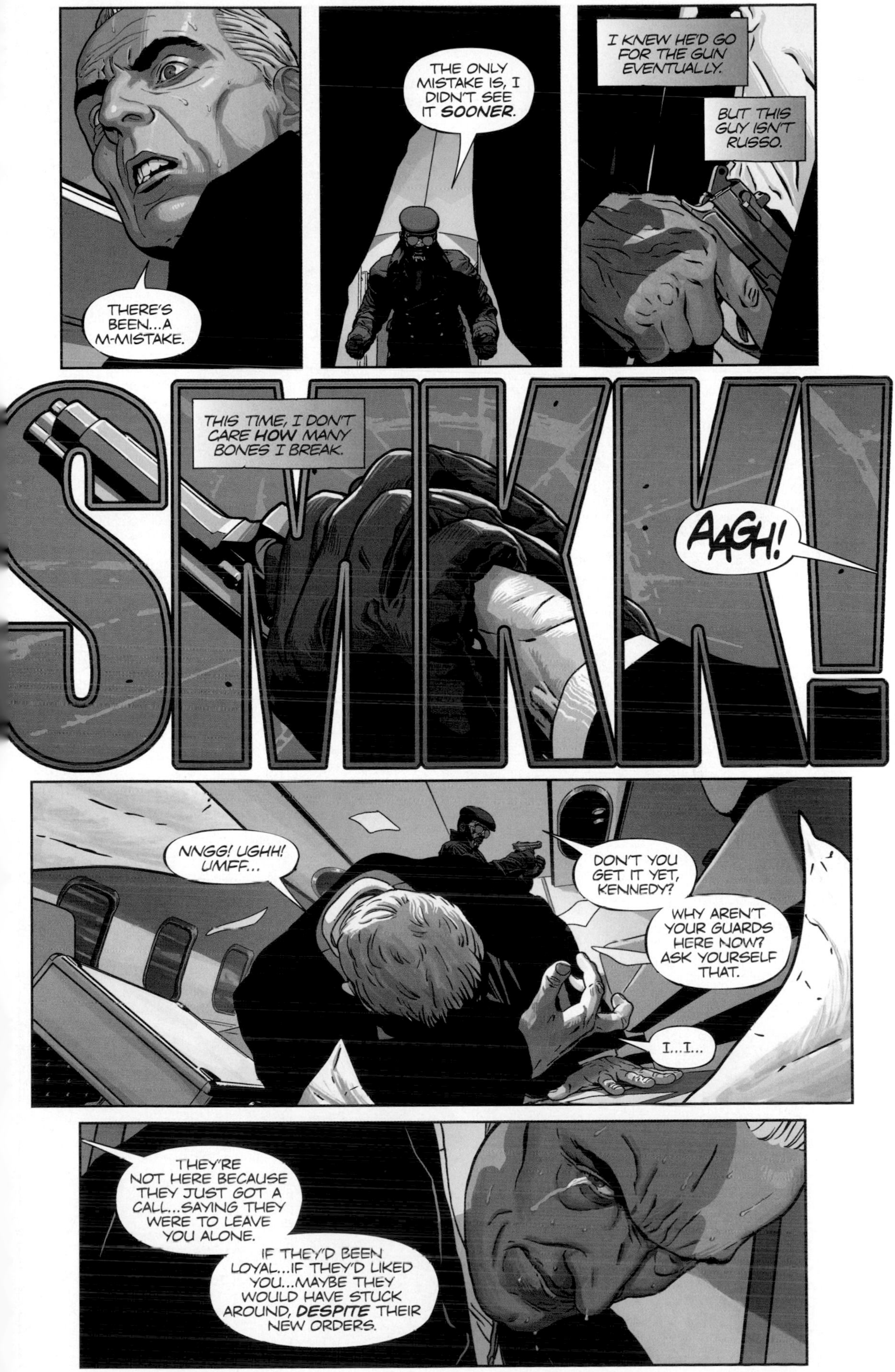
THERE'S BEEN...A M-MISTAKE.
THE ONLY MISTAKE IS, I DIDN'T SEE IT SOONER.
I KNEW HE'D GO FOR THE GUN EVENTUALLY.
BUT THIS GUY ISN'T RUSSO.
SMKK!
THIS TIME, I DON'T CARE HOW MANY BONES I BREAK.
AAGH!
NNGG! UGHH! UMFF...
DON'T YOU GET IT YET, KENNEDY?
WHY AREN'T YOUR GUARDS HERE NOW? ASK YOURSELF THAT.
I...I...
THEY'RE NOT HERE BECAUSE THEY JUST GOT A CALL...SAYING THEY WERE TO LEAVE YOU ALONE.
IF THEY'D BEEN LOYAL...IF THEY'D LIKED YOU...MAYBE THEY WOULD HAVE STUCK AROUND, DESPITE THEIR NEW ORDERS.

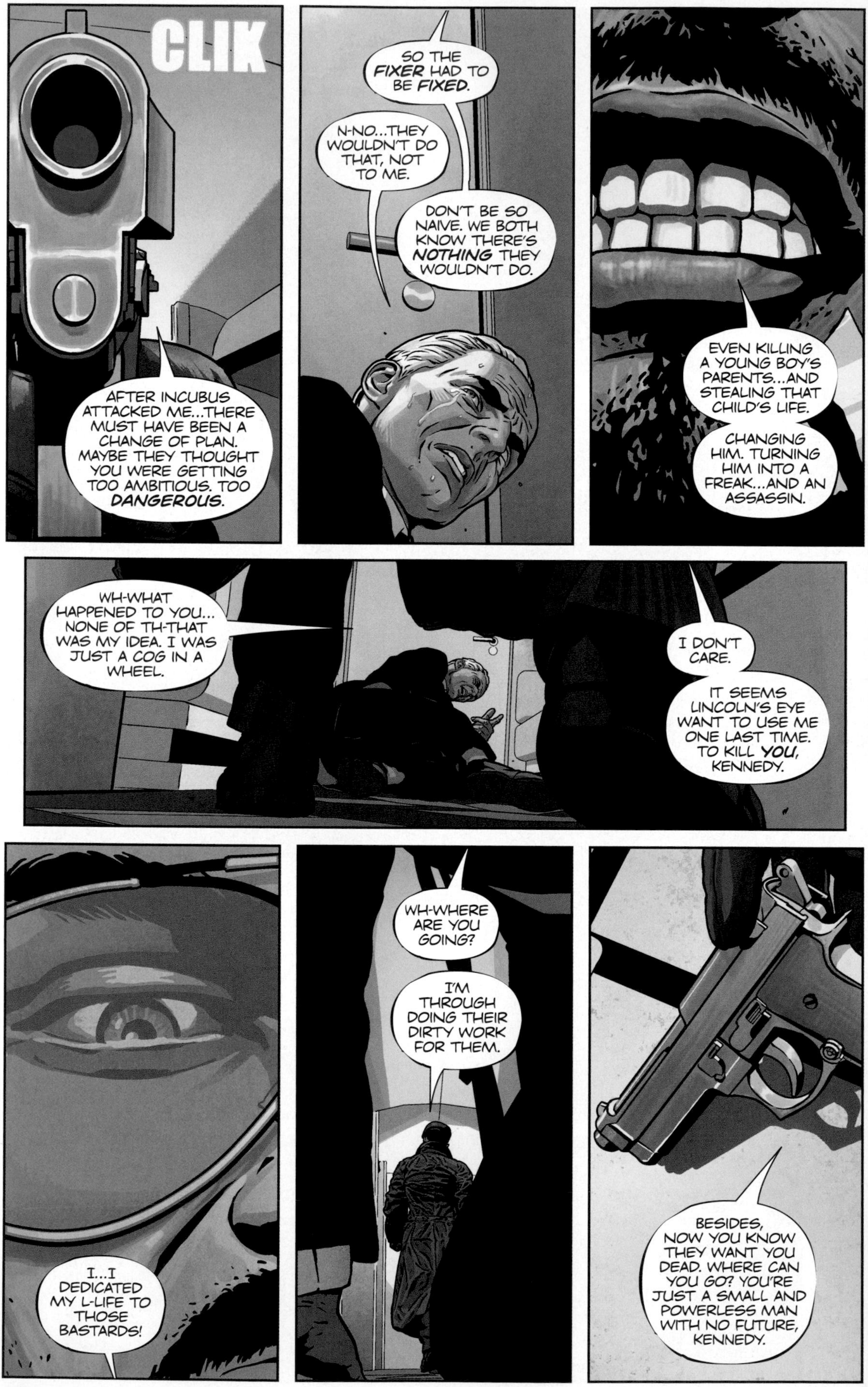
CLIK
AFTER INCUBUS ATTACKED ME...THERE MUST HAVE BEEN A CHANGE OF PLAN. MAYBE THEY THOUGHT YOU WERE GETTING TOO AMBITIOUS. TOO DANGEROUS.
SO THE FIXER HAD TO BE FIXED.
N-NO...THEY WOULDN'T DO THAT, NOT TO ME.
DON'T BE SO NAIVE. WE BOTH KNOW THERE'S NOTHING THEY WOULDN'T DO.
EVEN KILLING A YOUNG BOY'S PARENTS...AND STEALING THAT CHILD'S LIFE.
CHANGING HIM. TURNING HIM INTO A FREAK...AND AN ASSASSIN.
WH-WHAT HAPPENED TO YOU... NONE OF TH-THAT WAS MY IDEA. I WAS JUST A COG IN A WHEEL.
I DON'T CARE.
IT SEEMS LINCOLN'S EYE WANT TO USE ME ONE LAST TIME. TO KILL YOU, KENNEDY.
I...I DEDICATED MY L-LIFE TO THOSE BASTARDS!
WH-WHERE ARE YOU GOING?
I'M THROUGH DOING THEIR DIRTY WORK FOR THEM.
BESIDES, NOW YOU KNOW THEY WANT YOU DEAD. WHERE CAN YOU GO? YOU'RE JUST A SMALL AND POWERLESS MAN WITH NO FUTURE, KENNEDY.

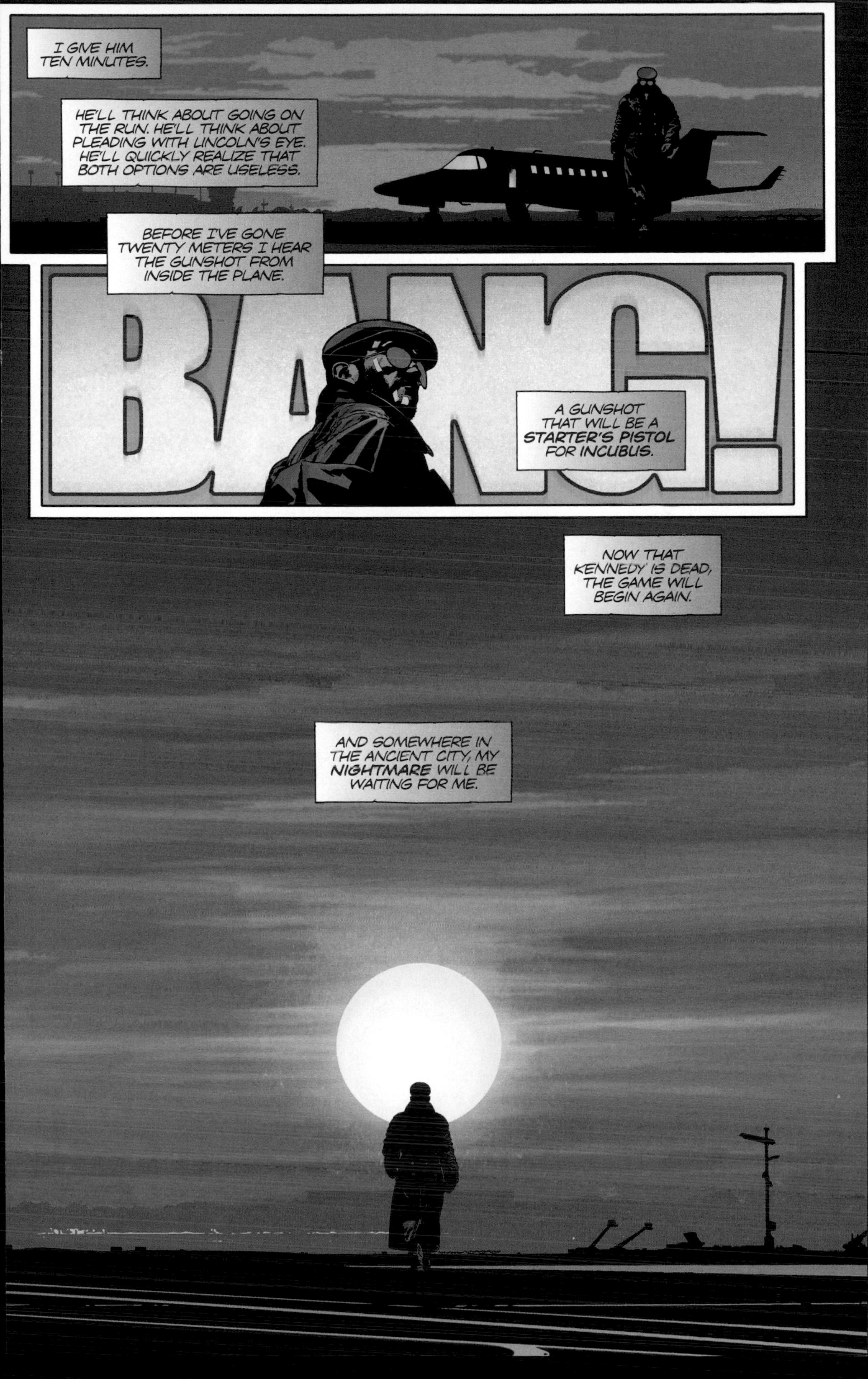
I GIVE HIM TEN MINUTES.
HE'LL THINK ABOUT GOING ON THE RUN. HE'LL THINK ABOUT PLEADING WITH LINCOLN'S EYE. HE'LL QUICKLY REALIZE THAT BOTH OPTIONS ARE USELESS.
BEFORE I'VE GONE TWENTY METERS I HEAR THE GUNSHOT FROM INSIDE THE PLANE.
BANG!
A GUNSHOT THAT WILL BE A STARTER'S PISTOL FOR INCUBUS.
NOW THAT KENNEDY IS DEAD, THE GAME WILL BEGIN AGAIN.
AND SOMEWHERE IN THE ANCIENT CITY, MY NIGHTMARE WILL BE WAITING FOR ME.

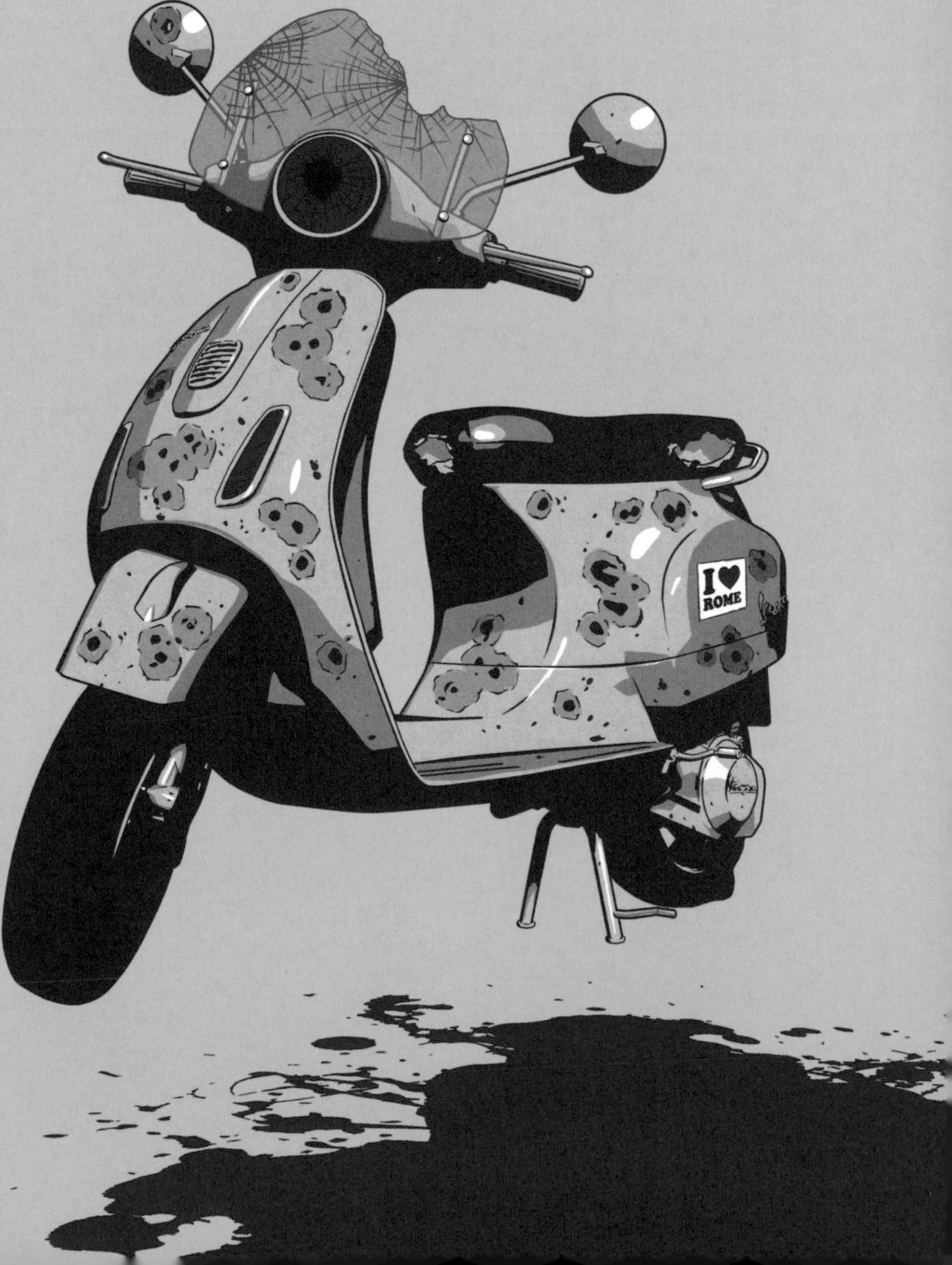
I ♥ ROME

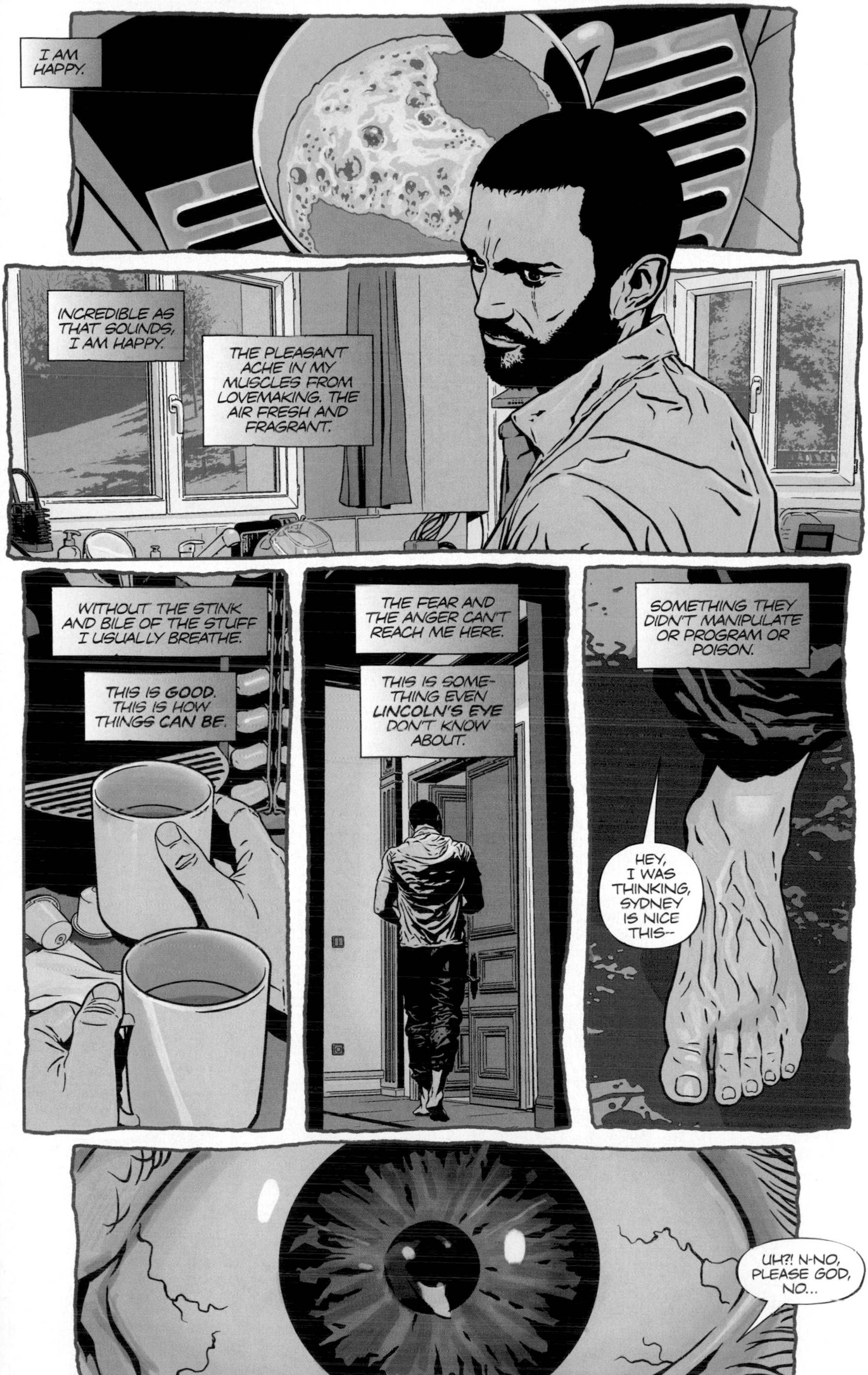
I AM HAPPY.
INCREDIBLE AS THAT SOUNDS, I AM HAPPY.
THE PLEASANT ACHE IN MY MUSCLES FROM LOVEMAKING. THE AIR FRESH AND FRAGRANT.
WITHOUT THE STINK AND BILE OF THE STUFF I USUALLY BREATHE.
THIS IS GOOD. THIS IS HOW THINGS CAN BE.
THE FEAR AND THE ANGER CAN'T REACH ME HERE.
THIS IS SOME-THING EVEN LINCOLN'S EYE DON'T KNOW ABOUT.
SOMETHING THEY DIDN'T MANIPULATE OR PROGRAM OR POISON.
HEY, I WAS THINKING, SYDNEY IS NICE THIS--
UH?! N-NO, PLEASE GOD, NO...

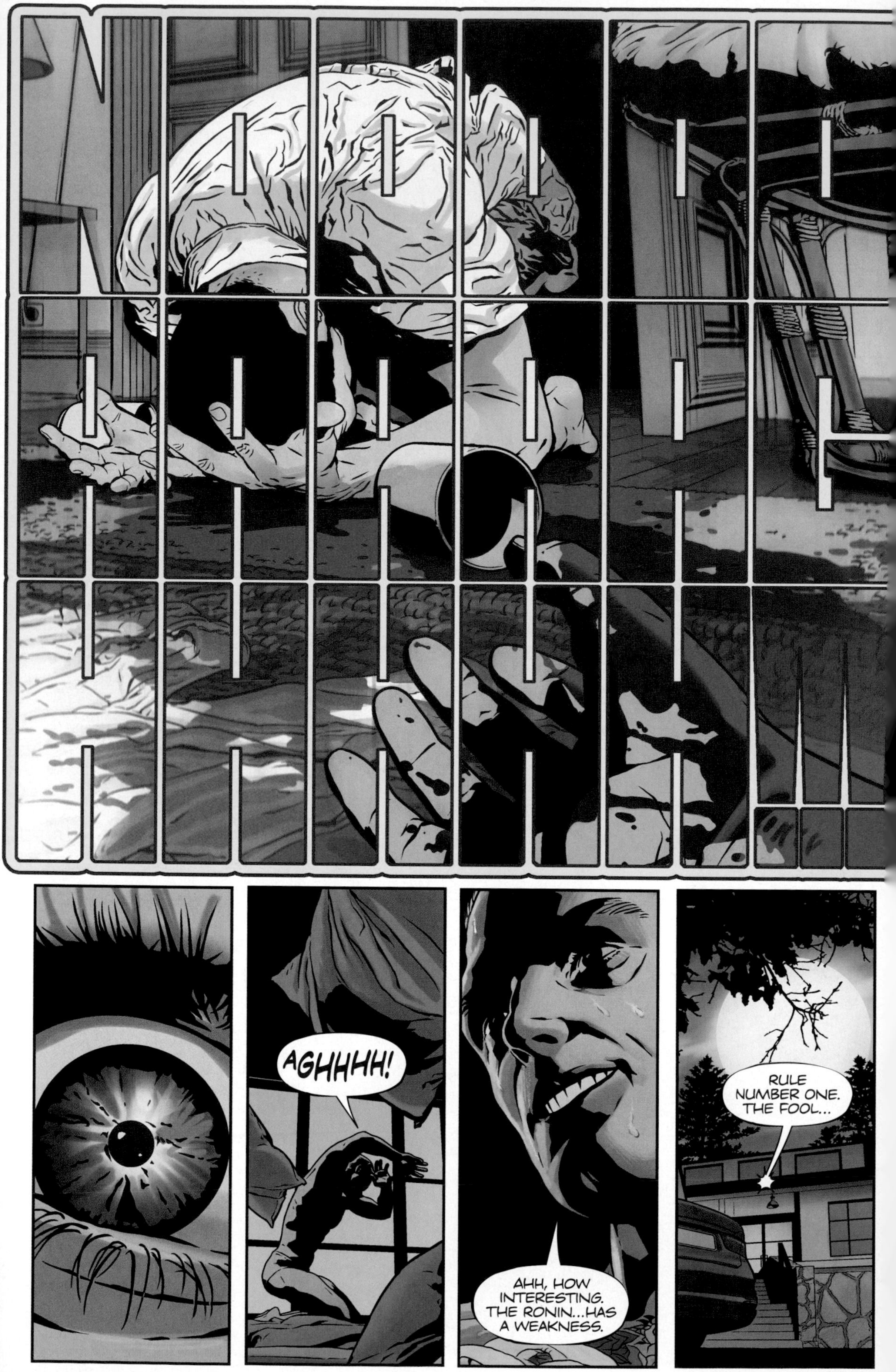
AGHHHH!
AHH, HOW INTERESTING. THE RONIN...HAS A WEAKNESS.
RULE NUMBER ONE. THE FOOL...

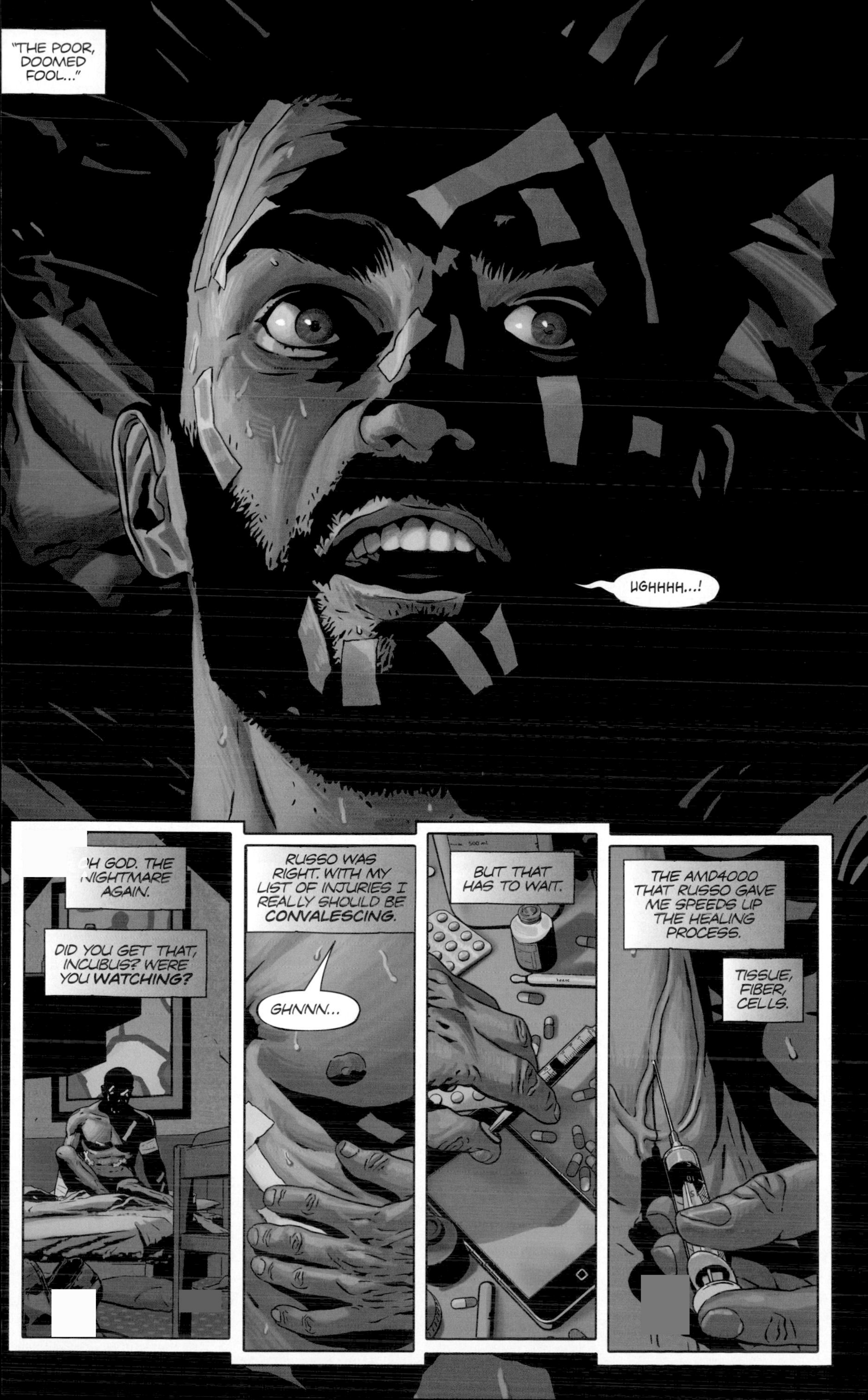
"THE POOR, DOOMED FOOL..."
UGHHHH...!
H GOD. THE NIGHTMARE AGAIN.
DID YOU GET THAT, INCUBUS? WERE YOU WATCHING?
RUSSO WAS RIGHT. WITH MY LIST OF INJURIES I REALLY SHOULD BE CONVALESCING.
GHNNN...
BUT THAT HAS TO WAIT.
THE AMD4000 THAT RUSSO GAVE ME SPEEDS UP THE HEALING PROCESS.
TISSUE, FIBER, CELLS.

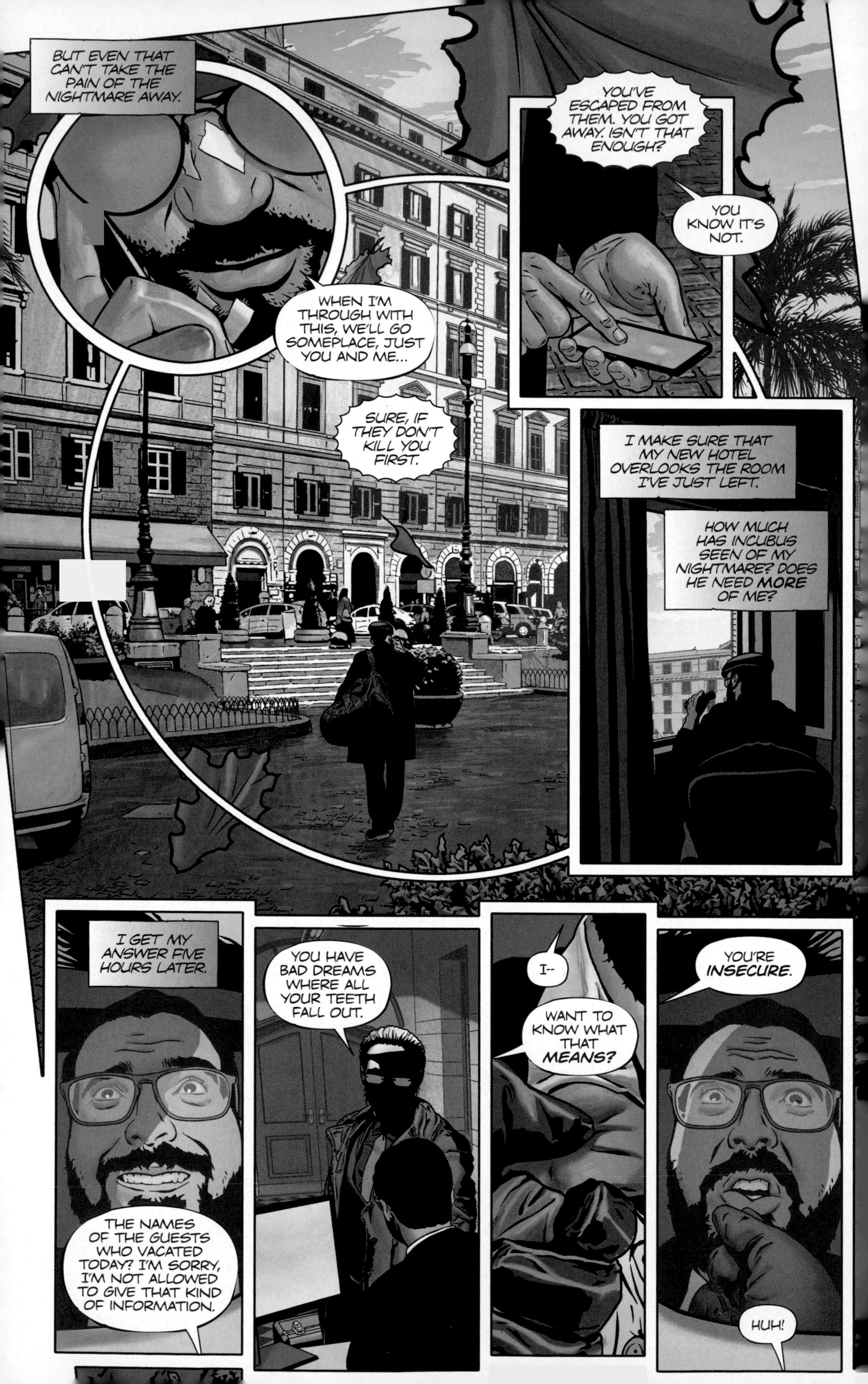
BUT EVEN THAT CAN'T TAKE THE PAIN OF THE NIGHTMARE AWAY.
WHEN I'M THROUGH WITH THIS, WE'LL GO SOMEPLACE, JUST YOU AND ME...
SURE, IF THEY DON'T KILL YOU FIRST.
YOU'VE ESCAPED FROM THEM. YOU GOT AWAY. ISN'T THAT ENOUGH?
YOU KNOW IT'S NOT.
I MAKE SURE THAT MY NEW HOTEL OVERLOOKS THE ROOM I'VE JUST LEFT.
HOW MUCH HAS INCUBUS SEEN OF MY NIGHTMARE? DOES HE NEED MORE OF ME?
I GET MY ANSWER FIVE HOURS LATER.
THE NAMES OF THE GUESTS WHO VACATED TODAY? I'M SORRY, I'M NOT ALLOWED TO GIVE THAT KIND OF INFORMATION.
YOU HAVE BAD DREAMS WHERE ALL YOUR TEETH FALL OUT.
I--
WANT TO KNOW WHAT THAT MEANS?
YOU'RE INSECURE.
HUH!

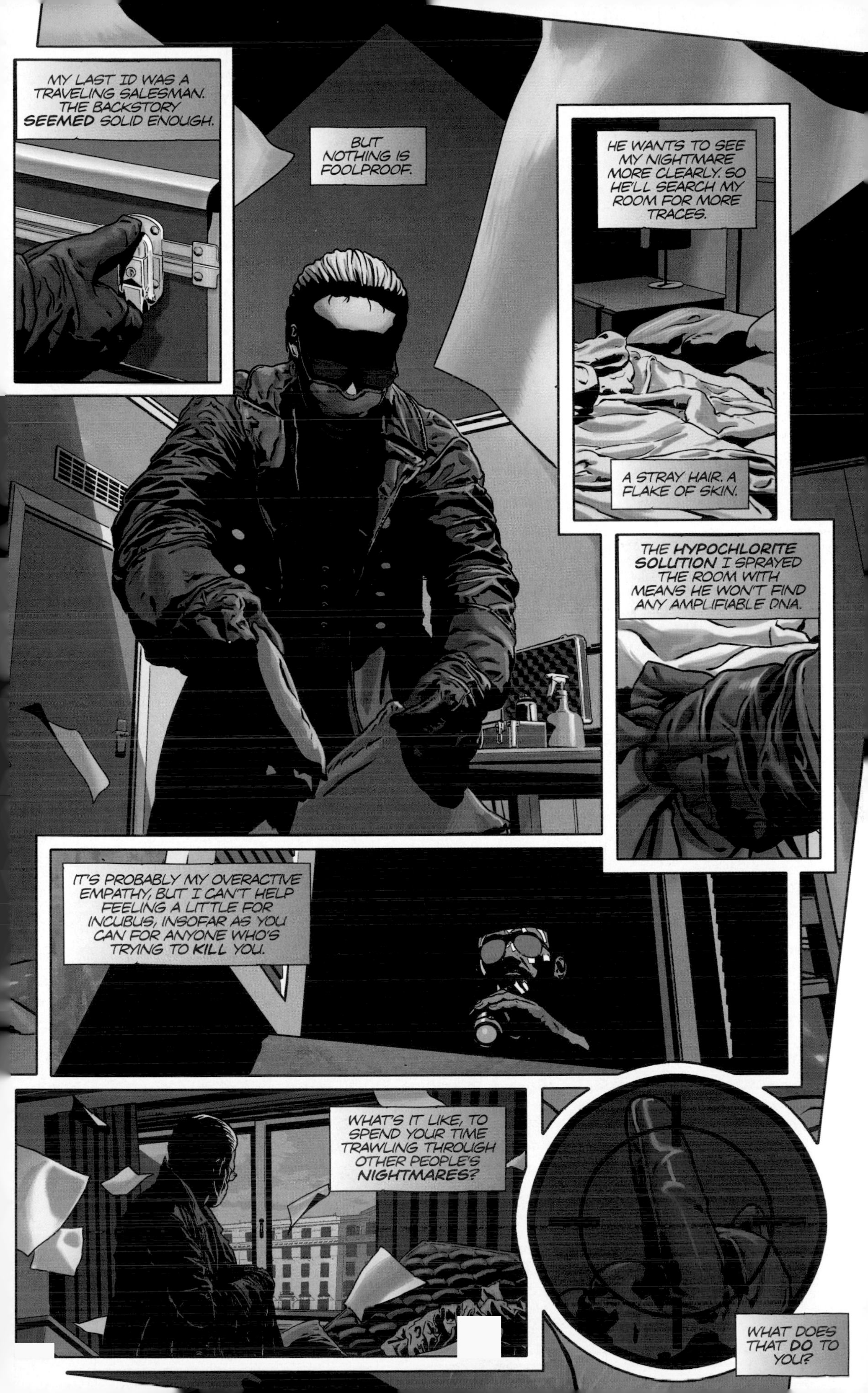
MY LAST ID WAS A TRAVELING SALESMAN. THE BACKSTORY **SEEMED** SOLID ENOUGH.
BUT NOTHING IS FOOLPROOF.
HE WANTS TO SEE MY NIGHTMARE MORE CLEARLY. SO HE'LL SEARCH MY ROOM FOR MORE TRACES.
A STRAY HAIR. A FLAKE OF SKIN.
THE **HYPOCHLORITE SOLUTION** I SPRAYED THE ROOM WITH MEANS HE WON'T FIND ANY AMPLIFIABLE DNA.
IT'S PROBABLY MY OVERACTIVE EMPATHY, BUT I CAN'T HELP FEELING A LITTLE FOR INCUBUS, INSOFAR AS YOU CAN FOR ANYONE WHO'S TRYING TO **KILL** YOU.
WHAT'S IT LIKE, TO SPEND YOUR TIME TRAWLING THROUGH OTHER PEOPLE'S **NIGHTMARES**?
WHAT DOES THAT **DO** TO YOU?

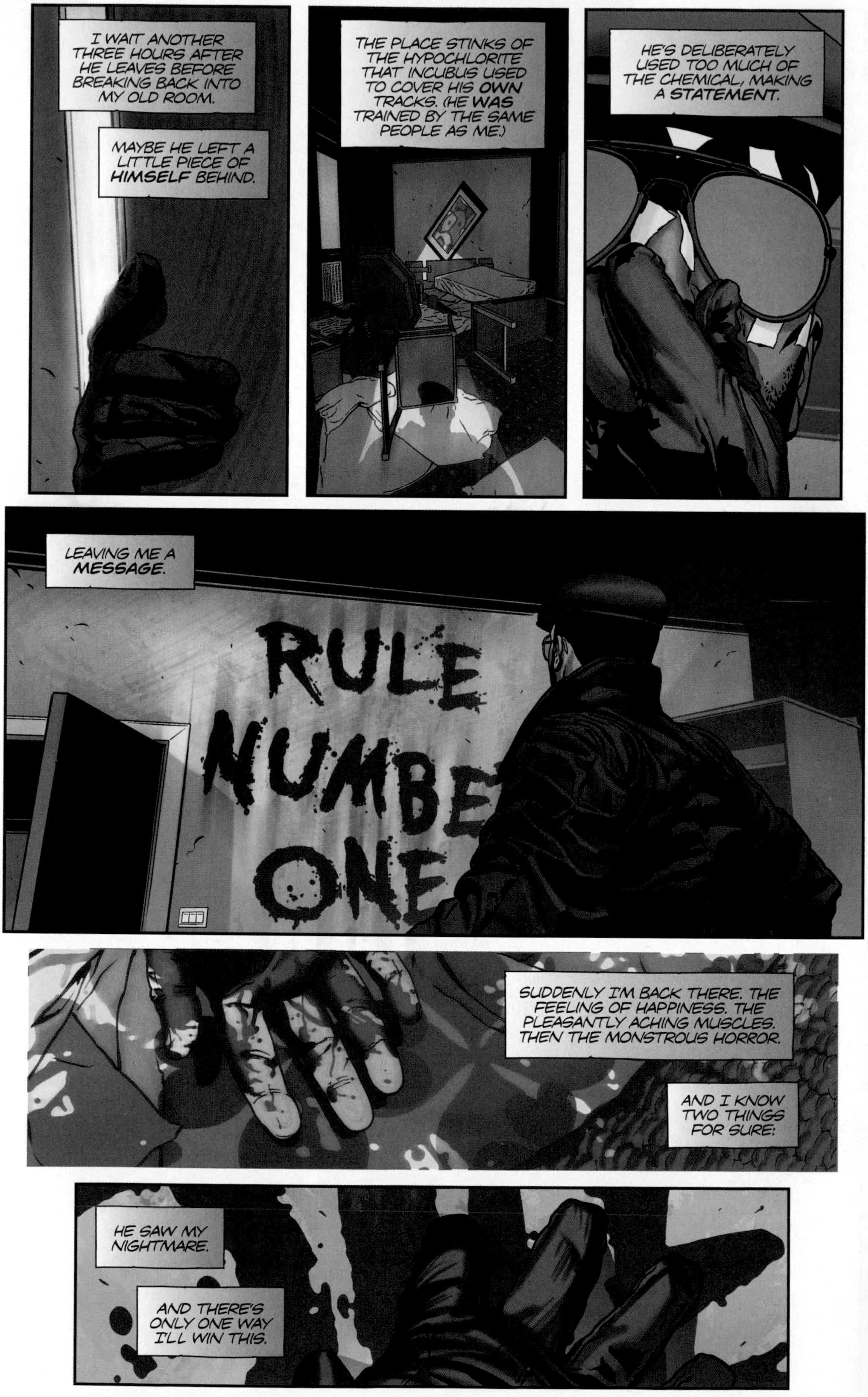
I WAIT ANOTHER THREE HOURS AFTER HE LEAVES BEFORE BREAKING BACK INTO MY OLD ROOM.
MAYBE HE LEFT A LITTLE PIECE OF HIMSELF BEHIND.
THE PLACE STINKS OF THE HYPOCHLORITE THAT INCUBUS USED TO COVER HIS OWN TRACKS. (HE WAS TRAINED BY THE SAME PEOPLE AS ME.)
HE'S DELIBERATELY USED TOO MUCH OF THE CHEMICAL, MAKING A STATEMENT.
LEAVING ME A MESSAGE.
RULE NUMBE ONE
SUDDENLY I'M BACK THERE. THE FEELING OF HAPPINESS. THE PLEASANTLY ACHING MUSCLES. THEN THE MONSTROUS HORROR.
AND I KNOW TWO THINGS FOR SURE:
HE SAW MY NIGHTMARE.
AND THERE'S ONLY ONE WAY I'LL WIN THIS.

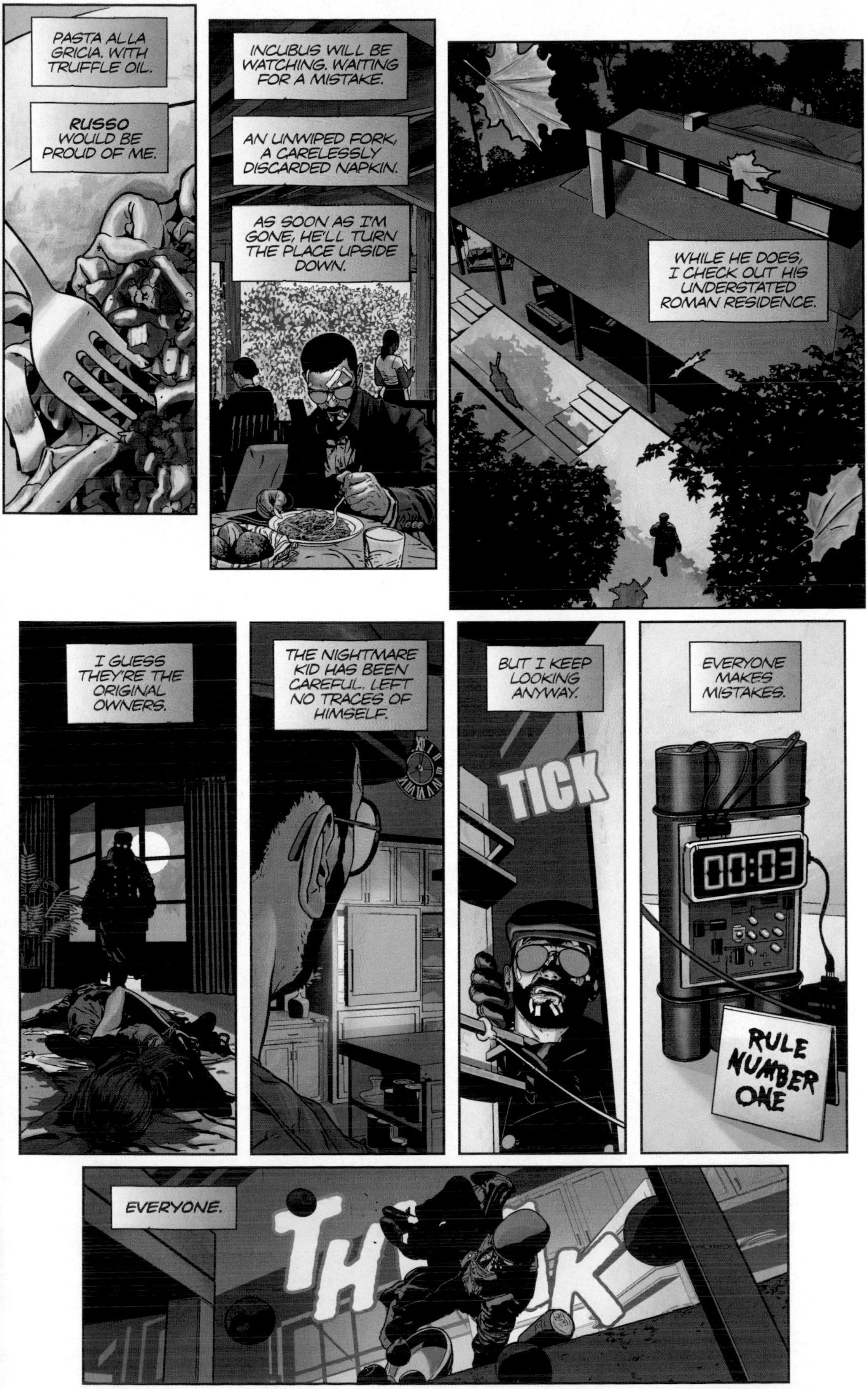
PASTA ALLA GRICIA. WITH TRUFFLE OIL.
RUSSO WOULD BE PROUD OF ME.
INCUBUS WILL BE WATCHING. WAITING FOR A MISTAKE.
AN UNWIPED FORK, A CARELESSLY DISCARDED NAPKIN.
AS SOON AS I'M GONE, HE'LL TURN THE PLACE UPSIDE DOWN.
WHILE HE DOES, I CHECK OUT HIS UNDERSTATED ROMAN RESIDENCE.
I GUESS THEY'RE THE ORIGINAL OWNERS.
THE NIGHTMARE KID HAS BEEN CAREFUL. LEFT NO TRACES OF HIMSELF.
BUT I KEEP LOOKING ANYWAY.
TICK
EVERYONE MAKES MISTAKES.
00:03
RULE NUMBER ONE
EVERYONE.

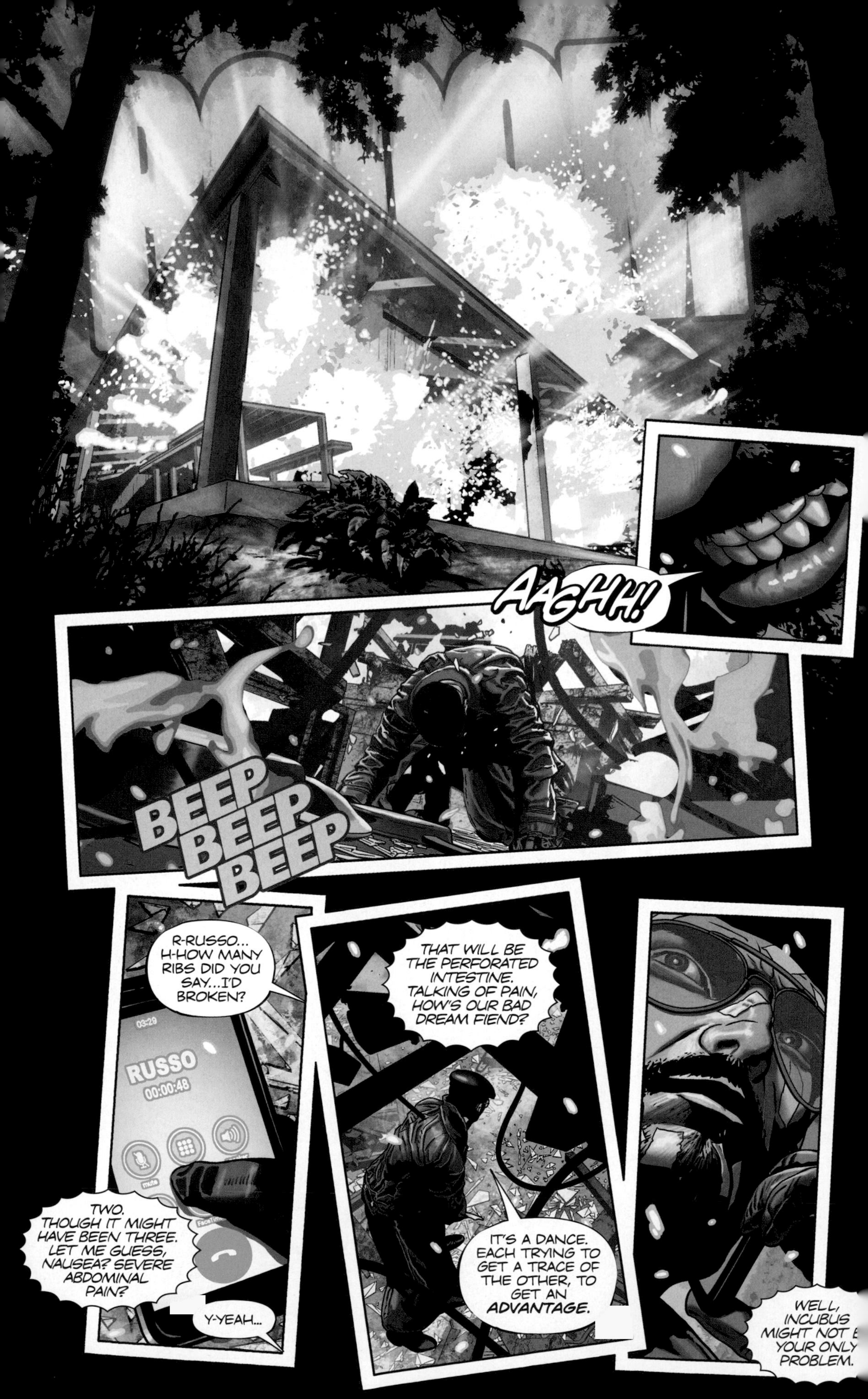
AAGHH!
BEEP BEEP BEEP
R-RUSSO... H-HOW MANY RIBS DID YOU SAY...I'D BROKEN?
03:29
RUSSO
00:00:48
mute
TWO. THOUGH IT MIGHT HAVE BEEN THREE. LET ME GUESS, NAUSEA? SEVERE ABDOMINAL PAIN?
Y-YEAH...
THAT WILL BE THE PERFORATED INTESTINE. TALKING OF PAIN, HOW'S OUR BAD DREAM FIEND?
IT'S A DANCE. EACH TRYING TO GET A TRACE OF THE OTHER, TO GET AN **ADVANTAGE.**
WELL, INCUBUS MIGHT NOT
YOUR ONLY PROBLEM.

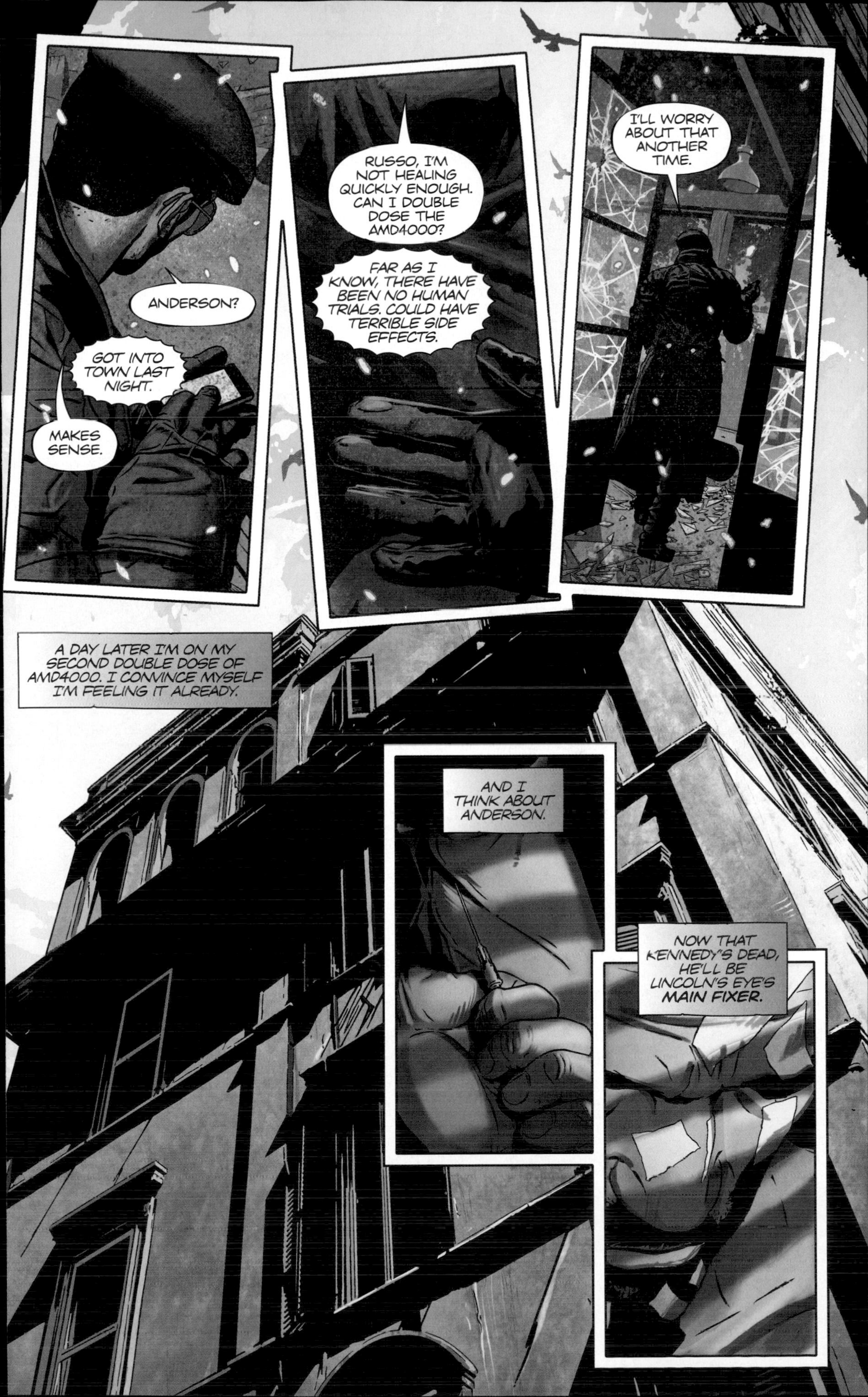
ANDERSON?
GOT INTO TOWN LAST NIGHT.
MAKES SENSE.
RUSSO, I'M NOT HEALING QUICKLY ENOUGH. CAN I DOUBLE DOSE THE AMD4000?
FAR AS I KNOW, THERE HAVE BEEN NO HUMAN TRIALS. COULD HAVE TERRIBLE SIDE EFFECTS.
I'LL WORRY ABOUT THAT ANOTHER TIME.
A DAY LATER I'M ON MY SECOND DOUBLE DOSE OF AMD4000. I CONVINCE MYSELF I'M FEELING IT ALREADY.
AND I THINK ABOUT ANDERSON.
NOW THAT KENNEDY'S DEAD, HE'LL BE LINCOLN'S EYE'S MAIN FIXER.

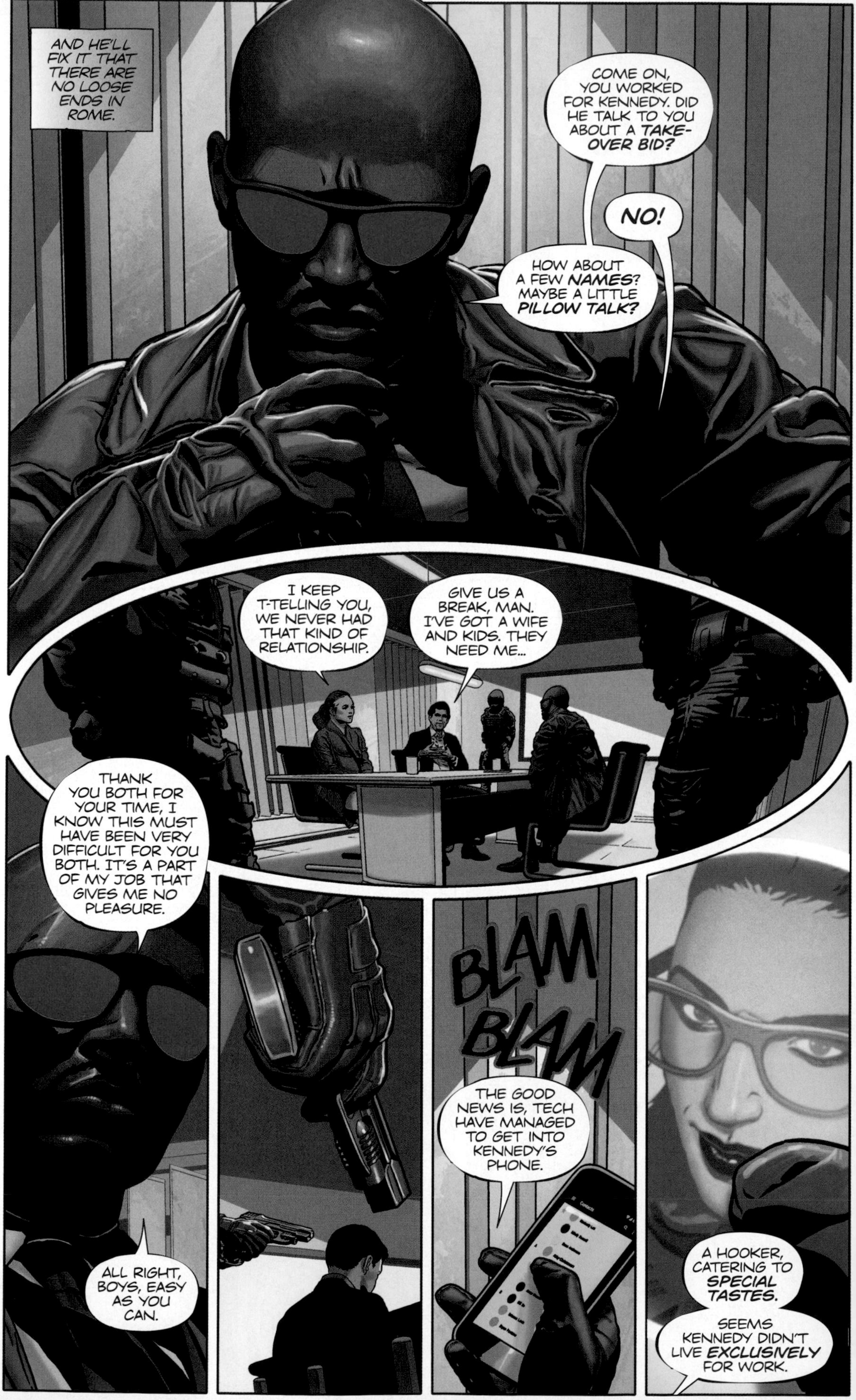
AND HE'LL FIX IT THAT THERE ARE NO LOOSE ENDS IN ROME.
COME ON, YOU WORKED FOR KENNEDY. DID HE TALK TO YOU ABOUT A TAKE-OVER BID?
NO!
HOW ABOUT A FEW NAMES? MAYBE A LITTLE PILLOW TALK?
I KEEP T-TELLING YOU, WE NEVER HAD THAT KIND OF RELATIONSHIP.
GIVE US A BREAK, MAN. I'VE GOT A WIFE AND KIDS. THEY NEED ME...
THANK YOU BOTH FOR YOUR TIME, I KNOW THIS MUST HAVE BEEN VERY DIFFICULT FOR YOU BOTH. IT'S A PART OF MY JOB THAT GIVES ME NO PLEASURE.
ALL RIGHT, BOYS, EASY AS YOU CAN.
BLAM
BLAM
THE GOOD NEWS IS, TECH HAVE MANAGED TO GET INTO KENNEDY'S PHONE.
A HOOKER, CATERING TO SPECIAL TASTES.
SEEMS KENNEDY DIDN'T LIVE EXCLUSIVELY FOR WORK.

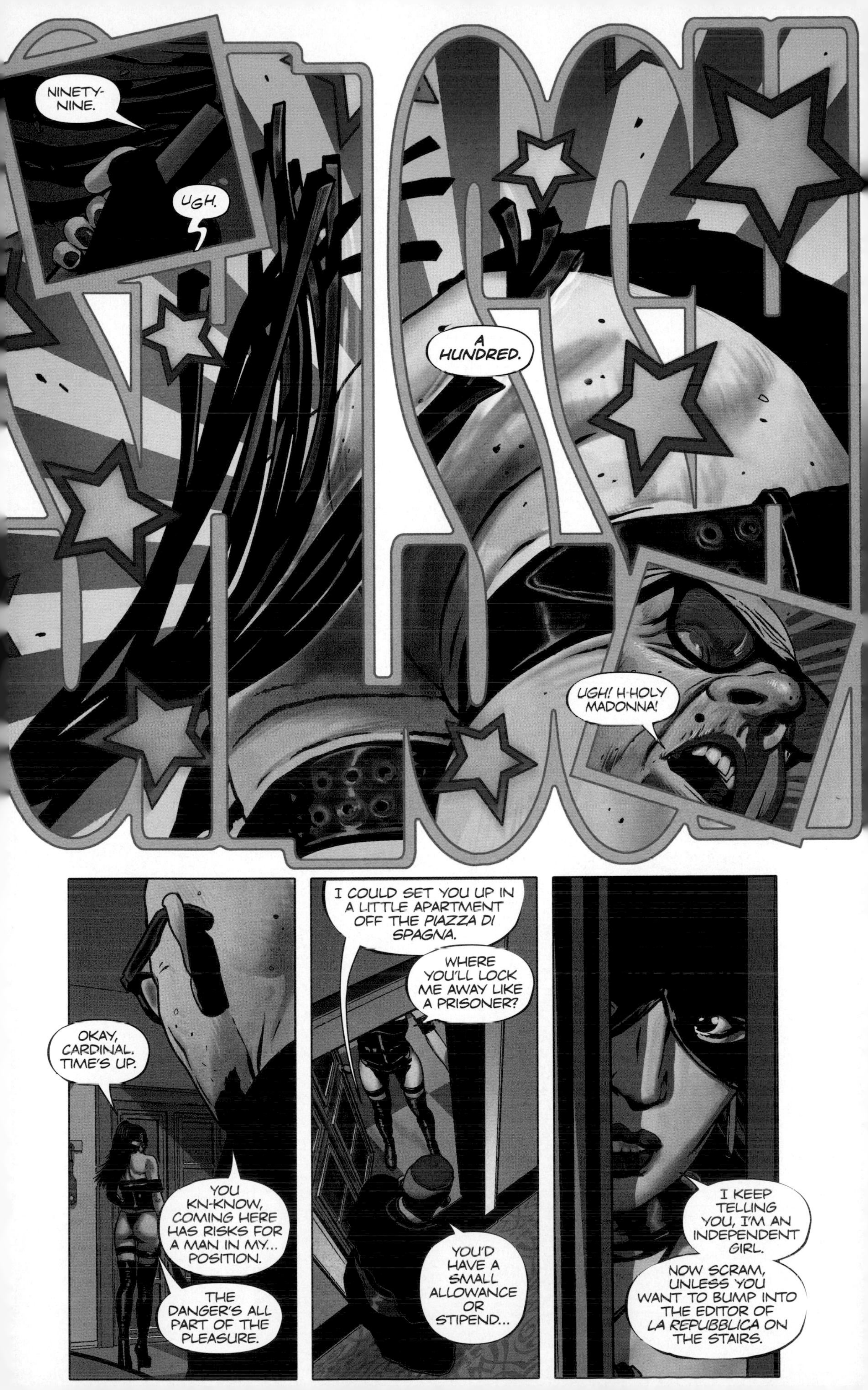
NINETY-NINE.
UGH.
A HUNDRED.
UGH! H-HOLY MADONNA!
OKAY, CARDINAL. TIME'S UP.
YOU KN-KNOW, COMING HERE HAS RISKS FOR A MAN IN MY... POSITION.
THE DANGER'S ALL PART OF THE PLEASURE.
I COULD SET YOU UP IN A LITTLE APARTMENT OFF THE *PIAZZA DI SPAGNA*.
WHERE YOU'LL LOCK ME AWAY LIKE A PRISONER?
YOU'D HAVE A SMALL ALLOWANCE OR STIPEND...
I KEEP TELLING YOU, I'M AN INDEPENDENT GIRL.
NOW SCRAM, UNLESS YOU WANT TO BUMP INTO THE EDITOR OF *LA REPUBBLICA* ON THE STAIRS.

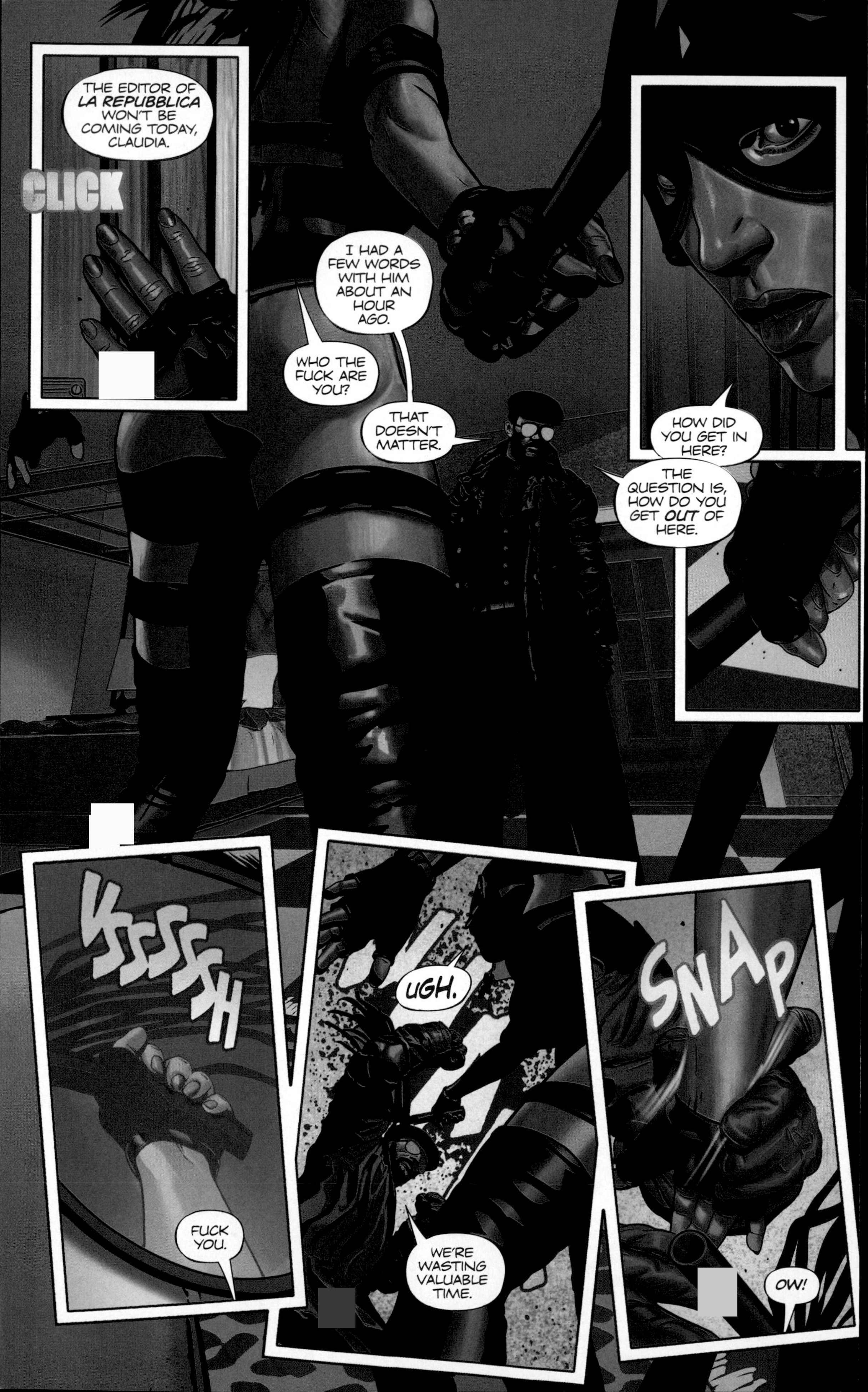

THE EDITOR OF *LA REPUBBLICA* WON'T BE COMING TODAY, CLAUDIA.
CLICK
I HAD A FEW WORDS WITH HIM ABOUT AN HOUR AGO.
WHO THE FUCK ARE YOU?
THAT DOESN'T MATTER.
HOW DID YOU GET IN HERE?
THE QUESTION IS, HOW DO YOU GET *OUT* OF HERE.
VSSSSSH
FUCK YOU.
UGH.
WE'RE WASTING VALUABLE TIME.
SNAP
OW!

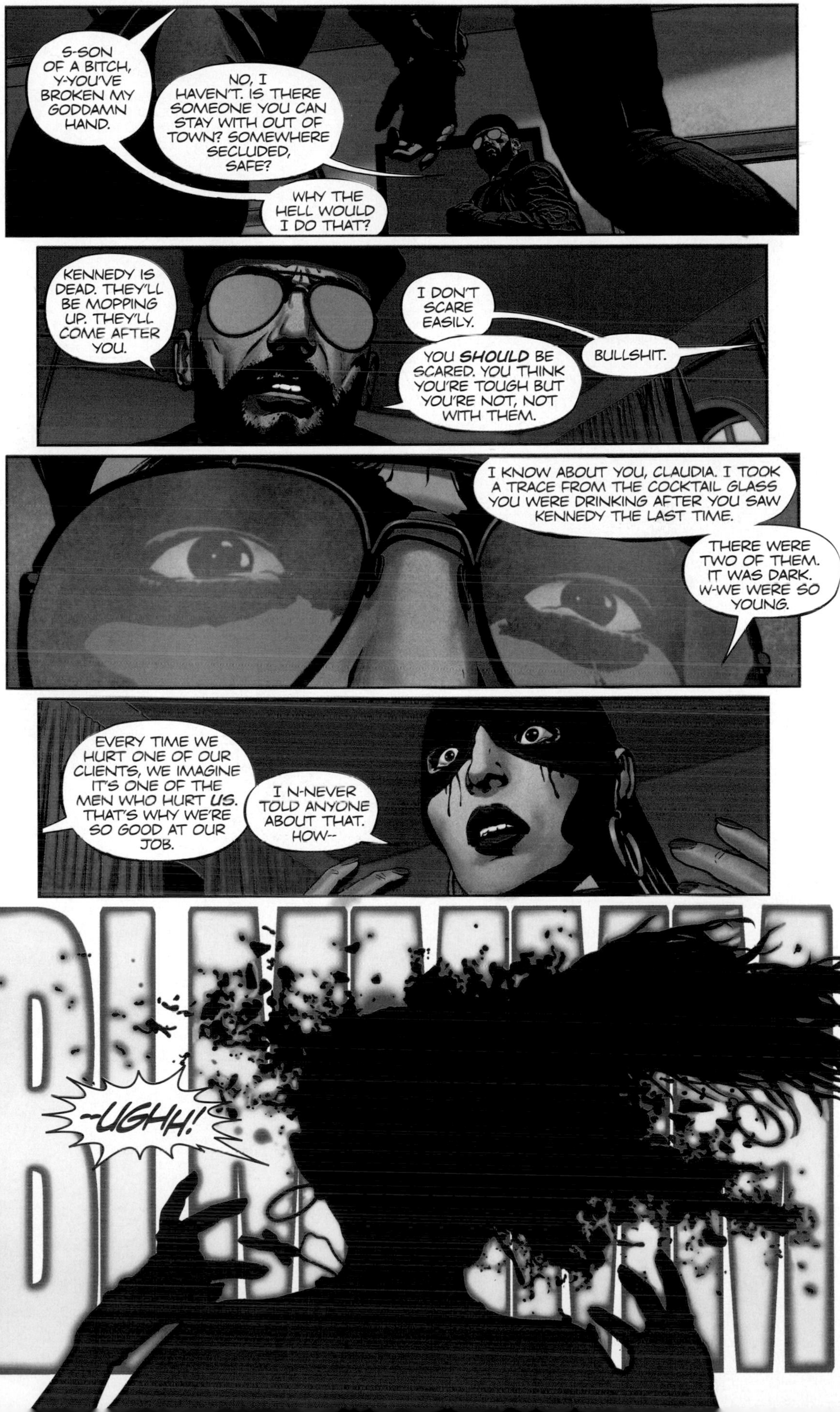
S-SON OF A BITCH, Y-YOU'VE BROKEN MY GODDAMN HAND.
NO, I HAVEN'T. IS THERE SOMEONE YOU CAN STAY WITH OUT OF TOWN? SOMEWHERE SECLUDED, SAFE?
WHY THE HELL WOULD I DO THAT?
KENNEDY IS DEAD. THEY'LL BE MOPPING UP. THEY'LL COME AFTER YOU.
I DON'T SCARE EASILY.
BULLSHIT.
YOU SHOULD BE SCARED. YOU THINK YOU'RE TOUGH BUT YOU'RE NOT, NOT WITH THEM.
I KNOW ABOUT YOU, CLAUDIA. I TOOK A TRACE FROM THE COCKTAIL GLASS YOU WERE DRINKING AFTER YOU SAW KENNEDY THE LAST TIME.
THERE WERE TWO OF THEM. IT WAS DARK. W-WE WERE SO YOUNG.
EVERY TIME WE HURT ONE OF OUR CLIENTS, WE IMAGINE IT'S ONE OF THE MEN WHO HURT US. THAT'S WHY WE'RE SO GOOD AT OUR JOB.
I N-NEVER TOLD ANYONE ABOUT THAT. HOW--
--UGHH!

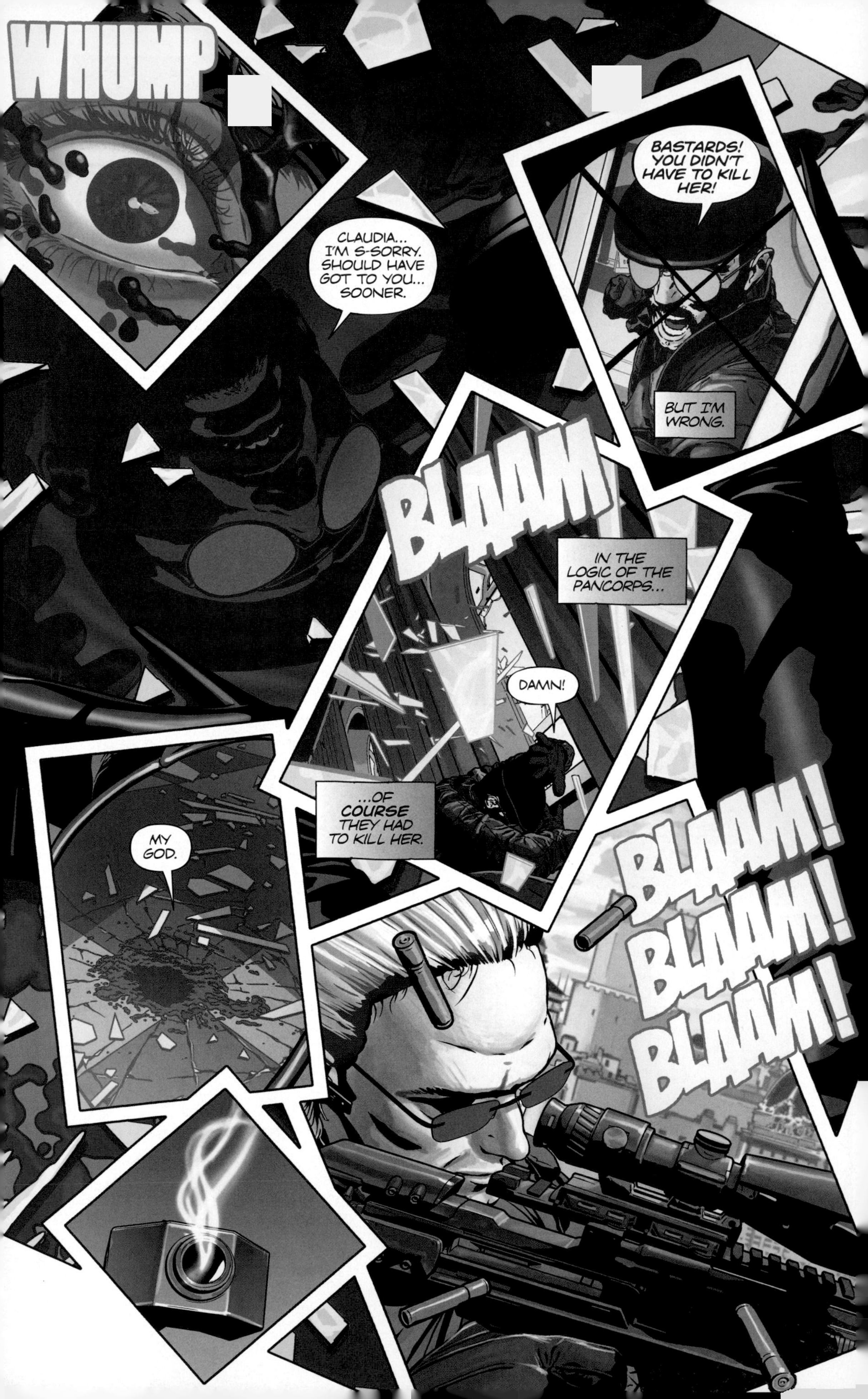
WHUMP
CLAUDIA... I'M S-SORRY. SHOULD HAVE GOT TO YOU... SOONER.
BASTARDS! YOU DIDN'T HAVE TO KILL HER!
BUT I'M WRONG.
BLAAM
IN THE LOGIC OF THE PANCORPS...
DAMN!
...OF COURSE THEY HAD TO KILL HER.
MY GOD.
BLAAM!
BLAAM!
BLAAM!

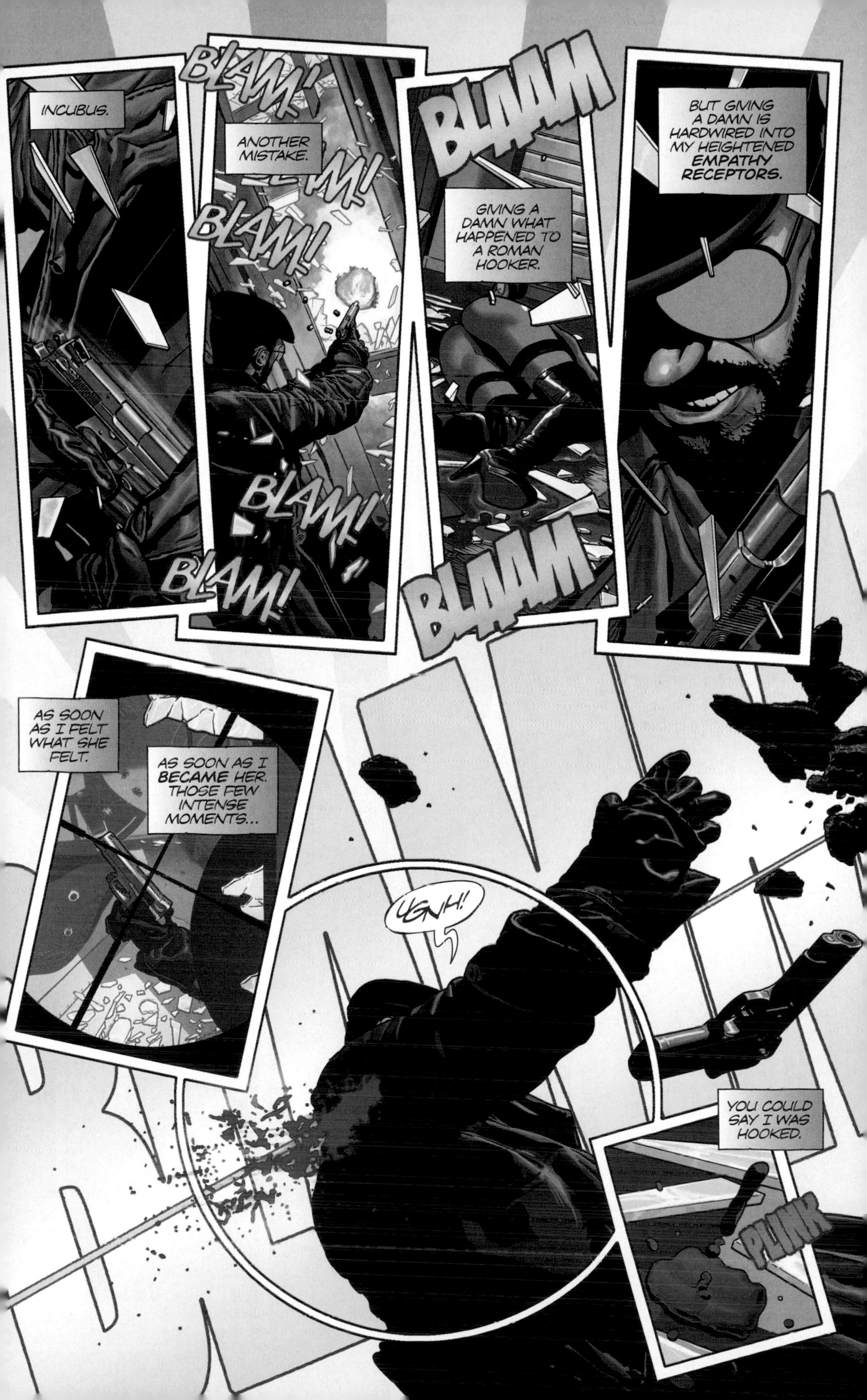INCUBUS.
BLAM!
ANOTHER MISTAKE.
BLAM!
BLAM!
BLAM!
BLAM!
BLAAM
GIVING A DAMN WHAT HAPPENED TO A ROMAN HOOKER.
BUT GIVING A DAMN IS HARDWIRED INTO MY HEIGHTENED EMPATHY RECEPTORS.
BLAAM
AS SOON AS I FELT WHAT SHE FELT.
AS SOON AS I BECAME HER. THOSE FEW INTENSE MOMENTS...
UGNH!
YOU COULD SAY I WAS HOOKED.
PLINK

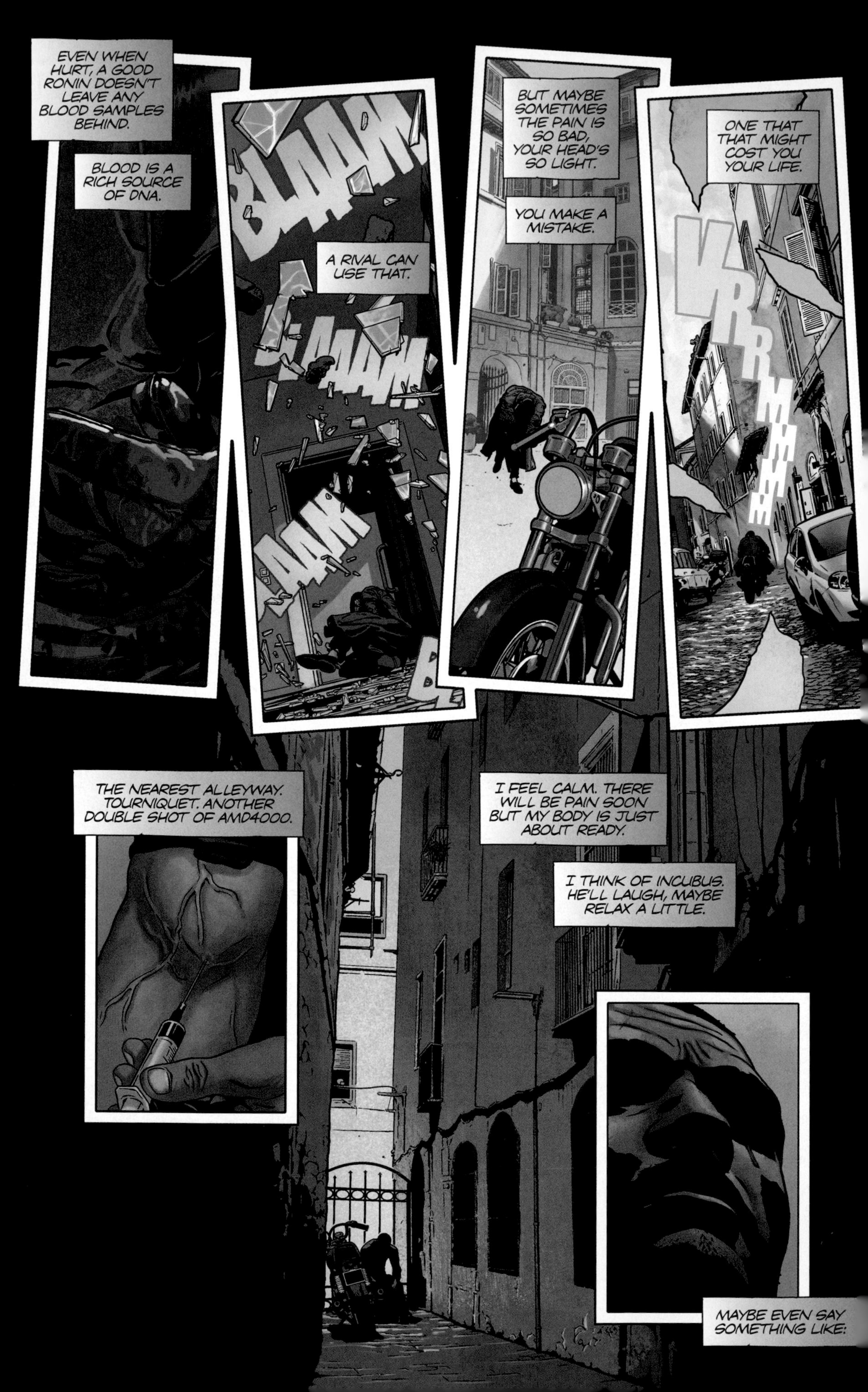
EVEN WHEN HURT, A GOOD RONIN DOESN'T LEAVE ANY BLOOD SAMPLES BEHIND.
BLOOD IS A RICH SOURCE OF DNA.
A RIVAL CAN USE THAT.
BUT MAYBE SOMETIMES THE PAIN IS SO BAD, YOUR HEAD'S SO LIGHT.
YOU MAKE A MISTAKE.
ONE THAT THAT MIGHT COST YOU YOUR LIFE.
THE NEAREST ALLEYWAY. TOURNIQUET. ANOTHER DOUBLE SHOT OF AMD4000.
I FEEL CALM. THERE WILL BE PAIN SOON BUT MY BODY IS JUST ABOUT READY.
I THINK OF INCUBUS. HE'LL LAUGH, MAYBE RELAX A LITTLE.
MAYBE EVEN SAY SOMETHING LIKE:

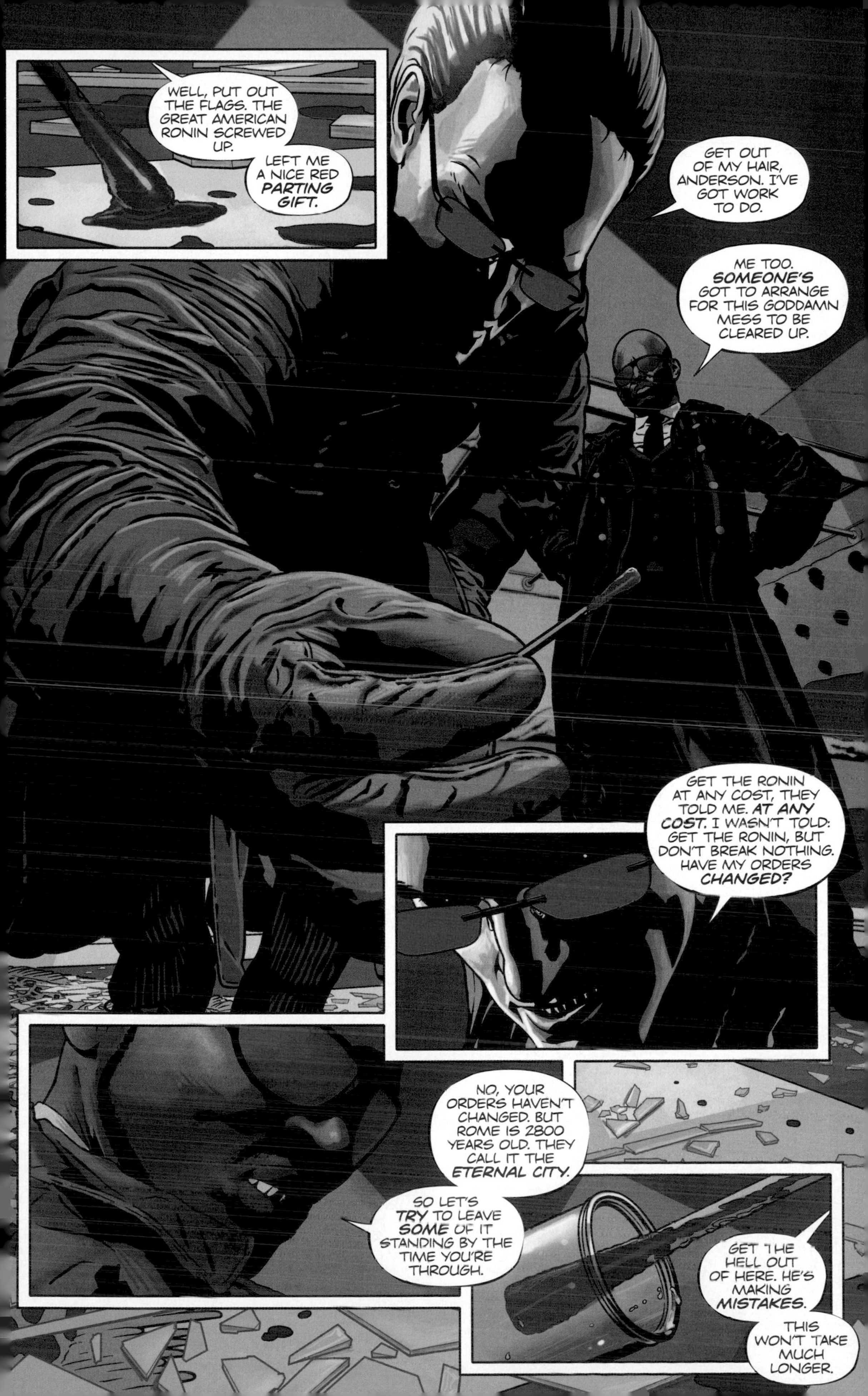
WELL, PUT OUT THE FLAGS. THE GREAT AMERICAN RONIN SCREWED UP.
LEFT ME A NICE RED **PARTING GIFT.**
GET OUT OF MY HAIR, ANDERSON. I'VE GOT WORK TO DO.
ME TOO. **SOMEONE'S** GOT TO ARRANGE FOR THIS GODDAMN MESS TO BE CLEARED UP.
GET THE RONIN AT ANY COST, THEY TOLD ME. **AT ANY COST.** I WASN'T TOLD: GET THE RONIN, BUT DON'T BREAK NOTHING. HAVE MY ORDERS **CHANGED?**
NO, YOUR ORDERS HAVEN'T CHANGED. BUT ROME IS 2800 YEARS OLD. THEY CALL IT THE **ETERNAL CITY.**
SO LET'S **TRY** TO LEAVE **SOME** OF IT STANDING BY THE TIME YOU'RE THROUGH.
GET THE HELL OUT OF HERE. HE'S MAKING **MISTAKES.**
THIS WON'T TAKE MUCH LONGER.

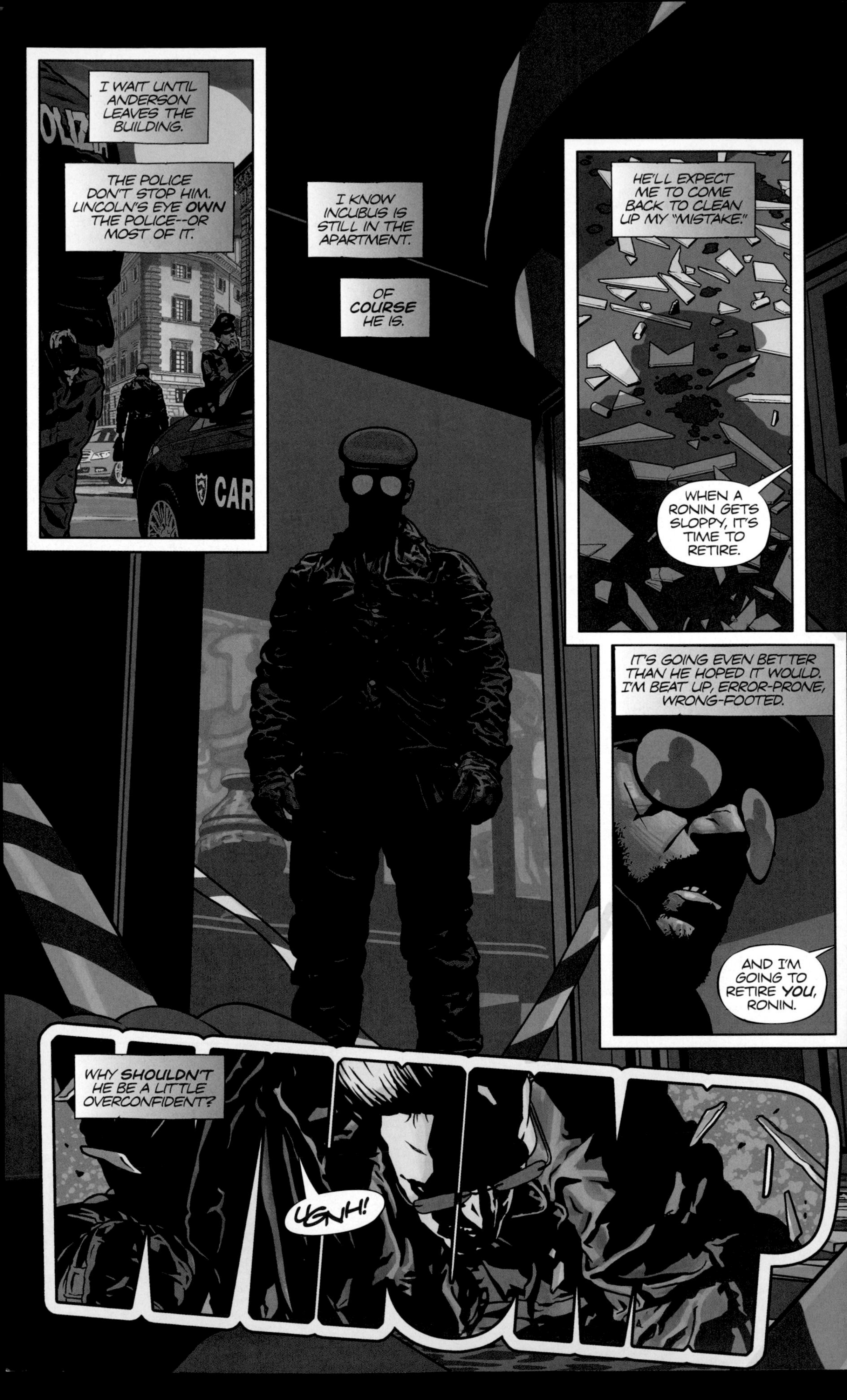
I WAIT UNTIL ANDERSON LEAVES THE BUILDING.
THE POLICE DON'T STOP HIM. LINCOLN'S EYE **OWN** THE POLICE--OR MOST OF IT.
CAR
I KNOW INCUBUS IS STILL IN THE APARTMENT.
OF **COURSE** HE IS.
HE'LL EXPECT ME TO COME BACK TO CLEAN UP MY "MISTAKE."
WHEN A RONIN GETS SLOPPY, IT'S TIME TO RETIRE.
IT'S GOING EVEN BETTER THAN HE HOPED IT WOULD. I'M BEAT UP, ERROR-PRONE, WRONG-FOOTED.
AND I'M GOING TO RETIRE **YOU**, RONIN.
WHY **SHOULDN'T** HE BE A LITTLE OVERCONFIDENT?
UGNH!

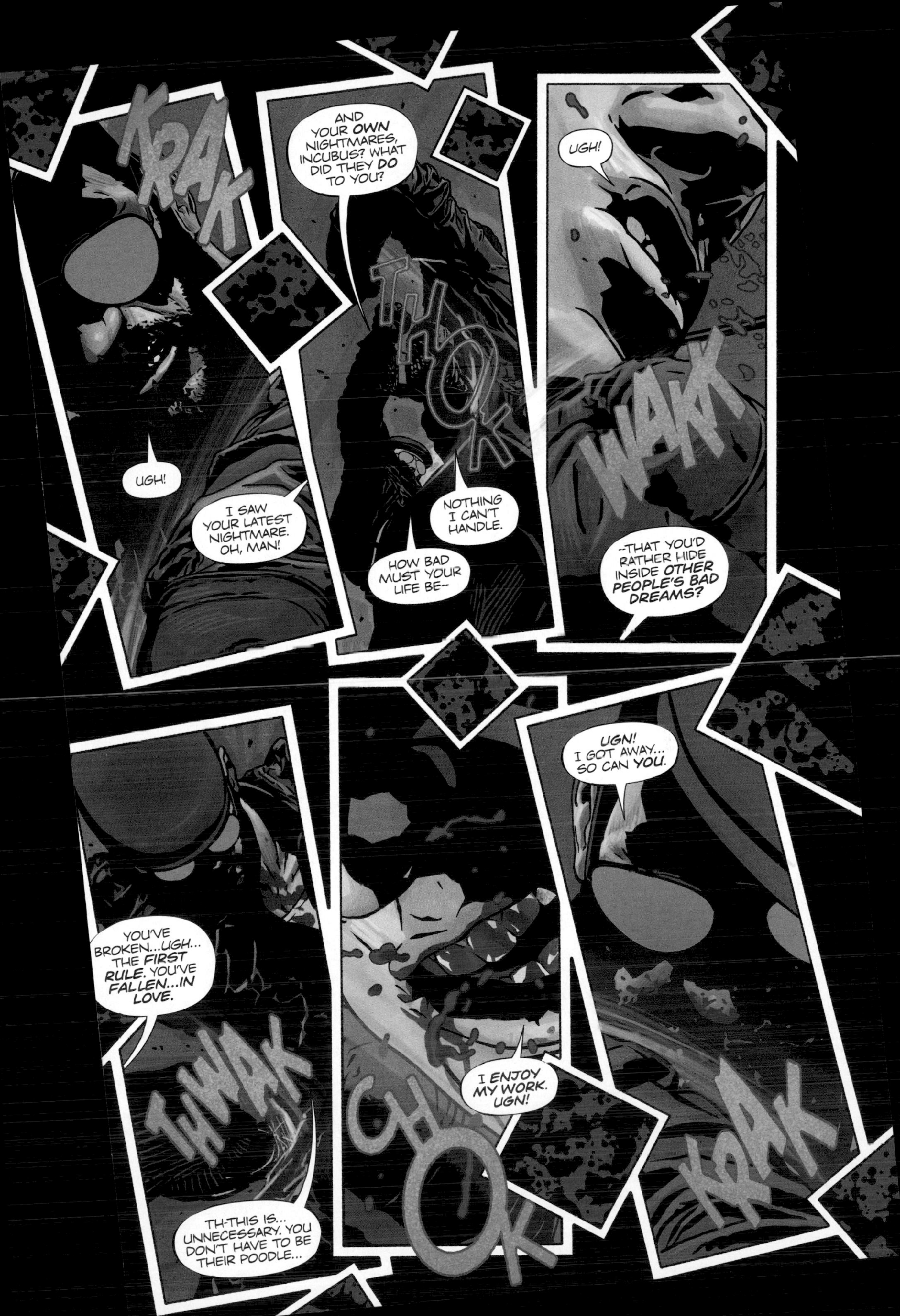

KRAK
UGH!
I SAW YOUR LATEST NIGHTMARE. OH, MAN!
AND YOUR OWN NIGHTMARES, INCUBUS? WHAT DID THEY DO TO YOU?
THOK
NOTHING I CAN'T HANDLE.
HOW BAD MUST YOUR LIFE BE--
UGH!
WAKK
--THAT YOU'D RATHER HIDE INSIDE OTHER PEOPLE'S BAD DREAMS?
YOU'VE BROKEN...UGH... THE FIRST RULE. YOU'VE FALLEN...IN LOVE.
THWAK
TH-THIS IS... UNNECESSARY. YOU DON'T HAVE TO BE THEIR POODLE...
I ENJOY MY WORK. UGN!
CHOK
UGN! I GOT AWAY... SO CAN YOU.
KRAK

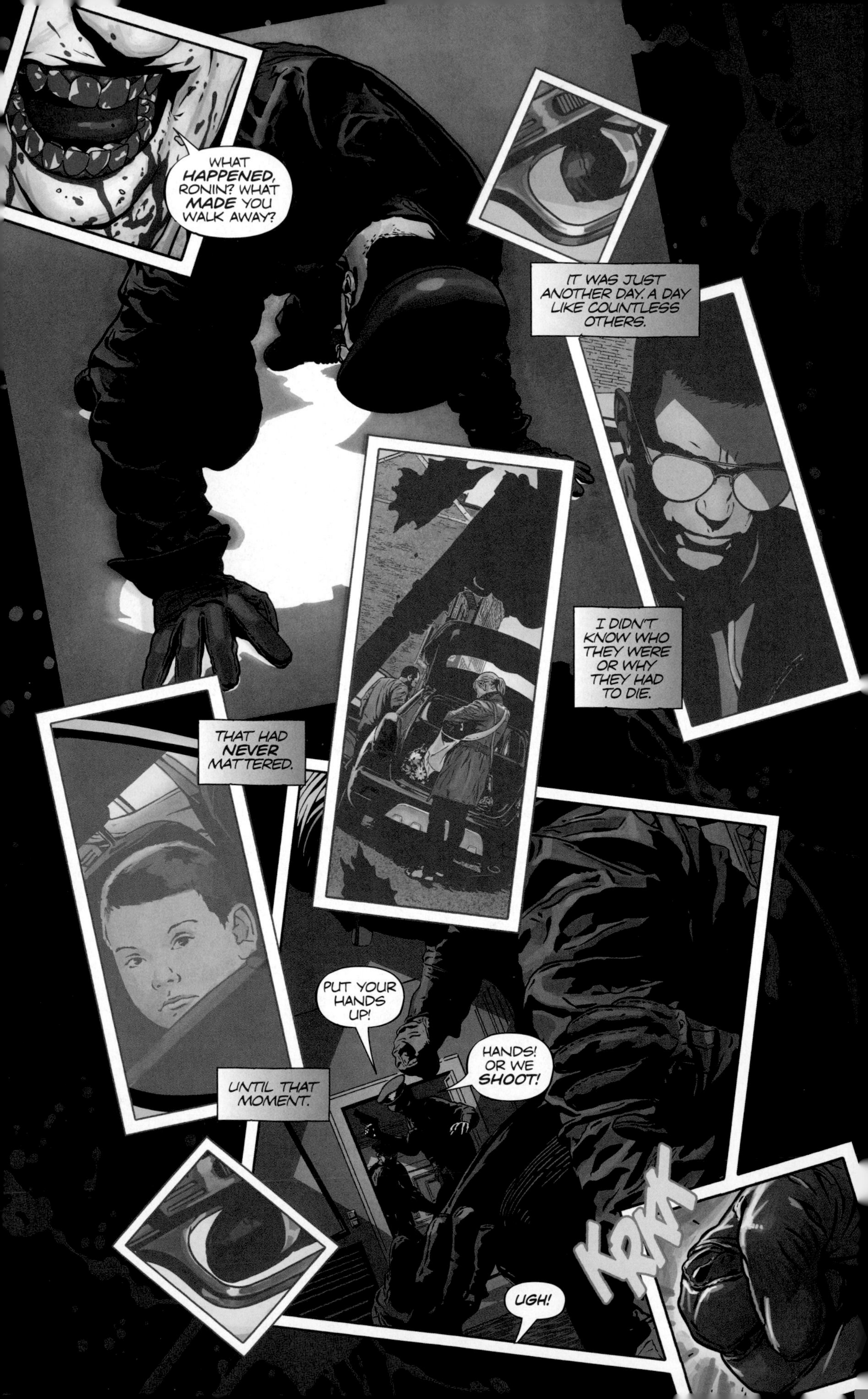
WHAT HAPPENED, RONIN? WHAT MADE YOU WALK AWAY?
IT WAS JUST ANOTHER DAY. A DAY LIKE COUNTLESS OTHERS.
I DIDN'T KNOW WHO THEY WERE OR WHY THEY HAD TO DIE.
THAT HAD NEVER MATTERED.
UNTIL THAT MOMENT.
PUT YOUR HANDS UP!
HANDS! OR WE SHOOT!
KRAK
UGH!

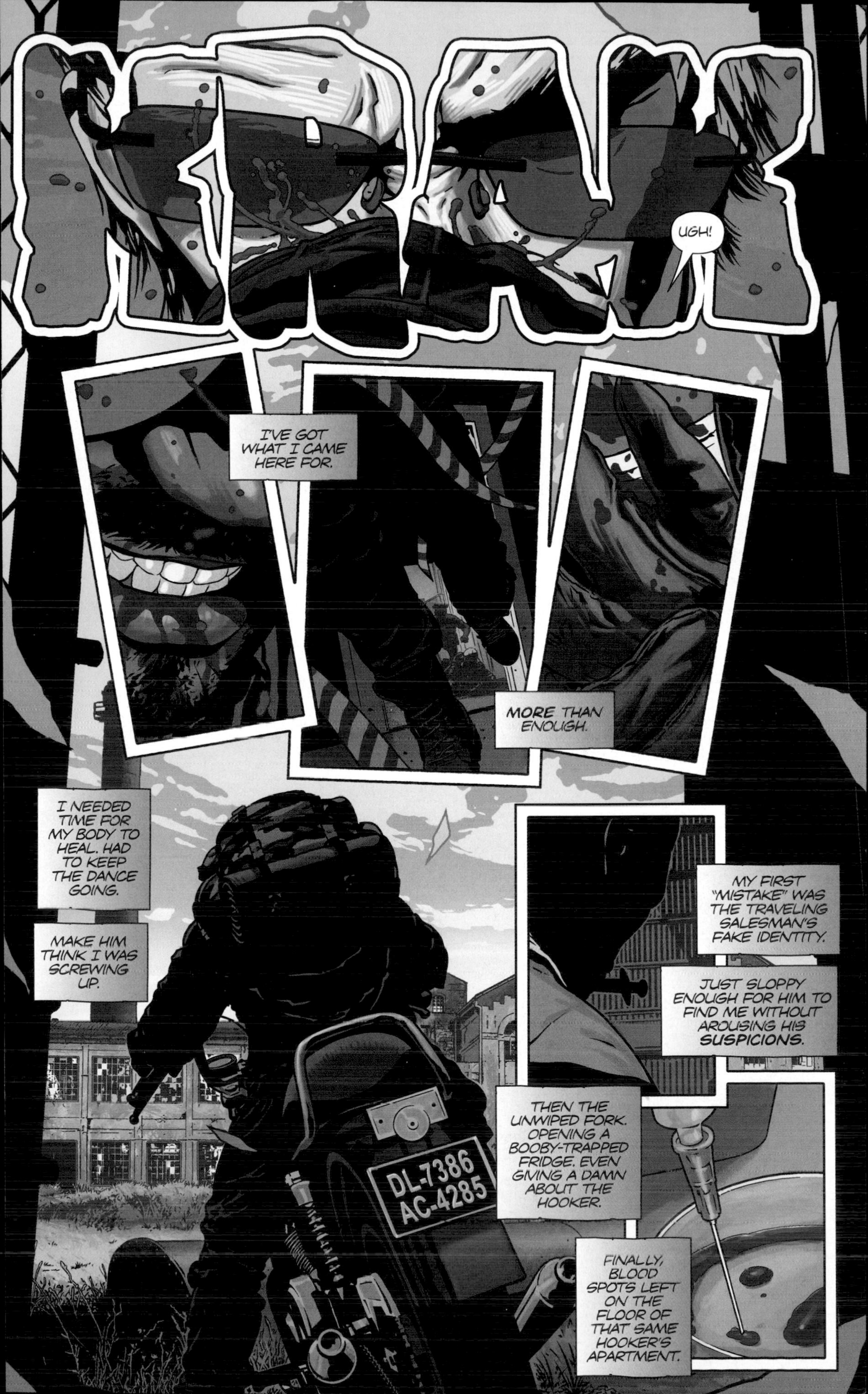
UGH!
I'VE GOT WHAT I CAME HERE FOR.
MORE THAN ENOUGH.
I NEEDED TIME FOR MY BODY TO HEAL. HAD TO KEEP THE DANCE GOING.
MAKE HIM THINK I WAS SCREWING UP.
DL-7386
AC-4285
MY FIRST "MISTAKE" WAS THE TRAVELING SALESMAN'S FAKE IDENTITY.
JUST SLOPPY ENOUGH FOR HIM TO FIND ME WITHOUT AROUSING HIS SUSPICIONS.
THEN THE UNWIPED FORK. OPENING A BOOBY-TRAPPED FRIDGE. EVEN GIVING A DAMN ABOUT THE HOOKER.
FINALLY, BLOOD SPOTS LEFT ON THE FLOOR OF THAT SAME HOOKER'S APARTMENT.

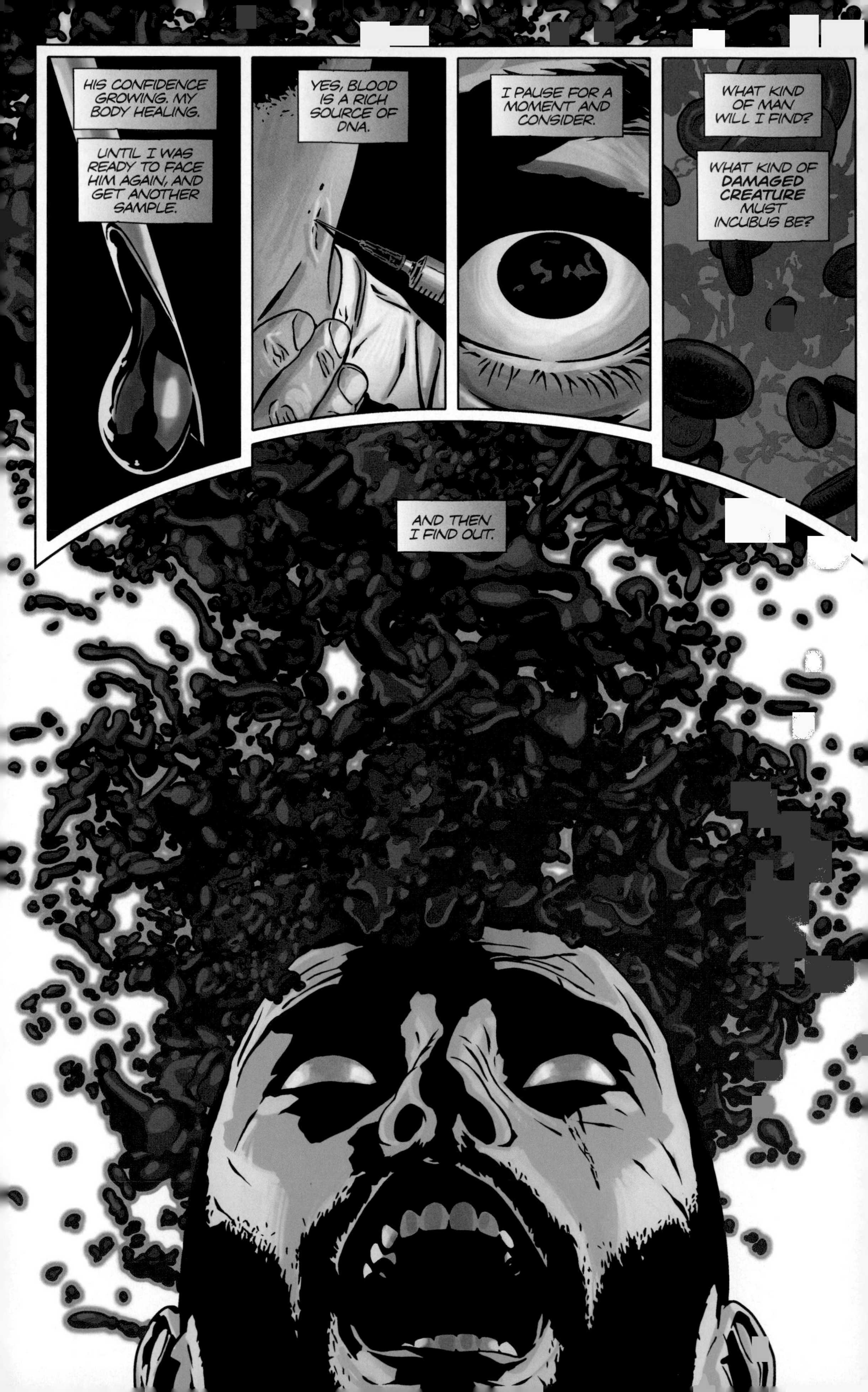
HIS CONFIDENCE GROWING. MY BODY HEALING.
UNTIL I WAS READY TO FACE HIM AGAIN, AND GET ANOTHER SAMPLE.
YES, BLOOD IS A RICH SOURCE OF DNA.
I PAUSE FOR A MOMENT AND CONSIDER.
WHAT KIND OF MAN WILL I FIND?
WHAT KIND OF DAMAGED CREATURE MUST INCUBUS BE?
AND THEN I FIND OUT.

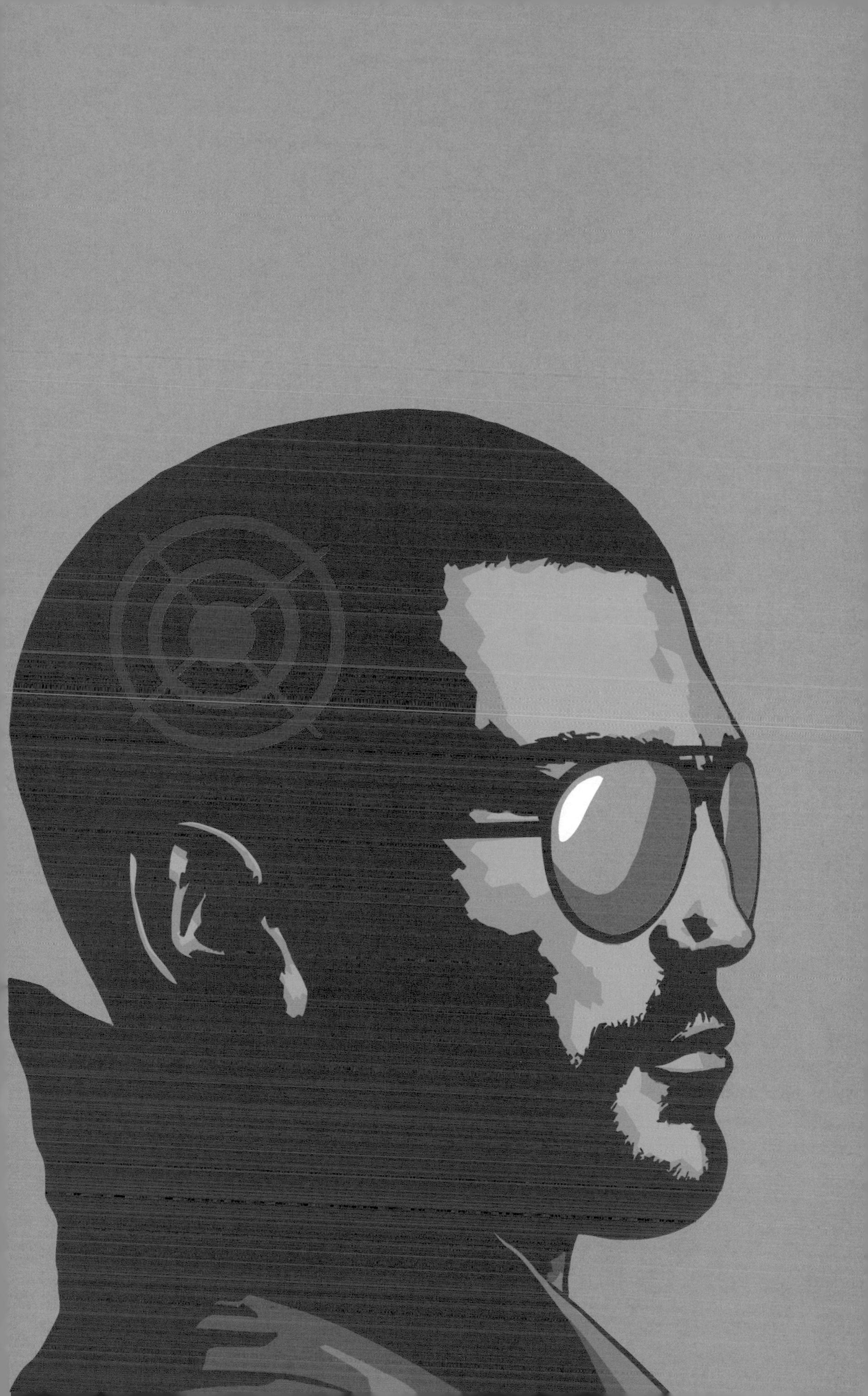

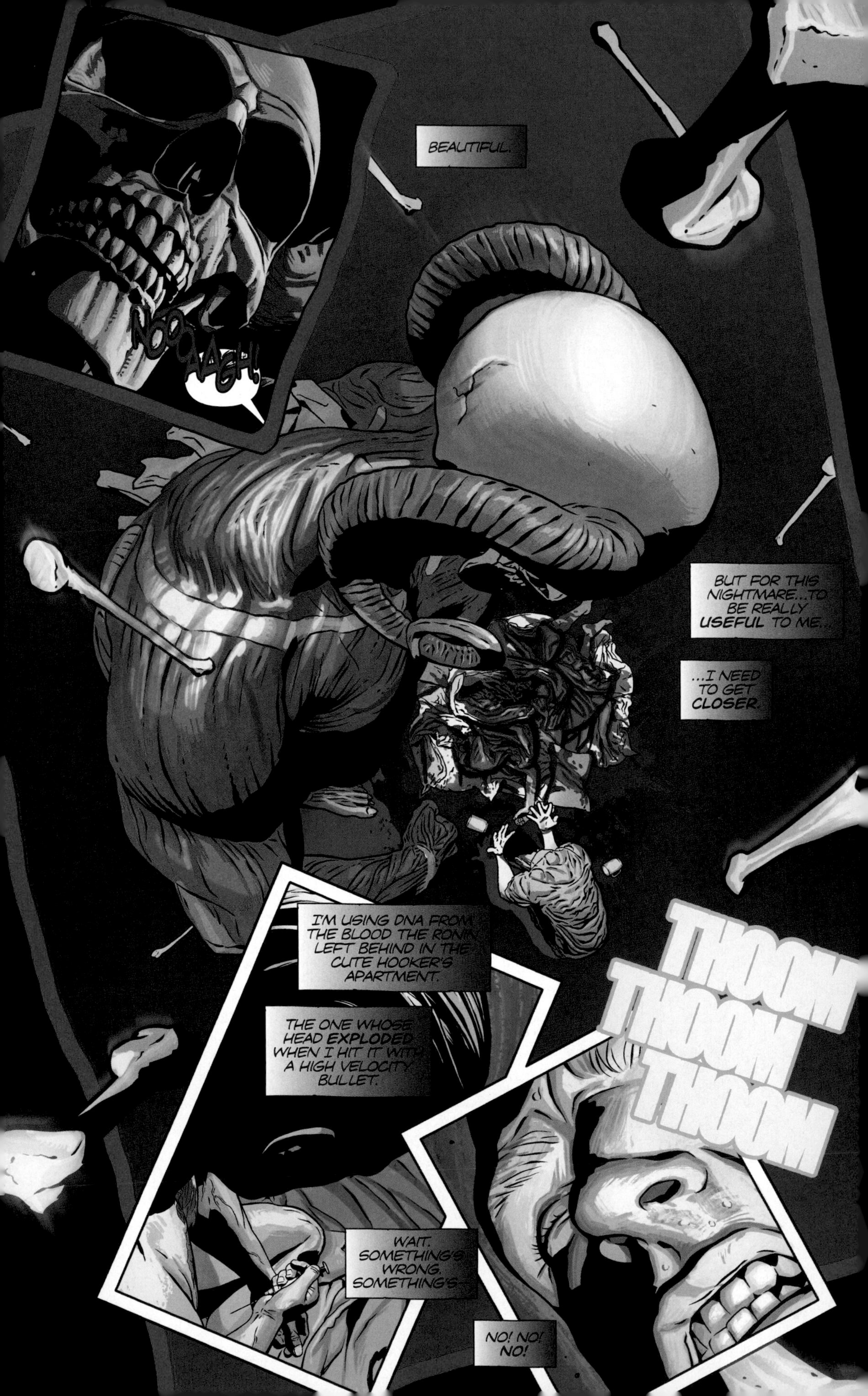
NOOOAAGH!
BEAUTIFUL.
BUT FOR THIS NIGHTMARE...TO BE REALLY USEFUL TO ME...
...I NEED TO GET CLOSER.
I'M USING DNA FROM THE BLOOD THE RONIN LEFT BEHIND IN THE CUTE HOOKER'S APARTMENT.
THE ONE WHOSE HEAD EXPLODED WHEN I HIT IT WITH A HIGH VELOCITY BULLET.
THOOM THOOM THOOM
WAIT. SOMETHING'S WRONG. SOMETHING'S--
NO! NO! NO!

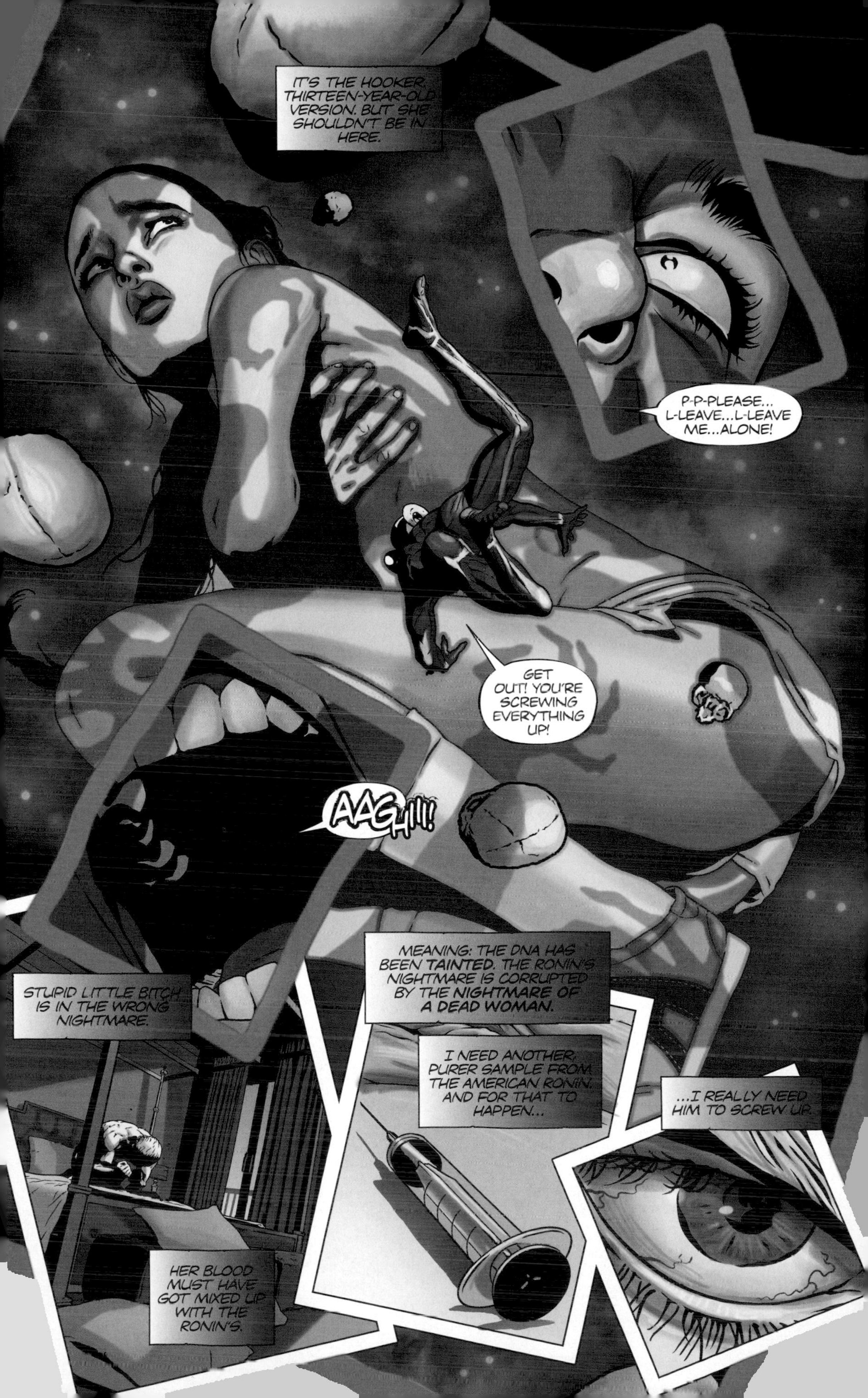
IT'S THE HOOKER. THIRTEEN-YEAR-OLD VERSION. BUT SHE SHOULDN'T BE IN HERE.
P-P-PLEASE... L-LEAVE...L-LEAVE ME...ALONE!
GET OUT! YOU'RE SCREWING EVERYTHING UP!
AAGH!!!
STUPID LITTLE BITCH IS IN THE WRONG NIGHTMARE.
HER BLOOD MUST HAVE GOT MIXED UP WITH THE RONIN'S.
MEANING: THE DNA HAS BEEN TAINTED. THE RONIN'S NIGHTMARE IS CORRUPTED BY THE NIGHTMARE OF A DEAD WOMAN.
I NEED ANOTHER, PURER SAMPLE FROM THE AMERICAN RONIN. AND FOR THAT TO HAPPEN...
...I REALLY NEED HIM TO SCREW UP.

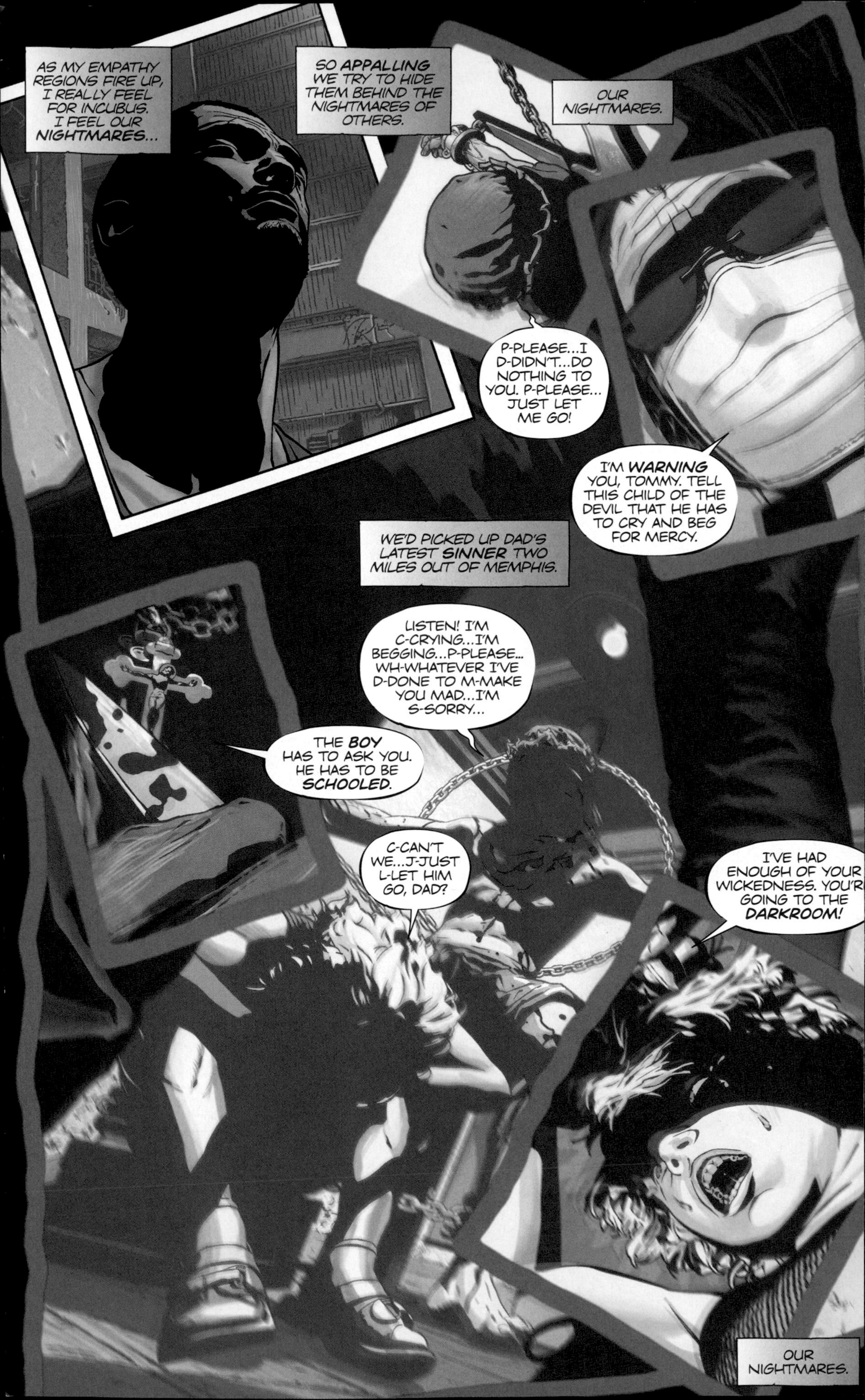
AS MY EMPATHY REGIONS FIRE UP, I REALLY FEEL FOR INCUBUS. I FEEL OUR NIGHTMARES...
SO APPALLING WE TRY TO HIDE THEM BEHIND THE NIGHTMARES OF OTHERS.
OUR NIGHTMARES.
P-PLEASE...I D-DIDN'T...DO NOTHING TO YOU. P-PLEASE... JUST LET ME GO!
I'M WARNING YOU, TOMMY. TELL THIS CHILD OF THE DEVIL THAT HE HAS TO CRY AND BEG FOR MERCY.
WE'D PICKED UP DAD'S LATEST SINNER TWO MILES OUT OF MEMPHIS.
LISTEN! I'M C-CRYING...I'M BEGGING...P-PLEASE... WH-WHATEVER I'VE D-DONE TO M-MAKE YOU MAD...I'M S-SORRY...
THE BOY HAS TO ASK YOU. HE HAS TO BE SCHOOLED.
C-CAN'T WE...J-JUST L-LET HIM GO, DAD?
I'VE HAD ENOUGH OF YOUR WICKEDNESS. YOU'R GOING TO THE DARKROOM!
OUR NIGHTMARES.

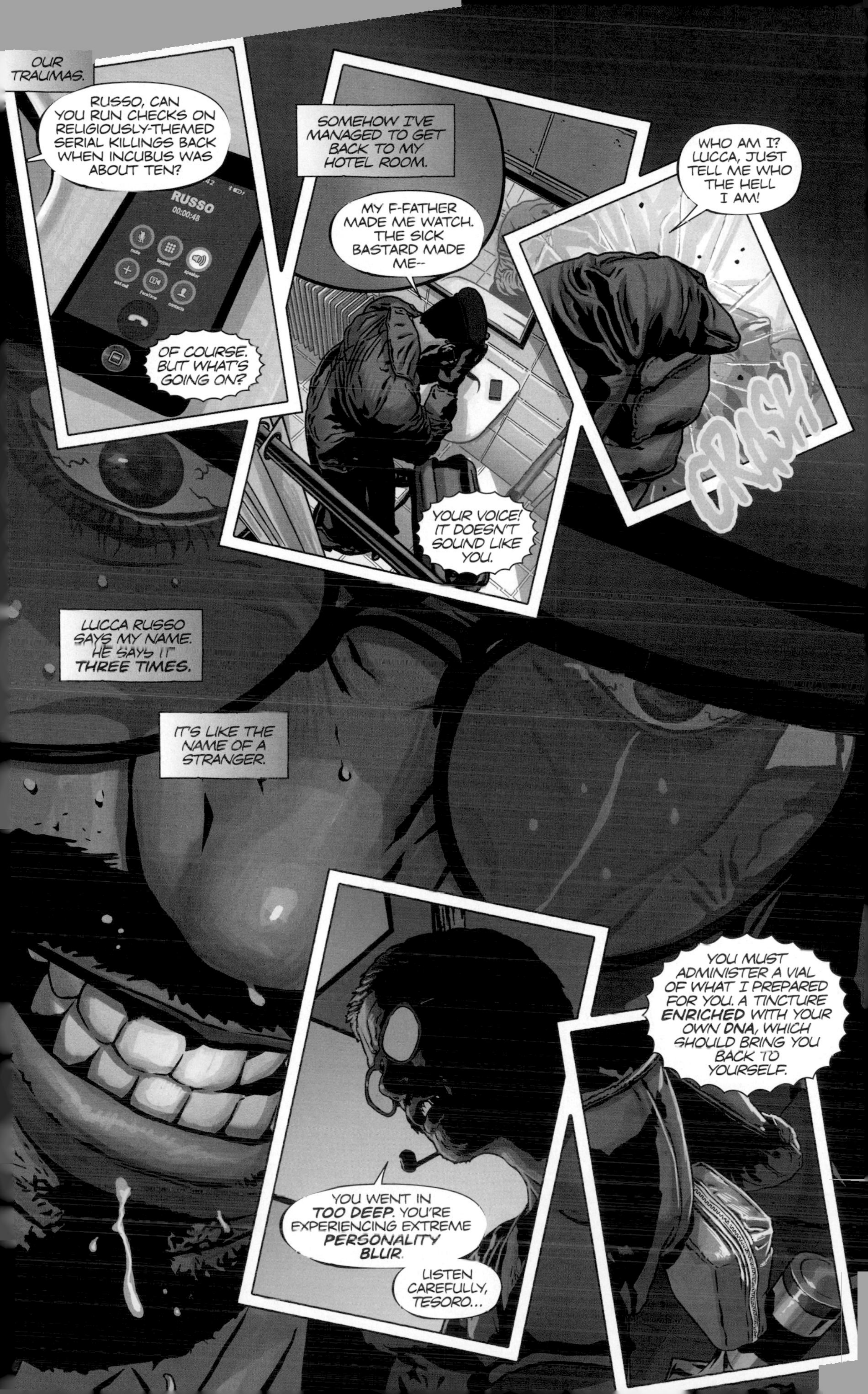
OUR TRAUMAS.
RUSSO, CAN YOU RUN CHECKS ON RELIGIOUSLY-THEMED SERIAL KILLINGS BACK WHEN INCUBUS WAS ABOUT TEN?
RUSSO
00:00:48
OF COURSE. BUT WHAT'S GOING ON?
SOMEHOW I'VE MANAGED TO GET BACK TO MY HOTEL ROOM.
MY F-FATHER MADE ME WATCH. THE SICK BASTARD MADE ME--
YOUR VOICE! IT DOESN'T SOUND LIKE YOU.
WHO AM I? LUCCA, JUST TELL ME WHO THE HELL I AM!
CRASH
LUCCA RUSSO SAYS MY NAME. HE SAYS IT THREE TIMES.
IT'S LIKE THE NAME OF A STRANGER.
YOU WENT IN TOO DEEP. YOU'RE EXPERIENCING EXTREME PERSONALITY BLUR.
LISTEN CAREFULLY, TESORO...
YOU MUST ADMINISTER A VIAL OF WHAT I PREPARED FOR YOU. A TINCTURE ENRICHED WITH YOUR OWN DNA, WHICH SHOULD BRING YOU BACK TO YOURSELF.

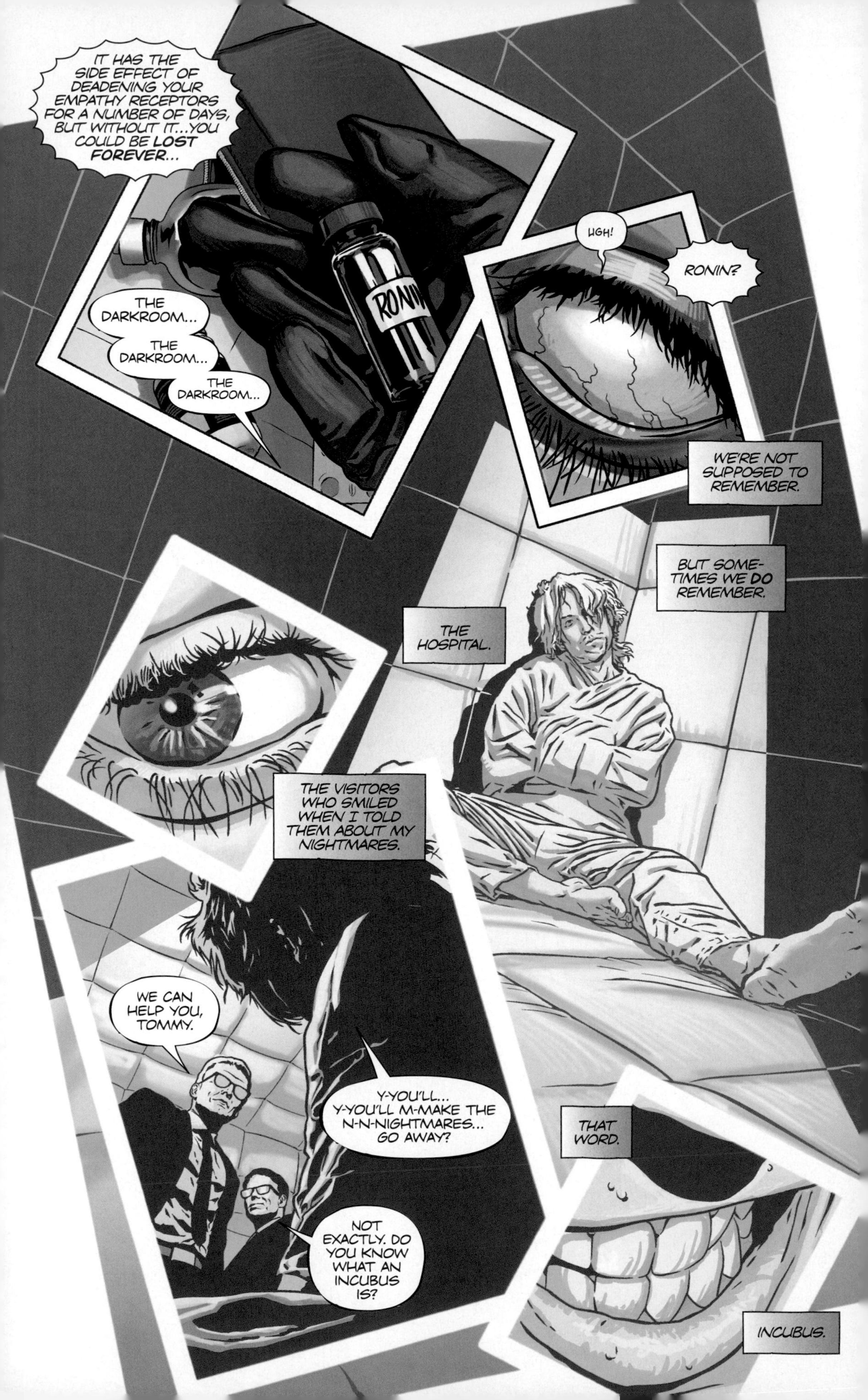
IT HAS THE SIDE EFFECT OF DEADENING YOUR EMPATHY RECEPTORS FOR A NUMBER OF DAYS, BUT WITHOUT IT...YOU COULD BE LOST FOREVER...
RONIN
THE DARKROOM...
THE DARKROOM...
THE DARKROOM...
UGH!
RONIN?
WE'RE NOT SUPPOSED TO REMEMBER.
BUT SOMETIMES WE DO REMEMBER.
THE HOSPITAL.
THE VISITORS WHO SMILED WHEN I TOLD THEM ABOUT MY NIGHTMARES.
WE CAN HELP YOU, TOMMY.
Y-YOU'LL... Y-YOU'LL M-MAKE THE N-N-NIGHTMARES... GO AWAY?
NOT EXACTLY. DO YOU KNOW WHAT AN INCUBUS IS?
THAT WORD.
INCUBUS.

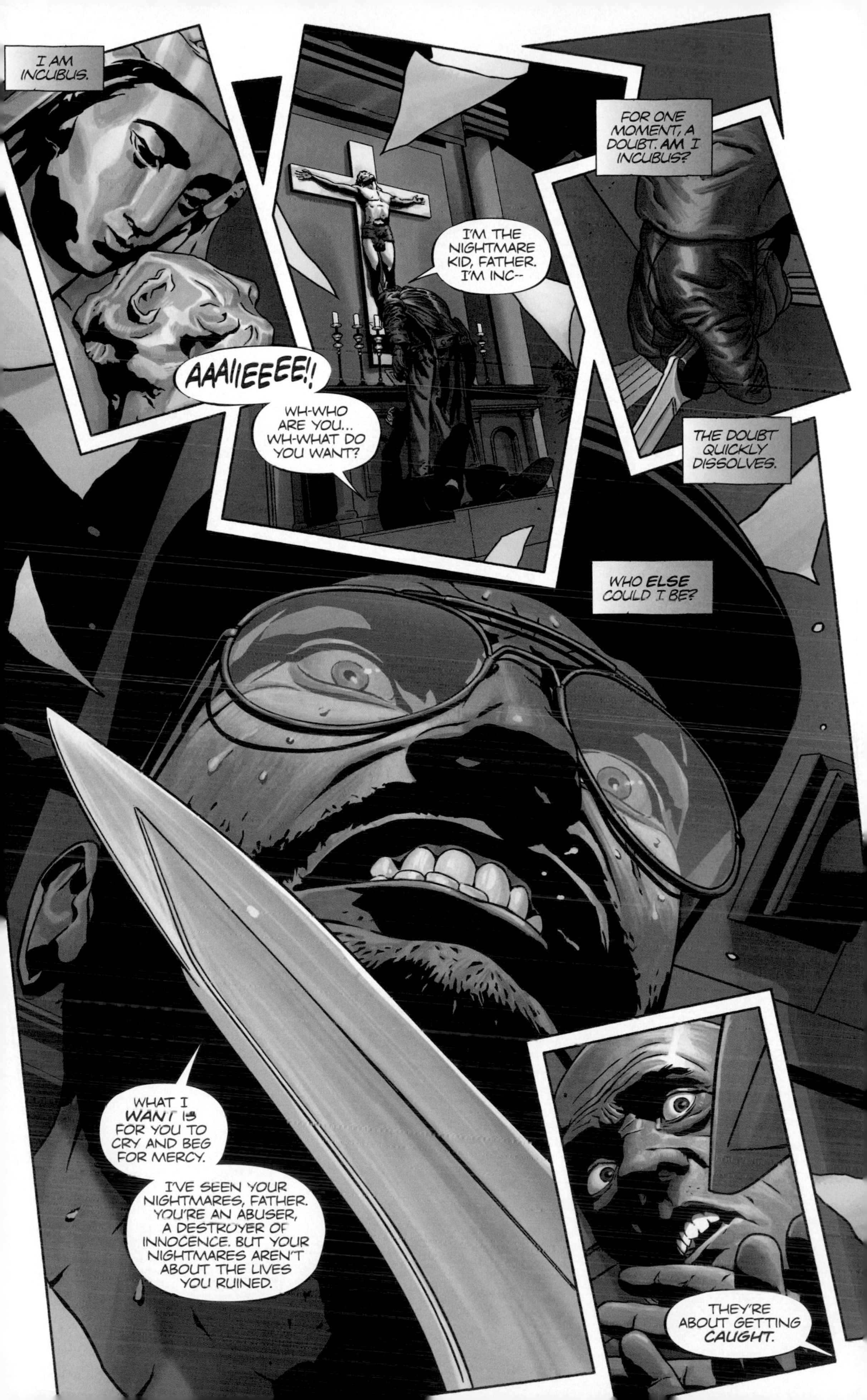
I AM INCUBUS.
AAAIIEEEE!!
WH-WHO ARE YOU... WH-WHAT DO YOU WANT?
I'M THE NIGHTMARE KID, FATHER. I'M INC--
FOR ONE MOMENT, A DOUBT. AM I INCUBUS?
THE DOUBT QUICKLY DISSOLVES.
WHO ELSE COULD I BE?
WHAT I WANT IS FOR YOU TO CRY AND BEG FOR MERCY.
I'VE SEEN YOUR NIGHTMARES, FATHER. YOU'RE AN ABUSER, A DESTROYER OF INNOCENCE. BUT YOUR NIGHTMARES AREN'T ABOUT THE LIVES YOU RUINED.
THEY'RE ABOUT GETTING CAUGHT.

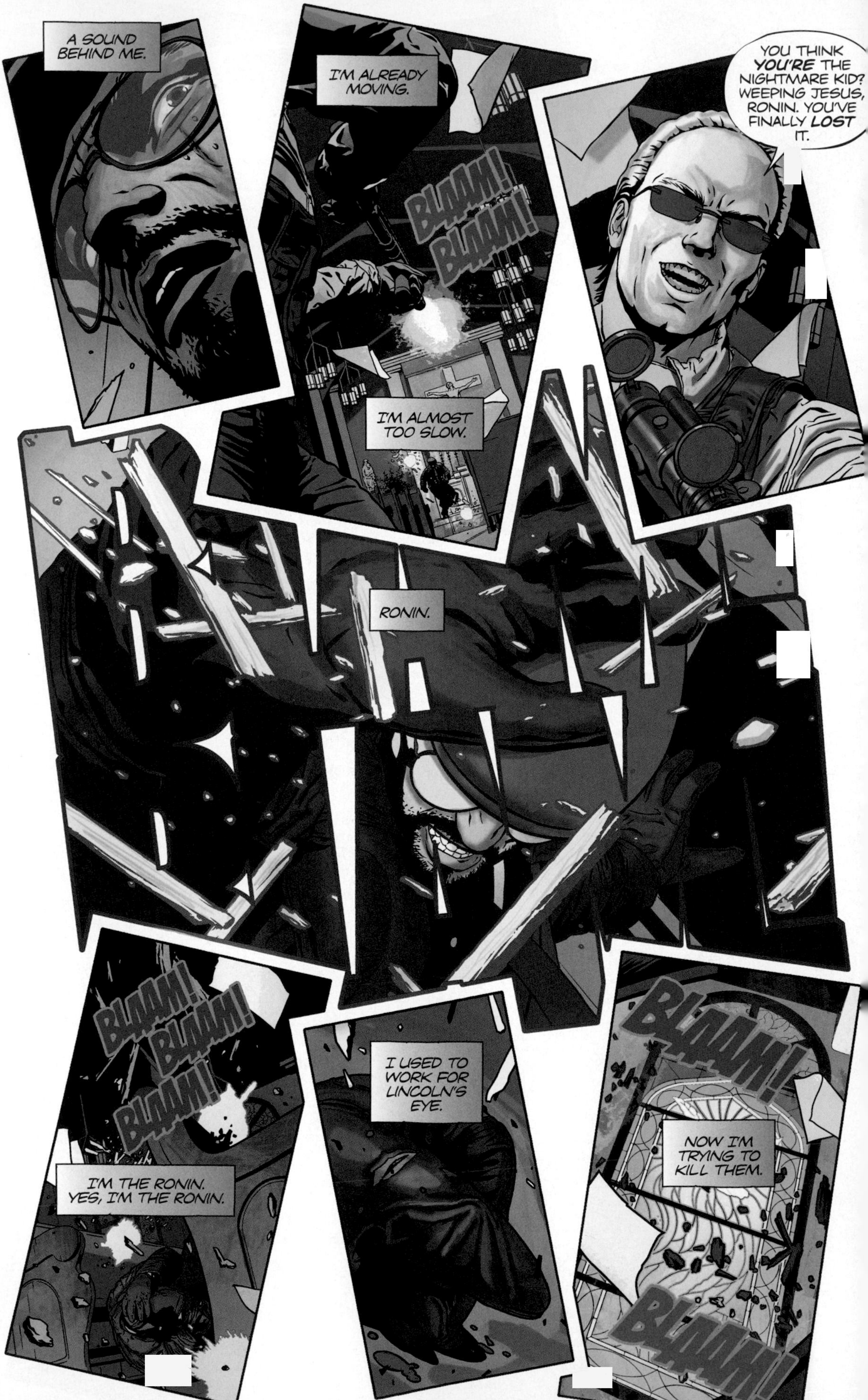
A SOUND BEHIND ME.
I'M ALREADY MOVING.
BLAAM! BLAAM!
I'M ALMOST TOO SLOW.
YOU THINK YOU'RE THE NIGHTMARE KID? WEEPING JESUS, RONIN. YOU'VE FINALLY LOST IT.
RONIN.
BLAAM! BLAAM! BLAAM!
I'M THE RONIN. YES, I'M THE RONIN.
I USED TO WORK FOR LINCOLN'S EYE.
BLAAM!
NOW I'M TRYING TO KILL THEM.
BLAAM!

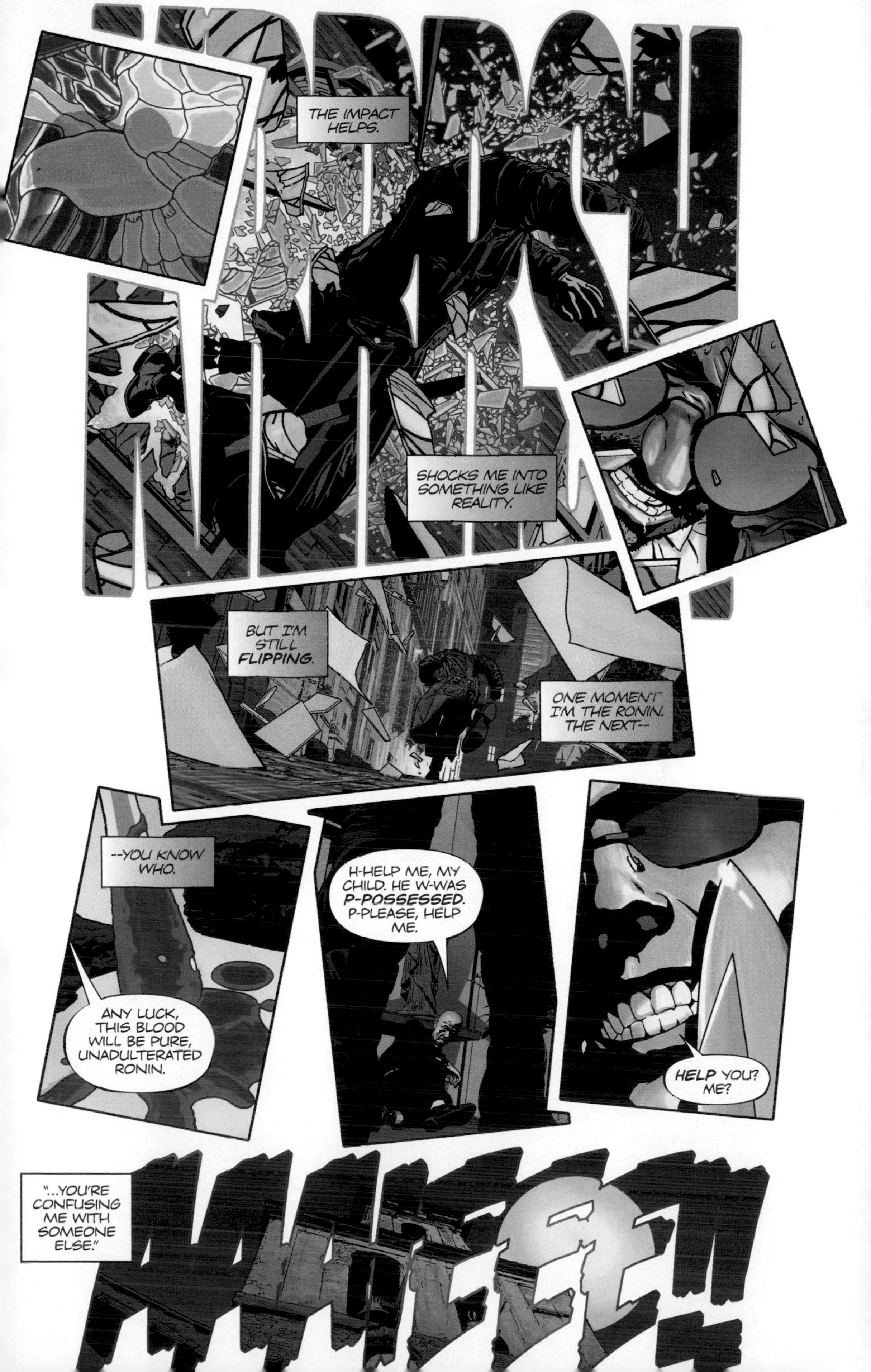
THE IMPACT HELPS.
SHOCKS ME INTO SOMETHING LIKE REALITY.
BUT I'M STILL FLIPPING.
ONE MOMENT I'M THE RONIN. THE NEXT--
--YOU KNOW WHO.
ANY LUCK, THIS BLOOD WILL BE PURE, UNADULTERATED RONIN.
H-HELP ME, MY CHILD. HE W-WAS P-POSSESSED. P-PLEASE, HELP ME.
HELP YOU? ME?
"...YOU'RE CONFUSING ME WITH SOMEONE ELSE."

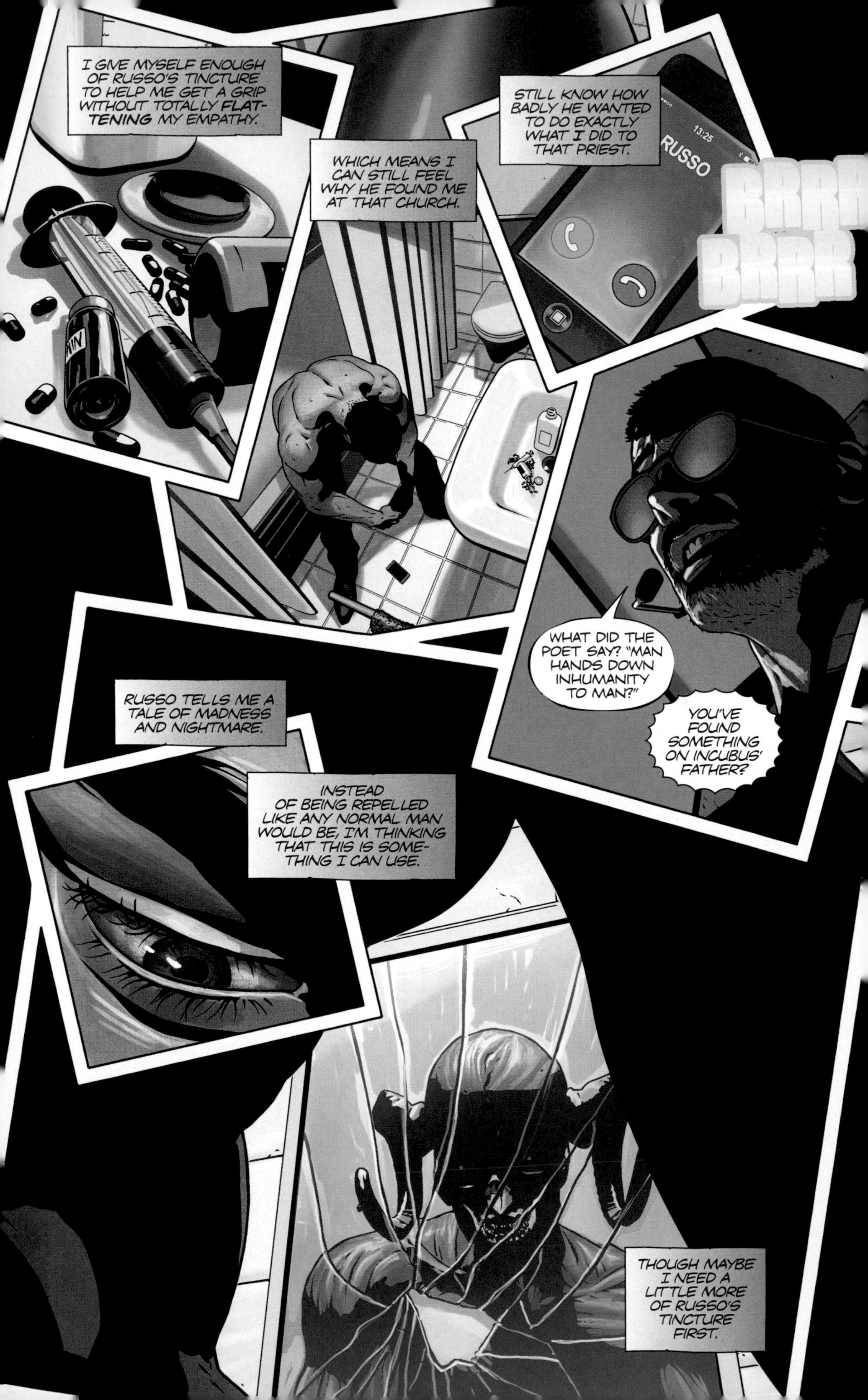
I GIVE MYSELF ENOUGH OF RUSSO'S TINCTURE TO HELP ME GET A GRIP WITHOUT TOTALLY FLATTENING MY EMPATHY.
WHICH MEANS I CAN STILL FEEL WHY HE FOUND ME AT THAT CHURCH.
STILL KNOW HOW BADLY HE WANTED TO DO EXACTLY WHAT I DID TO THAT PRIEST.
13:25
RUSSO
BRRR BRRR
WHAT DID THE POET SAY? "MAN HANDS DOWN INHUMANITY TO MAN?"
YOU'VE FOUND SOMETHING ON INCUBUS' FATHER?
RUSSO TELLS ME A TALE OF MADNESS AND NIGHTMARE.
INSTEAD OF BEING REPELLED LIKE ANY NORMAL MAN WOULD BE, I'M THINKING THAT THIS IS SOMETHING I CAN USE.
THOUGH MAYBE I NEED A LITTLE MORE OF RUSSO'S TINCTURE FIRST.

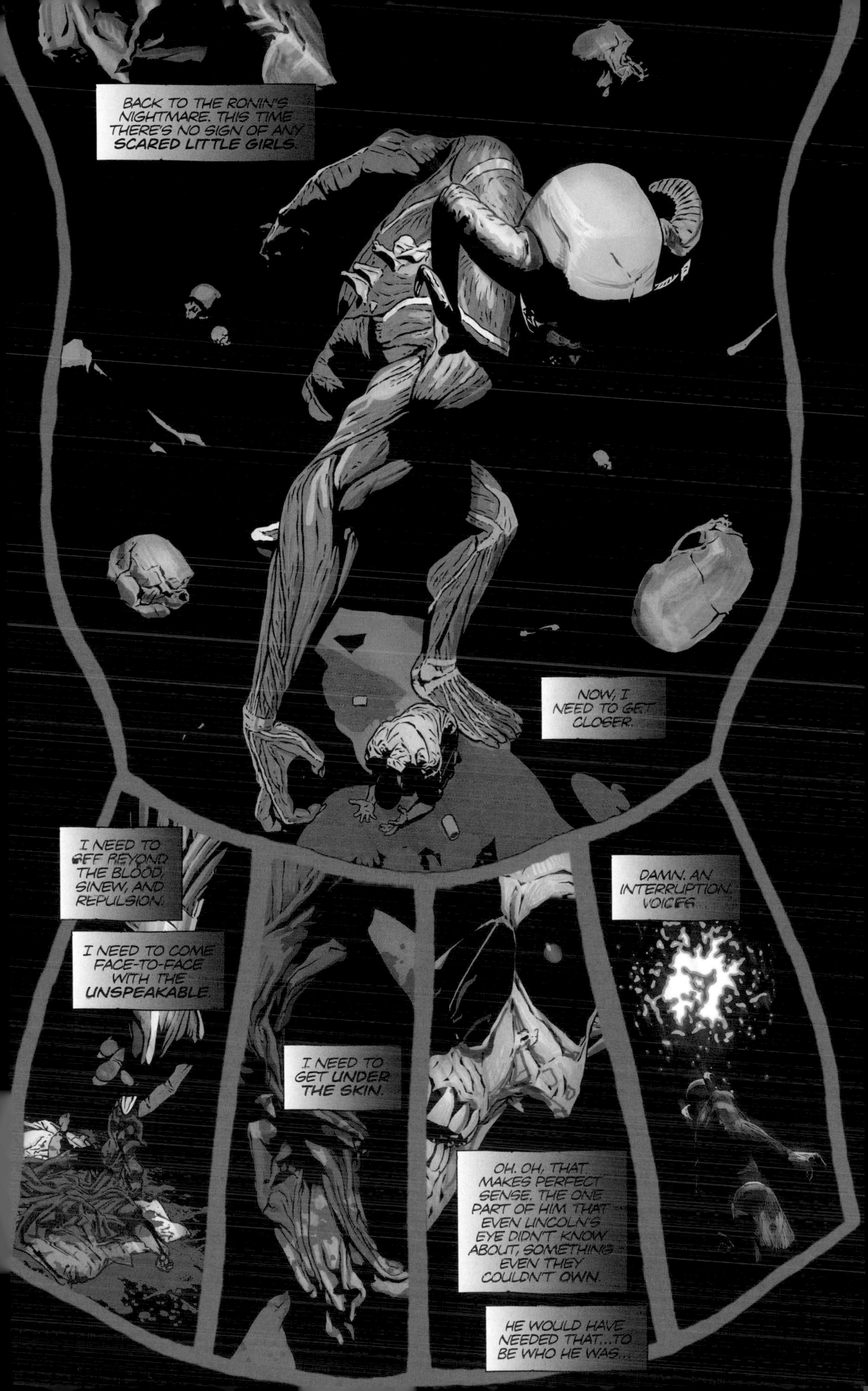

BACK TO THE RONIN'S NIGHTMARE. THIS TIME THERE'S NO SIGN OF ANY SCARED LITTLE GIRLS.
NOW, I NEED TO GET CLOSER.
I NEED TO GET BEYOND THE BLOOD, SINEW, AND REPULSION.
I NEED TO COME FACE-TO-FACE WITH THE UNSPEAKABLE.
I NEED TO GET UNDER THE SKIN.
OH. OH, THAT MAKES PERFECT SENSE. THE ONE PART OF HIM THAT EVEN LINCOLN'S EYE DIDN'T KNOW ABOUT, SOMETHING EVEN THEY COULDN'T OWN.
HE WOULD HAVE NEEDED THAT...TO BE WHO HE WAS...
DAMN. AN INTERRUPTION. VOICES.

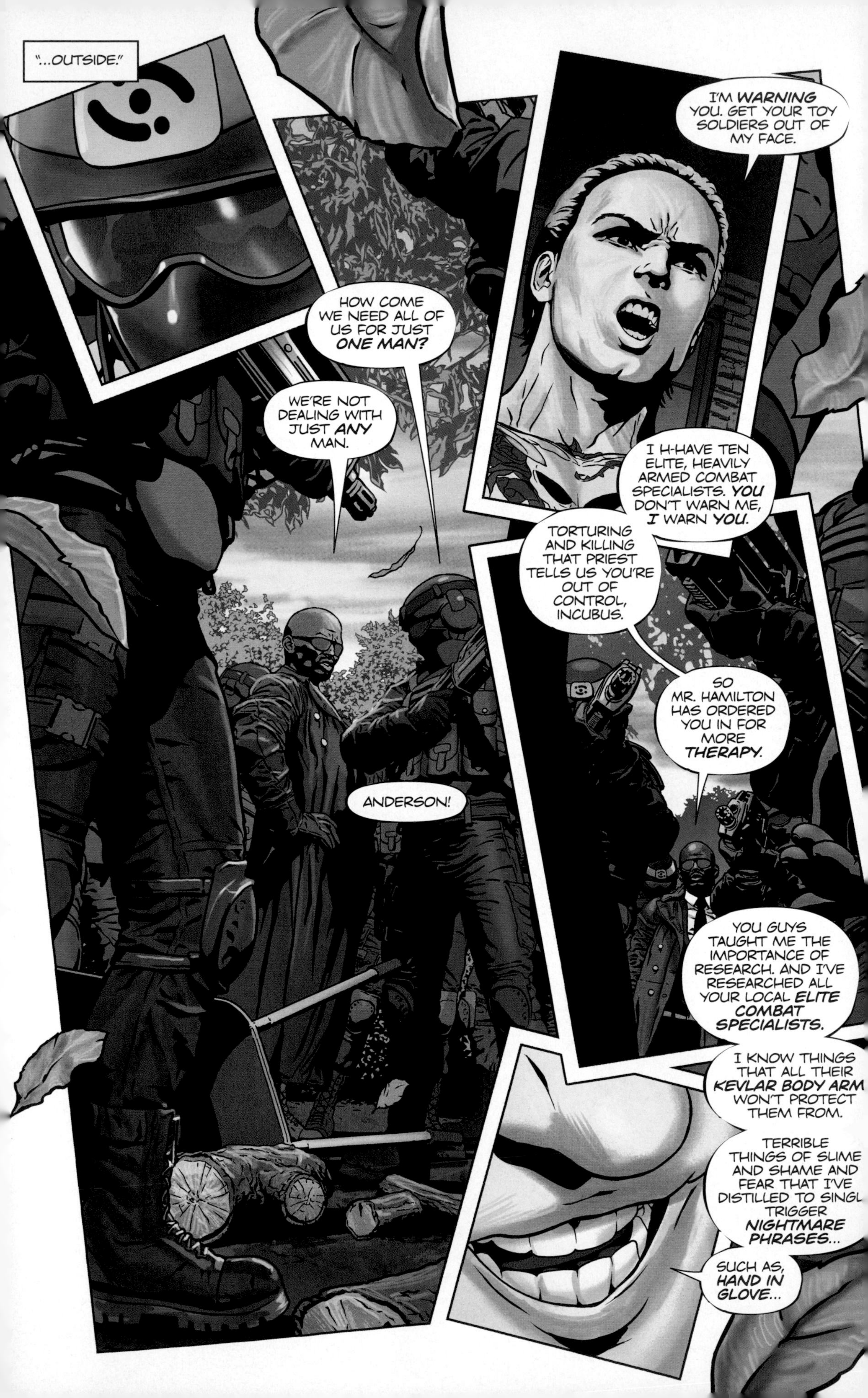
"...OUTSIDE."
HOW COME WE NEED ALL OF US FOR JUST ONE MAN?
WE'RE NOT DEALING WITH JUST ANY MAN.
ANDERSON!
I'M WARNING YOU. GET YOUR TOY SOLDIERS OUT OF MY FACE.
I H-HAVE TEN ELITE, HEAVILY ARMED COMBAT SPECIALISTS. YOU DON'T WARN ME, I WARN YOU.
TORTURING AND KILLING THAT PRIEST TELLS US YOU'RE OUT OF CONTROL, INCUBUS.
SO MR. HAMILTON HAS ORDERED YOU IN FOR MORE THERAPY.
YOU GUYS TAUGHT ME THE IMPORTANCE OF RESEARCH. AND I'VE RESEARCHED ALL YOUR LOCAL ELITE COMBAT SPECIALISTS.
I KNOW THINGS THAT ALL THEIR KEVLAR BODY ARM WON'T PROTECT THEM FROM.
TERRIBLE THINGS OF SLIME AND SHAME AND FEAR THAT I'VE DISTILLED TO SINGL TRIGGER NIGHTMARE PHRASES...
SUCH AS, HAND IN GLOVE...

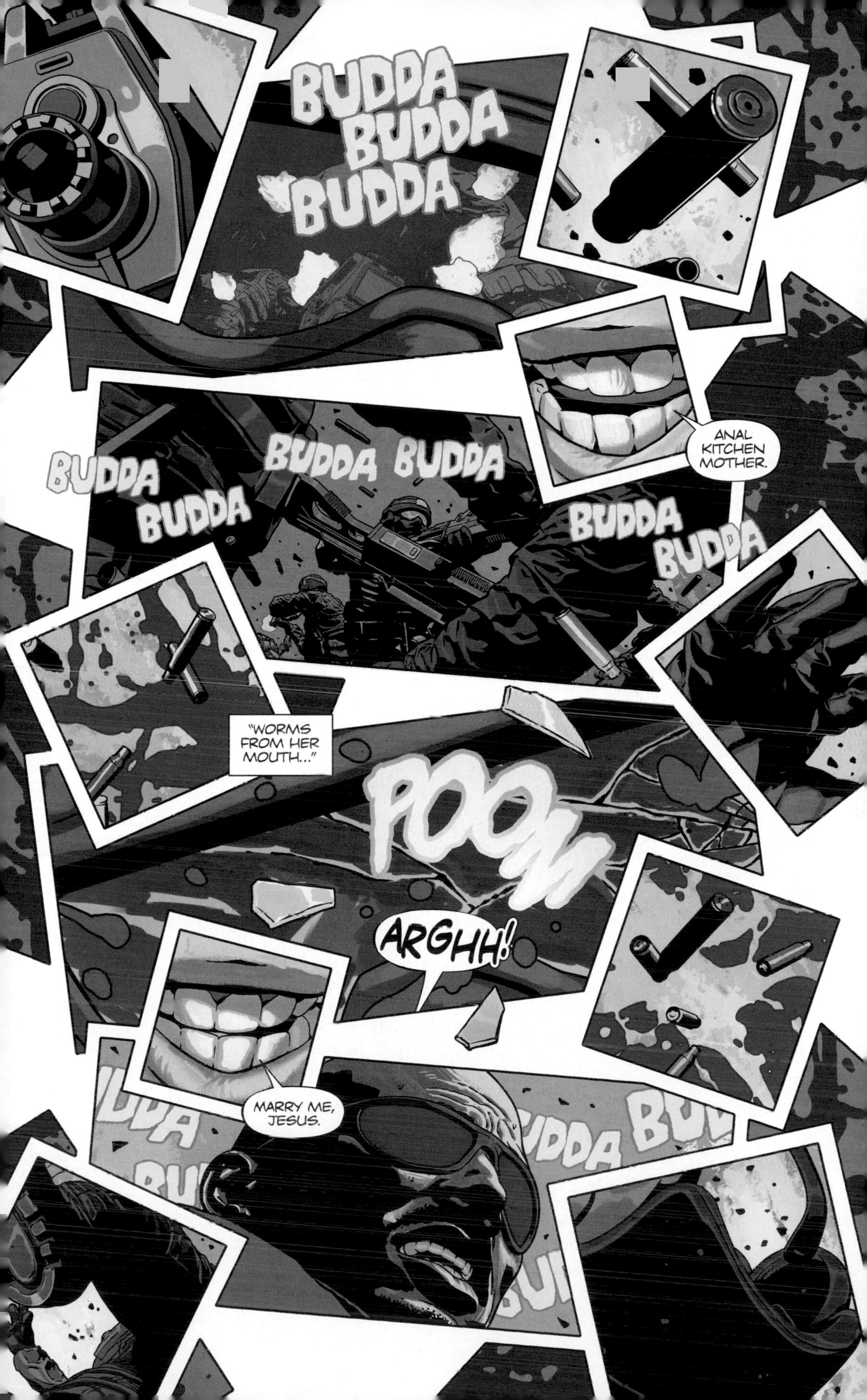
BUDDA BUDDA BUDDA
ANAL KITCHEN MOTHER.
BUDDA BUDDA
BUDDA BUDDA
BUDDA BUDDA
"WORMS FROM HER MOUTH..."
POOM
ARGHH!
MARRY ME, JESUS.

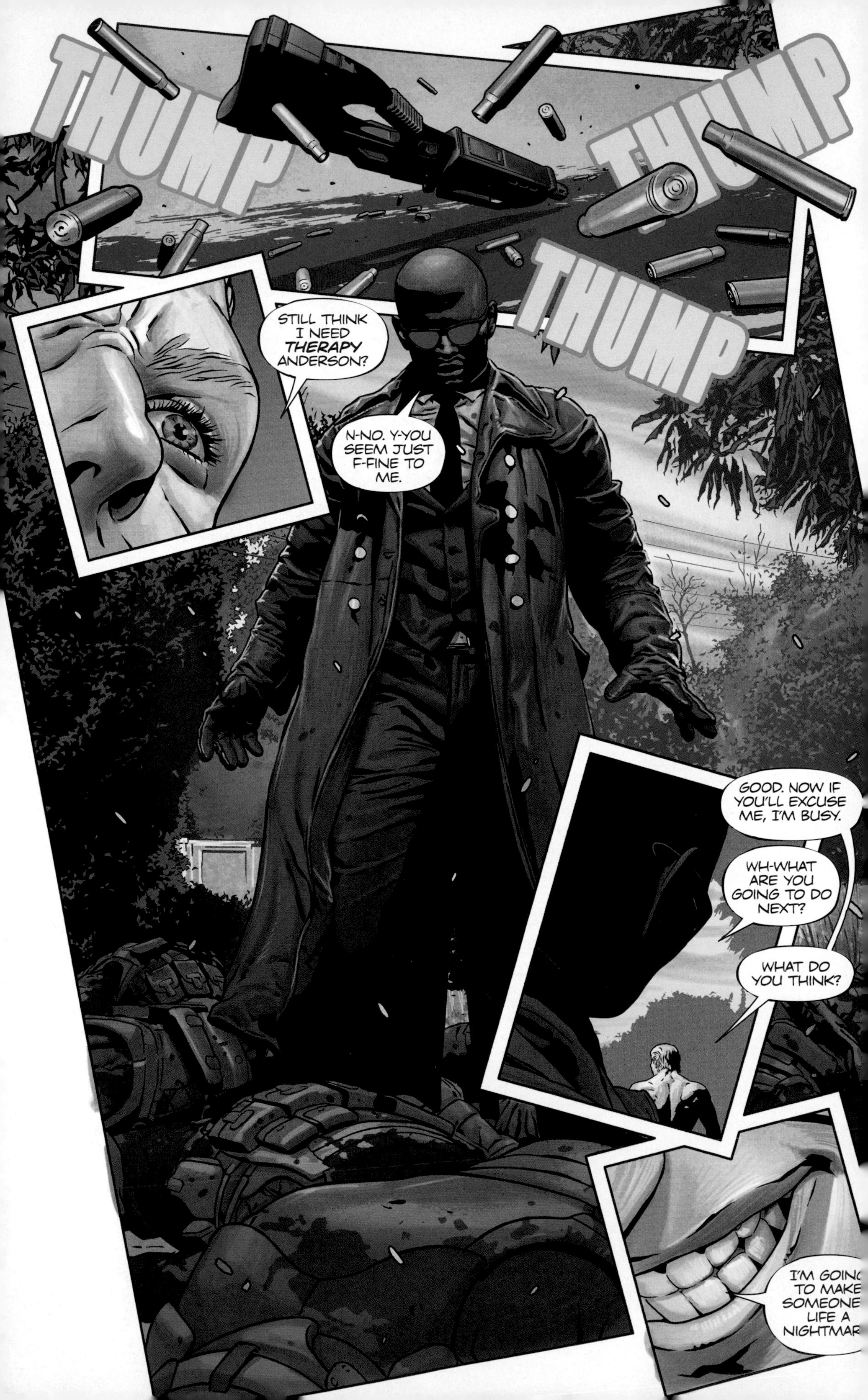
THUMP
THUMP
THUMP
STILL THINK I NEED THERAPY ANDERSON?
N-NO. Y-YOU SEEM JUST F-FINE TO ME.
GOOD. NOW IF YOU'LL EXCUSE ME, I'M BUSY.
WH-WHAT ARE YOU GOING TO DO NEXT?
WHAT DO YOU THINK?
I'M GOIN TO MAKE SOMEONE LIFE A NIGHTMAR

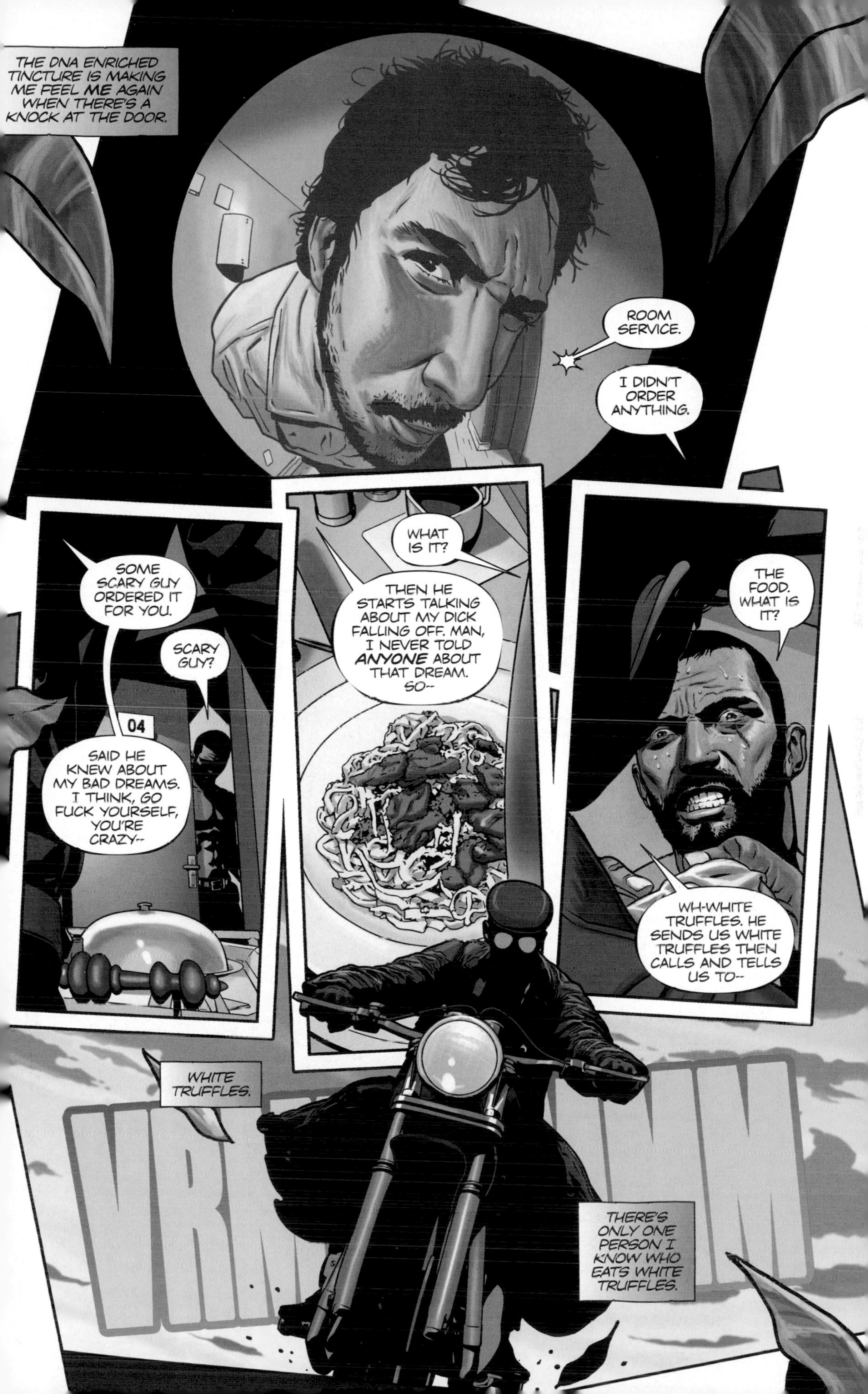
THE DNA ENRICHED TINCTURE IS MAKING ME FEEL ME AGAIN WHEN THERE'S A KNOCK AT THE DOOR.
ROOM SERVICE.
I DIDN'T ORDER ANYTHING.
SOME SCARY GUY ORDERED IT FOR YOU.
SCARY GUY?
04
SAID HE KNEW ABOUT MY BAD DREAMS. I THINK, GO FUCK YOURSELF, YOU'RE CRAZY--
WHAT IS IT?
THEN HE STARTS TALKING ABOUT MY DICK FALLING OFF. MAN, I NEVER TOLD ANYONE ABOUT THAT DREAM. SO--
THE FOOD. WHAT IS IT?
WH-WHITE TRUFFLES. HE SENDS US WHITE TRUFFLES THEN CALLS AND TELLS US TO--
WHITE TRUFFLES.
THERE'S ONLY ONE PERSON I KNOW WHO EATS WHITE TRUFFLES.

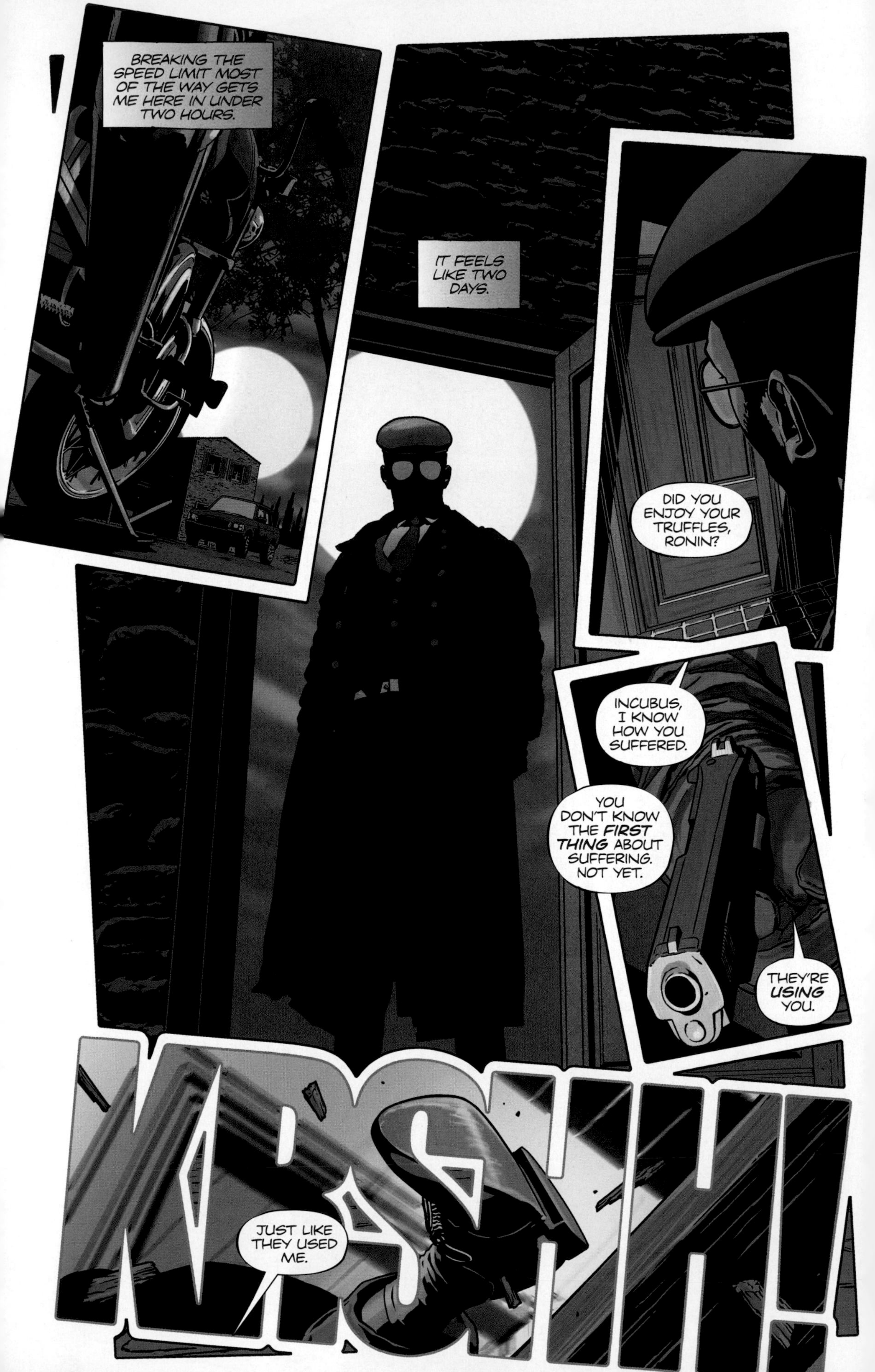
BREAKING THE SPEED LIMIT MOST OF THE WAY GETS ME HERE IN UNDER TWO HOURS.
IT FEELS LIKE TWO DAYS.
DID YOU ENJOY YOUR TRUFFLES, RONIN?
INCUBUS, I KNOW HOW YOU SUFFERED.
YOU DON'T KNOW THE FIRST THING ABOUT SUFFERING. NOT YET.
THEY'RE USING YOU.
KRSSHH!!
JUST LIKE THEY USED ME.

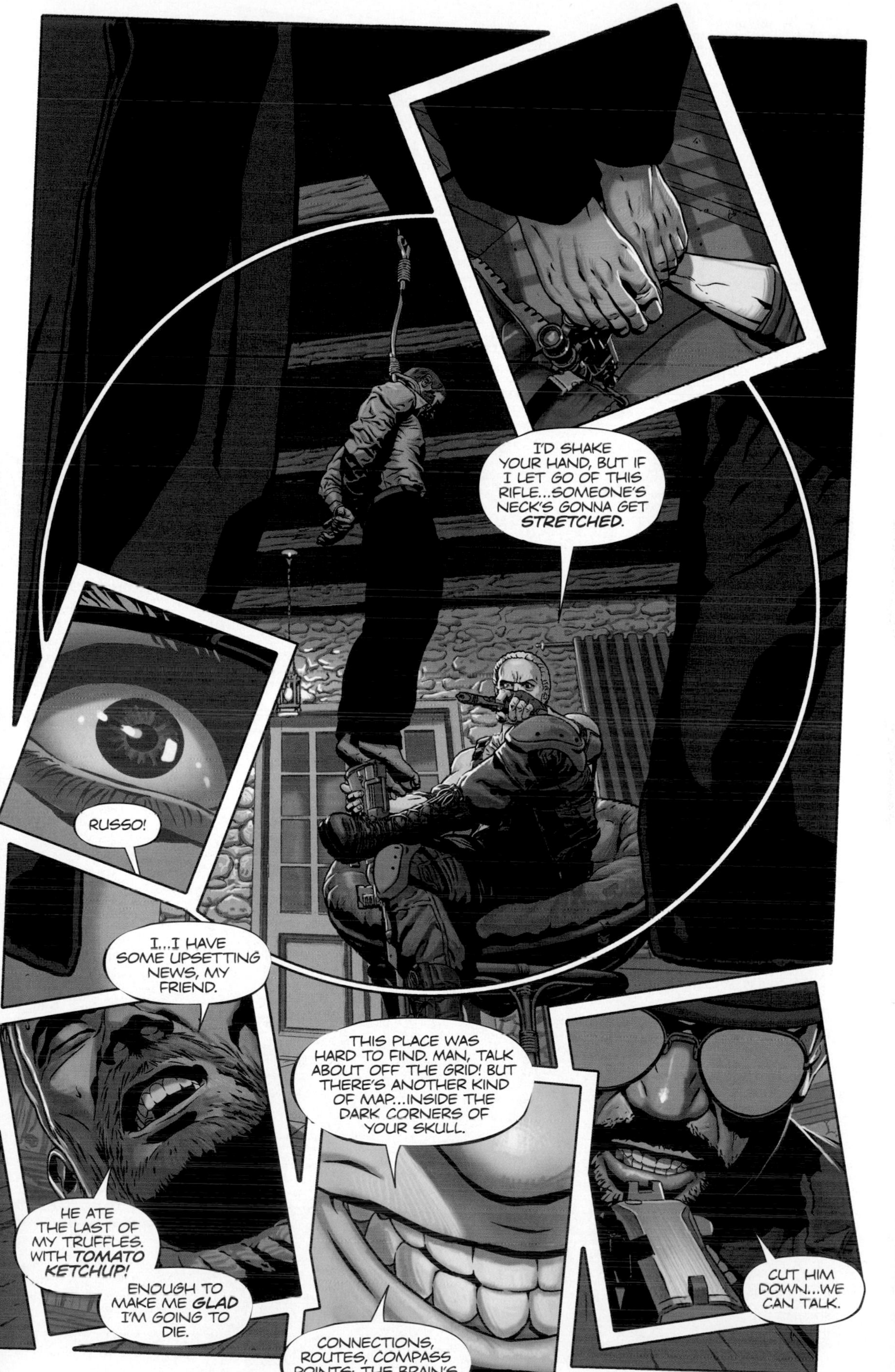
I'D SHAKE YOUR HAND, BUT IF I LET GO OF THIS RIFLE...SOMEONE'S NECK'S GONNA GET **STRETCHED**.
RUSSO!
I...I HAVE SOME UPSETTING NEWS, MY FRIEND.
HE ATE THE LAST OF MY TRUFFLES. WITH ***TOMATO KETCHUP!***
ENOUGH TO MAKE ME ***GLAD*** I'M GOING TO DIE.
THIS PLACE WAS HARD TO FIND. MAN, TALK ABOUT OFF THE GRID! BUT THERE'S ANOTHER KIND OF MAP...INSIDE THE DARK CORNERS OF YOUR SKULL.
CONNECTIONS, ROUTES, COMPASS POINTS: THE BRAIN'S OWN GPS.
CUT HIM DOWN...WE CAN TALK.

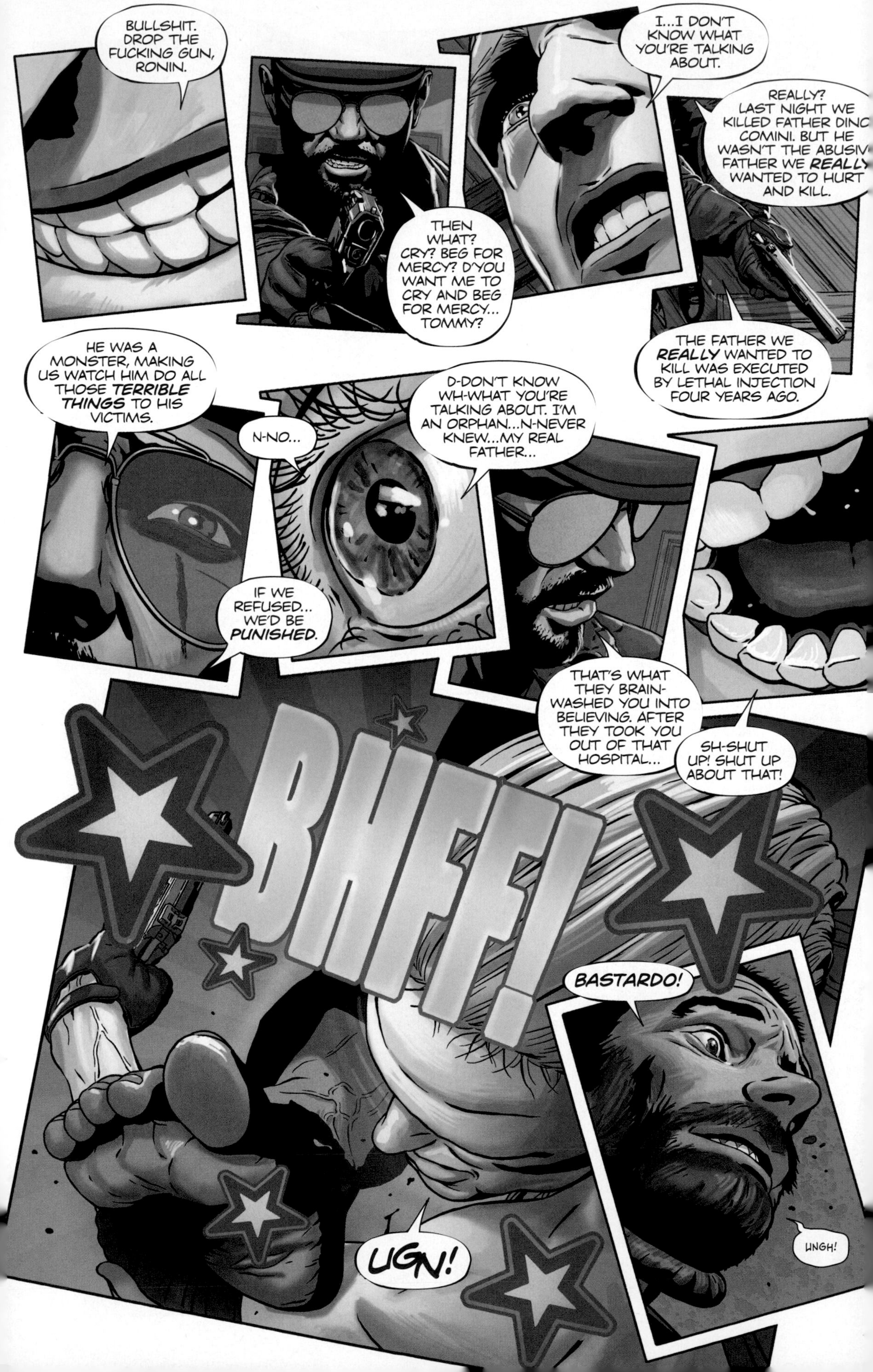
BULLSHIT. DROP THE FUCKING GUN, RONIN.
THEN WHAT? CRY? BEG FOR MERCY? D'YOU WANT ME TO CRY AND BEG FOR MERCY... TOMMY?
I...I DON'T KNOW WHAT YOU'RE TALKING ABOUT.
REALLY? LAST NIGHT WE KILLED FATHER DINO COMINI. BUT HE WASN'T THE ABUSIVE FATHER WE REALLY WANTED TO HURT AND KILL.
THE FATHER WE REALLY WANTED TO KILL WAS EXECUTED BY LETHAL INJECTION FOUR YEARS AGO.
HE WAS A MONSTER, MAKING US WATCH HIM DO ALL THOSE TERRIBLE THINGS TO HIS VICTIMS.
IF WE REFUSED... WE'D BE PUNISHED.
N-NO...
D-DON'T KNOW WH-WHAT YOU'RE TALKING ABOUT. I'M AN ORPHAN...N-NEVER KNEW...MY REAL FATHER...
THAT'S WHAT THEY BRAIN-WASHED YOU INTO BELIEVING. AFTER THEY TOOK YOU OUT OF THAT HOSPITAL...
SH-SHUT UP! SHUT UP ABOUT THAT!
BHFF!
BASTARDO!
UGN!
UNGH!

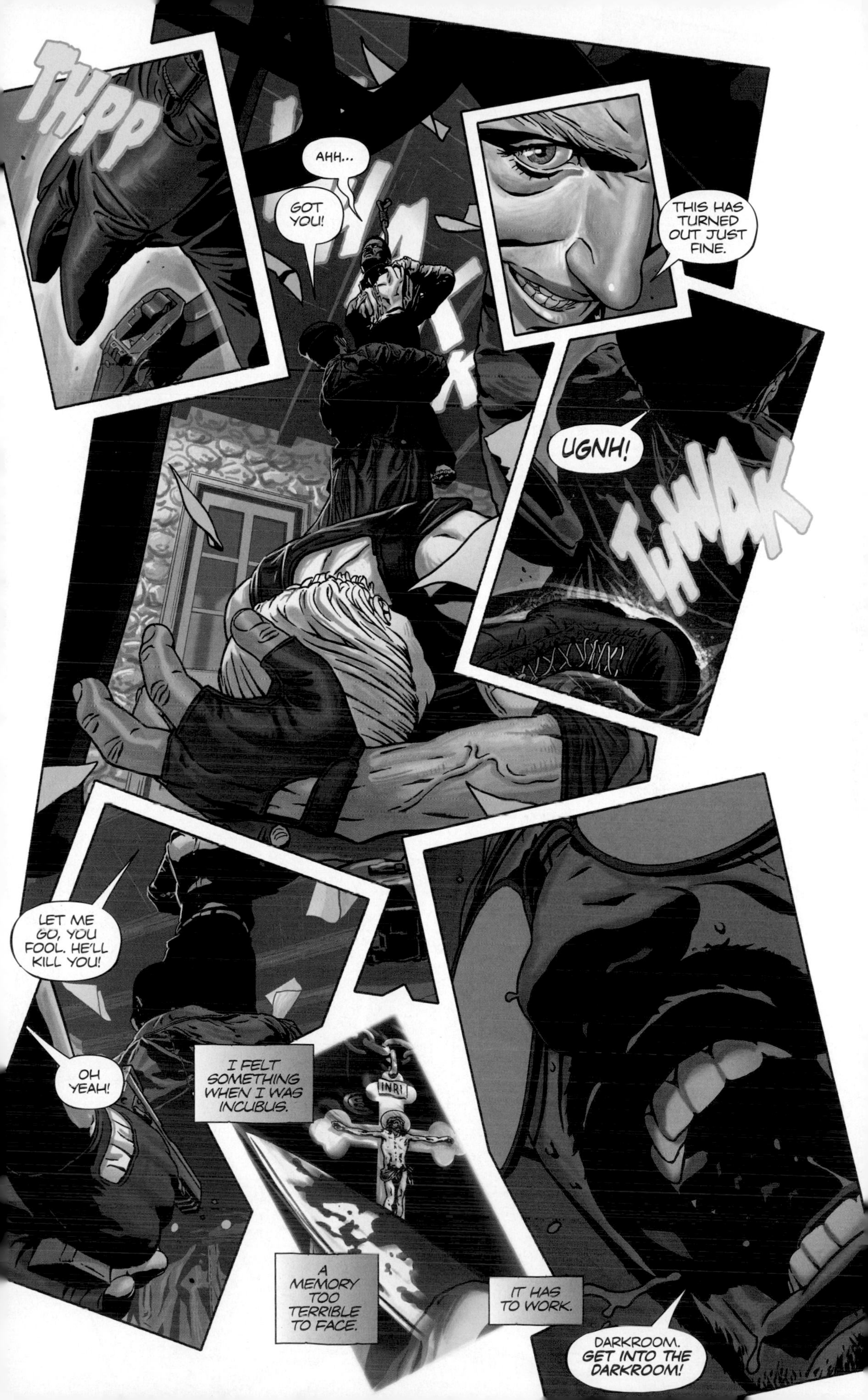
THPP
AHH...
GOT YOU!
THIS HAS TURNED OUT JUST FINE.
UGNH!
THWAK
LET ME GO, YOU FOOL. HE'LL KILL YOU!
OH YEAH!
I FELT SOMETHING WHEN I WAS INCUBUS.
INRI
A MEMORY TOO TERRIBLE TO FACE.
IT HAS TO WORK.
DARKROOM. GET INTO THE DARKROOM!

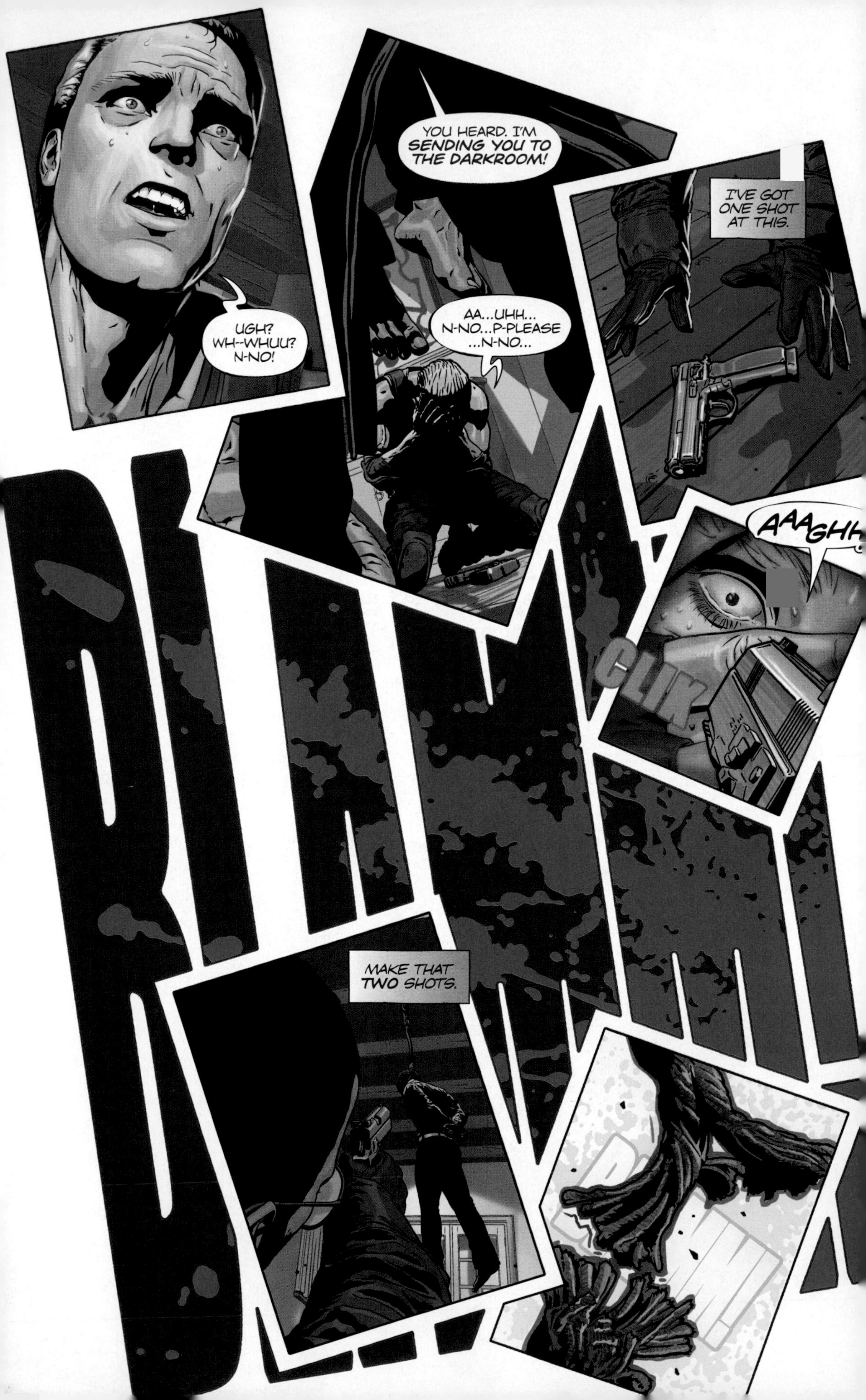
UGH? WH--WHUU? N-NO!
YOU HEARD. I'M SENDING YOU TO THE DARKROOM!
AA...UHH... N-NO...P-PLEASE ...N-NO...
I'VE GOT ONE SHOT AT THIS.
AAAGHH
CLIK
MAKE THAT TWO SHOTS.

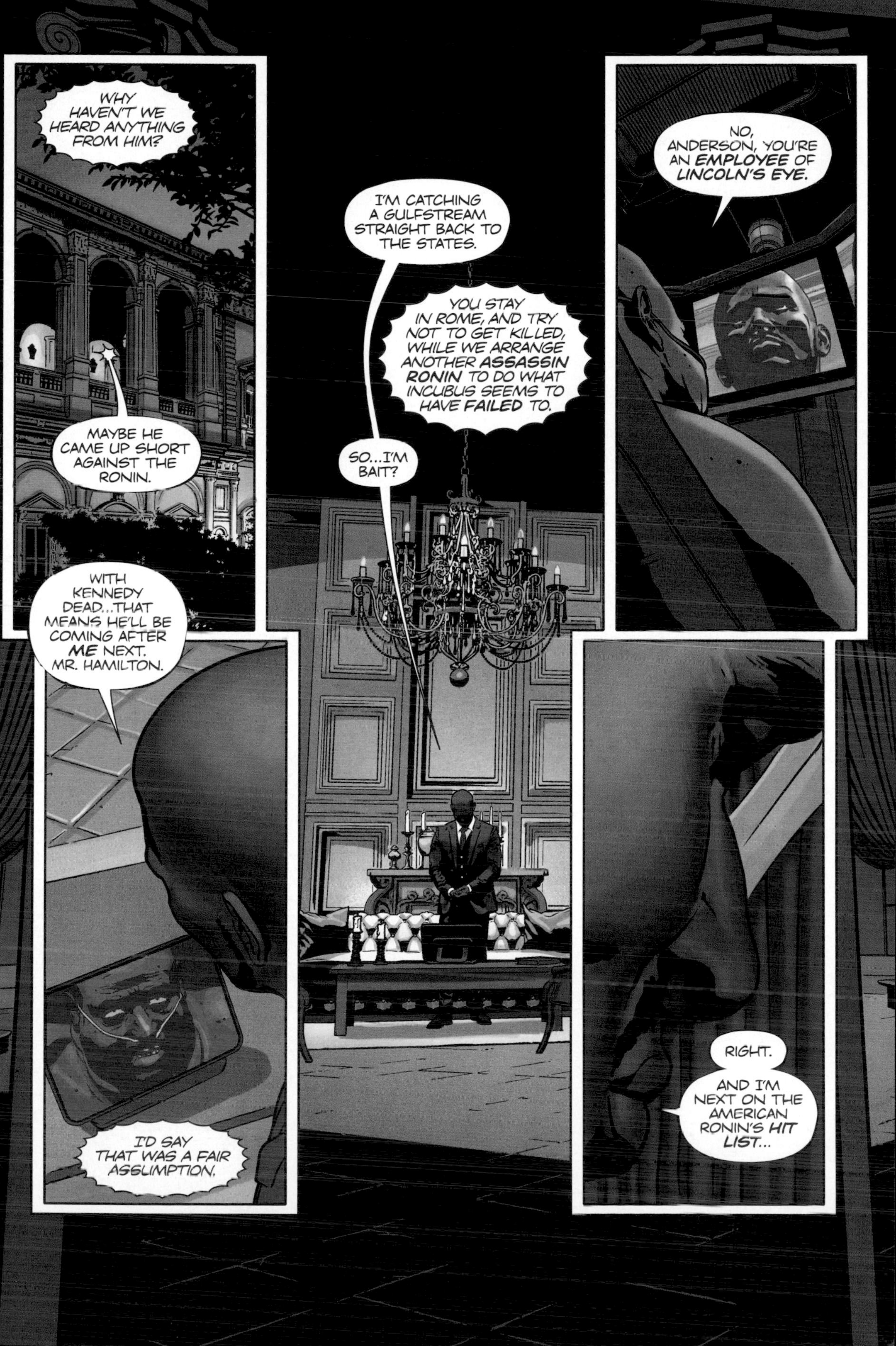
WHY HAVEN'T WE HEARD ANYTHING FROM HIM?
MAYBE HE CAME UP SHORT AGAINST THE RONIN.
I'M CATCHING A GULFSTREAM STRAIGHT BACK TO THE STATES.
YOU STAY IN ROME, AND TRY NOT TO GET KILLED, WHILE WE ARRANGE ANOTHER **ASSASSIN RONIN** TO DO WHAT INCUBUS SEEMS TO HAVE **FAILED** TO.
SO...I'M BAIT?
NO, ANDERSON, YOU'RE AN ***EMPLOYEE*** OF ***LINCOLN'S EYE.***
WITH KENNEDY DEAD...THAT MEANS HE'LL BE COMING AFTER ***ME*** NEXT. MR. HAMILTON.
I'D SAY THAT WAS A FAIR ASSUMPTION.
RIGHT.
AND I'M NEXT ON THE AMERICAN RONIN'S ***HIT LIST***...

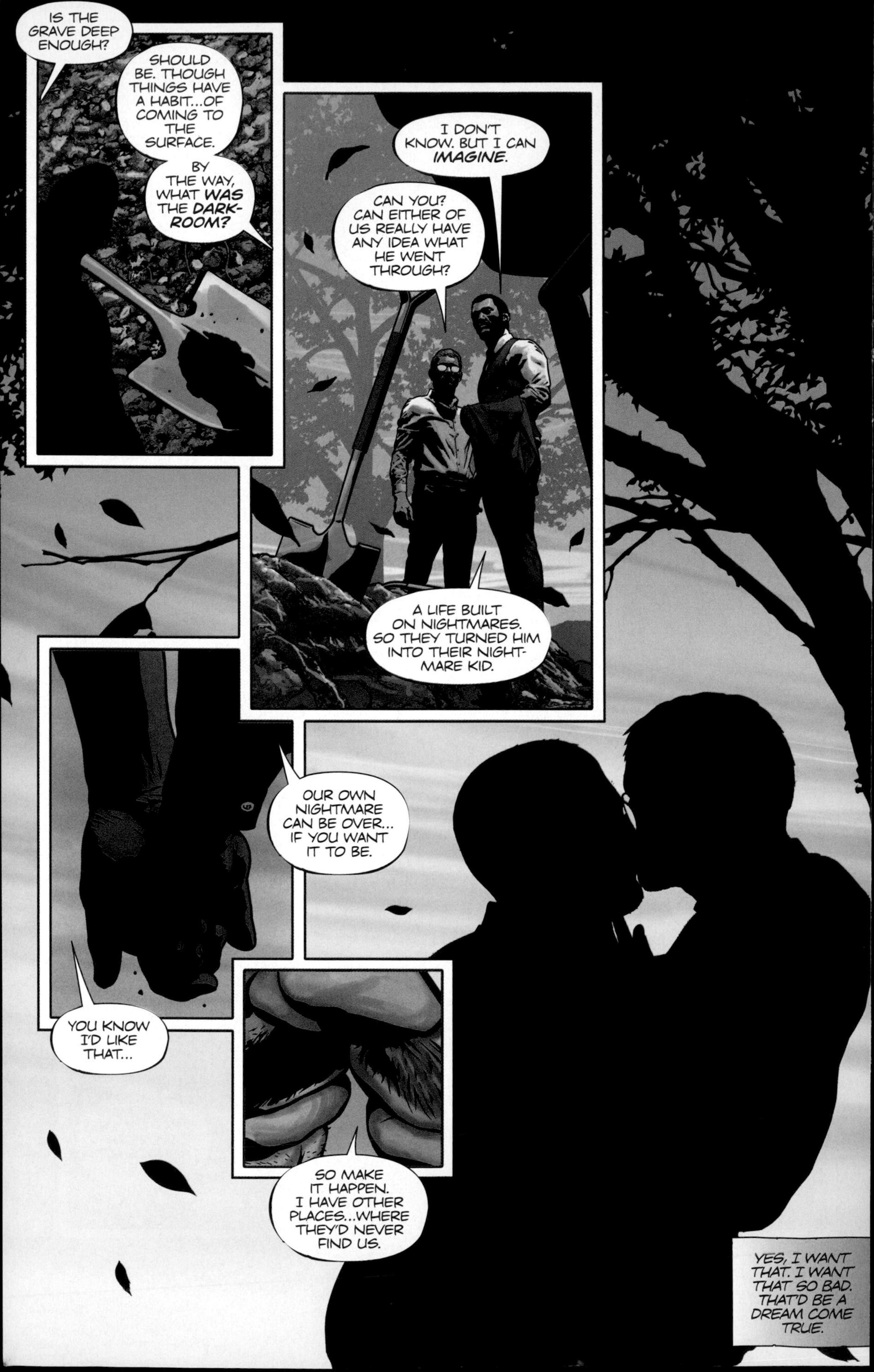

IS THE GRAVE DEEP ENOUGH?
SHOULD BE. THOUGH THINGS HAVE A HABIT...OF COMING TO THE SURFACE.
BY THE WAY, WHAT WAS THE DARK-ROOM?
I DON'T KNOW. BUT I CAN IMAGINE.
CAN YOU? CAN EITHER OF US REALLY HAVE ANY IDEA WHAT HE WENT THROUGH?
A LIFE BUILT ON NIGHTMARES. SO THEY TURNED HIM INTO THEIR NIGHT-MARE KID.
OUR OWN NIGHTMARE CAN BE OVER... IF YOU WANT IT TO BE.
YOU KNOW I'D LIKE THAT...
SO MAKE IT HAPPEN. I HAVE OTHER PLACES...WHERE THEY'D NEVER FIND US.
YES, I WANT THAT. I WANT THAT SO BAD. THAT'D BE A DREAM COME TRUE.

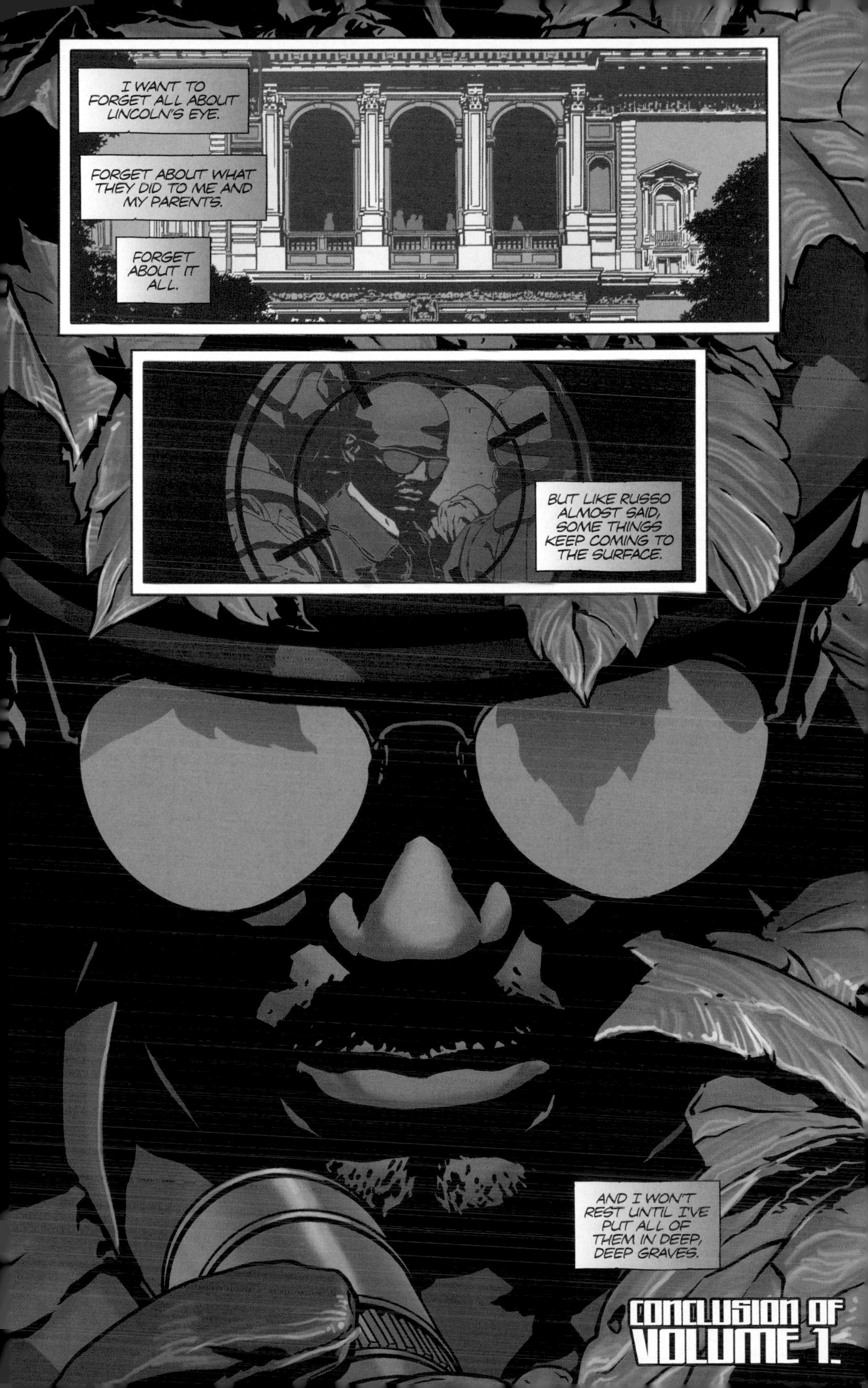
I WANT TO FORGET ALL ABOUT LINCOLN'S EYE.
FORGET ABOUT WHAT THEY DID TO ME AND MY PARENTS.
FORGET ABOUT IT ALL.
BUT LIKE RUSSO ALMOST SAID, SOME THINGS KEEP COMING TO THE SURFACE.
AND I WON'T REST UNTIL I'VE PUT ALL OF THEM IN DEEP, DEEP GRAVES.
CONCLUSION OF VOLUME 1.

LETTERS FROM THE CREATORS OF

AMERICAN RONIN

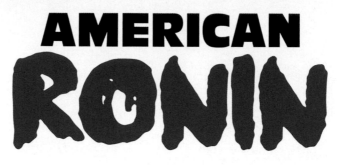

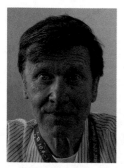

Peter Milligan

I KNOW HOW YOU FEEL.

I am a writer. I sit at my desk and look at my characters and try to bring them to life. I try to bring them to life by understanding who they are, by entering their consciousness, by making them believable, whole people with a consistent or sometimes consistently inconsistent set of behaviours, thoughts, dreams, weaknesses.

As a writer interested in character and identity this process has engaged me for a long time. In *Human Target* I tried to explore the creative process of understanding or becoming a character by writing about Christopher Chance, who so deeply and so thoroughly impersonated his 'targets' that in some strange and indefinable way he became them.

In *Enigma* I explored this process by watching Michael Smith experience himself changing as he pursued the favorite comic book hero of his youth. Michael wasn't so much becoming gay as stripping away the layers of self-deceit and ignorance and discovering his true, beautiful self. I am not gay so in writing about this journey I had to do what all writers do. I imagined myself into Michael. I did my research, I based Michael's journey a little on someone I knew, but ultimately I had to make that creative leap from me to Michael. In short, I had to try to make him a living, breathing human.

This ability to empathize, to imagine ourselves as someone else, to feel what they're feeling, that ultimately makes us human.

But there's the rub. For what is it to be human? Not simply to be a Great Ape who walks upright and has a large, wrinkly brain. To be human.

What makes me me, and you you? How can we ever bridge the yawning chasm that exists between two people, between two consciousnesses, each with its own set of memories, dreams, and fears?

The answer, of course, is empathy. Empathy might not allow us to walk a mile in an-

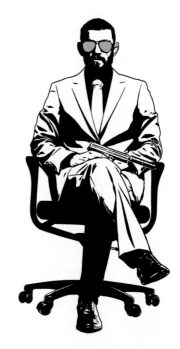

other man's shoes, but it at least lets us try on those shoes for size. And maybe it's this, this ability to empathize, to imagine ourselves as someone else, to feel what they're feeling, that ultimately makes us human (and, sometimes, writers).

The American Ronin is good at empathy. He takes empathy to a whole different level. In a comic book world full of violently-weaponized characters with the powers to punch, blast, scorch, laser, and incinerate, here is a man with that most human of powers.

He knows how you feel.

Here's how it works. You eat lunch at a diner. By the time you're finished your DNA is all over the knife and fork you used, the chair you sat at, the glass you drank from. You do not notice the man slip into the restaurant after you and pocket your fork. Maybe money is exchanged, a few coins to a waiter buys your glass.

And now the American Ronin gets to work. Extracting your DNA. Mixing it in the required solution, and INJECTING it into his blood-

stream. Fast track to exploding, surgically-enhanced empathy regions of his brain.

And then the magic happens.

The magic of becoming: a kind of creative transcendence.

Cut to a few years ago. I'd just had some kind of disagreement with one of my brothers—nothing serious, it didn't quite come to blows, and it was entirely his fault. As a dizziness-inducing mental exercise I tried to see things from his side. I really did.

And I think I probably failed.

And afterwards I was struck by how hard it is to really see the world from someone else's POV. To put on those ill-fitting shoes we're supposed to walk a whole bloody mile in. Sure I could empathize—up to a point. I was human, wasn't I?

But could I ever really have such a deep connection with someone else—as Christopher Chance did—that my own self dissolved and for a while I really became them? Knew their thoughts, felt their dreams, shivered at their nightmares?

And I saw then how much of my work has

been about this 'becoming someone else' thing. And I knew I wanted to explore it further, go even deeper.

And at that moment the first zygote cell of a life that would become *American Ronin* came into being.

But what kind of world would *American Ronin* be born into?

If the American Ronin's "power" was that most human of abilities, empathy–albeit empathy with a rocket strapped to its ass–I knew the universe he operated in would have an in-

> I'll tell you what I love about this book. For all its James Bond, *Bourne Identity*, large screen, violent, exotic location, mega-corporation, explosive craziness... at the heart there's a man. A man who can know how you feel.

human, or dehumanized flavor. It would be our world, but pushed to the breaking point.

Just as the American Ronin, this feeling-machine, would be pushed to the breaking point.

In the global financial crisis of 2008, one thing that became apparent–besides the obvious fact that most banks and stock market cowboys were lying, risk-addicted, avaricious bastards–was how little power national governments and democracies really had compared with the transnational, many-armed hydra that was Money, with its banks, hedge funds, schemes, and markets.

A number of years later and the even more deadly crisis of Covid-19, and we once again see democracies and states struggling to cope with something that respects no national borders.

This is not a criticism of democracy. If anything it's a call to make democracy stronger and to protect it against multinational threats and tin-pot dictators.

But let's get real. Democracy's, and therefore our own, ability to influence the world we're living in is being eroded. That's the world of *American Ronin*. A world where true power resides in huge pan-national companies, with names like Lincoln's Eye and War And Peace. These behemoths wage a closet war against each other: assassinations, murders, blackmails. It's like the Cold War, except the agents now are surgically-enhanced Ronins, each with their own specific power or ability. One has the ability to step inside your nightmares and know what you really fear. Another has the ability to make anyone love or trust her.

And one, the one called American Ronin, does his thing with empathy.

I'll tell you what I love about this book. For all its James Bond, *Bourne Identity*, large-screen, violent (sometimes very violent), exotic location, mega-corporation, explosive craziness...at the heart there's a man.

A man who can know how you feel. A man who's determined to kill the very people who made him the way he is. A man who dies a little inside every time he kills someone.

And I'm still waiting for my brother to apologize.

- Peter Milligan

In recent years I have worked for publishers where the toys belonged to others and where the deadlines demanded every minute of my time. In the long run it has caused me a lot of personal problems so I needed a break. It was at that precise moment when I received the proposal from Axel Alonso to join his new editorial project, AWA, and I did not hesitate for a second to get on this boat. One of the incentives to join was the possibility of being able to work with some of the creators that I admire the most in the industry and being able to develop our own stories and characters. When I learned that *American Ronin* was going to be written by Peter Milligan, then I had no doubts. Peter is a comic book legend and the author of many of my favorite books. He has worked with such incredible artists that it made me dizzy to think if I was going to be up to it. Luckily for me, both Peter and the AWA team have made things much easier for me and presented me with a project in which to develop my work in the best possible way. Having my usual inker by my side, David Lorenzo, has given me greater security. Each page he returns is full of details and improves my pencils incredibly. Having Dean White as a colorist has been a great experience. I have wanted to work with him for years and being able to see my pages with his style is incredible. He really is a superstar. Sal Cipriano's work as a letterer is well known and I can only be grateful to have someone of that quality for this story. *American Ronin* is the combination of many talents and a series that has required a lot of work and attention, in which the setting plays an important role with cities such as Hong Kong and Rome. These are wonderful settings full of elements on their streets and at the same time so different that they give greater visual richness to the whole of the story. Making the world bigger has always seemed like a success. And the Ronin, our protagonist, is a lot of fun to draw. He moves away from the canon of spy or secret agent and it shows that his life has not been easy.

> Showing a ruthless as well as fragile character is always a challenge, as we are too used to invincible heroes.

Showing a ruthless as well as fragile character is always a challenge, as we are too used to invincible heroes. This time working on *American Ronin* has been a breath of fresh air for me and I am looking forward to showing you more projects at AWA and Upshot Studios. I hope that you, reader, enjoy our work on *American Ronin* and that you are sure that we wanted to give you our best version. I hope you enjoy it and thanks for being there.

- ACO

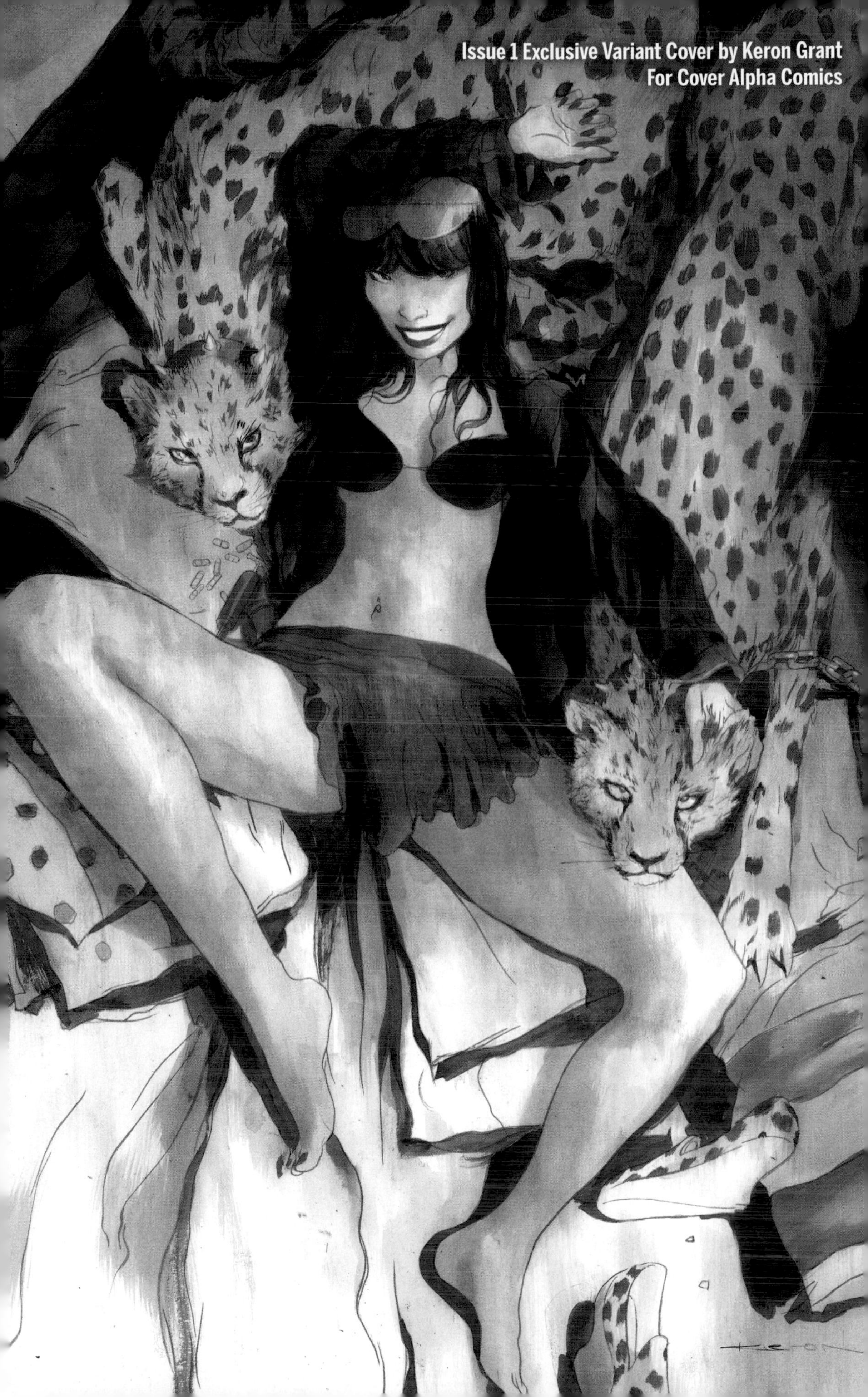

**Issue 1 Exclusive Variant Cover by Keron Grant
For Cover Alpha Comics**

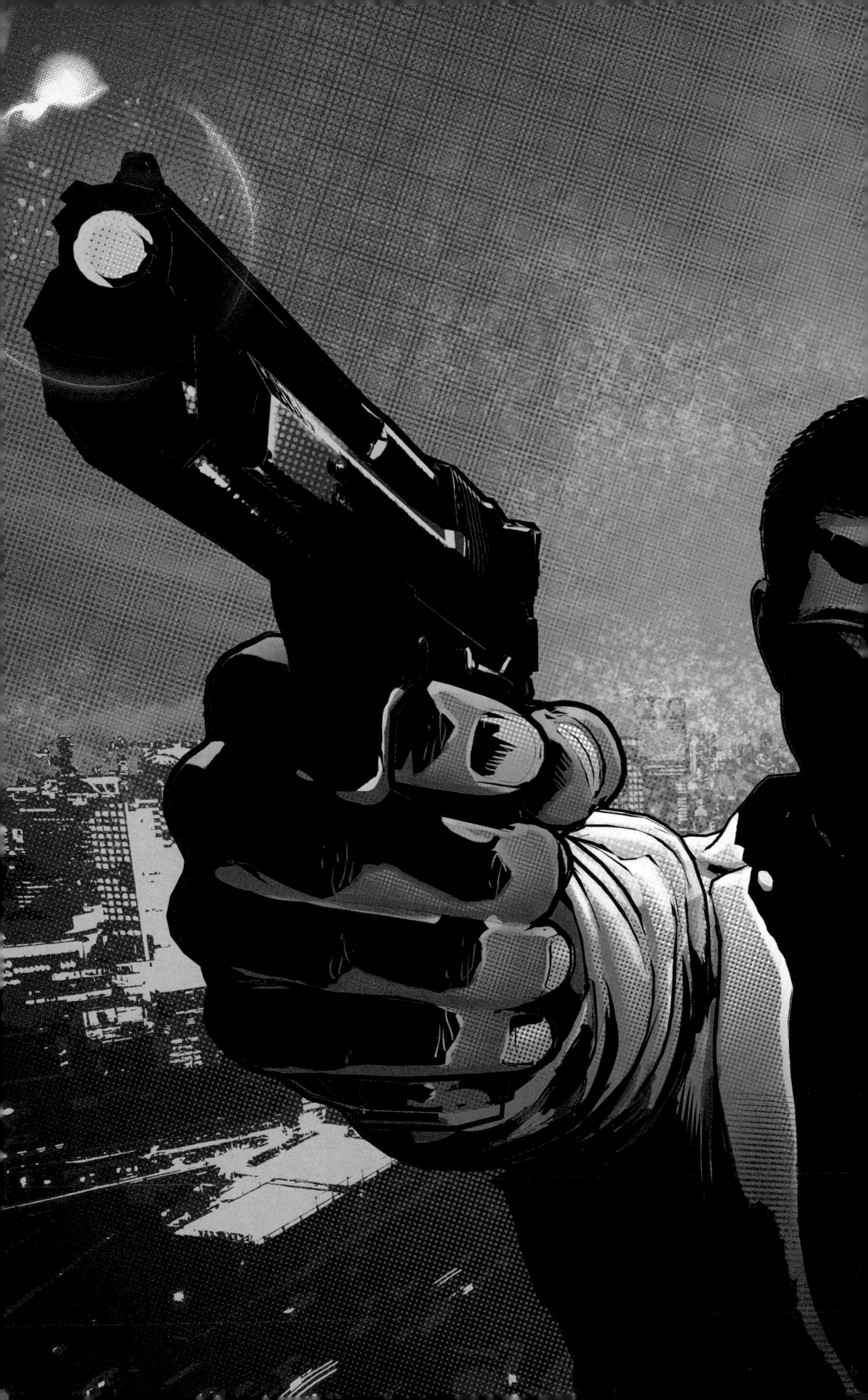

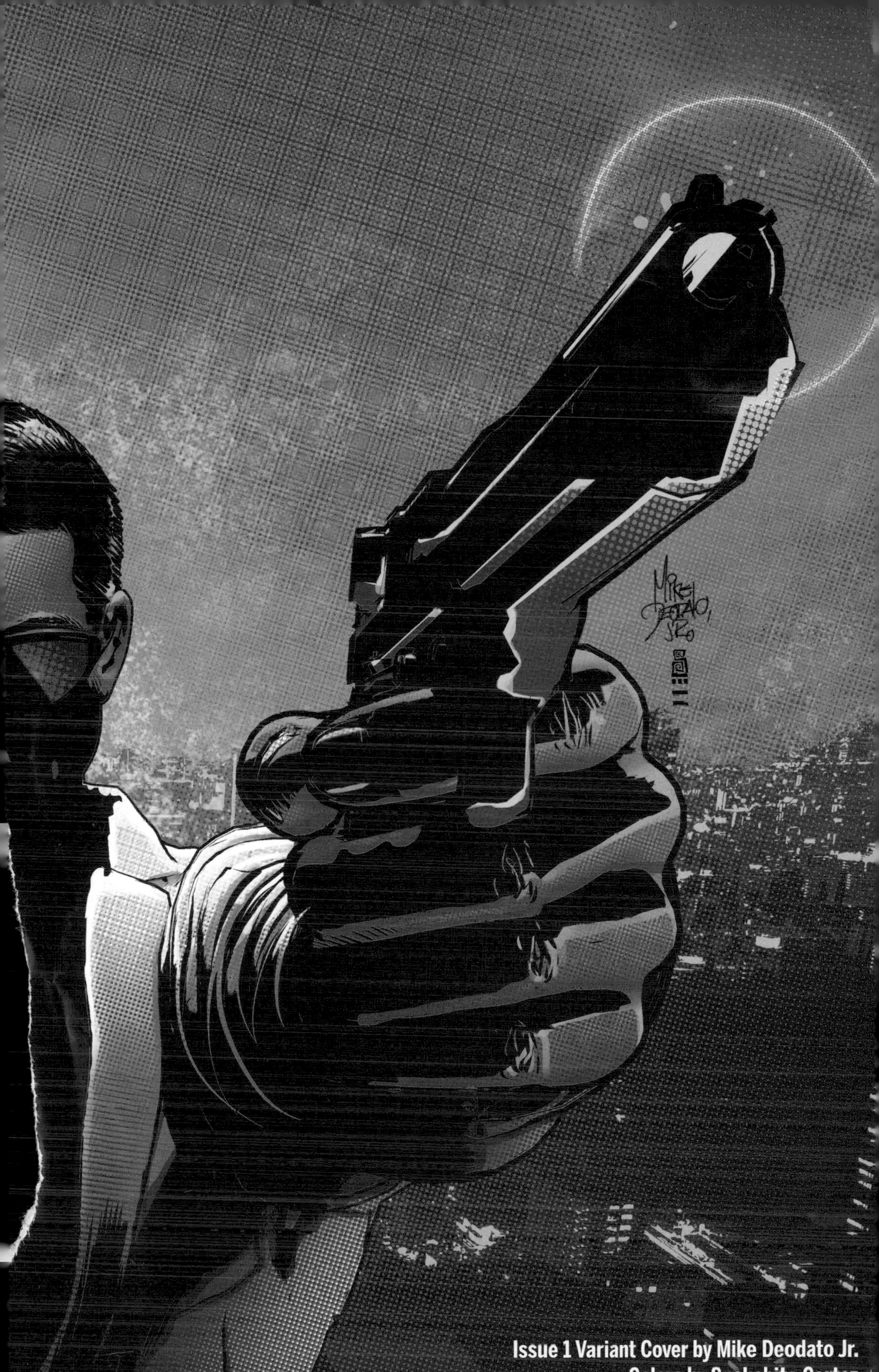

Issue 1 Variant Cover by Mike Deodato Jr.
Colors by Snakebite Cortez

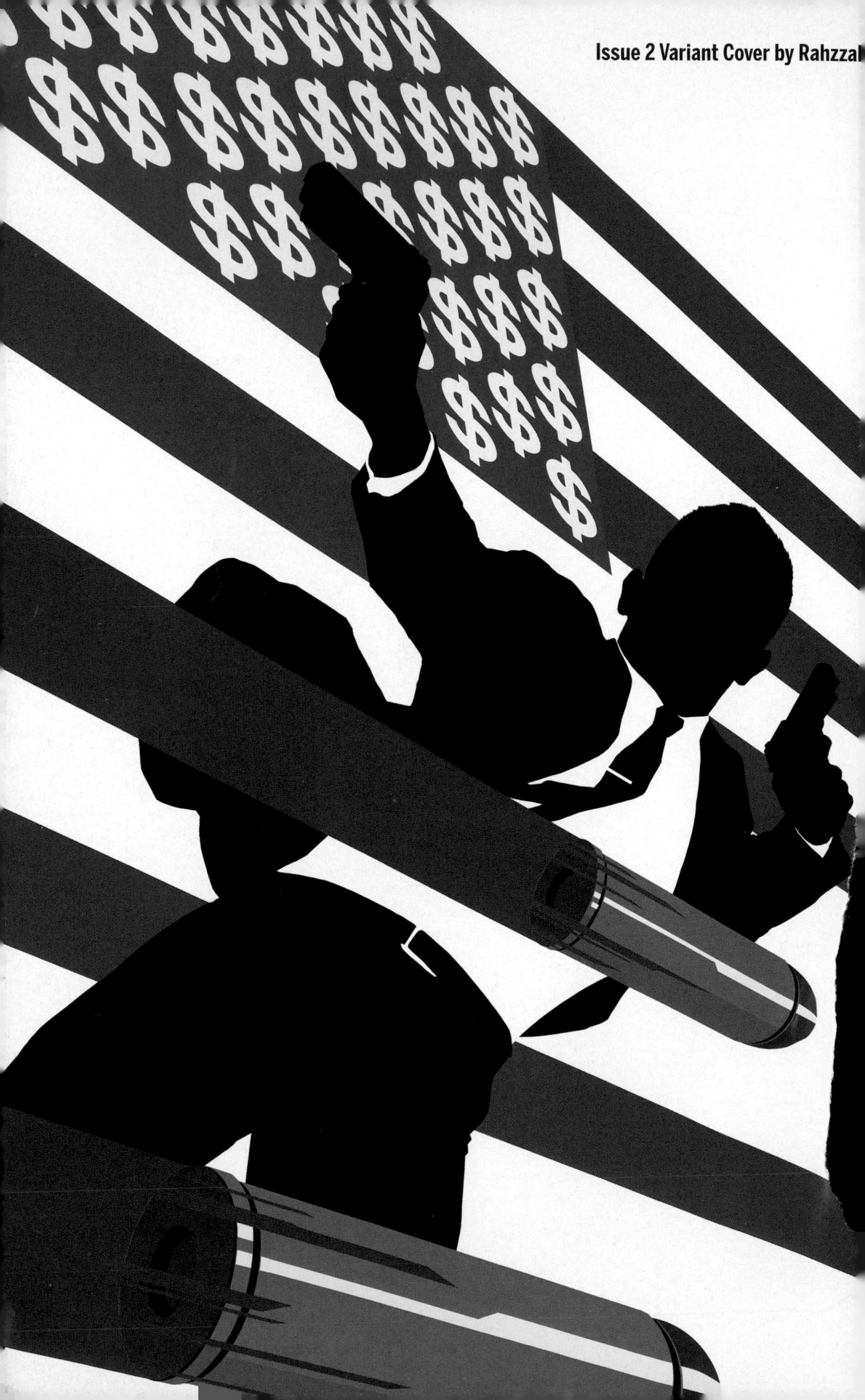

Issue 2 Variant Cover by Rahzzal